The National Bet

Also by Bob McCarty

The Clapper Memo

Three Days In August

The National Bet

by

Bob McCarty

Pump Lamp Press

Saint Louis

Bob McCarty, L.L.C.
P.O. Box 1423
Saint Charles, MO 63302-1423
BobMcCarty.com

Note to Readers: This is a work of fiction. Names, characters, places, and incidents are a product of the author's imagination. Locales and public names are sometimes used for atmospheric purposes. Any resemblance to actual people, living or dead, or to businesses, companies, events, institutions, or locales is completely coincidental.

The National Bet / Bob McCarty

ISBN-13: 978-0692245309
ISBN-10: 0692245308
First Edition Printed in the United States of America.

This book is dedicated to my first and only wife of 29 years. Thank you for putting up with my writing affliction for so many years.

1

"K-man! K-man! Wake up! We've gotta go!" Waking to those words, Master Sergeant Josh Kastens knew the day was about to get serious.

A twelve-year veteran who had reached his current rank almost two years ahead of his peers, Josh was a member of the elite Air Force pararescue fraternity known as "PJs." Assigned to the 347th Rescue Group at Moody Air Force Base near Valdosta, Georgia, he was pulling his first six-month tour in Somalia even as most Americans didn't realize members of their country's military had been deployed to the African nation since 2007.

Being rousted out of bed at "oh-dark-thirty"—2:15 a.m. local time on this occasion—usually meant an aircraft was down and a pilot needed rescue—or, in PJ vernacular, "saved."

"A viper flamed out," said Captain Eddie Hoskins, speaking loud and being unmistakably clear. "Briefing room in five!"

During the briefing, Josh learned the mission would take him and his crew from their base near Berbera on the coast of the Gulf of Aden to an insurgent stronghold almost fifteen miles west of Saylac and ten miles south of Somalia's border with Djibouti.

By 2:30, their HH-60G Pave Hawk helicopter was airborne. Estimated time to target: twenty minutes.

Outside the chopper, the early morning temperature was a stifling ninety-seven degrees Fahrenheit. Inside, the heat was even more oppressive as engine noise drowned out everything but the headset chatter between crewmembers.

Two gunners stood ready at their GAU-2/B miniguns, while Josh and his PJ partner, Staff Sergeant Stu Duckworth, sat with their legs hanging out opposite doors, M-4 carbines across their laps. Just in case.

Josh had made six saves during previous combat tours in Afghanistan and Iraq, but something about this new battlefield gave him the creeps.

Flying fast and low at a ten o'clock heading, the chopper pilot followed instructions from controllers aboard an E-3B Sentry Airborne Warning and Control Systems aircraft flying high above, and they reached the downed pilot's location without incident.

Due to the latest round of Pentagon budget cuts that had dramatically reduced the number of rescue aircraft in theater, only one chopper participated in this mission. And, thanks to misguided Rules of Engagement that no longer allowed gunners to use preliminary fire to clear landing zones of bad guys, every LZ was considered hot.

Approaching the LZ, the pilot took his chopper down at a steep angle while making a number of irregular turns designed to make it more difficult for anyone to shoot his bird down. Then, after dropping the PJs in a clearing, he climbed back into the sky. The entire process took less than forty seconds, and his chopper took no incoming fire. Now, he and his crew would keep watch over the area as the PJs went to work.

Equipped with night-vision goggles, the PJs reached the downed pilot quickly after spotting him crouched behind an abandoned truck some fifty yards north of the LZ.

"Are you hurt?" Josh asked the pilot, Captain Bud McGowan, who showed no signs of serious injury but was understandably nervous.

"No, but I think there are some bad guys out there," the pilot replied, motioning with his eyes toward the east. "I heard them shouting to each other, so they can't be too far away."

Captain McGowan's F-16C Fighting Falcon had lost hydraulic pressure in its lone engine. As a result, he had to eject in an area only a few miles away from an enemy base where, a short time earlier, members of the terror group al-Shabaab had been on the receiving end of one of his laser-guided five-hundred-pound bombs. Now, instead of being the hunter, he'd become the prey, hunted by dark-skinned men now less than half a mile away and closing fast.

After attaching a harness to the pilot, Josh radioed the chopper to return for an immediate pickup. As the word "copy" left his lips, a single shot rang out and, out of the corner of his eye, he saw Sergeant Duckworth—"Duck" to his friends—reach up with his left hand to the side of his head. A large chunk had been ripped out of the PJ's helmet, but it didn't appear as if the bullet had penetrated his partner's skull. It did, however, cause him to be disoriented and have a hard time keeping his balance.

"Mama bear, we're taking fire!" Josh screamed into his radio. "Duck's hit! Duck's hit! We need cover! East, one hundred yards! We need cover!"

More shots rang out, but all missed.

As Josh half-carried his partner toward the makeshift LZ, Captain McGowan fired his 9 mm Beretta in the direction of the attackers who had cut the distance between themselves and their prey in half.

"How many are--" Josh began to ask Captain McGowan before stopping in mid-sentence as an AK-47 round grazed the left side of his neck. Then another round hit him inches above his right hip. Adrenaline surging, a quick assessment confirmed neither wound was life threatening.

Seconds later, the chopper—their lifeline to the world—appeared out of nowhere from over a ridge to the south. After the helo's right-side gunner spotted the rebels through his night-vision goggles, he unloaded a barrage of 7.62 mm rounds on the enemy positions and declared over the radio, "Enemy destroyed!"

Such an outcome had been made possible only after a U.S. Marine Corps three-star general had taken over as commander of the International Security Assistance Force in Afghanistan and succeeded in convincing his superiors in the chain of command to allow crews aboard casualty-evacuation choppers (a.k.a., "CASEVACs" or "dustoffs") to defend themselves in hot LZs.

Upon hearing the E-D announcement, the chopper pilot dropped his aircraft to the ground within twenty yards of the PJs and the aviator they had come to save.

Ignoring his own wounds, Josh partnered with Captain McGowan to load Sergeant Duckworth onto the chopper. As they began lifting him up to the floor of the chopper, three more gunshots rang out in quick succession and Josh felt more pain. Looking down as he began to collapse, he saw his left leg nearly severed above the knee.

For what seemed an eternity, Josh watched through his night-vision goggles as his own warm blood poured from the leg, yielding a bright-red thermal-infrared signature. Less than a minute after he was hit, he lost consciousness.

Responding to the burst of unexpected gunfire, the chopper's right-side gunner quickly located and eliminated its source, another Somali sniper who seemed to appear out of nowhere some sixty yards northeast of the LZ. But it was too late for Josh.

While both PJs stayed true to their warrior fraternity's creed, "That Others May Live," only one survived.

2

On the other side of the world, Gary Kastens wrapped up another long day as day-shift manager at Illinois Chemical Company and looked forward to unwinding.

Upon completing the ten-minute drive south to his home on the north edge of Effingham, Illinois, he checked the mailbox at the end of the driveway before turning in and parking his twelve-year-old Ford Ranger pickup in the center of his two-car garage. After carrying his daily stack of mail—most of it junk—into the house, he promptly changed out of his work clothes into a pair of comfortable blue jeans and a t-shirt. He hoped to finish mowing the one-acre lot surrounding his three-bedroom ranch before sundown and put a mental checkmark next to the one chore he had failed to complete the previous weekend. In addition, he was counting on the vibration of his riding mower's fifteen-horsepower engine to help dissolve the stress of another long day at the plant. At best, he had two and a half hours of daylight to get it done—unless, that is, the sun decided to shine past 6:30.

Kastens mowed the smaller backyard and then the larger front yard before deciding to tackle the ten-feet-wide strip of grass between the front edge of his property and the blacktop road that ended twenty feet beyond his driveway. Technically, the strip belonged to the city of Effingham, but those in charge of maintaining it seemed to forget about their responsibility as often as they remembered.

As Kastens completed his first pass along the edge of the blacktop road, the sight of a car approaching his once-rural home from the east distracted him. Though he couldn't hear it yet, he could see it.

The only resident living at the end of the two-mile stretch of blacktop that protruded like a finger along the side of the new Walmart Super Center, he knew anyone driving down his road was either lost or looking for him. Whatever the reason, he didn't like cars on *his* road.

As Kastens watched the car come closer and closer, dark thoughts began to fill his mind, the sound of the car's engine grew louder, and his stomach began turning backflips. Much like the photos his Polaroid camera had spit out thirty years earlier, the image in front of him began to develop. Slowly.

"A blue government sedan," he whispered as he brought the mower to a stop and turned off its engine. "Please, God, don't let this...."

Before completing the thought, his mind went numb. The fifty-five year old who, only a short time earlier, had planned to spend an uneventful evening in front of his television, now stood in disbelief for what seemed an eternity as the lone automobile approached.

"Don't let this..." he whispered again, now able to see two shadowy silhouettes of individuals in the car's front seat as it came within a quarter-mile of his home. "Please, no."

Kastens climbed off the mower and began walking toward his driveway, all the while looking back over his right shoulder until the car passed him. Keeping an eye on his unwelcome visitors as they parked in the driveway, he soon found himself standing face to face with two men dressed in blue suit-and-tie uniforms. A third man, previously unnoticed by Kastens, remained in the backseat of the car.

The men in front of Kastens were Air Force lieutenant colonels, both sporting silver oak leaves on their shoulders, specialty insignias on their left chests and name tags on their right.

Jake Michels, the taller of the two officers, wore a silver maintenance officer badge above four rows of ribbons earned during nineteen years in uniform. The other, Noah Galbraith, sported a shiny chaplain's cross above two rows of ribbons. Unbeknownst to Kastens, the men had departed Scott Air Force Base in nearby Belleville, Illinois, some ninety minutes earlier, on a mission to deliver heart-wrenching news.

"Sir, are you Mr. Gary Kastens?" Colonel Michels asked.

Detecting the slightest hint of a nod, the colonel continued, looking the father straight in the eyes as he spoke.

"Mr. Kastens, the Chief of Staff of the Air Force asked me to express his deepest regrets and inform you that your son, Master Sergeant Joshua L. Kastens, was killed in action in Africa, on Monday, April 7, 2014."

After pausing only momentarily upon seeing the shocked expression on Kastens' face, Colonel Michels continued. "Your son died heroically while rescuing a fellow American, a fighter pilot, who'd been forced to eject from his aircraft and soon found himself surrounded and under attack by enemy combatants.

"Despite being struck by enemy fire, your son saved both the pilot's life and that of a fellow pararescueman before succumbing to his wounds. Your son was a hero, Mr. Kastens. The Chief of Staff extends his deepest sympathy to you and your family during this time of loss."

Stunned and unable to make sense of the colonel's words, Kastens couldn't think of anything to say that might justify the effort. Instead, he turned slowly, shuffled toward the front door of his home and walked inside, his legs weak under the weight of the news he'd received. The sun was going down—on this day and on life as he had known it.

Sensing Kastens might require help, Master Sergeant Mike Nolan emerged from the back seat of the car and followed the other men as they followed Kastens into the house. Dressed in the enlisted man's version of the uniform worn by the colonels, the noncommissioned officer carried a black medical bag and stood ready to administer aide to the new Gold Star father.

Previous experience had taught all three airmen to be prepared for every possibility and to expect the unexpected from family members with whom they shared the worst kind of news. Though today's recipient didn't collapse physically as many had done in the past, he appeared he might collapse in other ways. And who could blame him.

✝

Determining the appropriate time to leave was never easy for casualty-notification officers, especially when the person notified was alone and/or without relatives or friends by his side. By the look of things, their stay at the Kastens home would not—and should not—end soon.

"Mr. Kastens, is there anyone you need to call to let them know about your son?" Colonel Michels asked.

What had seemed like a good question—the first of many he would ask that day—led to little in the form of a useful answer.

"I need to call his mother, but I don't know where she is," Kastens replied.

"Is she at work? Maybe we can call…"

"We divorced twenty-eight years ago, and I haven't seen or heard from her since," Kastens answered, aware that his unexpected guests didn't know much about his personal life.

"Is there anyone else?" Colonel Michels continued, leaning forward from his spot next to the chaplain on the living room sofa.

"No," Kastens replied from the seat of his front porch-perfect rocking chair opposite the airmen. "Josh was the only family I had." A long pause followed before the father spoke three more words. "All I had."

"Do you have any church friends or anyone else we can call?" asked Chaplain Galbraith, hoping to learn of at least one person Kastens regarded as a friend or confidant.

"No," the distraught father replied, his eyes communicating a nonverbal message that said, "Back off!"

Chaplain Galbraith understood exactly what the broken man had said—but not why—and spoke few words during the remainder of the visit. Instead, he opted to pray silently.

Colonel Michels took the nonverbal dagger aimed at the chaplain as his cue to re-enter the conversation.

"Mr. Kastens, this is Master Sergeant Nolan," he said, motioning to his left where the NCO in charge of the base hospital's outpatient clinic sat next to the chaplain. "He's here to help you if you need it."

Kastens acknowledged the sergeant's introduction with another barely detectable nod, but said nothing.

While Air Force protocol dictated that a medical technician be part of every casualty notification team, it also specified the technician maintain a low profile unless summoned by one of the commissioned officers to provide assistance. Sergeant Nolan sensed he couldn't be called upon to provide assistance on this day, and Colonel Michels reached the same conclusion.

An aircraft maintenance officer whose less-than-perfect vision had prevented him from earning a coveted pilot slot upon graduation from Texas A&M University so many years earlier, Colonel Michels had performed this additional duty nearly a dozen times since September 11, 2001, and the launch of Operation Enduring Freedom that came soon after. Short of a national emergency, it would always take priority over his other duties. And he didn't mind. In fact, he thrived under the unique kind of pressure that accompanied such work. It was part of what made him different.

"Josh must have meant a lot to you," Colonel Michels said, shifting gears and hoping to elicit some kind of response from the grieving father.

"He did," Kastens replied, his voice barely audible as he choked back what he knew could morph into a wave of uncontrollable sobs and tears. "Everything."

"I understand, Mr. Kastens," Colonel Michels replied, wanting to say more but holding back as he watched Kastens slowly give in to his overwhelming need to cry.

"Even I have someone," the colonel thought to himself as he walked over and stood next to the chair into which Kastens had settled.

Putting his hand on the man's shoulder as a friend would, the colonel's thoughts drifted to his eighty-one-year-old mother who, in maintenance officer terms, was slowly slipping out of "MICAP"—mission-capable—status.

Kastens sobbed and cried for several minutes and then, somewhat abruptly, stopped. Keeping both eyes closed, he began rocking and, as he rocked, rubbing his thumbs into the arms of the rocking chair and into the deep depressions his thumbs had worn into those arms during many previous sessions.

The rocking chair, it appeared to Colonel Michels, was his place of refuge, the place where he went to relax, recharge and think. Never before had he needed it more than now.

Several hours passed and few words were spoken as Kastens continued to rock. With the tacit approval of their host, the uniformed visitors helped themselves to occasional glasses of water in the kitchen, ever mindful of the fact they were the last people on earth this man wanted in his home.

Some fourteen hours after their arrival, the sun breached the horizon and peeked through a large picture window into the living room where the Air Force men had spent the night with Kastens. It would soon be time for them to leave.

Before departing, Colonel Michels left Kastens an official casualty notification letter along with details about how he would be contacted—probably within twenty-four hours—by representatives from the Air Force Casualties Office in San Antonio and from the Mortuary Affairs Office at Scott Air Force Base.

The colonel also left a three-by-five card upon which he had written both his name and the chaplain's name as well as phone numbers where both men could be reached anytime—today, tomorrow or a year from now. Though leaving the card wasn't in line with official protocol, both officers had agreed to go the proverbial "extra mile."

As the men walked out the door, Kastens acknowledged their departure with a slightly more noticeable movement of his left hand. At the same time it had conveyed subtle messages of "thank you" and "goodbye," the gesture said, "Please leave." Kastens wanted to be by himself as he continued to grieve.

Soon after the men drove away, Kastens stood in his entryway, slowly tearing in half the card Colonel Michels had left behind, knowing he would never contact them—or anyone else—for help. Instead, he would return to his rocking chair and begin reliving in his mind the years he had shared with his son.

Gary Kastens remembered how two-year-old Josh never seemed to understand why his mother left without saying goodbye; how, for years, Josh would ask if his mother would be coming to see him on his birthday; and how, in response, he always found a way to tell his son, "No," without painting the boy's mother in too negative a light.

He remembered making the decision to sell their house in a nearby town so he and Josh could buy a new home closer to his work, make a fresh start, and make new memories— happy memories.

He remembered the day thirteen-year-old Josh watched "Blackhawk Down," a film about U.S. Army Rangers battling Muslim rebels on the streets of Mogadishu, and wondered out loud why other Soldiers didn't rescue their pinned-down comrades. And he remembered the day five years later when his son told him he was going to join the Air Force and become a PJ after high school.

"What in the world is a PJ?" he'd asked his son after hearing about his plans.

"Pararescue jumper," Josh had answered. "PJs are the guys who rescue pilots who've been shot down."

Josh had learned about them by watching a program on cable about elite units in the U.S. military. By becoming a PJ, Josh had believed he could do his part to make the world a better place by keeping another Somalia from happening.

Finally, Kastens remembered a promise he had made to Josh in one of the many letters they exchanged during Josh's most-recent overseas tour. Not only the most important promise he'd ever made, it was also the one he never imagined having to keep.

Josh made his dad promise to do everything he could to prevent the United States from settling for defeat against Islamic extremists in Afghanistan, Iraq, Africa and anywhere else—including the United States—if he didn't return alive. Though a tall order for one man, it was a promise Kastens told his son he would keep until it was fulfilled or until he died trying. And he was a man of his word.

3

News of Josh Kastens' death spread quickly. Newspaper and television accounts, including ones offered in major news network reports, confirmed the hometown boy was a national hero. For the people of Effingham, he was *their* hero.

Throughout the community, flags were lowered in Josh's honor, and it seemed nearly every citizen in the small farming community of nearly thirteen thousand wanted to pay respects to the father he had left behind.

The outpouring of love and respect so overwhelmed local florists that they had to tap the resources of colleagues in nearby communities in order to fulfill the demand. Nearly every rose, mum, tulip and potted plant within three hundred miles seemed destined for delivery to one Effingham address.

By sunset on the first full day after receiving the bad news, Gary Kastens had grown weary of the parade of visitors—among them, several coworkers and a few men with whom he had served years earlier as a West Effingham Fire Protection District volunteer firefighter. Most of the visitors, however, had been strangers who hoped, in some small way, to soften the burden of his loss.

After receiving far more than his refrigerator and freezer could hold by mid-afternoon, Kastens retreated to his garage to do something constructive. That was, after all, how he had always battled bouts of loneliness since Josh had left home a dozen years earlier.

Finding a four-by-eight-foot sheet of plywood leaning against the wall inside his garage, he grabbed it with both hands and carried it out to the grass alongside his driveway.

Returning to the garage, he removed a can of red spray paint from the shelf above his workbench and began shaking the can while walking back toward his makeshift canvas. Seconds later, he sprayed out a polite three-line message— *"Please, no more meals. Thanks, Gary"*—and leaned the plywood sheet against the mailbox at the end of his driveway where it would be impossible for anyone to miss as they approached his home.

†

Two days after Kastens had received the bad news in person, a package arrived by overnight mail from the Air Force Casualty Affairs Office in San Antonio. Along with a signed letter of condolence from the Air Force Chief of Staff, the package contained forms for the Gold Star father to fill out in order to claim his son's personal belongings, most of which—including the black 2010 Honda Pilot he had bought one week before deploying to Africa—were in storage in Georgia. The letter also included instructions to follow in order to collect on his son's $400,000 Servicemembers' Group Life Insurance policy.

Kastens knew he would have to take care of details like that and thought about putting them off until after the funeral or after his grief had subsided. Upon realizing he might never stop grieving, he decided to complete the paperwork while it was in front of him.

Within two to four weeks, according to the Air Force, he would receive a letter confirming that an account had been set up in his name with a balance much larger than any he had ever maintained. In addition, he would receive a package containing step-by-step instructions for claiming Josh's personal property from temporary storage at the base in Georgia.

4

Josh Kastens' body arrived in Effingham some seventy-two hours after his death. It had been accompanied the entire way home—through military bases in Germany, Dover, Delaware, and Belleville, Illinois—by Captain McGowan, the Air Force Academy graduate-turned fighter pilot Josh rescued during his final mission.

On the final leg of its journey, the fallen hero's body was transported by motorcade from Scott Air Force Base to Effingham in the back of a black hearse, escorted by eight Illinois State Police troopers and nearly one hundred motorcycle-riding members of the Patriot Guard Riders who had traveled from several surrounding states to honor the fallen PJ.

People from Mulberry Grove, Pocahontas, Saint Elmo and other neighboring communities assembled on overpasses to wave their American flags and hold up hand-painted signs of admiration and encouragement as the motorcade passed on I-70 below. By the time the motorcade reached the crematory and funeral home in Effingham, thousands of people had assembled to offer a similar display of support.

The following afternoon, according to his father's wishes and arrangements he had made with the funeral home, Josh would be buried in Effingham with full military honors during a noon-hour service.

A military funeral meant a lot to the citizens of Effingham. Extracurricular events at the high school were cancelled, and most shopkeepers closed their doors. Even the Walmart Super Center shut down for four hours.

As they had the day before, many stood outside the funeral home as the motorcade departed toward the cemetery. Others carried American flags as they stood for hours, lined up along the motorcade route. Thousands more, including Josh's high school classmates and his dad's Illinois Chemical Company coworkers, attended the funeral. Complete strangers did, too.

The funeral would be remembered as one of the largest outpourings of sympathy in Effingham since April 1949 when seventy-four people perished in a late-night fire at Catholic Saint Anthony's Hospital.

✝

Print, broadcast and multimedia journalists came from nearby towns and faraway cities to cover the funeral.

Most took note of the solemn and respectful pace at which the event took place, complete with four color guard members who presented the American and United States Air Force flags and six pallbearers who carried the flag-draped casket to the grave site.

Most felt a sense of awe as they watched seven members of an Honor Guard unit from Scott Air Force Base fire three volleys each as directed by the NCO in charge of the detail.

Most listened as taps played over a loudspeaker system, the result of the Air Force, like the other military branches, abandoning the effort to maintain adequate numbers of trained bugle players after almost thirteen years of war and too many funerals had stretched the ranks of volunteer buglers beyond thin.

Following taps, most watched silently as Colonel Blaze Fitch, the 347th Rescue Group commander who had flown in from North Africa to attend the funeral, presented Gary Kastens with the American flag that had draped Josh's casket.

After the flag presentation, most watched members of the Honor Guard march away slowly, signaling the end of the service.

Only a few members of the media waited around long enough to notice one person had remained behind. Standing alone by his son's casket, Gary Kastens watched as cemetery workers lowered his son's casket into the ground and covered it with dirt. Some would mention it in their stories.

✝

J.C. Champlin had never attended a military funeral, and the twenty-three-year-old *Effingham Courier* reporter wasn't there simply to pay respects. Instead, she was on a mission.

During the ceremony, Champlin noticed a man dressed in an Air Force blue uniform sitting next to the grieving father and suspected he might be the fighter pilot Josh Kastens had saved on his final mission. She based her suspicion on something she read. Military sources cited in a *Stars and Stripes* newspaper article said Josh's PJ partner was still recovering in a hospital bed at the Army-operated Landstuhl Regional Medical Center in Germany.

"That means he must be the pilot," she told herself.

Convinced the story had all the earmarks of a patriotic tearjerker, Champlin tried to keep her eyes on the man she hoped was the pilot as the service came to an end. Before she could get close enough to ask questions, however, she lost sight of him.

Thinking fast, Champlin alternated between speed walking and jogging to get to her car as quickly as possible while trying not to attract too much attention. Along the way, she scanned the crowd, looking for any glimmers of sunlight reflecting off the railroad track-like rank insignia on the shoulders of the man's uniform. About to give up hope, she spotted him behind the wheel of a white, four-door Chevy Malibu in a long line of vehicles approaching the cemetery's main exit. That's when she decided she would follow him to wherever he was going.

To speed things up, she climbed into her car and drove toward the back of the cemetery. Earlier in the day, she had spotted a maintenance gate that might allow her a quicker exit and access to the I-70 service road that fronted the cemetery. Now, she hoped it was unlocked.

When Champlin arrived at the gate, she climbed out of her car and found the gate unlocked. After quickly pushing it open, she drove through, slammed her car's gearshift back into PARK, and climbed out again to close the gate behind her. In less than a minute, she made it to the service road well ahead of the man in the white car.

Two minutes passed while Champlin sat parked on the shoulder, waiting for the man's car to reach the front of the line. Once he reached the exit, he turned left on the service road and passed within six feet of her door. Her plan was working.

Champlin followed the man's car to the I-70 on-ramp and west for another thirty miles until he pulled into a Steak 'n Shake restaurant at the first Vandalia exit. Once inside, she approached him at his table, introduced herself by name and asked if she could join him. He said, "Sure," and, by the way he looked back at her, she knew her hunch had been correct.

"Where ya headed?" she asked, soon after getting the green light to join him.

"I'm on my way to Saint Louis," he replied. "There's a flight to New Orleans at eight in the morning, and I hope to be on it."

Between bites of his steak burger, the man explained that he had thirty days of leave to burn before returning to Africa and that he planned to spend most of it at his parents' home near Baton Rouge, Louisiana.

Champlin guessed he would want to get to the airport at least ninety minutes early in order to return his rental car and get a bite to eat. If her quick mental math was accurate and she played her cards right, she might be able to keep this guy engaged for two hours or more.

"Oh, I'm sorry," Champlin piped up. "I failed to mention I'm a reporter for the *Effingham Courier.*"

"Bud McGowan," he countered, "but I get the feeling you know who I am."

"I think you're the pilot Josh Kastens helped rescue on his last mission. Am I right?"

"Yes, you are" he replied. "Captain Bud McGowan."

Several seconds—maybe a minute—passed as Champlin tried to figure out where to go with the interview. While thinking about her next step, she pretended to concentrate on her food—that is, until the captain broke the silence.

"Everyone told me I shouldn't feel guilty," he explained, "because the plane's engine quit, not me. But I can't escape feeling like I should have done something more or been more vigilant. Something."

Hoping to get him to talk, she began exercising proven interviewing techniques (i.e., nods of understanding and long periods of silence after asking questions) that even the most-tortured souls had been unable to resist. Before long, she found Captain McGowan unable to resist her journalistic spell. She would carve another notch in her number two pencil later.

The pair talked for a while about events leading up to Josh's death and those immediately following it, then Champlin abruptly changed the course of the conversation.

"Have you spoken to Sergeant Kastens' family?"

"Only briefly," the pilot said before describing Josh's father as "pretty shook up."

"I can't imagine."

"I thanked his dad for his incredible sacrifice and delivered some of his son's personal effects, including a letter he had written to his father."

"Do you know what was in the letter?" she asked, sensing Captain McGowan might have something poignant to share.

"I do, but I'm not at liberty to discuss the details. I'm sure you understand."

"Of course."

"Are you going to talk to him before you write your story?" the captain asked.

"I hope to, but our paper has a long-standing policy of not allowing reporters like me to push for interviews with people who've recently lost loved ones," Champlin said. "In fact, we usually wait at least a month before we approach them— if we approach them at all."

Secretly, Champlin hated the family-owned newspaper's policy, believing it might keep serious small-town reporters like herself from being able to write the gripping, emotional stories that earn awards and lead to jobs on the staffs of big-city papers in places like Chicago, Cleveland and Saint Louis. Until the policy changed, she would continue paying her dues in Southern Illinois journalism.

"That sounds like a pretty decent policy if you ask me," Captain McGowan said. "Do you need anything else?"

"No," she said, "but I'd like to get a phone number and email address where I can reach you if I have other questions or, you know, need to clarify anything."

Though realizing he was obligated to run requests for interviews and other news media opportunities through his unit's public affairs officer, Captain McGowan gave Champlin his cell number and personal email address anyway. Seconds later, he shook her hand and walked out the door.

For Champlin, the interview was over, but the story still had to be written. And she would pour her heart into it.

†

To people who read her article in the *Effingham Sunday Courier*, printed and delivered Saturday afternoon to extend the life of advertisements for local merchants, it seemed Champlin had soaked up each of the tears she and Captain McGowan had shed during the interview and arranged them as an emotional stream of word pictures, each capturing a different element of the story behind a young man's life-saving sacrifice and his hometown's response.

Well-written, Champlin's article was the type many people would forward to family members and friends during the days and weeks to come. Why? Because it conjured up strong feelings, especially among those with military experience and/or loved ones in uniform.

By e-mail message and old-fashioned news clipping, the article became the fodder of many kitchen table conversations and country café bull sessions. And it was the kind of story that went viral after being shared hundreds of thousands of times on social networking sites like Facebook, Twitter and Pinterest.

Barely one year into her career as a professional journalist, Champlin struck pay dirt. Her article went viral, published by hundreds of newspapers and becoming content for thousands of legitimate and illegitimate news outlets worldwide.

Meanwhile, other reporters writing about the same topic struck different chords. Some found ways to weave coverage of anti-war sentiment into their coverage. Even worse, others used the story of Josh's death as a platform from which they could segue into sensationalized stories related to military justice cases and about other topics they lumped into "more disturbing news from the war zone." Almost every story, however, included a mention of the two-hundred-year-old community being home to the world's largest cross—198 feet tall, made of 180 tons of steel and standing along I-70 west of town.

5

Champlin was still in bed Sunday morning when her cell phone rang at a few minutes past 10. It was her editor, Kurt Hassler, calling to tell her Josh Kastens' father had left a voicemail message on the newspaper's Reader Hotline that morning.

"He wants to speak with you," Hassler said.

"Are you serious, Kurt? What did he say?"

"He's tired of the way most people are reporting about his son's death, but he liked the interview you did with that pilot and thinks he can trust you."

"Whaddya mean, he *thinks* he can trust me? You know darn well he can trust me!"

"He said it, not me!"

"Okay, what's his number?"

Hassler gave Kastens' number to Champlin and walked away, happy to see some spirit in a young reporter.

Normally, Champlin didn't work on Sundays. She would, however, make an exception on this day, because opportunities like this one were few and far between at the *Courier*.

"Hello, Mr. Kastens," she began after hearing him pick up his phone. "This is J.C. Champlin at the *Courier*. I understand you left a message for me."

"Yes, I did," Kastens replied. "Can we get together and talk?"

"Certainly. What's on your mind?" she asked, despite having a pretty good idea already.

"Ms. Champlin—"

"Please, call me J.C."

"Okay, J.C., I read your article yesterday and found it was different from most of the others I've seen about my son," he began. "After I read it, I also called Captain McGowan and talked over a few things with him. During our conversation, he told me you asked about the letter Josh wrote—the one Captain McGowan delivered to me."

"Yes," Champlin said ever so subtly, prompting him to continue.

"I'd like to share the contents of that letter with you, Ms. Champlin—err, uh, J.C."

To Josh's dad, nothing on earth could have been more disturbing than the news he had struggled with during the previous four days. And when he began to see journalists and others including his son's name in mudslinging conversations about whether American involvement in so many wars was justified, it made him sick to his stomach. By sharing Josh's story with Champlin, he hoped to set the record straight.

"I appreciate that, Mr. Kastens."

"Please, call me Gary," he said. "Where can we meet?"

"Can I come to your house?" she asked. Not waiting for a reply, she continued, "I'd like to see where Josh grew up and take a look at pictures you have—stuff like that. Would that be alright?"

"Yes, why don't you come over and we can talk over lunch? I have enough food over here to feed the whole town."

"That sounds good. Let me get my things together, and I'll be there, let's say, by eleven?"

"Sounds fine," Kastens said. After giving Champlin directions to his home and exchanging few pleasantries, both hung up and the line went dead. That was Champlin's cue to get ready. She had thirty-five minutes until the interview. She hoped that would be enough time.

After a ten-minute shower, Champlin fixed her hair in five minutes and put on her face—that's how she described the process of applying foundation, mascara, etc.—in four. She laid out her clothes—her favorite pair of blue jeans, thin white pullover, denim jacket and pair of brown loafers—and dressed in another three minutes.

With a final look in the mirror, she let out a sigh of relief upon realizing she now had about eight minutes to write down a list of questions for the interview and five minutes to drive to the Kastens home. During the drive, she reasoned, she would outline in her mind a game plan for the interview.

Though she rarely stuck to an outline, she was loyal to the organized interview process she had perfected while working as a reporter for the student newspaper at Southern Illinois University-Edwardsville.

"What if he just wants to vent? What if he goes postal? What if?"

A flurry of questions raced through Champlin's mind as she waited for the stoplight to change to green at the intersection of Banker Road and West Fayette Street. Traffic was backed up three cars deep—a traffic jam by local standards—and she needed to get going. After what seemed an eternity with her foot on the brake pedal, she realized traffic was something she couldn't control, and then she had an epiphany.

Rather than try to control the interview process, she decided she would trust her instincts instead. This, after all, might be her first "story of a lifetime."

The red light eventually changed and, thanks mostly to Champlin's devotion to being on time, she found herself pulling into Kastens' driveway promptly at 11.

Her interview subject had seen her approaching in the powder blue 2008 Volkswagen Beetle her dad had bought her to drive to SIUE. When she came to within a half mile, she saw Kastens walking out his front door and across the lawn to wait next to his pickup truck at the top of his driveway. Only after she turned into the driveway and brought her car to a stop did she notice him begin to walk toward her.

"Hi," Champlin said as she climbed out of her car, pen and paper in hand. "You must be Gary."

"That's right," Kastens nodded, extending his hand to her as they came within arm's reach.

"J.C. Champlin," she said, making a point to smile, but not too widely as she sensed her interviewee was a bit nervous and likely had little experience with reporters. A pregnant pause followed as they stood still in front of her car, then Champlin tried to break the ice with light fare.

"You're right about this being the only home behind the Walmart," she said while taking small, follow-me steps toward the house.

"Yes," he replied, catching on to her prompt and beginning to walk alongside her. "As long as you can find the Walmart, you can find my place."

The two walked across the front lawn, still a bit soggy from a steady rain the night before. Upon reaching the front door, Kastens held the door open for Champlin as both wiped the bottom of their shoes on the welcome mat before entering.

Once inside, the reporter couldn't help but notice the abundance of flower arrangements. Everywhere, from the front door to the back door and in every direction—except for a narrow walking path—it seemed flowers had replaced carpet and furniture inside the home.

Kastens noticed her look of amazement.

"You wouldn't believe it, but I've turned away almost as many deliveries as I've accepted," he told Champlin before pulling the condolence card from one of the flower arrangements and locating the sender's information.

"They've come from as far away as Okinawa, Japan," he said while holding up the card.

"Wow, that must mean a lot to you."

"It does, I guess, but I'd trade it all in a heartbeat to have Josh back."

"I'm sure you would."

Another awkward moment of silence followed, then it appeared as if Kastens wanted to say something but struggled to let it out.

"Gary, I know this must to be hard to talk about," Champlin began, exhibiting a kind of wisdom that belied her youth, "but I get the feeling you have something really important to share with the world about your son, something you want the world to know about him."

Hearing those words, the man looked at the young reporter and sensed right away that she understood his pain.

"I do," he said. At the same time, he realized he should probably clear a place for the two to sit down so they could talk.

"Would you like to sit at the table here?" he asked after swallowing back his emotions. "I can clear the table off a bit."

"That would be great. Let me help you."

Together, the two began relocating flower vases and potted plants until there was enough room for each to pull up a chair and be able to see each other across the table.

"Are you hungry?"

"To be honest, I am. I haven't had anything to eat yet today."

"Well, you can take your pick," he said. Displaying a slight bit of theater, he waved his left hand as he opened the right-side door of his refrigerator-freezer with his other hand. "I have almost anything a hungry person might want when it comes to food."

The refrigerator was packed, and it had been a long time since the underpaid and overworked reporter had seen so many menu options. She chose an entrée that wouldn't interfere with taking notes.

"Would you mind if I have some of that pasta salad?" Champlin asked.

"Not at all. Plate or bowl?"

"Bowl, please."

Kastens grabbed a large bowl from the cabinet above and, using a spoon from the nearby silverware drawer, began scooping pasta salad from the Tupperware container.

Because his back was to her as he doled out the pasta salad, Champlin could only imagine how much he was scooping. Then, when he turned around, she saw he had filled the bowl several inches deep and almost as wide across as a dinner plate.

"Wow, that's a lot," she said, laughing at the thought of finishing such a large portion. "It could last me a week!"

"You're welcome to take home more if you like," he countered as he handed her a fork and spoon. "I'm not much of a pasta guy."

"Thank you, I will."

Kastens fixed himself a plate of sliced ham and baked beans and, after warming it up for a minute in the microwave, sat down and began eating. At the same time, he tried to anticipate the questions that were certain to follow, hoping he could answer them well.

"I hope you don't mind if I ask you questions and take notes while we eat," Champlin said, not expecting opposition.

When Kastens nodded, his mouth full, she took that as her "go" signal.

"Did Josh grow up here?"

"For the most part," he began after pausing to finish a bite. "We moved here when he was four. That was about twenty-six years ago."

"Can you tell me about him—you know, what was he like as a boy, as a young man and so on?"

"More than anything else, Josh cared for other people," the father began while looking straight into the eyes of the reporter. "When the Air Force men came to tell me Josh had died, I wasn't at all surprised to learn the circumstances of his death."

"What did they tell you?"

"They told me," he began before stopping a minute to collect his thoughts and begin anew. "They told me he died during a combat search-and-rescue mission.

"He'd been shot several times, but he still made sure the person he had been sent to rescue, Captain McGowan, made it out alive. That's the kind of person Josh is. Was."

"Was he always this way or did the Air Force mold him into the type of man he became?" Champlin probed, hoping her question might cause Kastens to exhibit the kind of pride most fathers love to express about their children—especially their sons.

"Yes, he was. From about the time he was thirteen, I had the feeling that saving lives would be an important part of his future."

"What happened then?"

"Josh watched a documentary on television that showed the bodies of American Soldiers being dragged through the streets of Somalia, and then he asked me why other Soldiers didn't save them. Four years later, he told me he was going to join the Air Force right after he finished high school."

"It sounds like Josh discovered his purpose in life pretty early on," Champlin said, hoping to elicit more details.

"He did," Kastens replied while leaning forward on his elbows and staring right into the eyes of his interviewer. "He saw something noble in the teamwork and camaraderie of the military and, at the same time, he saw his job in the Air Force as an opportunity to save lives."

"You must be very proud of your son."

"Of course, I am. I only wish he could hear me say so," he said, his voice trailing off.

"Can you tell me about Josh's mother?" Champlin asked, not sure about the backstory of her absence at the family home but feeling the need to know.

"She left us when Josh was two," Kastens explained, emotionless, "just a baby, really."

Anticipating Champlin's next question, Kastens offered an answer.

"No explanation. Never tried to contact either of us again."

"What is her name?"

"First name was Carla. Maiden name Coulson."

Sensing a need to change the direction of the interview, Champlin decided to ask some basic questions about Josh (i.e., schools he attended, his hobbies, his friends, etc.) and his dad (i.e., occupation, background, etc.). That detour took about ten minutes, and then she decided to ask Kastens to tell her about the letter he had received from Josh.

"Captain McGowan said he delivered a letter to you from Josh, and I think you mentioned it when we spoke earlier. Would you be willing to share what Josh wrote in that letter?"

"I would," he replied eagerly, holding up a well-worn number ten envelope for Champlin to see. "They said Josh carried it inside one of the zipper pockets of his flight suit and had it with him when he died."

Champlin could see Josh had written his father's name and address in blue ink in an effort that took up nearly half of the space on the front side of the envelope. And in the upper left corner of the same side, he had written his name and unit address. Below that, a handwritten message: *In the event of my death, please deliver to my dad at the address shown.* The envelope had no postage stamp on it—a sign Josh had known someone in his unit would ensure it was delivered personally.

"Josh told me to remember the promise I'd made to him in a letter last August," Kastens began. "In the event he didn't return from Africa, I would do everything within my power to prevent the United States from settling for defeat against Muslim extremists. Of course, I told him I would, but I never imagined I might have to fulfill that promise."

"That's a tall order—and please don't take this the wrong way—for an ordinary guy in a small town like Effingham," Champlin countered, hoping it would spur a response.

Champlin paused when she saw Kastens clench his jaw a bit upon hearing her words. His expression didn't look like one of anger, she thought. Perhaps it was anguish. To find out for sure, she asked the question in a different way, more directly.

"How are you going to live up to the promise?"

Though the question would haunt him the rest of his life, Kastens believed he knew how to answer it for Champlin.

"I know one man like me, working alone, can't overcome the type of evil we've seen displayed so often by terrorists and insurgents who would love nothing more than to see this country perish," he said. "If, however, others join me, I know I can keep the promise I made to my son, and I'm going to do everything within my power to fulfill that promise."

"It's probably too soon," Champlin countered, "but have you figured out any specifics about how you plan to fulfill the promise?"

"I've thought about a lot of things, a lot of options, you know, but I haven't finalized anything if that's what you're asking."

"Will you let me know when you decide upon something?" she asked, trying to keep the tone in her voice from sounding skeptical before realizing she had failed.

"J.C., I know you might think I'm way out on a limb here, one man thinking he can make a difference, but I truly believe I'll find a way."

It was at that instant Champlin felt the hair stand up on the back of her neck.

It wasn't necessarily the words he had used, but it was the combination of his words and his body language—elbows on the table, fists clenched in from of him—accentuated by a piercing stare that caused her to sense for the first time that the father of this town's latest fallen hero might be full of rage, ready to come unhinged.

Maybe he was angry at his fellow citizens for what he perceived to be their apathy and ignorance about wars being fought around the world by people like Josh. Or, perhaps, he was simply upset about losing his son in the war. Either way, she sensed an emotional cauldron boiling deep inside the man, and it was making her uneasy.

Champlin began to think it was time to take some photographs, wrap up the interview and, using one of her favorite clichés, "get the hell out of Dodge."

She double-checked the spelling of several names, verified some details about Josh's life and asked if she could borrow a few photos Kastens had shown her during the interview. Then, with his permission, she made her selection before thanking him for his willingness to share so much information about Josh during such a difficult time. After that, she made a beeline for the door, trying to avoid appearing as if she was in the hurry that she was.

By 2 p.m., Champlin was driving down the blacktop road again, oblivious to the fact she had forgotten the bowl of pasta salad Kastens had said she could take. Oh well, she had a story to write, and it wasn't exactly the story she thought she would be writing when she had arrived three hours earlier.

When Champlin walked through the back entrance to the newspaper building at 9 a.m. Monday, her editor was the first to greet her.

"So how did it go?" Hassler asked, fully anticipating some kind of melodramatic response from his promising young reporter.

"Kinda strange," she began as she walked toward her desk in the far corner of the newsroom, Hassler by her side. "It's one thing for a man to be saddened by his son's death, but it's quite another for him to be angry. Angry to the point that— "

"Wait a minute," Hassler said, stepping in front of her and looking straight into her eyes. "You say this guy was angry and not grieving? What gave you that impression?"

"He said he made a promise to his son that he would do everything within his power to prevent the U.S. from settling for defeat against Islamic extremists."

"So what? A lot of people would make that kind of promise."

"I think you're wrong, Kurt."

With that, she stepped around her editor and walked a few feet until she was able to deposit herself in the chair behind her desk and elaborate.

"This guy has a gap-toothed grin like David Letterman and seemed really nice at first. But after he started talking about keeping the promise to his son, I couldn't help but think he might be one of those guys you hear about on the evening news—you know, the guy all the neighbors say was 'friendly, but kept to himself a lot' after they hear about him being arrested for committing some heinous crime."

"I think you're confusing sadness with insanity, J.C. Losing a loved one—especially a first-born son—can cause people to behave strangely."

"*Only* son!" Champlin barked. "And *only* close relative to boot!"

"By the way," Hassler added as he walked away, realizing his decades of experience were not about to convince Champlin otherwise, "I want your story on my screen by noon Wednesday. That's forty-eight hours by my watch."

"Fifty-one hours!" Champlin shouted before leaning back in her chair and staring at the moisture-stained tiles in the drop ceiling above her. She suspected it might take every second of those hours to finish the job at hand—and it did.

†

The front page of the *Effingham Sunday Courier* was typically divided into thirds. The space above the fold of the broadsheet newspaper was usually reserved for something of national or international importance, enhanced with a powerful photo or graphic to catch the eyes of readers. Below the fold and to the right, a story of local importance would appear, intended to drag readers to an interior page of the newspaper that happened to be laden with advertisements. The rest of the front page usually consisted of news and feature briefs designed to catch a reader's attention and cause him to dive deep into the newspaper's interior pages to finish reading the stories and, not coincidentally, see more ads.

Unlike her story the week before, Champlin's latest piece occupied prime "real estate"—that is, front page above the fold—in the newest Sunday edition of the newspaper. It qualified as the prototypical small-town newspaper reporter's ultimate scoop.

Accompanied by a chronological set of photos revealing Josh's transformation from innocent child to handsome war hero who had given his all for his country, the young reporter's story read ever so smoothly.

6

Though Illinois Chemical owed Gary Kastens more than six weeks of vacation, he decided to return to work after an absence of only two. He thought doing so might take his mind off his loss. Barely halfway through his first day back at work, however, he realized it did not.

With the encouragement of his boss, Plant Manager Dan Christie, Kastens left work early and decided to use a few more days to try and sort things out.

At home by noon, he flipped on the television and found a cable news anchor interviewing Brad Binkholder. A financial expert and best-selling author, Binkholder began by using the phrase, "slow-motion train wreck," to describe the early stages of the U.S. economic collapse that had paralleled President Barack Obama's first six years in office. Soon after, he resorted to another metaphor.

"If Chinese leaders follow through on their threats to dump U.S. debt—and I think they will," he said, "the U.S. economy will more closely resemble a Japanese bullet train going downhill without brakes. Our national debt interest payments will soar, inflation will skyrocket, the dollar will become nearly worthless and Americans—especially the elderly living on fixed incomes—will struggle like they've never struggled before."

On another channel, a news anchor talked over an on-screen graphic depicting how nearly seventy percent of

American voters, according to one poll, believed the United States needed to bring its warfighters home from their overseas deployments.

"The survey results show most Americans want their men and women in uniform to come home from the predominantly Muslim countries where they are fighting," the anchor continued as viewers watched B-roll footage of American Soldiers and Marines who appeared to be fighting somewhere in the Middle East. "We asked Americans what they think."

"So many have died already, and we've spent billions on what?" said a middle-aged ironworker, interviewed outside a delicatessen on Cicero Street near Chicago's Midway Airport. "We need to get outta there now!"

"Let them fight it out amongst themselves," said a thirty-something image consultant wearing a Brooks Brothers suit and walking in New York City's financial district. "It's time to bring our troops home!"

Others, including a teacher's aide interviewed outside an Austin supermarket and a college student at Brigham Young University in Provo, Utah, shared similar views.

The news anchor concluded his report by stating that large majorities in both houses of Congress, "including several who only recently began their first terms in office," had reached the same isolationist conclusion. What he failed to explain, however, was that decisions made by the politicians had been driven largely by what their pollsters had told them would win votes among Americans mostly unaware of any specifics related to President Obama's reckless approach to foreign affairs.

That approach had included announcing in advance our timelines for withdrawing troops from Iraq and Afghanistan; supporting a Muslim Brotherhood takeover in Egypt during the so-called "Arab Spring" of 2011; arming al-Qaeda-aligned rebel groups in Syria; failing to send military help to Benghazi, Libya, after Islamic extremists attacked the U.S. Consulate there and killed four Americans, including Ambassador Christopher Stevens; and recklessly withdrawing forces from Iraq and Afghanistan only to see both countries fall back into disarray, their citizens under the thumbs of Islamic extremists.

While Kastens knew little about foreign policy or terrorism, he did remember one day on which the two had intersected.

"How could everyone have forgotten September 11th?" Kastens asked himself in disbelief as he began to realize the magnitude of the battle that awaited him as he struggled to fulfill his promise to his son. He also realized failure wasn't an option.

After watching a seemingly endless parade of anti-war, pro-withdrawal news stories and stump speeches, Kastens decided the best way to start attacking the problem was by writing letters to those elected officials purporting to represent his interests in Washington, D.C.

All three members of *his* Illinois delegation in the nation's capitol were men—one a Republican, two Democrats, all self-centered.

The redheaded son of Irish immigrant parents, Democrat Representative Robbie Mauk called Altamont his home but was even willing to negotiate that for the right price. Serving his fifth term as the voice of Illinois' 19th Congressional District, his friends called him "Red" and his enemies called him "Red-handed"—as in caught that way—due to a long list of allegations he benefited frequently from under-the-table deals with individuals and organizations with ties to organized crime. Though censured once by his House colleagues, he somehow managed to avoid genuine prosecution.

From the affluent Chicago suburb of Naperville, Democrat Senator Charles L. Slott looks the part of a fat cat career politician. Though he weighs in a pie slice over three hundred pounds, it's his political weight that he never hesitates to throw around. As the one-time head of the state's most-powerful teachers union, the Democrat twisted enough arms and compiled enough dirt on his challengers to win four consecutive six-year terms. So far.

The American-born son of Chinese immigrants, Senator Bing Yee moved to Illinois from San Francisco after graduating from UC-Berkley. He speaks Chinese fluently and owes most of his professional and political success to corporate interests outside of his district. In political circles, the Republican who calls Carol Stream home is known to return favors to constituents who treat him well, and the best way to do that is by contributing to his re-election bids every six years. No ancient Chinese secret in that formula.

During a seven-hour marathon session in front of his barely-used three-year-old desktop computer, Kastens typed and retyped a letter several times until he felt like it made sense without being too confrontational. Finished at 3 a.m. Tuesday, April 22, the body of his letter read:

I'm writing this letter today for deeply personal reasons.

Several months ago, my son, Air Force Master Sergeant Joshua L. Kastens, sent me a letter from a base somewhere in Africa. In his letter, he asked me to do one thing for him. In the event he didn't return, he asked me to promise him I would do everything within my power to prevent the United States from settling for defeat against Muslim extremists wherever they were in the world. I responded by sending a letter back to him, promising him that I would honor his request.

Then, on April 7, 2014, Josh and a fellow pararescueman were shot while performing a combat search and rescue mission in Africa. Sadly, my son died of his wounds, but not until he and his partner had completed the rescue of the downed pilot they had been sent to save. (See the attached newspaper clipping.)

After burying Josh at a cemetery in Effingham 11 days ago, I now have to honor the promise I hoped I would never have to keep. Not knowing how or where to begin, I decided to write this letter to you and to the other members of the Illinois delegation in Washington D.C.

Please help me honor the promise I made to my son by assuring me you will oppose any and all efforts to withdraw U.S. troops from Afghanistan, Africa, the Middle East and other places where Americans serve before the mission to defeat Islamic extremism is accomplished. By making this pledge, you'll be telling Americans that my son, and thousands of other courageous Americans just like him, did not sacrifice their lives in vain.

I trust you will do the right thing and look forward to your reply.

After Kastens was satisfied with the content of the letter, he customized the address blocks and salutations for each recipient before adding his signature to each letter and preparing the envelopes to go in the mail the next day. Then he breathed a sigh of relief.

He had finally taken the first step—albeit a small one—toward fulfilling his promise to his son. Now, he would wait for his elected officials to respond.

†

One week after mailing the letters, Kastens' awoke from the state of near-sleep he had struggled with for most of a month. It was 5:15 a.m. on the first day of his second attempt to return to work at Illinois Chemical. His to-do list included making a call to Senator Slott's office in Washington, D.C., during his lunch break. Because folks in the nation's capitol were working an hour ahead, he decided to take an early lunch, hoping to increase his chances of success.

Kastens wasn't calling the senator to thank him for his response to the letter he had sent two weeks earlier, though it was the only response he had received from any member of the Illinois delegation; instead, he wanted to explain how he felt as if he had been written off by the senator and his staff—a bunch referred to by many as the "Slott Machine" because they took in a lot of money and gave back little in return.

Kastens imagined someone on the senator's Capitol Hill office staff had only glanced at the letter he had written, seen the word, Africa, and concluded that a form letter outlining the senator's stance on foreign aid to Africa would suffice. That someone turned out to be wrong.

"Senator Slott's office, what is your zip code, please?" answered a young female receptionist, using a time-tested Washington method for screening calls.

"Six-two-four-zero-one," Kastens replied.

"Please hold."

A two-minute medley of the senator's campaign sound bites filled Kastens' ear, backed up by patriotic music. Then, as if on cue, the audio package ended and Kastens heard the voice of another female staffer.

"Good morning, may I help you," she said, careful not to offer her name so as not to have it linked to a constituent unhappy with her reply.

"Who am I speaking with?" Kastens asked.

"This is Tiffany," she answered curtly. "How may I help you?"

"Tiffany, my name is Gary Kastens, and I'm calling to voice my concerns to Senator Slott."

"Sir, I'm going to have to ask you to visit our web site, Slott dot senate dot guv—that's g-o-v. We have a comment tool on the website you can use to express your concerns directly to the senator."

"I don't want to use the website, Tiffany! That's why I called you today!"

"Sir, please hold."

Kastens spent the next five minutes on hold, this time listening to recorded audio of a recent appearance the senator had made on a Sunday morning news show. When Tiffany came back on, she was decidedly ruder than before.

"Okay, sir," she said, speaking to Kastens as if his call had interrupted her busy schedule. "What do you need?"

"Tiffany, I sent a letter to Senator Slott two weeks ago and, yesterday, I received a form letter about foreign aid!" he began, determined not to let Tiffany interrupt him again. "My son was killed in Africa last month, young lady, and I think I deserve more from my senator than a form letter that doesn't address my concerns. Don't you?"

Incredibly, Tiffany's tone remained unchanged as she issued a final plea to the senator's concerned constituent.

"Sir, I'm so sorry about your loss, but the senator receives thousands of letters each week and simply doesn't have the staff to answer each of them personally. The best way to reach Senator Slott is by using the comment tool on the website."

As Kastens began to speak again, his ear filled with the sound of a dial tone. Tiffany had hung up on him.

"Unbelievable!" he shouted before pushing the END button on his pre-paid cell phone and putting it back into the tool pocket of his favorite blue-denim painter's pants.

At this point, Kastens reached the conclusion that his elected officials were out of touch and that he would have to meet with them face to face in order to get his point across.

7

Gary Kastens' boss had told him he could take more time off if he needed it, so he decided to take him up on his offer and asked for two more days off—Tuesday and Wednesday of the following week—and got them.

After ending his shift Monday, May 5, 2014, Kastens drove 109 miles to Saint Louis to catch a nonstop flight to Baltimore on Southwest Airlines. After arriving early at Baltimore-Washington International Thurgood Marshall Airport, he made his way to the curbside pickup area and boarded a shuttle van that whisked him to his motel, a Holiday Inn Express a few blocks from the airport. Within thirty minutes, he had checked in, made it to his fourth-floor room, cleaned up, and turned down the sheets on his king-size bed.

If his day went as planned, he would take a shuttle to the train station early in the morning and, from there, take the Penn Line to Union Station in the heart of the District. Following a short walk toward Capitol Hill, he would darken the doorways of each of his elected representatives in the U.S. Senate and House of Representatives. After wrapping up his meetings by 4 p.m., he would return to Union Station in time to catch the 4:15 train back to the station at the airport. Once there, he would catch the 7:25 flight back to Saint Louis, make it home by a decent hour, and have all day

Wednesday to process what he had been told by his elected officials.

Sleep came quickly. So did Tuesday morning. Though Kastens had scheduled a 6 a.m. wake-up call with the front desk, he found himself up and about a full hour before the call came. He couldn't wait to meet with his elected officials.

Ten minutes before 6, Kastens entered the motel's first-floor lobby/dining room to find a crowd of early risers enjoying the free continental breakfast buffet. Like most others in the room, he was wearing a suit. For him, however, it wasn't the kind of comfortable attire he preferred.

After eating a hot breakfast of eggs, bacon, toast and coffee, Kastens boarded a complementary shuttle to the train station where, ten minutes later, he stood on a platform with nearly two hundred others and waited. After train 407 arrived, he found a backward-facing seat and stared out the window until the train reached Union Station—within walking distance of the White House and Capitol Hill—at 7:30.

His first stop, the Russell Senate Office Building, was less than a mile away, according to a map of the capitol complex he had found online and printed the previous day.

Carrying a small overnight bag that resembled a backpack, Kastens began walking and watching. Never before had he seen such a variety of people, including several who managed to balance newspapers, cell phones, PDAs and steaming cups of coffee while pulling wheeled suitcases and dollies loaded with boxes full of who-knows-what.

Among those not drinking coffee and/or managing heavy loads, he saw were panhandling homeless people and $10-an-hour protesters who marched in circles and carried message-laden signs outside government buildings while expressing half-hearted support for the cause du jour employer who had hired them. No, this wasn't Effingham by a long shot.

Almost ten minutes into his walk, Kastens reached the entrance to what he thought might be the most appropriately named building in the capitol. On his map, its name appeared as "Russell SOB." Though he couldn't remember any person named Russell who deserved to have his name on a Senate Office Building, he believed the SOB acronym suited Senator Slott perfectly.

Kastens walked up the steps and through the building's entrance only to learn he couldn't pass through security without authorization from someone in Senator Slott's office.

"I flew all the way from Saint Louis to talk to my senator!"

"I'm sorry, sir," a guard replied without giving details about the skyrocketing number of threats made against members of Congress during the previous year. "Due to heightened security measures, we can't let anyone past the checkpoint without an appointment. I suggest you call your senator's office."

Though discouraged by this turn of events, Kastens thanked the guard for his advice and took it.

Standing outside the building's entrance minutes later, he dialed the number for Senator Slott's office which he had brought with him just in case. A squeaky-voiced female staffer answered, and he explained his predicament.

"I'm sorry, but the senator is booked solid for the next two weeks."

"My son gave his life for this country, and you're telling me my senator doesn't have time to meet with me for just a few minutes?"

"Not without an appointment, sir," she answered coldly. "I suggest you visit the senator's website and put in your request."

"But I'm standing on the steps of your office building, and I don't have a doggone computer!"

Cutting him off, she replied, "That's your best chance, sir. Goodbye," and Kastens heard another dial tone.

To save himself from any more unproductive travel by foot, Kastens called the offices of Senator Lee and Representative Altamont and received treatment eerily similar to that doled out by the Slott Machine staffer.

Adjectives failed to adequately describe his emotions at that point, and Kastens realized he could count on no one else when it came to fulfilling the promise to his son.

Members of Congress had become more interested in exercising control over every aspect of Americans' lives and keeping themselves in power than in being responsive to a single constituent; more focused on polling results, cast into the public arena by special-interest groups, than on what was best for the nation; and more eager to ensure their own short-term political gains than long-term national security.

Soon after—and completely unrelated to—Kastens' visit to D.C., they began demanding what public opinion polls showed most Americans wanted: a complete withdrawal of U.S. troops from the Middle East, Southwest Asia, Africa and the Muslim world.

Despite the fact a withdrawal would make it easier for Islamic extremists to expand their global reach and wage jihad against American interests worldwide, Kastens believed the poll results reflected how ignorant most of his fellow citizens had become about the Constitutional principles upon which the country was founded, about how to conduct foreign policy, and about the right and proper use of military might to safeguard national interests.

"Does anyone understand what we're up against?" he asked himself. "The Jihadists are winning, and things will only get worse. What will it take for Americans to wake up?"

It wasn't long until he received a partial answer to his litany of questions.

While starting his walk back to Union Station, Kastens noticed something he had not seen while walking along the same route earlier that day. People. Throngs of people.

Many were dressed in the usual suit-and-tie attire of Capitol Hill staffers and K Street Northwest lobbyists. Just as many, however, were not dressed to impress. Instead, they appeared as if they had traveled far, from places as remote as Effingham.

Carrying signs, folding chairs, coolers and other gear, they seemed to be on their way to a rally or protest of some sort, and prepared to stay a while. Likewise, they did not appear to belong to any specific activist group hoping to gain media exposure for a specific issue or cause. Instead, they reeked of being grassroots activists who had come to the nation's capitol with hopes of seeing someone held responsible for the rapid downward spiral of the republic.

With his schedule unexpectedly wide open, Kastens decided to follow the crowd and, within minutes, realized they were headed to the mall area near the Lincoln Memorial and Reflecting Pool.

Upon arrival at the site made famous by so many events over the years, he heard someone describe the current protest as "ten days old and growing" and "exponentially larger than 'Operation Patriot Rising 2013,'" a grassroots effort that had failed to draw much in the way of participants or media attention a year earlier despite having had the impeachment of President Obama and removal of other top officials from office as its stated goals.

Kastens wondered how he had missed news reports about this massive protest. Then he looked around and found network television news crews nowhere in sight. Instead, only a handful of local and niche media outlets had dispatched reporters to the event.

Members of the nation's largest national news media outlets (a.k.a., "the mainstream media") had apparently opted to stick to their decades-old practice of serving as propaganda organs for elected officials and special interest groups devoted to the government-knows-best ideology. As a result, only those who witnessed such events firsthand or paid attention to alternative news sources (a.k.a., "the new media") were likely to know the true extent to which their elected officials and the MSM had failed them.

One question remained on Kastens' mind: What would it take to wake the American people?

Kastens observed the protest for a couple of hours before making his way back to the airport, catching his nonstop return flight to Saint Louis and arriving home a few minutes before 10:30 Tuesday night.

After spending the next day reflecting upon his D.C. visit and thinking about what he might do next, Kastens returned to work Thursday. There, Christie shared some news.

"Gary, I know it's been a tough road lately, and I can't imagine what you've gone through," he began, "and, because I expect things to get much busier during the next few months, I'm gonna make some temporary changes."

"What kind of changes?" Kastens countered.

"I'm moving Burt to day shift, and having you run the graveyard shift for a while. It's slower and less stressful, you know. Maybe that'll help you out a bit."

"Dan, it's your call, and it is temporary, right?"

"Just a few months, Gary, then we'll switch things back."

"You know I haven't been a night owl for years," Kastens said, trying to lighten the moment while realizing his boss probably felt worse about it than he did. "When do we start?"

"Sunday night. You'll have a few days to prepare yourself."

"Have you told Burt yet?" Kastens asked, referring to Burt Abramov, the graveyard shift manager.

"Not yet, but I'll talk to him tonight when he comes in," Christie said while rising to his feet. "You know he'll want it to be permanent, right?"

"As long as you promise me it's not, I won't worry," Kastens said as he walked out the door.

"It's only temporary, Gary. I promise."

8

Located off I-57 almost five miles north of Effingham, Illinois, Benson Wood College was home to about eleven hundred students when Michael del Rosario arrived on campus in August 2010, three weeks ahead of the first day of fall semester classes, so he could participate in orientation for international students.

A nineteen-year-old freshman everyone would come to know as Rosy, he didn't know much about the history of the school or its namesake, a long-since-dead local politician. And that was about the only thing he shared in common with most of his fellow students, the majority of whom came from homes less than two hundred miles away.

One of only a handful of students from the Republic of the Philippines, Rosy became homesick almost immediately after his arrival in the Land of Lincoln. At the same time, he knew in his heart that his father had wanted only the best for him when he had put him on the airplane that would take him halfway around the world, cut off from all he knew and loved, and drop him smack in the middle of the American heartland—a place many Americans referred to as "flyover country."

For the most part, returning students, faculty and staff tried to make good first impressions on new students. Unfortunately, their efforts began to wane only a few weeks into the first semester, and Rosy began to feel less welcome with each passing day. That's when a fellow Filipino took notice.

A junior business major from the southern Philippines island of Mindanao, Manuel Romanillos had experienced feelings similar to Rosy's after his arrival in the U.S. two years earlier. In response, the Catholic-since-birth Filipino had sought out a sense of belonging and found it in a most-unexpected place. Only eight months after arriving on campus, he had converted to Islam and, as part of his effort to conform to the tenets of his new religion, had changed his name to Mohamed Abu Nadal. By design, the initials of his new name would allow him to keep using his beloved nickname, Manny.

Anyone who watched Manny on a daily basis would have been hard-pressed to describe the short and stocky Filipino's post-conversion routine as that of a devout Muslim—except for when he was trying to recruit others to Islam.

On a brisk December day near the end of the 2010 fall semester, Manny began sharing his newfound ideology with Rosy. Without naming it, he described Islam as a "unique opportunity to become part of something big" and went on to explain that its beauty lies in the fact it runs completely counter to the values Rosy's parents had tried to instill in him and his younger siblings—three brothers and two sisters—since birth. Rosy, however, didn't buy the sales pitch.

Having grown up in a devout Roman Catholic household, Rosy decried Manny's recruiting efforts, once going so far as to compare his unholy worldview to those of his countrymen in the Northern Philippines province of Pampanga who, for more than sixty years, had drawn thousands of tourists to their bloody annual reenactments of the crucifixion of Christ.

Because his father and so many other Catholics had detested the Good Friday events, Rosy had detested them, too.

During the next two school years, the Filipinos continued their education, and Manny continued working on Rosy as if whittling a piece of wood with a dull pocket knife. It wasn't until the spring semester of Rosy's senior year that Manny, then pursuing his MBA at the college, realized his young target might have reason to be more receptive to his message.

Less than three months before he was set to graduate, Rosy told Manny how, during a video chat with his parents, he had asked his father if he could return home for Christmas that year; how, by asking ten months in advance of the holiday after spending three Christmas breaks in a row far from his family, he had hoped to improve his chances of receiving a positive response; and, how he had received an answer identical to those he had received on several earlier occasions dating back to the first fall break after his plane carried him away from Ninoy Aquino International Airport.

"Michael, your education is more important than coming home for Christmas," his father told him. "You can come home when you finish your master's degree. I'm sorry, but it's best that way."

His father's unwillingness to budge had put the dark-haired twenty-three year old over the proverbial edge, ready to take his life in a new direction. Still several months from receiving his bachelor's degree in chemical engineering, Rosy didn't know which direction he might follow, but he liked to think it would follow a path independent of his father and his authority.

After hearing a distraught Rosy tell him about his father's decision, Manny sensed opportunity like never before.

During an intense three-hour conversation that followed, Manny described Islam as a means via which Rosy could serve notice to his sometimes-overbearing father that he was going to be his own man. In addition, he carefully outlined how Islam would allow Rosy, once and for all, to end what he described as the "toxic relationships" he had with members of his family— especially his father.

"If your father really loved you, he wouldn't have forced you to leave home and stay away for so long," Manny said, carefully driving a wedge between the young man and the man he had once regarded as his hero. "If you would like to be part of something better, a bigger family, become a Muslim like me. Become my brother in Islam."

Though not ready to commit immediately, Rosy began attending meetings of the Muslim Students League on campus.

During six weeks of often-heated discussions with Manny and others at the meetings, Rosy's objections began melting away. Gradually, he found himself caving to relentless pressure from MSL members who seemed so interested in his future, teetering on the brink of deciding that a religion whose followers recognized Jesus had walked this earth more than two thousand years earlier couldn't be all wrong.

One month before his undergraduate days at Benson Wood were set to end, Rosy found himself seriously considering whether or not he should convert to Islam.

In his still-forming young adult brain, Rosy viewed his father as someone who had pushed him away and seemed not to want him back. Conversely, he saw Manny as someone who had spent endless hours with him, expressing what seemed to be heartfelt interest in his future.

Though Rosy knew such a major life decision would likely result in him cutting all ties to his family, he finally gave in to Manny's non-stop recruiting effort and converted to Islam.

Soon after witnessing Rosy's conversion, Manny urged his new Muslim friend to sit down and write a letter to his father, a devout Roman Catholic businessman who owned and operated a small printing business in Manila.

"You and your ways are dead to me. I am now a Muslim," Rosy declared in the letter, dated Wednesday, April 9, 2014. "Had you truly loved me, I might not have discovered the truth. Now, I am thankful for your hatred and thankful we shall never meet again. Praise be to Allah! Allahu Akbar!"

The new convert ended his painfully-brief letter by writing the name given to him at birth by his parents and then crossing it out with red ink that Manny said represented blood. Next to it, he used the same pen to write his new Muslim name, Yusaf Abdul Sharif.

Once the letter reached his parents, Rosy—he still couldn't think of himself as Sharif—knew it would cause them terrible pain. And, if sent too soon, he knew it might cause him pain as well.

Fearful his father would cut off the funding of his educational pursuits as soon as he received the letter, Rosy found temporary relief in the fact that his father had already paid his room, board and tuition expenses for his first semester of grad school that would begin in July. To be safe, however, he decided against mailing the letter until such time as his tuition payments at the school had become fully non-refundable. Mailing it sooner, he feared, might result in his father demanding the school return the money.

Rosy folded the letter into an envelope and stuck it into the pages of the Holy Bible that had been collecting dust on a shelf above his bed for many months.

✝

Graduation came and, during the two-week break that followed, Rosy focused more of his attention on studying the Koran and the radical teachings of the local imam than on preparing for graduate school. If he continued on this path, however, the young man knew it couldn't be a lack of finances that would end his pursuit of a master's degree in chemical engineering. It would be poor grades.

To avoid such an outcome, he put everything else on the back burner and worked on a contingency plan to deal with the financial challenges he would surely encounter as soon as his father discovered he had converted to Islam and cut off his financial support. He went looking for a place to live and a job to pay the bills.

Through a Muslim Students League contact, Rosy hooked up with three other Muslim students who had a spare bed in the apartment they rented near campus.

In addition, a friend at the school registrar's office helped him land a part-time janitorial job at Illinois Chemical Company. Though working Tuesday, Thursday and Saturday nights couldn't pay well, required a twenty-minute bike ride or a one-hour walk to and from work each way, and seemed to hold little possibility of upward mobility, he sensed the job might offer some hidden opportunities. With no other offers in sight, Rosy started working at Illinois Chemical Saturday, May 4, 2014.

After learning what was expected of him on Day One, Rosy took only a few days to develop an efficient routine. He would arrive at the plant by 10:45 p.m., sweep the floors, empty the trash cans and, during the hours that followed, mop and polish the concrete floor that was nearly the size of a football field. The routine usually left him with at least an hour at the end of shift during which he could read or study.

Because he found his work mind-numbing at times, Rosy frequently stared up at the ceiling, mesmerized by the maze of pipes through which raw materials flowed from temperature-controlled storage tanks outside the building to processing lines inside. Ever curious, he wanted to learn as much as possible about how the company's products were produced before being delivered to customers.

It didn't take long before Rosy's approach caught the attention of his graveyard-shift coworkers. They noticed he completed in six hours the same amount of work his predecessor had needed eight to finish. And he did a better job.

Soon, everyone at the plant came to know Rosy as the hard-working Filipino who, while nervous on his first day, had slipped up and said they could call him by his old nickname instead of by his Muslim name, Yusaf.

One man who took notice of Rosy's work was Christie. After watching him work hard and efficiently for several weeks, the plant manager engaged him in conversation about his career plans.

"What do you plan to do after you get your master's degree?" Christie asked his newest employee one night, shortly before his shift ended.

"My goal is to obtain an H-1B visa that will allow me to stay in the United States and work full-time after graduation," Rosy replied.

"What is it you're studying again?"

"Chemical engineering. As a boy, I found it fascinating to watch my father as he mixed inks at his printing company to produce different colors. Now, I want to do more than just mix the ink. Perhaps, I can develop new processes for making the ink itself."

The kind of guy who liked to help people simply for the good feeling it gave him, Christie didn't know much about the specialty occupation visa Rosy had mentioned, but he did know the company wanted to find a replacement for one of it's senior engineers who was planning to retire in a couple of years. At the same time, he recognized the young man's demonstrated work ethic, advanced education, and minority status would fit all of the company's needs. On top of that, he had heard good reports from his shift managers about Rosy's work.

Two days later, Christie asked him if he would be interested in an apprenticeship.

"Of course, I would. Does that mean I would continue to work nights?"

"Sometimes, but not as a janitor. You'd be an engineer in training, working different shifts every six months while the company pays your college bills."

"Wow!" Rosy replied, shocked at the turn of events.

"In exchange, you'd be asked to sign a contract that says you'll commit to working at Illinois Chemical part-time while you're in school and for at least six years after you finish your graduate program. It might even require a move to Chicago in a few years. How's that sound?"

"I'm all in!"

Christie told Rosy he would submit the paperwork to the company's Chicago headquarters and, if everything went well, someone from human resources would contact him "sometime soon" about setting up a meeting and finalizing the deal. After that, the two parted ways.

Rosy knew such an opportunity might open doors for him. At a minimum, he knew it would enable him to climb out from under his father's financial thumb. He even began to believe his conversion to Islam might have played a role.

Whether or not he was being completely honest with himself on that point still gnawed at his conscience.

9

Though technically on vacation two days after Christmas, Christie came in to work for early-morning meetings with three employees.

During the first meeting, he would share good news. During the second meeting, he would make someone happy. During the third meeting, he would deliver bad news. There was, however, little he could do to prevent it.

Christie approached Rosy an hour before the young man was due to clock out and long after he had finished all of his cleaning duties.

"Merry Christmas, Rosy—if you celebrate the holiday, I mean."

"I hope you had a good holiday, sir," Rosy replied in a low-key manner while dodging the awkward issue of the religious holiday. After waiting more than twenty weeks for news about the apprenticeship, he had all but given up.

"Thank you, I did, and it looks like I have a present for you. The folks at headquarters approved your apprenticeship, Rosy. You're in!"

Rosy was floored by the news.

"Oh, thank you so much, Mr. Christie," he said, almost crying while reaching out and grabbing Christie's right hand with both of his own. "I will work very hard for you. Thank you! Thank you!"

"I'm sure you will, Rosy. I'll need you to stop by Human Resources and sign some papers during the day tomorrow, and then you can start your new job next week. Sound good?"

"Oh yes, Mr. Christie! Thank you so much!"

✝

Fifteen minutes later, Christie found Kastens on the plant floor.

"Are you ready to return to the day shift, Gary?" Christie asked as he came within earshot of Kastens.

"I think I am, Dan. As ready as I'll ever be, I suppose."

"I appreciate the way you've handled the graveyard shift, but look forward to having you around during the day again."

"So, when do we make the change?"

"If it works for you, Monday the fifth."

"Count me in, Dan—and thanks!"

✝

Christie's third meeting began soon after he returned to his office and found Burt Abramov walking through the glass double doors at the main entrance of the plant. It was 6:25.

"Burt, can I talk with you a second?" Christie asked while leaning out into the hallway from his office.

"Sure," said the fifty-two year old who had enjoyed the day-shift manager position for more than seven months. "Let me grab a cup of coffee, and I'll be right there."

Abramov returned to Christie's office a few minutes later.

"What do you need, Mr. Christie?" asked Abramov, not addressing his boss by his first name because he believed doing so might be interpreted as a lack of respect.

"Burt, I need to talk with you about a change I'm making next week. I'm gonna move Gary back to the day shift."

Christie could have said more, but both men knew all they needed to know as soon as those words had been spoken.

"Next week?" Abramov asked, the calm tone of his voice belying the angry expression that began taking over his face as he placed his coffee mug on the edge of Christie's desk.

"Monday."

Hearing Christie's answer, Abramov stood up and stormed out of the room, out of the building, and to his car in the parking lot. Never looking back, rage filled his mind as he raced out of the parking lot toward the plant's entrance.

Christie understood why Abramov was upset. The move back to the graveyard shift would mean he would spend less time with his children. But Christie could do little to change that.

Something else Christie could do little to change was Abramov's short temper. If the man didn't return in time to manage that day's shift, he wouldn't have a future at the plant. Both men knew that; therefore, Christie didn't worry about whether Abramov would return. He knew the man had no choice.

10

A few minutes past noon on May 11, 2015, President Barack Obama shocked the nation during an announcement carried live on all of the major television and radio networks as well as PBS, C-Span, YouTube and thousands of new media outlets.

Barely two years after the nation's forty-fourth president had proposed a cap on lifetime contributions to individual retirement and 401(k) accounts at "about three million dollars for someone retiring in 2013," he told Americans something that cut even deeper.

"The American economy is on the verge of collapse and, after consulting with members of my cabinet, I decided to take swift action to avert disaster. A few minutes ago, I signed an Executive Order that effectively places the Treasury Secretary in what I like to describe as a guardianship role over the retirement savings plans of all Americans."

Hearing the news, Americans braced themselves for what he would say next.

"So, what does that mean? It means this: if you have an IRA, a 401K, a pension or any other type of retirement plan, it means it will now be held in trust, safe, by the United States Government. And it means you can sleep comfortably tonight knowing it is safe."

Unlike the never-implemented proposal the president had pitched in May 2013 as a way to prevent the people he called "wealthy individuals" from accumulating "substantially more than is needed to fund reasonable levels of retirement savings," this executive order—the most recent of more than two-hundred he had signed since taking office—left Americans feeling as if a sacred trust had been broken.

After the fine-print details of the order—conveniently omitted by the president during his television address—became public, Americans became angry, feeling as if they had been robbed of their retirement nest eggs. In turn, they began directing their anger at anyone remotely connected to Washington, D.C.

Even those in charge of newsrooms across the country showed interest. Finally, it seemed, they realized they could no longer ignore the damage done by too much government intrusion into the lives of its citizens; they could no longer look the other way as dishonest politicians got away with legislative and regulatory murder; and they could no longer ignore their own decades-long failure to be objective in their reporting. After all, *it* was about to affect their financial futures in much the same way it would those they had so often referred to as "workers" and "ordinary" Americans.

The days of lobbing softball questions had come to an end. There would be no more fluff pieces about First Lady Michelle Obama's efforts to make fat kids eat healthy food and no more reports about congressional hearings that seemed little more than feeble attempts to pacify angry Americans demanding swift prosecution of senior Obama Administration officials for their involvement in myriad scandals.

Finally, members of the mainstream media began doing their jobs as journalists.

Newspapers began offering objective front-page reports, and news magazines began offering the kind of long-form stories that had almost disappeared from the journalism landscape. Most importantly, details about several scandals that had been overlooked during the previous six years—including, but not limited to, Benghazi, "Extortion 17," and "Fast and Furious"—began to emerge.

Life in the United States changed dramatically following President Obama's announcement on the day that would be remembered in history books of the future as Black Monday: non-perishable food items virtually disappeared from store shelves, snapped up by anxious and fearful Americans; hundreds of long-haul trucks and freight trains full of food and other vital necessities fell victim to armed robbers; supply chains were disrupted; and Secret Service agents lost count of the number of threats made against officials in all three branches of government. Perhaps most importantly, the protest Kastens had witnessed in the nation's capitol more than a year earlier had gone viral.

Often seeming leaderless and usually conducted without seeking permits from any government agencies, protests raged like never before in Boston, Miami, Seattle and every major city in between. Everyone, including members of the military and law enforcement agencies, had had enough.

In public squares, in farm fields and on the steps of taxpayer-owned buildings in cities across the country, the American people joined forces and vented anger in ways not seen in this country since Paul Revere had shouted from horseback, "The British are coming!"

Tea Party and Occupy Movement. Liberal and conservative. Union and non-union. Republican and Democrat. All had reached the conclusion that government was out of control and deserving of the title, Public Enemy Number One.

Elected officials across the nation—and especially in the nation's capitol—felt the heat like never before. Many, including Illinois' Senators Slott and Yee and Congressman Mauk, made themselves unavailable to reporters and ordered their spokespersons to say they were "in closed-door sessions, working hard to resolve the crisis in bipartisan fashion."

No longer willing to accept such political posturing and double-speak, Americans began calling for resignations and launching recall petitions.

Amidst news reports about ammunition and body armor sales going through the roof, the nation's top elected officials began to sense the end was near, that the tipping point had finally arrived. And they were right.

On Tuesday, June 30, 2015, President Obama, Vice President Joe Biden and leaders of both the House and Senate heard from members of Congress, state governors, and others from a wide array of academic, business and professional groups of a loose-knit coalition of people with long track records of supporting limited government. Their demands were clear: resign immediately or face criminal prosecution on a laundry list of charges, up to and including treason.

Though the process did not adhere to the letter of the law as set forth in the Constitution, those given the option to resign quickly realized they were facing opponents who represented the vast majority of the American population— and, for what it was worth, had the tacit approval of the Joint Chiefs of Staff and a majority of Supreme Court justices.

President Obama was the first to resign at 5 that evening. Within hours, members of the president's cabinet and White

House leadership team resigned, too. By midnight, the Republican Speaker of the House and the Democrat Senate Majority Leader had followed suit.

Members of Congress still standing after the resignations realized they would have to adapt quickly to the new normal if they were to stand any chance of keeping their jobs. In addition, they would have to distance themselves from their track records as RINOs (a.k.a., "Republicans In Name Only") and tax-and-spend Democrats. The old ways of doing business would no longer be tolerated. The American people had had enough, and the 2016 primary elections were not far away.

Of course, everyone in the nation's capitol knew matters could have gotten worse—like they had a few years earlier in Iceland when citizens staged a peaceful revolution. Protests there had resulted in indictments of the country's president and several bankers as well as the election of a new Congress. On top of that, several members of the country's political elite had been ordered to leave the country.

11

With the line of succession to the presidency obliterated, surviving members of the U.S. House and Senate met for five days straight to discuss a one-time, extra-Constitutional means for resolving this never-before-experienced crisis. They were joined by a select number of individuals from outside the legislative branch who had been instrumental in securing the top-level resignations. Together, they worked to select a successor to serve out the remainder of President Obama's second term.

Minus any smoke signals, several rounds of papal election-style voting took place during an exhausting three-day period until one man, a proven leader without the baggage of a Beltway insider, emerged from the pack.

Governor Franklin G. Rivera was a second-term governor from Wyoming who some people—but not the man himself—liked to refer to as "FGR." Far more conservative than the three-term president who, decades earlier, had been associated with a similar three-letter acronym, Governor Rivera's public approval ratings were higher than any other statewide office holder in the country.

With much trepidation, the governor accepted the job just a few minutes before noon Saturday, July 4, 2015.

After taking the oath of office behind closed doors and without fanfare, the nation's first Latino president addressed the nation at 3 p.m., delivering the first of many difficult messages he would be called upon to share as Commander-in-Chief:

My fellow Americans, many of you have suffered tremendous losses during the past several months. To you, I offer a sincere apology on behalf of every elected official in Washington.

Members of Congress have, with the cooperation of too many American presidents, gotten away with robbery for far too long. They've allowed taxing and spending to get out of control. And they've allowed government regulation to trample common sense and decency. As a result, we've all paid a price higher than most of us care to calculate.

During the next twelve months, I pledge to work tirelessly to establish legal safeguards in our system via which we will do more than simply prevent members of Congress from increasing the national debt. The safeguards I propose will involve imposing stiff financial penalties on individual members of Congress who choose to waste taxpayers' dollars on any projects or programs that increase the national debt and the burden on our children and grandchildren.

Even more important than that, however, is my top priority—ensuring that all of your assets, taken from you illegally by the previous administration, are returned to you as quickly as possible.

I've set July 4, 2016, as the date by which your money, the money that is rightfully yours, will be returned, with interest, to your bank accounts, to your 401K accounts and to your other retirement savings vehicles. It will be a Financial Independence Day when government no longer has its hands on your money.

President Rivera's speech resonated with the justifiably jaded American people.

After learning more about the energetic sixty-year-old president's background via biopic news and feature reports that surfaced following his appointment, most Americans seemed genuinely appreciative of the fact his legal-immigrant parents had set a good example for their oldest son and his five younger siblings, all of whom had been born in the United States.

Not surprisingly, they liked knowing Rivera's parents had realized success as farmers, growing mostly wheat and soybeans on the flatlands of eastern Colorado. And they liked the fact that the new president's four adult children seemed to be decent, well-educated people not seeking to ride their father's political coattails.

In addition, they liked the fact he had become successful through hard work, determination and a steadfast refusal to run with the pack when the pack was heading in the wrong direction. And they liked how he seemed to take time to think before opening his mouth to speak and refused to compromise his Christian faith.

Most importantly, they liked how President Rivera's early actions spoke even louder than his personal history.

In addition to signing an executive order on Day One that banned the use of taxpayer dollars on inaugural activities, he signed another that prohibited all federal employees from participating in inaugural activities, public or private.

The new president also completed the process of appointing cabinet members within two days and warned members of Congress not to waste any time in approving his nominees, saying, "We have important business to take care of!"

During his first year in office, President Rivera worked too hard and slept too little while waging a gallant effort to restore stability. Not a single round of golf was played, and vacations were off limits for White House staffers and all who remained employed on Capitol Hill.

In addition to pushing across-the-board spending cuts through Congress and filling hundreds of foreign relations potholes, President Rivera signed an Executive Order that replaced the previous administration's so-called Affordable Care Act (a.k.a., "ObamaCare") with common-sense healthcare reforms, many of which were made possible by tort reform legislation he championed. Nearly as important, he walked a federal Right-to-Work law and a loser-pays legal reform measure through both houses of Congress and signed the bills into law as soon as each reached his desk.

Some were quick to paint Rivera as another Ronald Reagan, but he rejected the comparison outright, saying, "I've never been an actor, and I'll never read words on a teleprompter."

12

During his first six months as an apprentice, Rosy shadowed Christie and learned the roles and responsibilities of people in key areas of the plant, including accounting, administration, and operations, in order to understand what the plant manager described as the "big picture" at Illinois Chemical.

To Rosy, it seemed as if he was being groomed to be the plant manager, and he liked that idea. He also liked his flexible daytime hours. As long as he put in twenty hours per week, he simply had to give Christie two weeks advance notice about what those hours would be. Simple as that.

Hardly a day went by without Rosy seeing a bit of his father in Christie. Though they bore no physical resemblance to each other—Christie had brown hair, was almost six feet tall and looked like he had never missed a meal, while Rosy's dad was a short Filipino with jet-black hair who was built sturdy, but not overweight—they approached business in much the same way.

"Follow the Golden Rule," Rosy's father had always told him, "and you will get the gold!"

While Rosy never heard Christie speak those exact words, he heard plenty of similar statements from the man and quickly came to respect him.

Another man he came to respect was Gary Kastens.

Rosy shadowed Kastens during the second six months of his apprenticeship and noticed the day-shift manager seemed to go out of his way to show him the intricacies of his job and to teach him things a young engineer would likely never learn in a classroom or by reading a textbook.

On occasion, Kastens' exorbitant kindness made Rosy wonder whether or not the shift manager might be seeing a bit of his late son in him. After all, what else could explain why the man had shown so much compassion to a young man from the other side of the planet?

Rosy dared not raise such a possibility in conversation, because he barely knew Kastens. Instead, he simply counted his blessings, thankful for everything the man had taught him.

By the time his second shadow period ended on the final day of 2015, Rosy felt as if he could probably run the plant.

†

Following his second Christmas as a Muslim, Rosy became more convinced than ever his conversion had been a mistake. His new feelings coincided with the beginning of his third shadow period during which he returned to the graveyard shift and followed Burt Abramov.

Though Rosy had read his Bible and the Quran many times each and understood both Christians and Muslims recognized Jesus had walked the earth more than two centuries earlier, he grew increasingly more troubled by the Islamic description of Jesus as only a man and not the Son of God. Along the way, Abramov fanned the flames of Rosy's frustration.

A Muslim since birth, Abramov was the only employee at the plant who called Rosy by his Muslim first name, Yusaf, instead of by his pre-conversion nickname. And he was, Rosy believed, the only other Muslim employee at the plant.

Whenever the two were alone and out of earshot of coworkers, Abramov liked to ask his apprentice one question more often than any other.

"Why do you let everyone call you Rosy instead of making them call you by your Muslim name?"

In reply, he would explain that, ever since he had let it slip out that his friends had always called him Rosy, he had grown tired of correcting people.

"And those who know me know my true heart," he told Abramov.

Only days into the new year, it became apparent to Rosy he should be careful not to cross Abramov and that he should go to great lengths to avoid lengthy conversations with his new mentor. The man had, after all, almost singlehandedly caused him to regret his conversion to Islam.

After arriving at work the evening of Thursday, May 1, 2016, it didn't take long for Rosy to notice Abramov acting more irritable and spewing more anti-infidel rhetoric than usual. For most of the next eight hours, he watched the man. Ignoring the tiny voice inside his head that was telling him to do otherwise, he decided to ask his mentor if anything was wrong as their shift was about to end. Then, in an instant, the man's demeanor seemed to turn on a dime. It was as if something had clicked in his head.

"No, of course not, Yusaf," Abramov replied while exhaling a deep-throated chuckle. "I can see the future, and it looks bright. In fact, so bright, I think it's time for you to learn how to mix batches of product all by yourself. You need to know this to be an engineer, right?"

Though Rosy didn't appreciate the Jekyll-and-Hyde change in Abramov's behavior, he nodded and smiled to be polite. After all, he wanted to learn how to mix batches of product by himself, something neither of his other mentors had allowed him to do during the previous year.

"We start tomorrow!" Abramov exclaimed while putting his arm around Rosy and walking him back to the spot where, like the plant's hourly workers, he was expected to wave his radio-frequency identification chip-equipped employee badge in front of a scanner so that his departure from the plant could be recorded for posterity like his arrival had some eight hours earlier.

Rosy found himself in front of the same scanner thirty-six hours later, careful to make sure company administrators knew he had arrived on time for yet another day of work and education.

"Hello, Yusaf!" Abramov said enthusiastically as he stepped into the hallway outside his office and spotted the Filipino. "Are you ready to mix it up?"

"Yes, sir!"

Piggybacking on the young man's enthusiasm, Abramov spent many hours teaching Rosy everything he thought the future engineer should know about mixing large quantities of chemicals. Though the apprentice often wondered why his mentor spent so much time on each step, he appreciated the thoroughness of his teaching nonetheless.

"Timing is essential," Abramov told Rosy frequently, often adding the reminder, "Too much or too little time on certain steps can ruin a batch, and that costs the company money."

Abramov had Rosy rehearse the process over and over, adding a new step daily to the mixing sessions he liked to call "dry runs," because they didn't involve mixing actual products.

Unlike any of the earlier steps, the final step—which Abramov emphasized as being "most important"—involved the addition of a stabilizer agent required those involved to wear protective rubber suits, complete with face masks, respirators and hoods while working in a somewhat-cramped space inside a small clean room.

Located on a platform near the top of the giant vat inside which products were mixed, the clean room was roomy enough for two average-size people. It was only during training, however, that more than one employee was allowed to enter the room at the same time.

13

As the sun began to rise July 1, 2016, Petty Officer First Class Tom West began his daily routine, leaving his Trident Park Condominiums bachelor pad and making the four-minute commute to work at Naval Submarine Base New London. On this Friday morning, however, the twenty-eight-year-old master diver, who had spent most of the previous two years teaching sailors how to escape from submarines, couldn't shake the feeling something was wrong.

Up until this point in his ten-year Navy career, "too sick to work" was a phrase never used by the bachelor from Denver who regularly competed in marathons and triathlons and, along the way, attracted a lot of female attention with his chiseled physique, close-cropped blonde hair and eyes the color of faded blue jeans. On this day, however, the five-eleven, 180-pounder felt as if he might never jog again.

After waking up dizzy and feeling a headache grow more painful with each passing minute, he noticed tingling on his skin during his morning shower. Instead of going directly to work, he decided he would turn off Crystal Lake Road, pass through the security checkpoint at the base's East Gate, and follow a winding path—right on Tang Avenue and left on Tautog Avenue—to the health clinic at the base. Unfortunately, his plan fell through.

After struggling to stay conscious behind the wheel of his red brick-colored 2008 Toyota FJ Cruiser, West passed out after turning off Crystal Lake Road. His SUV, however, kept going and began picking up speed.

Guards at the checkpoint began paying close attention to the SUV as it approached the checkpoint—in the left lane of two lanes through which all incoming traffic flowed—and showed no signs of slowing down.

Though attuned to spotting danger after serving stints in Iraq and Afghanistan, one guard was slow to decide whether or not the driver constituted a threat. Another guard, however, reached a different conclusion, quickly firing six rounds into the SUV's engine compartment and three more into its windshield, causing it to veer left, cross a narrow strip of wet grass and collide with a concrete barrier separating inbound and outbound traffic.

No longer moving forward, the SUV's tires continued to spin—the result of the driver's foot remaining on the gas pedal—and steam spewed from under its hood.

Uncertain how many rounds he had left, the guard who had fired at the SUV slapped a new fifteen-round magazine into his Beretta M9 as he approached the vehicle. His colleagues, meanwhile, began closing all entrances and exits to the base and implementing a host of emergency actions that far beyond the Force Protection Charlie procedures put in place two years earlier after it was confirmed that members of several Islamic terror groups had infiltrated the nation's southern border on more than one occasion.

Gun drawn as he reached for the vehicle's front passenger door, the guard kept his eyes on West, motionless and slumped over the steering wheel with blood dripping from a deep cut on his lip, as he opened the door.

Realizing he posed no threat and appeared unconscious, the guard reached across the front seat and, while careful not to touch West's body, turned off the SUV's engine before quickly backing out.

"Call an ambulance!" he shouted to his colleagues after climbing back out of the car quickly. "Tell 'em this guy's covered in a rash like nothin' I've seen before."

After pausing, he added, "And tell 'em they're gonna need protective gear!"

Though West escaped being hit by any of the 9 mm rounds fired in his direction, he might have been better off if he had. Things didn't get any better for him after he was transported to the base hospital. He was declared dead on arrival at 6:01 a.m.

†

One hundred and thirty miles south, Jon Peters and Eric Ryan finished their ninety-minute set as the headliner band at Freddie's, a popular indie music venue in Brooklyn, New York, a few minutes before 3 a.m. Wasting little time, the Saint Louis-based musicians—known around indie music circles as Quake—loaded their amps, microphones, instruments and other equipment into a small pull-behind trailer before entering a destination address into Ryan's smartphone's map app.

Twelve hours earlier, their manager had sent them a text message containing the address of Lucy Marcelli, a twenty-six-year-old call center manager who had responded favorably to a classified ad—"Rockers Need Crash Pad"—on Craigslist a few days earlier.

Not yet rich or famous as a result of the contract they had signed a year earlier with a small record label in Wisconsin, Peters and Ryan appreciated having a place to sleep that night after reaching the halfway point of their thirty-stop East Coast summer tour. After a short drive to Marcelli's tiny Brooklyn apartment, the twenty-three year olds would simply hope things worked out as planned.

On the way to the apartment, Peters and Ryan stopped at the first convenience store they found open. While Peters stayed behind the wheel of his seven-year-old Volvo wagon, Ryan went inside to buy bottles of water for immediate consumption and some gifts of appreciation to serve as an icebreaker upon their arrival. While working their way through college, the two had learned few things were more awkward and uncomfortable than showing up empty-handed at a generous stranger's home.

Upon arrival in the vicinity of the apartment building, Peters followed instructions about where to park their car and trailer that Marcelli had shared with their manager. Though mildly concerned about the lack of security, he knew he could do little to change or improve the situation and decided to press on.

Peters and Ryan retrieved their overnight bags, laptop computers and c-store items from the backseat before locking the car, double-checking the locks on the trailer, and walking around to the front side of the twenty-four-unit building. There, a cloudy night and blacked-out streetlights combined to make finding the entrance challenging.

Using his iPhone's flashlight feature, Peters spotted the words, APT 202, written in black magic marker on a piece of faded-yellow masking tape affixed to a brass faceplate above a small, pearl-colored button. Expecting to hear a doorbell chime after he pushed the button, he was startled to hear the irritating sound of a buzzer instead. It was 3:27 a.m., never a good time to hear the sound of a buzzer.

No one answered after the first try, so Peters pushed the button again and waited. Same result.

A quick review of the instructions confirmed they were in the right place and had the correct apartment number, so Peters pushed the buzzer again, only to discover the phrase, "third time's a charm," would not apply to this situation.

"Who the hell is buzzing me at four in the morning?" a female voice screamed through a loudspeaker mounted in the wall next to two-dozen mailboxes.

Ryan, who had majored in theater in college, decided he was best qualified to handle the situation and leaned forward toward the speaker box.

"Uh, yes, this is Eric Ryan. I'm with--"

"Who the frick do you think you are, buzzing me at this hour?" the female voice interrupted. "I'm about to call the cops!"

Whispering in Peters' ear, Ryan said, "I think someone forgot to tell someone else we were coming." That someone was Marcelli's roommate, Rita Falcone. The two women had met two years earlier at a nearby community college and struck up a friendship that led to becoming roommates.

As they were about to walk away, they heard a new voice over the loudspeaker.

"I'm so sorry," Marcelli said before pressing a button that remotely unlocked the deadbolt and allowed Peters and Ryan to enter. "Come on in, fellas. I'll be right down."

Marcelli threw on a tattered green terrycloth robe and walked to the second-floor landing, a vantage point from which she could see the men waiting inside the exterior door at the bottom of a long, dark and narrow flight of stairs. Not wanting to wake any of her neighbors, she waved for the boys to come up.

"Sorry about that. I couldn't remember exactly when you were supposed to arrive, and I guess I forgot to tell Rita,"

Marcelli said as Peters and Ryan reached the top of the stairway. "I'm Lucy, and you are?"

As the musicians followed Marcelli to her apartment, they began to sense the bowling pin-shaped woman was more than excited about their presence; in fact, they concluded, the raven-haired hostess seemed to have deemed them flirtworthy.

Once inside her apartment, Peters and Ryan presented Marcelli with the gifts they had purchased—a case of beer and a lottery ticket—and she, in turn, thanked them and pointed out everything she thought they might need during their stay.

"This is the kitchen," she explained before removing the beer bottles from the case and putting them on the bottom shelf of her refrigerator one at a time. "We don't keep much food around, but you're welcome to whatever you can find."

Based on the near-empty appearance of the refrigerator, Peters and Ryan didn't challenge Marcelli on her claim about the food supply. Instead, they spoke silently—the way they often did on stage—by reading each other's lips.

"If they don't keep much food around, they must eat out," Peters mouthed to Ryan.

"A lot," Ryan replied silently.

Regardless, the musicians were happy to have a cheap place to stay. Even after the costs of the beer and the lottery ticket, the lodging turned out to be less expensive than any decent motel they might have found. And it seemed fairly safe. Little else mattered beyond that.

"One of you can have the couch, the other the recliner," Marcelli continued as she walked from the kitchen toward her bedroom door. "See you in the morning, and thanks for the beer—and the ticket!"

Exhausted, the musicians—Ryan on the couch and Peters on the recliner—fell asleep quickly only to be awakened less than five hours later by a female voice full of panic and fear.

"Lucy, are you okay?! What's wrong, girl?!" screamed Falcone, the twenty-seven-year-old whose screaming intercom voice had been the first to greet the musicians earlier that morning. "Is anyone out there?"

"Uhh, we are," Ryan replied, sitting on the edge of the couch, feeling groggy and uncertain about what was going on only steps away inside the cramped apartment's only bedroom.

"I need help!" barked Falcone, a woman who, from the neck down, appeared to be a clone of Marcelli. "I don't know what you guys did to her last night, but this girl needs to get to a hospital right now!"

Confused, Ryan shuffled his socked feet across the hardwood floor to the doorway of the bedroom and opened the door. Inside, he found a seventy-five-watt compact fluorescent bulb protruding from the popcorn ceiling and casting on odd color of light on the tense situation unfolding below.

"Jon, call for an ambulance!" Ryan screamed upon seeing Falcone in a well-worn nightshirt kneeling over Marcelli.

Lying on the floor unconscious, Marcelli's skin was covered with red blotches. Ryan knew something was seriously wrong.

After trying unsuccessfully to shake the cobwebs out of his head, Peters dialed the emergency number and was describing the scene to the emergency operator when he abruptly changed the course of the conversation.

"What's your address?" he shouted to Falcone after failing to remember it from hours earlier.

"Seven-seventeen Flushing!" she screamed, "Flushing Avenue! Brooklyn!"

Seven minutes after Peters had dialed 911, a two-man ambulance crew arrived to find him holding open the door to the building's ground floor entrance while waving for the first responders to hurry. In less than a minute, they had made their way up the stairs, gurney and all, to the apartment.

A twenty-something EMT with muscles as thick as a New York phone book checked Marcelli's vitals before sharing serious concerns with his partner, a woman who appeared to be at least fifteen years his senior.

"I've never seen anything like this. Heart racing. Breathing shallow. We need to load her up quick!"

"I should've called in sick today," the female EMT replied as she and her partner began the arduous task of loading the plus-size woman on the gurney and carrying her down the single flight of stairs for the four-minute ride to the Brooklyn Hospital Center.

The oldest hospital in town, BHC was also the closest. But it wouldn't matter. An emergency room physician declared Marcelli dead a few minutes past 10 a.m.

†

Two hundred and fifty miles north of Brooklyn, Pastor Ron French accomplished little during the first half of the day. He was, after all, following the steps of a risky plan concocted less than twenty-four hours earlier. If successful, his plan would breathe new life into the nondenominational River of Life Church in Concord, New Hampshire. If not, things would get worse. Much worse.

Pastor French had spent many hours the previous month contemplating what he might recommend to the seven lay members of the church's budget committee when it came time to hammer out the budget for the next fiscal year. Now, with the committee's meeting less than thirty days away, he couldn't stop thinking about what might take place and had begun associating the likely outcome of the meeting with the title of a movie he had watched a few years earlier: "There Will Be Blood."

Why? Because his plan hinged on a long-shot solution for fixing one of the many things that had gone wrong at the church of almost three-hundred souls; at the church in which he had been raised during the 1960s and 1970s; and at the church to which he had returned forty years later to serve as senior pastor.

Though his plan did not represent the kind of thinking church members expected from Pastor French, it was the kind of thinking that had dominated the fifty-two-year-old pastor's thoughts for some time.

Pastor French had always practiced sacrificial giving, going above and beyond the ten percent figure mentioned so often in the Bible. Conversely, most members of his congregation had not. Proof of their shortcomings could be found in the collection plate each and every Sunday morning.

Fewer than fifteen percent of the church's members tithed on a regular basis, and fewer still matched or exceeded the ten percent figure. As a result, the financial outlook for the church appeared bleak.

Translated into pie charts that appeared atop page two of the church bulletin each week, updated versions of that outlook reflected a growing disparity between need and reality. In fact, it showed large slices of the Holy pie disappearing every seven days without being replaced.

Pastor French knew he would have to cut something—people, not pie—from the church budget if attitudes did not change soon. Specifically, he knew Jesse Povelones, his worship leader, was the staffer most likely to be cut. Worse still, he knew the recent seminary graduate and his twenty-something wife Lou were expecting their first baby any day.

Beyond the pain of cutting Povelones, Pastor French knew something even worse might follow—either he would have to find a volunteer to do the job or he would have to fill in as worship leader until the economy improved and/or the hearts of church members changed. With good volunteers hard to find, neither option looked good to the man at the top of the church's org chart.

Against the backdrop of a continuing decline in membership that had taken place since he had been brought in two years earlier to revive the church, Pastor French's plan involved doing something that ran 180 degrees counter to the theological position he had advocated from behind the pulpit on dozens—if not hundreds—of occasions.

In an effort to ensure no one—especially not his devoted wife Brenda or any of their four teenage children (Jonathan, June, Joan and Jacob)—ever learned about his plan, he decided to execute it in a faraway town during a block of time normally reserved for some of his more-spiritual pursuits.

Though, technically, he had the day off, Pastor French told his wife he wanted to stick to his normal Friday afternoon schedule that included visiting homebound and hospitalized members of the church. After finishing a healthy salad she had prepared for him as lunch, he climbed behind the wheel of his 2006 Infiniti i30 sedan—one of the aging spoils leftover from his pre-clergy days as a semi-successful real estate broker in Saint Petersburg, Florida—and was on the road by 1 p.m.

Instead of visiting church members, however, the pastor drove north on I-93 for forty-seven minutes until he reached Campton, a town of thirty-three hundred residents. According to the latest annual River of Life Family Directory, none of them were members of the church.

Arriving in Campton a few minutes before 2, Pastor French pulled into the parking lot of the first convenience store he spotted and, upon entering, was greeted by Chris and Mikey Ketmering, two twenty-something men working behind the counter: "Welcome to Maple Mart!"

The manner in which the young men had greeted him— almost in unison—made Pastor French wonder if some sort of motion sensor had triggered their greeting. It didn't seem as if their hearts were in the delivery. And they weren't.

Full-time MBA students at the nearby University of New Hampshire in Durham, the brothers had been enjoying a three-week break between classes when both their mother Janet and their older brother Alex said they weren't feeling well and asked them to mind the store. They gladly stepped in, knowing they'd be able to get some studying done between customers.

Upon hearing their greeting, Pastor French gave a quick nod to be polite, but nothing more. Being on a clandestine mission, he didn't want to engage anyone in conversation if he could avoid it. Unfortunately for the pastor, the Ketmering brothers couldn't keep themselves from conversing with customers. They had been raised that way.

After the pastor picked up some snack food and a drink for the return trip, he walked up to the counter and found out just how folksy the Ketmering boys could be.

"Is that all you need today, sir?" said Chris, the older of the two extremely fit brothers.

"I need one of those, too," the pastor said while pointing to an item featured on a wall poster above point-of-purchase displays for beef jerky, bubble gum and other mostly unhealthy fare.

"Those are really good," Mikey said, pointing to the bag of mixed nuts the customer had placed on the counter.

Pastor French remained silent.

"That'll be one-oh-three ninety-nine, sir," Chris said before bagging the pastor's items.

Making only brief eye contact, Pastor French pulled two bills from his wallet—one featuring Benjamin Franklin's likeness, the other Abraham Lincoln's—and waited for his change. After pocketing it, he walked out the door rather quickly, hoping he had not drawn any unwanted attention to himself.

Seconds later, he climbed back into his car and began the forty-five-minute return trip to Concord. By 3, he had made it back to his neighborhood.

After pulling into his private parking space behind the church instead of his own driveway across the street, the pastor had only one step remaining in his plan before he would walk home. With much trepidation, he sat behind the wheel of his car and executed that step. Almost immediately, he learned his plan had failed, utterly and completely. Now, all he had was an empty cup and a belly full of nuts.

"Perhaps this was God's way of teaching me a lesson," he thought to himself before leaning his head against the steering wheel and silently asking forgiveness for his latest sin.

Pastor French's short across-the-street commute followed, and he used the remainder of the afternoon to mow the yard, toss a football with his thirteen-year-old son, Jonathan—the only one of his children to have shown an interest in athletics—and cook hamburgers and bratwursts on the grill. After that, he watched a chick flick with his wife.

Before the movie reached the point at which everyone in the audience knew whether or not there would be a happily ever after, Pastor French acted out of character and told his wife he needed to go to bed early. When she asked if was feeling okay, he told her he probably needed a good night's sleep and walked away.

After cleaning up and getting ready for bed, he went to his knees on the side of his bed and offered a prayer. Not only did he promise God he would never pull such an unholy stunt again, but he thanked God for blessing him with a large and loving family, each member of which had a relationship with Jesus Christ as his or her Savior.

At a few minutes past 7 the next morning, Brenda French rolled over in bed toward her husband who was laying on his right side and facing away from her. Realizing he had slept far longer than usual, she decided to wake him.

"Don't you think eleven hours of sleep is enough, Ronnie?" she asked, calling him by the name she had used since their first meeting at college more than thirty years earlier. She knew he would want to enjoy a full day off before it was time to preach again Sunday morning.

Not receiving a response after putting her hand on his left shoulder, Brenda sensed something was terribly wrong and sat up so she could lean over her husband. When she did, she found all visible parts of his six-foot two-inch frame—his face, neck, hands and feet—covered by a rash.

Acting quickly, she grabbed her husband's cell phone from the lamp table on his side of the bed and dialed 911 in a panic.

"I need you to send an ambulance right away! My husband is sick! Please hurry!"

An ambulance crew arrived six minutes later and rushed Pastor French to the local twenty-five-bed hospital. There, despite Herculean efforts to save him, the emergency room physician on duty pronounced him dead at 7:27 a.m.

His life on earth was over, he had fulfilled the last promise he had made to God and, although his wife was in tears, his secret seemed as if it might be safe—at least for a little while.

✝

Like Tom West, Lucy Marcelli and Ron French, most Americans looked forward to the Fourth of July weekend and extra time off. In fact, many had looked forward to a four-day weekend until they began experiencing strange symptoms.

At first wondering if they might be suffering from some new type of allergy, they became concerned after noticing no one around them experiencing similar symptoms. That's when they began asking questions, including the big one, "Why me?"

Within hours of noticing the initial symptoms (i.e., extreme fatigue and red, blotchy skin), things worsened. Their heads began to ache, and they couldn't breathe enough air into their lungs.

Some sought medical help right away while others waited, hoping their symptoms would pass. But they did not.

One by one, their internal organs began to shut down. Only those who made it to advanced-care facilities quickly would live for more than a day, thanks largely to the electric currents powering life-support technology at their bedsides. Those who delayed seeking care died even sooner. There simply wasn't enough life-support equipment available to handle the tsunami of critically ill patients.

By the end of the first day of July 2016, doctors and nurses across the Northeast realized they had something in common with those under their care who were suffering from this mysterious killer; they were exhausted and full of questions. All had seen their hospitals, offices and minor emergency clinics overtaken by record numbers of patients; all had worked round-the-clock shifts as they tried to cheat death; and all had failed miserably.

Something or someone unknown was wreaking havoc on the population, and not even the new-and-improved healthcare system that had replaced ObamaCare seemed able to fight it.

14

When Joseph L. "Joe-L" Wilson awoke at 5:30 a.m. July 1, 2016, he turned on the television in his D.C. motel room and found his attention drawn to breaking news reports about thousands of Americans dying mysteriously while the rest of the world slept. Needless to say, the reports captured the thirty-nine-year-old FBI agent's attention.

While waiting at Dulles Airport a short time later, Wilson continued to follow the news by watching television monitors near his gate. Anticipating what the news would mean for him, he called his wife Lori before boarding his flight home to Charlotte and told her he wouldn't be coming home right away after his plane landed. As she had so many times before, she told him she understood the unique nature of his job and that it required flexibility—and she did. After ending the call, he began writing a mushy love letter that he would drop in the mailbox near his office as soon as he made it there.

Wilson's plane was the last one to leave the nation's capitol before Homeland Security officials closed airports nationwide as a precaution against whatever it was that had killed so many Americans during the day's first seven hours.

After landing in Charlotte, he hailed a cab to take him to his office on the south side of town where he hunkered down with a handful of other agents for what all expected would be a marathon shift. Before walking into the building, however, he dropped a love letter in the mailbox outside.

Along with agents in Charlotte and across the country, Wilson worked around the clock, analyzing leads of every shape and size in an effort to unravel the mystery behind the wave of deaths. Twenty-four hours later, he managed to escape the office for a few hours so he could shower, change clothes and give Lori her sixteenth anniversary gift: a two-carat diamond ring he'd picked up two days earlier in the nation's capitol. What he didn't give her that day was another gift—a $100 scratch-off lottery ticket—he'd purchased on his way to the airport in D.C. before getting on his flight home. If his plan worked out, she would find out about it the next day when she checked the mail. By then, he hoped, the worst of the bad news casting a cloud over their special day would be over.

†

In response to news about the wave of deaths, municipal officials, theme park owners and others across the nation cancelled their Independence Day parades and fireworks displays. Other public events, ranging from baseball games to county fairs, were cancelled, too, as fear gripped the nation.

Amidst much hand wringing, many were quick to suspect Islamic terrorists were somehow behind the deaths but had no evidence upon which to base their suspicions. Others suspected homegrown terrorists but couldn't explain who they were or how they might have carried out such an attack. In reality, no one knew who or what was to blame. Americans were simply nervous and scared.

Wilson, on the other hand, maintained a calm demeanor throughout the crisis. Though it was taking place on a much larger scale than any previous case in which he had been involved, he would treat it no differently than he had previous major cases.

15

Eighteen years and six months after his birth on Christmas Day 1976, Wilson received his high school diploma and doubled down on his personal mission to make his parents proud.

Not only did he work forty hours a week as manager of the same horse farm where he had gotten his start shoveling horse manure, but he put twenty thousand extra miles on his truck going back and forth on nights and weekends as he studied at Lindenwood University in nearby Saint Charles. In only three years, he completed his undergraduate degree in criminal justice and became certified to work as a law enforcement officer in Missouri.

Five months after turning twenty-one, he paid a visit to the office of Sheriff Grover Small, hopeful he could take his first step toward a career in law enforcement.

"What brings you here, Joe-L?" asked Small, a man who was halfway into his third four-year term as sheriff after serving as a deputy for ten years before winning his first election.

"I heard you're looking to hire another deputy," Wilson said before handing his already-impressive resume to the sheriff.

"Don't you have enough work to do already?" Small asked with little more than a passing glance at the document.

"I'm ready to move up to more serious work, sheriff."

"I bet you are," the sheriff said, already familiar with the young man's demonstrated work ethic. "You're hired!"

"Excuse me?" Wilson replied, caught off guard.

"I said you're hired, Joe-L. Don't make me explain myself!"

"No, sir, I won't."

"You'll start bright and early one week from today. Between now and then, you'll need to get with Deputy Thomas to fill out your paperwork and get your uniforms ordered."

"Yes, sir."

"And you'll need a gun, too. You can use one of your own or one we issue. So, let Aaron know if you'll need one when you meet with him."

"Yes, sir."

"Any questions?"

"No, sir."

"Alrighty, then we'll see you here a week from Monday at 6:30 sharp."

"Thank you, sir! I won't let you down."

Wilson set up a meeting the following morning with Deputy Aaron Thomas, the department's operations officer, and the two of them whittled away at items on his pre-employment checklist until everything he needed had been ordered, signed for or otherwise processed. One week later, Wilson arrived in the tan uniform of a deputy, ready to work.

He wore black, military-style boots that laced up the front; on his head, a black ball cap with SHERIFF embroidered in gold for all to see.

Attached to a wide, black leather belt around his waist were tools—every tool he might ever need—including a department-issued Glock 19 with a fifteen-round magazine and several extra clips.

†

During his first week as a deputy sheriff, Wilson's work sometimes made him feel as if he was participating in a glorified ride-along program instead of doing actual police work.

On the first day, Sheriff Small took him on a four-hour cross-country tour with stops in Arrington and several nearby communities. Between stops, the sheriff seemed to spend as much time talking about his own law enforcement philosophies as he did introducing his new deputy to people he thought he should know.

"It's not always what you know, Joe-L. It's who you know. Remember that," Small told him. Wilson took mental notes.

During the remainder of that week, Wilson rode with a different deputy each day and participated in everything from traffic stops to domestic disturbance calls. And he learned two of the most important things a cop could ever learn: there's no such thing as a routine traffic stop, and "danger" doesn't begin to describe what one might encounter during a domestic disturbance.

As months rolled by, Wilson showed he was smart, much like a good bird dog, eager to learn. He also displayed people skills that would change his life forever.

While assigned to late-night patrol duty October 1, 1998, Wilson came across a twenty-one-year-old woman, Lori Ann White, standing beside her car on the shoulder on the east side of the two-lane highway that split Arrington in half. She had parked a couple of miles from downtown, near the sign that marked the northern edge of the city limits and near a small wooden cross that marked the spot where her parents had died in a car crash almost one year earlier, victims of a drunk driver.

Because it was almost eleven o'clock and every store in town had closed, Wilson stopped to see if she needed help and discovered she simply needed a shoulder to cry on.

During the next six months, Wilson discovered even more about Miss White, including the fact she had a weakness for men in crisp, tapered uniforms. One thing led to another, a relationship blossomed and, eventually, Wilson asked her to be his bride, and she said, "Yes!"

Fifteen months later, they tied the knot, and July 2, 2000, became a day they would remember fondly and forever.

†

Five years into his law enforcement career, Wilson earned a promotion of sorts by being named the department's credibility assessment officer. While the position came with only a nominal pay increase, it required him to receive training in how to conduct polygraph exams—something he thought might give him an edge as he competed for future promotions.

Unbeknownst to Wilson, however, his boss didn't put much faith in the century-old polygraph technology's reliability or effectiveness. Instead, he had put his newest deputy in charge of the one-man polygraph unit simply as a means to make him feel as if he had, in lieu of a significant pay bump of any kind, been rewarded for his hard work.

When it came time to consider the results of polygraph exams Wilson administered, the sheriff opted to ignore Wilson's findings most of the time.

Two years after Wilson completed his training as a polygraph examiner, Sheriff Small decided to send him to South Florida to learn how to conduct exams using a different kind of credibility assessment technology, the Computer Voice Stress Analyzer.

Sheriff Small's decision came after a sheriff in a neighboring county purchased CVSA for his department and, according to more than one headline on the front page of the *Arrington American*, began realizing incredible results. Sheriff Small didn't want to be outdone by any of his counterparts, so he ordered his own equipment and tapped Wilson as the man he would rely on to know how to use it.

Unfortunately, no technology on earth could change the results of what happened in Arrington the night of September 8, 2005. Less than twenty-four hours before Wilson was set to complete his two weeks of training in West Palm Beach, he received a phone call from Sheriff Small. During the call, he learned both of his parents had been killed, execution-style, by single gunshots to the backs of their heads.

Because neither of Wilson's parents had had any known enemies, the sheriff jumped to the conclusion they had simply fallen victim to desperate meth addicts who had staged a home invasion as a means of scoring money to buy drugs and feed their insatiable need to get high.

"Probably just drifters," he said before citing the Show-Me State's reputation as one of the top states in the country when it comes to producing and distributing crystal methamphetamine.

Regardless of how the sheriff looked at the tragedy, Wilson couldn't ignore the fact that his father and mother, 56 and 53, respectively, were gone.

Now, in addition to having his job and his wife, the six-year veteran of law and order had a burning desire to find the person or persons responsible for killing his mom and dad. At the same time, however, he had no opportunity to pursue it.

Though struggling with feelings of anger and depression, Wilson wasn't the type of person to let those feelings drive him to the psychiatric ward or cause him to "go postal." Instead, he knew his feelings, while painful and difficult to deal with, were normal, and that time would eventually bring some sort of healing and closure. He hoped it would anyway.

At the same time, he struggled with the kind of guilt known only by law enforcement officers who blamed themselves for not having prevented horrific crimes.

Wilson wanted to be meaningfully involved in the hunt for his parents' killer or killers, but Sheriff Small told him that wouldn't be wise since he was too close to the victims. On top of that, he cited Wilson's lack of experience as an investigator. It was at that moment in time Wilson's respect for, and trust in, the sheriff began to wane, and he began to see the man in a different light.

†

During the next few years, Wilson came to realize Sheriff Small, a man in whom he had once placed so much faith and trust, was more interested in satisfying local powerbrokers than catching criminals and putting them behind bars.

On one occasion in 2008, Wilson found Sheriff Small working in cahoots with a member of the Arrington Town Council as they waged a sort of legal jihad against Dolly Sherwood.

An eighty-nine-year-old woman who had outlived her only husband but not her knowledge of right and wrong, Sherwood had called 911 to report a neighborhood boy had been riding his motorcycle across her lawn and damaging her landscaping.

Perhaps because the fifteen-year-old teenager's father was both a longtime friend of Sheriff Small *and* an elected member of the county council, the sheriff responded to Sherwood's call by having one of his deputies pay the woman a late-night visit.

During that visit, the deputy tried to persuade Sherwood to drop her complaints against the boy and, after she refused, handed her a summons. She would have to appear in municipal court to answer allegations she had thrown a fifteen-ounce can of baked beans at the boy while he was riding his bike on the sidewalk in front of her home.

When Sherwood appeared in court, she attempted to bolster her claims of innocence by shining the light of justice on her hands, both of which had been ravaged by arthritis for thirty years.

"Your honor, I can barely grip a pencil, much less grip a can and throw it over the fence, and the only beans I keep in my pantry are Lima beans!"

Despite Sherwood's arguments and the lack of evidence or impartial eyewitnesses to the alleged incident, the judge found her guilty of disturbing the peace, fined her $150 and sentenced her to one year of probation during which she had to attend mandatory anger management classes.

Rather than hire a lawyer and spend thousands to fight the bogus conviction, Sherwood sought local news media coverage about her case but failed to garner any interest beyond that of a local blogger willing to champion her cause.

Seemingly given a green light, the neighborhood punk continued to harass Sherwood for another fourteen months until she was forced to call for help again.

This time, Sherwood told the 911 operator the teenager had thrown rocks through several ground-level windows of her home *and* destroyed her mailbox. Though a deputy responded immediately and filed a report, the complaint yielded nothing for four days. Then, on the fifth day, she found herself in receipt of yet another summons.

According to the latest summons, delivered to her home by the same deputy as before, an anonymous someone claimed to have seen Sherwood driving her car recklessly and at a high rate of speed in an Arrington school zone.

Sherwood appeared in court to refute the charges and shared two important facts with the judge: first, she had been in the hospital having major surgery on the day the driving violations were alleged to have taken place; and, second, she had been recuperating at home on the day two weeks later when the deputy stopped by to harass her.

Setting aside those arguments for a moment, Sherwood also questioned how she could have been speeding in a school zone on a hot summer day when schools were not even in session. In response, the judge ordered what turned out to be a permanent recess, leaving the case in legal limbo and Sherwood fearful she would face more harassment in the future.

Another case Wilson uncovered involved a more serious matter.

Hamilton Heath was a twenty-two-year-old former football star at Leonard County High School when he died under suspicious circumstances on a cold and snowy February day in 2010.

Numerous eyewitnesses reported seeing another of the school's former gridiron athletes, Wes Perkins, punch Heath before chasing him on foot as he fled the parking lot of a popular Friday night gathering place. Those same witnesses reported Perkins returned a short while later, boasting about giving Heath "a good whoopin'" during a violent encounter estimated to have lasted nine to ten minutes.

Heath, the only local boy ever to have earned an NCAA Division I football scholarship, did not return from the fight. Instead, his body was found the next morning, face down in a snowdrift on the side of a little-traveled dirt road half a mile from the spot where the altercation had begun.

In his report, the medical examiner mentioned Heath had suffered many injuries, including a broken collarbone, several broken ribs and a collapsed lung. Incredibly, however, he claimed the young athlete had fallen into the snowdrift, hit his head on a rock and fell unconscious before drowning in a two- to four-inch-deep puddle formed by melting snow sometime during the night. The official cause of death appearing on his death certificate: Accidental Drowning.

In a joint statement drafted to respond to news media inquiries, Sheriff Small and Leonard County Prosecutor Preston Troop cited the county medical examiner's cause-of-death determination as justification for not investigating the case further and for not pursuing criminal charges against anyone—including Perkins. Unmentioned in their statement was their apparent willingness to ignore several eyewitness accounts of what had transpired on the night Hamilton died.

Wilson believed Troop's decision had something to do with the fact Perkins' father, Stanley "Big Papa" Perkins, had a reputation as a bully that dated back almost three decades to his student days at LCHS.

Now a powerful businessman in town, Big Papa made a practice of collecting sensitive personal information about individuals in town only to turn around years later and use it to blackmail them while, at the same time, protecting his own interests.

Though he didn't yet have any hard evidence to prove it, Wilson suspected Big Papa must have had dirt on both the prosecutor and the county's top cop. And when he wasn't called upon to administer either a polygraph or a CVSA exam—or both—to Wes Perkins following Heath's death, he became more suspicious than ever. It seemed Wes Perkins might get away with murder, and Wilson felt like he was watching a cover-up unfold.

Knowledge of these cases and others caused Wilson to struggle with whether or not he wanted to keep working as a sheriff's deputy beyond the thirteen-plus years he had already served. Other factors weighed heavily on his decision as well.

Bart Coleman, a headhunter representing Bi-State Life & Property of Evansville, Indiana, contacted Wilson in January 2012, saying his company was looking to hire a full-time investigator to conduct personnel background checks and perform other tasks, most of which would be tied to insurance fraud investigations in several states in the Midwest.

Having seen Wilson's profile on a popular social networking site, Coleman said his qualifications— particularly his dual polygraph and CVSA certifications— matched his client's needs and, as a result, he had been authorized to offer Wilson three times what he was earning as a deputy if he would come to work at Bi-State.

Wilson considered the lucrative offer for almost two weeks before turning it down—and without even discussing it with his wife. He simply couldn't allow himself to walk away from the increasingly ugly situation in his hometown. That's not the way his father had taught him to handle things, and he felt obliged to do whatever he could to make things right.

Days after turning down the insurance company's offer, Wilson met someone who would play a big role in his life during the next few years. His name was Chuck Schmidt, and he was a decorated combat veteran who had retired from the Marine Corps in 2009 and, more recently, put down roots in Leonard County, not far from where his wife Barbara had been born and raised.

Wilson became fast friends with Schmidt and came to regard the man as the first person to come along in years who seemed capable of challenging Sheriff Small at the ballot box. Thinking he would have to convince him to run, he was surprised to learn in early February that Schmidt was already mapping out a plan to defeat the sixty-five-year-old incumbent.

Though careful not to violate the law by expressing his opinions or engaging in political campaign activities while in uniform or on duty, Wilson became an outspoken Schmidt supporter during the nine-plus months leading up to election day.

Along the way, Wilson and Schmidt learned they were not alone in their desire to rid Leonard County of corruption, graft, bribery and other types of wrongdoing by public office holders. Their friends and neighbors felt the same as they did. As a result, Schmidt won the election by a landslide— nine hundred votes in local terms.

After being sworn in as sheriff on the first business day of 2013, Schmidt promoted Wilson to detective and quickly came to rely upon him as his most-trusted ally.

Wilson's first assignment involved sifting through stacks of criminal cold case files previous investigators had allowed to go unsolved. Among the cases to which he paid particular attention was a 1999 case involving the disappearance of a twelve-year-old boy, Troy Stewart, from an area near his home in the rural northwest part of Leonard County.

He remembered the Stewart case as the first missing person investigation for which he had had a front-row seat. He also remembered it as the first case for which the outcome—or lack thereof—had left him wondering why more effort had not been expended to find the boy and the person or persons responsible for his disappearance and apparent murder.

Having had virtually no law enforcement experience at the time, Wilson's role in the investigation had been minimal, consisting primarily of paying attention to BOLO—Be On the Lookout—orders from dispatchers while on patrol duty. Now, almost fourteen years later, he could apply his wealth of experience and knowledge as he looked at the case with fresh eyes.

It took Wilson only three weeks to discover evidence previous investigators had either failed to uncover or opted to keep to themselves. He became convinced the boy had become a victim of area drug dealers wanting to send a clear message to the boy's parents: *"This is what we do to people who fail to pay us what they owe."* Soon, he found himself briefing Schmidt on how he had reached that conclusion.

"Boss, I paid a visit to Troy Stewart's mother, Marsha Stewart-Wilkerson. She's on her deathbed and seems ready to clear her conscience before she passes."

"Tell me more," Schmidt replied.

"She told me she's willing to sign a sworn affidavit and admit that it was her family's close relationship with Leroy and Harry Teague that put her son in mortal danger. And I believe her."

The sheriff remained silent as Wilson paused and flipped a page in his spiral notebook before continuing.

"I also discovered she was convicted on one count of child endangerment only a few years after her son's disappearance. It seems drug paraphernalia was found inside her home while her only remaining child, Lana Stewart Fry, was still living in the home."

"That's good stuff, but I don't think it's enough to get any convictions," the sheriff countered.

"I know, but there's more. I talked with another woman, Jenny Beth Morgan Teague. She's an ex-con and a mother of two small kids who was running with the Teague brothers back in their heyday. This woman's not quite as bad off as Troy Stewart's mom, but she's dying of cancer, too."

"Seriously?" the sheriff asked, prompting Wilson to continue without missing a beat.

"When I found out her friends in the drug trade, including her sugar daddy from India, had abandoned her because she was no longer contributing to their operation, I offered her an opportunity to come clean by testifying against the Teague brothers. I told her I thought the prosecuting attorney would allow her to plead guilty to a lesser charge for her role in the Stewart boy's murder. And did I tell you she was the boy's babysitter a short time before he disappeared?"

By the time Wilson uttered that last tidbit, he had already captured the sheriff's full attention. It was his final note, however, that sealed the deal.

"The key points are like this: she doesn't feel as if she owes any loyalty to her sugar daddy or any of the people she's been associated with during the past twenty years; she knows her kids are gonna be cared for by their biological father who's been fighting her for custody for almost ten years; and, she knows she's gonna die soon and wants to go out with a clean slate. Strike that. Let's say cleaner slate."

"She'll testify against the Teague brothers?" Schmidt asked.

"Absolutely! She has nothing to lose."

"Okay, then, I think we have a winner!" the sheriff replied before standing and reaching out to shake Wilson's hand.

Schmidt told Wilson to contact the prosecutor's office and set up a meeting as soon as possible so they could discuss filing charges against as many as three suspects in the kidnapping and suspected murder of Troy Stewart. Three weeks later at 11 a.m., the meeting began in the prosecutor's office.

A longtime area resident, attorney and consummate politician whose fence-straddling talents were unmatched, the recently reelected prosecutor listened quietly as Schmidt and Wilson shared their news. As soon as they had finished, however, he began playing Devil's Advocate.

"Gentlemen, I'm proud of the way the two of you --"

"It was Joe who did the legwork," Schmidt interrupted. "Just wanted to make that clear."

Though a bit perturbed by the interruption, Troop nodded slightly before leaning back in his high-back leather chair and starting over.

"I do appreciate all the hard work it appears you've put into trying to solve this case, but I'm afraid I'm gonna have to pass up this opportunity. I hope you understand."

"Could you tell us why, sir?" Wilson asked before his boss could get out his own version of the question.

"Well, between you and me, the men who investigated this case twenty years ago told me back then that their reluctance to prosecute wasn't due to lack of evidence; it was due to fear."

Schmidt and Wilson exchanged a quick glance, said nothing, and continued to listen.

"The Teagues were pretty big players with one of those Mexican drug cartels, and everybody—the police, the judges, you name it—was scared to death their families might suffer if the Teagues or any of their compadres were locked up for this crime," Troop continued. "Heck, I was scared, too!"

"So, you're telling me we had evidence, but—" Wilson began before the prosecutor interrupted.

"Not exactly, but we thought—I mean, the prosecutor at the time thought—he had enough corroborating testimony to convict at least one of the brothers of murder," Troop said, struggling to keep his role as assistant county prosecutor at the time of the boy's disappearance out of the discussion.

Wilson had long suspected Troop might know more than he was letting on about that role, but decided against bringing it up. Fortunately for him, Schmidt stepped in and offered a solution he hoped would sway the prosecutor to see things his way.

"Mr. Prosecutor, the Teague brothers are both serving long prison sentences right now for other crimes. In fact, one of 'em is in a wheelchair in a federal medical prison and, by now, both have probably been forgotten by whoever it is that's in charge of the cartel. On top of that, the third person at the scene of the crime—a woman who was once married to a third, younger Teague brother—is willing to testify against both of the older Teague brothers. So what do we have to lose by trying to get some convictions?"

"Well, first of all, we don't have a body," Troop countered. "On top of that, I really don't think it would be a good idea to open up such old wounds based on the words of a drug-dealing prostitute like Jenny Beth, and the costs--"

"Sir, do you know this woman?" Wilson interrupted, his tone a bit accusatory.

"No more than you just told me."

"But you mentioned her by her first name, middle name and profession."

"So. I only repeated what you had told me, didn't I?"

"I only mentioned her last name."

Thinking quickly, the prosecutor tried to cover his tracks before Wilson decided to follow them.

"Oh, I probably just saw her name on a rap sheet and popped it out without thinking."

Wilson already knew about Jenny Beth's track record of bribing public officials with drugs and sex—she was known to brag to others about her exploits. Now, he had reason to suspect Troop might be among the local elected officials with whom she had done "business." For now, however, he would keep his focus on the matter at hand.

"Sir, this case will remain unsolved forever if we don't prosecute now," Wilson challenged. "Do you want that on your conscience? I certainly don't!"

"Gentlemen, I think we're done here," a now-irritated Troop said, standing as he spoke. "Let me know when you find a case we can sink our teeth into."

With that, the sheriff and his trusted investigator walked out of Troop's office.

"There should be a law against cowards holding public office," Wilson whispered to Schmidt while holding open the door to the parking lot behind the courthouse.

"Where there is no vision, the people perish," Schmidt replied.

Upon hearing those words, Wilson didn't share with his boss everything he was thinking. Instead, he decided to employ an old tactic that had served him well over the years; he would ask for forgiveness later rather than permission now.

After work that night, he called Beth Allquist, a longtime friend and founder of an anti-socialism group that predated the Tea Party movement and was known for staging sidewalk rallies against all manner of government overreach and ineptness.

"Beth, I need your help," Wilson said before sharing a handful of publicly available details about the case with Allquist.

Not surprisingly, he received an immediate and supportive response.

"Joe-L, I'll have at least a dozen people a day protesting outside the courthouse Monday morning, and we'll keep it up for as long as it takes!"

Monday morning came, and Allquist delivered on her promise and then some.

Thanks largely to the fact that many members of her group were retirees with nothing but time and attitude on their hands, she was able to muster nearly fifty people at the courthouse, signs in hands, by 8 a.m. Fueled by coffee, baked goods and a few prescription medications, they stayed until noon.

Word-of-mouth efforts, combined with the power of its members' fledgling social media skills, enabled the group to continue its protest in the same manner every day—weekends included—during the first two weeks of February.

On any given morning, no fewer than three-dozen people could be found on the courthouse lawn, waving signs of protest and passing around a bullhorn through which they shouted their demand that charges be filed in the case. Coincidentally or not, no one in authority at the courthouse seemed inclined to demand leaders of the group obtain a permit. Certainly not the sheriff.

As the third Monday of the protests arrived, two Saint Louis television stations began covering the group's protest, and the county prosecutor found himself unable to stand the proverbial heat in the kitchen he had helped design and build. During a late-morning news conference on the cracked concrete steps of the Civil War-era courthouse, he addressed the protesters' demands.

"During the past several months of my campaign," Troop began, speaking without notes as his words were carried live during two noon newscasts, "I was approached by a number of my constituents who told me they wanted my office to revisit the mysterious 1999 disappearance of twelve-year-old Troy Stewart from his home near Arrington, Missouri. Suffice it to say, I took their requests seriously.

"Today, I want the citizens of Leonard County to know that, based on newly discovered evidence my office has uncovered, I plan to file new charges in the case of the disappearance and suspected murder of Troy Stewart very soon."

Not surprisingly, the prosecutor did not mention the role the protesters had played in his decision-making process during his news conference. Nor did he say anything about the efforts of anyone at the sheriff's department in compiling new evidence. Instead, he wanted everyone to think he was the man getting things done and making Leonard County voters safe.

Troop concluded his news conference by telling the assembled throng—including a handful of reporters who were outnumbered five to one by curious county employees he had asked to attend the impromptu event—he couldn't be able to answer questions or go into specifics of the new charges until after they were filed. In reality, he knew he would get more face time on television by spacing out his announcements. In addition, he figured the exposure couldn't help but "grease the skids" for a possible 2016 campaign for state attorney general.

Seven more days passed, and Troop held another news conference—inside the courthouse this time, because it was cold, wet and windy outside—and announced he had filed first-degree murder charges against two individuals whom he alleged had abducted and murdered the boy. Not surprisingly, the announcement set into motion the kind of high-profile courtroom drama about which many books have been written and movies made.

Murder charges might have been filed against three people if not for the fact Jenny Beth had agreed to testify against her two brothers-in-law, to admit she had been present at the scene of the boy's gruesome murder, and to plead guilty as an accessory to the boy's murder and kidnapping in exchange for a sentence that would not include the death penalty. After all, she was already facing death.

During tearful testimony that lasted more than two hours during the first trial and was more condensed during the second, thirty-eight-year-old Jenny Beth used graphic testimony to described the boy's murder. For instance, she told the court how the men had used a nylon rope to hang the boy by his neck from a wooden crossbeam some twelve feet above the dirt floor of an abandoned barn not far from the boy's home. Further, she explained how, while strung out on meth, they had used handsaws and axes to dismember the blonde-haired, blue-eyed boy's lifeless body before scattering his remains—"dozens of small pieces," she said—at more than a half-dozen rural locations miles apart.

With the help of Schmidt and Wilson, the prosecutor was also able to present a sworn affidavit, signed by Stewart-Wilkerson, during each of the trials. In it, the murdered boy's mother attested to everything she had told Wilson about her checkered past, including her family's ties to the Teague brothers that had cost her son his life.

Such admissions represented a radical departure from what Stewart-Wilkerson had told investigators and journalists during the previous thirteen-plus years, but it seemed she had to get out from under the burden of hiding those secrets before her days in hospice care came to an end.

Sixteen months after the charges were filed, and largely as a result of input from the two dying women, jurors found both of the forty-two-year-old Teague twins guilty of second-degree murder and sentenced both of them to life in prison.

The long-overdue convictions brought about forty-eight hours of national media attention to Leonard County, and those involved in obtaining the convictions were heralded as heroes. The post-trial attention Wilson received, however, would change his life forever.

In addition to local and national media interviews and a handful of honors bestowed by area politicians and civic clubs, Wilson received a phone call one Saturday afternoon in June 2014 from Special Agent-in-Charge Pamela Mazachek of the FBI Saint Louis Field Office.

A veteran of scores of complex investigations, Mazachek recognized how little FBI agents had contributed toward solving the case, both when it was fresh and even after it was more than a dozen years old. She also recognized who deserved most of the credit for the cold-case convictions.

"Joe-L, this is Pam Mazachek at the FBI in Saint Louis," she began, having learned of the detective's nickname by paying attention to news reports about the case. "I wanted to call and congratulate you for the great job you did on the Troy Stewart case."

"I appreciate that, Agent Mazachek. I really do."

Mazachek went on to invite him to her office in downtown Saint Louis so they could talk shop. He accepted her invitation and, nine days later, was prepared to make the ninety-minute drive to the city. When he opened his garage door, however, he found a black, late-model Chevy Suburban blocking his driveway.

"Need a lift?" Mazachek asked after rolling down the passenger window of her SUV. "Thought we might be able to talk on the way into town. Your boss said I can keep you all day if I want."

Wilson accepted the offer, and it didn't take him long to realize he was being recruited.

While driving east toward Saint Louis on I-70, Mazachek again told Wilson how impressed she was with his work on the Stewart case. Coffee and a tour of the Saint Louis office came next, followed by dining at Charlie Gitto's Italian restaurant on Shaw Avenue on The Hill.

During lunch, Mazachek told Wilson she believed he had everything necessary to become a top-notch FBI agent and that, because he was thirty-seven years old, he needed to act quickly if he was interested in applying. "I don't need an answer today, but you're gonna have to decide pretty soon, because the bureau doesn't grant many exceptions to the age limit."

She ended the working lunch by introducing Wilson to an FBI colleague who had arrived exactly at 1 p.m.

"Scout Miller will drive you home," Mazachek said, pointing to the colleague with whom she had developed a high level of trust after he saved her life twelve months earlier during a gunfight outside an East Saint Louis nightclub. "Ask him anything you want about the FBI, and he'll give you straight answers."

Wilson took Mazachek up on her offer and pelted Miller with several questions during the ride home. While the answers Wilson received helped him overcome his initial reluctance about changing horses so many years into his law enforcement career, he would think long and hard about this opportunity—and talk it over with Lori—before making a decision.

Not your typical elementary school librarian, Lori still had the striking good looks and curly blonde hair that had attracted Wilson's eye so many years earlier and helped keep the petite woman looking at least ten years younger than her husband.

Dropped off at his home a few minutes before 3 p.m., Wilson decided to surprise Lori when she walked in the door an hour later.

"Honey," he said as he walked toward the kitchen to meet her as she came in from the garage. "Someone made me an offer today."

"What kind of offer, big boy?" she said, flirtatious and laughing while looking up into her six-foot-tall husband's pale blue eyes.

"The agent in charge of the FBI in Saint Louis thinks I'd make a great agent, and she wants me to consider it seriously."

"Would we have to move?"

"I'm pretty sure we would," Wilson replied, still in the dark about which way his wife was leaning.

"That sounds exciting!" she squealed, ending any doubts. "I'm tired of teaching anyway, and no one on the board will miss me if I resign a few months early."

A first-term member of the illustrious local body known as the Board of Education, Lori had already grown tired of being the always-outnumbered conservative shouted down when she took stands against programs and concepts that focused more on test scores than on educating children.

Somewhat surprised by Lori's enthusiasm, Wilson told his wife he would apply but that she shouldn't tell anyone or quit either of her jobs until he had been accepted and had made it through training.

The following morning, Wilson called Mazachek to let her know he would be forwarding his application soon. In turn, she promised to endorse it before sending it to FBI Headquarters.

Five weeks and one background check later, Mazachek called Wilson again.

"It worked, Joe-L. You have a slot at Quantico," she said, referring to the FBI Academy Officer Candidate School on the banks of the Potomac River almost forty miles south of the White House.

"Thank you so much!" Wilson replied.

"Thank me when you finish the course, Joe-L," she told him. Despite being sure he would make it through with flying colors, she didn't want him to arrive overconfident. "You'll probably be the oldest guy there, and you're gonna have to hustle. Class begins in two weeks."

After hanging up with Mazachek, Wilson walked down the hall to tell Schmidt about the opportunity.

"We're gonna miss you around here, Joe-L," Schmidt said, "and, as long as I'm still here, the door will always be open if you want to come back."

†

Though a bit nervous about tackling one of the biggest professional challenges of his life, Wilson arrived at Quantico in early August to begin what he understood would be twenty grueling weeks of training. Not surprisingly, he excelled in almost every area and, two days before Christmas, graduated near the top of his class.

After leaving Quantico, Wilson returned to Missouri so he and Lori could pack their belongings and begin their new adventure. Within two weeks, they had packed up and moved to their first duty location: the FBI Field Office in Charlotte, North Carolina.

Realizing they would be expected to moves several times during their first decade of service, the Wilsons decided against buying and, instead, signed a one-year lease on a small Cape Cod-style home in a suburb of the nation's sixteenth-largest city—nicknamed the "Queen City" in honor of Charlotte of Mecklenburg-Strelitz, who had become queen consort of Great Britain the year before the city's founding.

More challenging than the move to Charlotte was Wilson's work after he arrived. He did not, however, disappoint anyone keeping track of his efforts.

During his first year on the job, Wilson's colleagues began to call him "Joe-L" after one of them heard Lori use the nickname in place of "Joe" or "Joseph."

Though unaware Wilson had been born on Christmas Day, they liked the nickname for several reasons. First, it sounded like "Noel" and reminded them of how he had dressed up like Santa Claus to deliver gifts to everyone in the office during his first Christmas in town; and, second, it reminded them of his effective and Santa Claus-like approach to complex criminal cases.

According to his fellow agents, Wilson's approach involved compiling a list of possible suspects, checking it twice and, with a high degree of accuracy, determining who had been naughty and who had been nice.

His full head of prematurely white hair—*"Yes, it's white, not gray,"* *he always told them*—simply added to his Santa Clause mystique.

16

Like Wilson, President Rivera had dealt with many crises over the years—most of them while serving as a governor. Nothing, however, could have prepared him for what was happening now—in his country and in his family.

During a nationally televised broadcast at noon July 2, 2016, he shared some deeply personal and painful news with the American people, holding back tears along the way:

My fellow Americans, I come before you today to share some terrible news.

Like so many of you have, I've lost someone very dear to me. Someone more precious to me than anyone else in the world. My darling Juanita, my wife and best friend of forty years, passed away this morning.

As is the case with so many other Americans in recent days, the cause of her death remains a mystery. But it will not remain a mystery forever. I promise I will not rest until we have answers. For Juanita, for my children and grandchildren, and for your loved ones and those left behind.

As we walk through these troubling times together, I thank you in advance for your kindness, for your patience, and for your understanding. God bless you, and God bless the United States of America.

In less than a minute, President Rivera had injected yet another piece of horrific news into what seemed a never-ending cycle of horror. Because of its timing and the tacit confirmation that she had died in the same manner as so many other Americans, the death of the First Lady sent a signal that all were vulnerable.

Thirty minutes after the president concluded his announcement, Dr. Dennis McKinney, director of the Centers for Disease Control, shared more bad news with Attorney General Stephen Daniels, Homeland Security Secretary Argus McQueen and FBI Director Pamela Mazachek: CDC experts were still unable to pinpoint what had killed nearly thirty thousand Americans so far.

At 1 p.m., the agency heads began sharing up-to-date details and information with the president who had appointed them. At the end of a thirty-minute videoconference, they received his approval to share some—but not all—of those details with the American people. An hour later, White House Press Secretary Rick Hammer announced that four high-ranking government officials had briefed the president and would hold a brief news conference that afternoon at FBI Headquarters in Washington, D.C.

Attorney General Daniels was the first to speak during the 3 o'clock news conference held inside a three-hundred-seat auditorium usually reserved for classroom training.

"I want to begin by expressing my heartfelt condolences to the American people, especially those who've been directly impacted by the events of the past thirty-six hours.

"Twenty-four hours ago, the Justice Department, with the FBI out front, began investigating the deaths of several thousand Americans during the past thirty-six hours. At this time, we are aware of deaths that have occurred in the District of Columbia and in the following eight states: Connecticut, Delaware, Maryland, Massachusetts, New Jersey, New York, Pennsylvania and Rhode Island.

"While we do not know the cause or causes of these deaths, we are working around the clock with local, state and federal agency officials nationwide in an effort to locate answers.

"This afternoon, Dr. Dennis McKinney of the Centers for Disease Control in Atlanta will address the process involved in reaching some of the conclusions we've reached to date. Afterward, I will take questions. Dr. McKinney."

"Thank you, Mr. Attorney General," the CDC director began. "During the past twenty-four hours, members of my staff have conducted toxicology tests on the bodies of more than fifty randomly selected victims, all of whom displayed nearly identical symptoms before dying July 1.

"Today, we are able to say with one hundred percent certainty that the cause of death in every single case so far has been the same. Because doing so might jeopardize the FBI's continuing investigation, I will not reveal specific details about that cause. Now, I'll turn things over to FBI Director Pam Mazachek."

"Thank you, Dr. McKinney," the FBI director said upon reaching the podium and looking out at the sea of reporters and photographers in front of her. "Though I know you have many questions about the cause of death identified by the CDC folks, I'm not at liberty to disclose those details at this time.

"I will, however, share three important observations: first, due to the fact that the rate at which deaths are being reported has declined with each passing hour, we believe the immediate crisis is over; second, we do not believe the unusually high number of deaths reported during the first thirty-six hours of July is natural or accidental in nature; and, third, I've assigned every available FBI agent to this case.

"Again, we believe the immediate crisis is over; the deaths were neither natural nor accidental; and FBI agents across the country are hard at work, trying to find answers. Thank you."

Reporters pummeled Mazachek with questions, and she deflected most of them easily by citing the "sensitive nature of the ongoing investigation." She did, after all, have good reason to be tightlipped.

Had the fifty-three-year-old native of Enid, Oklahoma, shared everything she knew about the deaths, she would have raised the level of fear in the country to new heights, and she certainly didn't want to do that. Things were bad enough already, and she wanted to keep her focus—and the country's focus—on capturing the person or persons responsible for the worst mass murder in U.S. history and bringing an end to the crisis that made the attacks of September 11 look like child's play.

Mazachek walked away from the podium after deflecting one final question, and Attorney General Daniels ended the news conference with a closing statement.

"At this time, I'd like to ask for help from the American people and members of the news media. I've been authorized by President Rivera to offer a tax-free, cash reward of fifty million dollars to anyone who provides my investigators with credible information that leads to the arrest and conviction of any individuals or groups responsible for the tragedy that has befallen this nation. Anyone with information regarding this matter, no matter how large or how small, is asked to call the FBI tip line or visit the FBI website to leave a tip."

After giving the phone number for the tip line and the address for the FBI website, Daniels ended the ever-so-brief news conference with a polite "thank you" and the agency heads departed in different directions.

17

Accompanied by the nine agents in her personal security detail, Mazachek used an elevator outside the auditorium to return to her fifth-floor office inside the crumbling, eight-story structure known as the J. Edgar Hoover Building.

Dedicated in September 1975 by President Gerald Ford and named for the man who had served as director for most of four decades, the building needed to be torn down and replaced, but no one who wanted to keep his job—or, in Mazachek's case, her job—dared ask for the money to make it happen.

Mazachek spent less than five minutes in her office before using a private elevator to access the roof where a UH-60 Blackhawk helicopter would carry her and members of her entourage away on a one-hour flight to Brooklyn. Not your ordinary law enforcement chopper, this rotary-winded wonder possessed all of the firepower and technological capabilities President Rivera believed his top criminal investigator might need—budget cuts be damned!

Earlier that day, Mazachek had instructed one of her deputies to work with the staff at the FBI's New York City Field Office to secure a flexible lease on an enormous, one-hundred-thousand-square-foot warehouse in Brooklyn, because the first mysterious death had been recorded in that borough.

Less than twelve hours later, the facility became operational as the FBI Special Task Force headquarters. Its Plymouth Street location—a stone's throw from the East River, less than an hour's drive from two major airports, and one river crossing away from the NYCFO—made it ideal.

†

Mazachek's flight to the warehouse afforded her yet another opportunity to overcome her single greatest fear— that is, her fear of flying.

It was something she had never told her physician about, because she feared a note appearing in her medical records— about it or about medications prescribed to deal with it— might somehow result in limits on her career options. In place of professional help, she dealt with aerophobia her own way.

Instead of conducting face-to-face meetings while aboard an aircraft, she conducted all of her business via secure phone lines and relied upon a wearable computer/headset with built-in microphone and eye-level monitor to keep her distracted. The hands-free approach made it possible for her to maintain a tight grip on both armrests most of the time while she was in the air.

Soon after takeoff, Mazachek placed the first of several white-knuckle phone calls, hoping she would soon hear the voice of an old friend.

"Hi, Joe-L. It's Pam. How are you?"

"I'm fine," Wilson replied, surprised to hear the FBI director's distinct and recognizable voice—the byproduct of a lifetime of smoking—and not yet comfortable addressing her by her first name. "To what do I owe this honor?"

"I need you to come to New York City as soon as possible. I want you to take charge of one of my special task forces."

Wilson realized the director's request probably had to do with the public health crisis making headlines around the world, so he opted against asking too many questions or prying for too many details. He'd be brought up to speed soon enough.

Likewise, he wasn't surprised by what seemed like an impulsive decision by Mazachek. She had, after all, developed a reputation as an innovator, open to blazing new trails during her brief time at the helm. Still, he couldn't help but wonder why she picked him.

"I'm flattered by your confidence in me, ma'am, but don't you think that might upset some of your old hands?"

"Joe-L, I think we both know you have more experience and street smarts than just about anyone in the bureau—myself included."

A pregnant pause followed—everyone on the call knew how much the director respected the field agent she had personally lured away from the Show-Me State—and Mazachek began to wrap up the call.

"I've already told your boss I'm gonna steal you for a while. In fact, my plane is waiting for you at the airport. Now, why don't you go home, pack your bags and tell your wife I'm sorry for having to call you up."

"Don't worry about her. She'll be fine."

"Thanks, Joe-L! See you tonight!"

With that, the director disconnected the line and moved on to her next call.

✝

Wilson went through the motions of letting Sean MacNab, the special agent in charge of the FBI Charlotte Field Office, feel as if he had had a say in what was taking place, though both men knew he didn't. And while MacNab appreciated it the gesture, he wasn't surprised to see Wilson called up. He was that good.

After the brief meeting ended, Wilson gathered the gear he thought he might need and walked out the door for what he suspected might be the final time.

Wilson phoned his wife as he drove out of the federal building's parking garage and asked her to locate the checklist he kept in the top drawer of his dresser and use it as a guide for packing his long-term suitcase. Arriving at his home, he went inside, fetched his suitcase and Lori, and put one in the trunk. The other would drive him to the airport after he sneaked into the kitchen and hid something.

A fifteen-minute drive to the airport followed, and Wilson kissed his wife goodbye before climbing out of the front passenger seat and removing his suitcase and a laptop bag from the trunk of the car. Walking into and through the general aviation terminal to the tarmac, he found the director's personal jet, a four-year-old Gulfstream G5, waiting. It was one of the FBI's few remaining aviation assets.

If all went well, Wilson would arrive at LaGuardia Airport in two hours. And all went well.

"Not bad," he thought to himself after realizing how easy it had been traveling early on a pre-Fourth of July Saturday when most frequent flyers were playing rounds of golf with their buddies, spending time outside with their children and enjoying cookouts with friends and loved ones.

✝

Lori returned home from the airport, fully expecting to spend the evening alone, drinking a glass of wine on the backyard deck and gazing lovingly at her new ring. Instead, she found a surprise when she checked the mailbox.

Inside an ordinary #10 envelope postmarked in Charlotte, she found a letter her husband had dropped in the mailbox outside his office one day earlier after returning from D.C:

My Dearest Lori, The past 17 years went by like a blur, and I can't think of anyone with whom I'd rather have spent those years and our years to come. You've always been the girl who makes me feel like a buzzillionaire, now I invite you to find the surprise I hid in the kitchen and see if you're gonna be one, too! Love always, Joe-L

Wilson didn't have to tell his wife where to look. She headed to the kitchen quickly and removed the lid from the yellow smiley-face ceramic cookie jar she had made as a teenager in art class more than two decades earlier. It was the place where her husband had always hidden things from his wife when he wanted her to find them. Inside, she found the $100 scratch-off lottery ticket he had purchased the previous morning in D.C.

She didn't mind that it had cost him more than any of the previous lottery tickets he'd brought home over the years. With plenty of money saved for retirement and no children to spend it on, they could afford the occasional extravagance. And it wasn't like they were big-time gamblers. Like four out of ten Americans, they bought tickets only once in a while, for fun, without ever expecting to win.

Before finding out if the scratch-off ticket was a winner, Lori decided to write a love letter to her husband.

Walking to the dining room, she opened the far-left drawer of the hutch and removed a sheet of pink stationery from a box of paper she reserved solely for letters to her husband. Favorite pen in hand, she cleared a space at the dining room table, organized her thoughts, and began writing.

Finishing a few minutes later, Lori signed her name at the end of the letter, careful to include a tiny heart as the dot over the "i" in her first name. Next, she planted a bright red kiss of lipstick next to her signature and sprayed the letter with a squirt of his favorite perfume. After that, she folded the letter over one time and sealed it inside a matching pink envelope before addressing it and putting a stamp on it. Finally, she carried the envelope into the kitchen and placed it in the wicker basket she used for outgoing mail. On Monday morning, she would put it in their curbside mailbox.

Now, however, she wanted to find out if the ticket her husband had left inside the cookie jar would change their lives forever.

Lori pulled a quarter from the coin jar they kept on the kitchen counter and returned to the living room. Sitting on the edge of the sofa, she used the fingers on her left hand to hold the ticket down on the top of the coffee table and began using the coin in her right hand to scratch the rubbery latex material from the front of the ticket.

18

Upon landing at LaGuardia, Wilson checked his phone and found a text message from Lori: *"You're the best! I love you!"* He took her excitement as a sign his letter must have arrived.

Though curious as to whether his wife's lottery ticket was a winner, he didn't waste any mental energy worrying about it. After all, he knew the lottery's success depended upon selling more losing tickets than winners. Winning was a long shot, and that's why he rarely bought tickets.

"Love U2" he replied before exiting the aircraft and retrieving his bags, thankful he didn't have to navigate the terminal and endure the mayhem in the baggage claim area at the seventy-five-year-old airport where workers were in the middle of tackling long-overdue renovations.

Before collecting his bags and walking down nine stair steps to concrete, Wilson expected to see an FBI driver waiting for him in a dark-colored, late model General Motors sport-utility vehicle—a Chevrolet Suburban or GMC Tahoe. Instead, he saw a tall, balding FBI agent standing next to the open trunk lid of a black 2012 Chevy Volt, the plug-in hybrid that had been mandated for use by federal agencies after sales to the general public fell flat.

Word around the agency was that they were stuck with the cars, despite the fact that they were ill equipped for use in law enforcement and were no longer being produced by the

General Motors subsidiary. Post-Black Monday budget cuts prevented agencies like the FBI from replacing vehicles every two years as had been customary for as long as most could remember. Wilson walked toward the car anyway.

"Joe Wilson," the FBI traveler said as he reached out to shake the hand of the familiar-looking agent.

"Scout Miller. Glad to meet you again."

Upon hearing Miller's baritone voice, Wilson remembered they had met in Saint Louis two years earlier.

As the men climbed into the car for the sixteen-minute drive to the FBI warehouse, Miller was first to break the ice.

"The director thinks you're quite the Kojak," he said, referring to the 1970s television cop show starring the late actor Telly Savalas in the title role as the lollypop-sucking New York City cop who always captured his man.

"You know better than to confuse me with a bald Italian," Wilson replied. "He was a lieutenant, too, and I never made it that high."

"They wanted to keep you as a working cop," Miller countered.

"You seem to know a lot about me," Wilson said after a brief lull in the conversation. "What's your story?"

"Well, I went to high school with Pam Mazachek, class of 1980 at Enid High School. In fact, we dated for a while in college. Even danced with her at the Nite Lite Club when there wasn't anything else to do—and, trust me, there wasn't much else to do in Alva, Oklahoma."

"Danced with the director, huh?" Wilson had a hard time imagining the giant of a man—he was six-four and two-forty—on the dance floor, especially with Mazachek. "I bet you're the only agent who can make that claim."

"Well, she wasn't the director back then. She was a member of the pom-pom squad, and I was on the basketball team. You know how that goes."

"I can see you playing basketball, being tall enough and all, but I find it difficult to envision the director as a cheerleader."

"Don't know what makes you say that. She tells me she's your biggest fan."

"Really?"

"You can't let her know I told you this, but she said you're probably the best investigator the bureau has."

"Trust me. I won't tell her you said it."

After earning a criminal justice degree—paid for, in part, by a basketball scholarship—at Northwestern Oklahoma State University in Alva, Miller served four years as an Oklahoma Highway Patrol trooper before joining the FBI. Despite thirty-two years in law enforcement, he looked as fit as he had the day he walked off the basketball court for the last time.

Wilson suspected Mazachek had assigned Miller to be his right-hand man—someone who would use his decades of FBI knowledge to prevent bureaucratic hurdles from hindering his investigative efforts. Only time would tell if he was right.

When the pair arrived at the warehouse, Miller parked in a nearby lot guarded by more than a dozen heavily armed men. Wilson, meanwhile, found himself in awe of the measures put in place to secure the facility. Included were portable lighting kits that made for a seamless transition from daytime to night and T-Walls surrounding the warehouse at ground level. Also known as "Bremer walls," the twelve-foot-high, portable, steel-reinforced structures came into fashion after extensive use by the U.S. military in combat zones during the previous decade. They would provide cover from a plethora of threats—bombs and bullets included—that might show up during this unsettling time.

What Wilson wouldn't learn until later was that his every move had been observed by several of the FBI's best snipers—men and women equipped with the latest killing technology and dressed in black—in rooftop positions at one-hundred-foot intervals for six blocks in every direction; that dozens of other agents were patrolling on foot along the waterfront of the nearby East River; that additional agents were keeping watch aboard personal watercraft and on armed patrol boats; and that others were positioned throughout the city, disguised as homeless people and food cart vendors while trying to blend in and keep their eyes and ears open.

Above the fray, FBI and NYPD helicopters conducted round-the-clock patrols of the restricted airspace established for three miles in every direction from the warehouse.

✝

After making it through the security checkpoint, Miller gave Wilson a quick tour of the facility, beginning with two key pieces of information: where to find a hot cup of coffee and where to go to get rid of it after it did its work. Beyond that, Miller pointed out several key features of the warehouse's efficient, hierarchical design, each of which was intended to boost efficiency and improve workflow during high-profile investigations.

Smack in the middle was a one-hundred-seat command center. Known as "The Ring" to agents who'd worked previous high-profile cases because of the verbal sparring that often took place there, it featured twenty-five computer workstations on each side of a square. Each workstation, in turn, provided access to every type of electronic information an agent might need or want while seated in an armless leather chair and staring at a seventeen-inch computer screen.

In addition to the workstations, four sixty-inch-diameter high-definition monitors hung from the ceiling on opposite walls, positioned high enough to provide big-screen viewing capability to all attendees without blocking any agent's ability to make eye contact with anyone else in the room.

Beyond The Ring's soundproof exterior walls, restricted-access hallways connected the offices of team leaders in charge of administration, intelligence, operations and support who were already cracking their whips.

In addition, white coat-wearing technicians from the FBI Laboratory at Quantico occupied one of the largest spaces in the warehouse—a mobile crime lab located in an area immediately outside of The Ring.

Between those offices and the building's exterior walls, dozens of smaller workspaces—some with walls and ceilings, others looking more like cubicles—housed staffers providing support to field agents working on the case. Most importantly, every office had at least one couch that doubled as a bed, and some had two.

Miller told Wilson everyone working inside the warehouse knew—or would eventually realize—those working closest to the building's exterior were, for lack of a better description, more expendable than those working closer to The Ring. Their offices were located along the same wall as a dozen customized motor homes, each equipped with locker room-style shower stalls, sinks and toilets, were parked for the duration.

"Just like being a cop," Wilson thought to himself. "Rank has its privileges."

After completing the warehouse tour, Miller led Wilson back to the office they would share, gave him a briefing book, and suggested he study it during the ten minutes remaining before his first STF meeting.

"Meet me in The Ring at seven," Miller said as he left the room.

"I'll be there with bells on."

†

Minus actual bells, Wilson entered The Ring with five minutes to spare. Other agents followed soon after.

Quick to recognize the seating arrangement had been determined in advance, each agent knew the director's chair would be located directly opposite the room's single entry point. Beyond that, it was a game of search and find as each of the one hundred laptop computer screens was lit up to display the name of a different agent. The names, however, were not in alphabetical order.

Wilson walked more than halfway around the room before finding his name on a screen in front of a chair sitting to the right of one reserved for the FBI director. Soon, he expected to learn more about the logic behind the arrangement.

As agents began finding their seats inside The Ring, Mazachek stepped off the helicopter that had touched down in the roped-off parking lot adjacent the warehouse. She was met by Hank Valenzuela, assistant director in charge of the FBI's New York City Field Office and the man who had been on the receiving end of the director's second white-knuckle phone call while en route to Brooklyn. During that phone call, Valenzuela told Mazachek everything there was to know about the warehouse but never mentioned the fact that he had been a finalist for the job Mazachek now had.

Two months shy of sixty, Valenzuela enjoyed being the FBI's top man in The Big Apple, especially after receiving a phone call directly from President Rivera an hour before

Mazachek's appointment had been made public. The president had told the veteran agent he was going to appoint Mazachek the FBI's first female director instead of him as the first Latino director. Why? Because he feared choosing a Latino might be construed as some sort of ethnic nepotism by the American people.

Rather than share that fear, the president told Americans his selection of Mazachek had been based solely only on his belief she was qualified to do the job and had nothing to do with filling a diversity square. The fact Mazachek had somehow never worked in the nation's capitol played the biggest part in his decision-making process, but he didn't speak to that either. Privately, the forty-fifth leader of the free world embraced hope that his new FBI director would look at everything in Washington, D.C., with a fresh set of eyes.

Valenzuela led the director's entourage to the building's entrance one hundred feet away and, barely thirty seconds later, every agent inside The Ring stood as Mazachek entered at 6:59 p.m.

Wearing dark slacks and a matching jacket over a nondescript white blouse, the director exuded confidence without appearing arrogant. Those who knew her well knew she wasn't the type to toot her own horn. They knew she preferred, instead, to let results speak for themselves and to ensure credit went to those who deserved it.

"Good morning, ladies and gentlemen," Mazachek said before sitting down and motioning for everyone else to do the same. "This will be the only time we meet this late in the day, and we won't meet in person tomorrow. Instead, senior staff meetings will, beginning Tuesday, take place at 8 a.m. unless circumstances dictate otherwise."

Mazachek paused for a few seconds as agents took note of her advisory.

"All of you are aware of why we are here. Before I get into any details about that, I want you to understand how this investigation is going to work, and I want it to stay in this room.

"Look around," she said, stretching her arms in front of her and then sweeping them back and down to her sides, "you'll see most of the agents in this room are fairly young by FBI standards. Seven out of ten of you have less than five years on the job. And that's intentional on my part."

Truth be told, she was at least thirty years older than most of the agents and nearly fifteen years older than Wilson.

"Since taking over as director, I've encountered a lot of opposition from two types of agents: those who have more headquarters experience than I have and those who have different reproductive organs than I have.

"Frankly speaking, I don't have time to let differences in seniority and gender impede this investigation, so I took the politically-incorrect path and assigned only certain types of agents to this case. In short, you are agents I believe are best suited to work on my team."

After pausing a moment to stand, Mazachek continued speaking. As she did, she tried to make eye contact with as many agents as possible without it seeming intentional.

"Moving forward, I want to introduce you to someone," she continued, without looking at the man sitting to her right. "Contrary to his aged appearance, he's been with the bureau less than two years. Still, he brings nearly twenty years of law enforcement experience to the table."

With those words, she looked around the room again briefly before turning to make eye contact with Wilson, who was silently hoping Mazachek didn't expect him to make a speech.

"Joe-L, please stand up," she said before pausing for a few seconds so everyone could get a look at the man in her spotlight. "Ladies and gentlemen, this is Special Agent Joseph L. Wilson."

After pausing again for effect, the director continued.

"When I spoke to Agent Wilson yesterday afternoon, I told him I needed him to fly up here and lead one of my Special Task Forces," she explained. "Joe-L, there's one thing I forgot to tell you: I only have one task force."

The roomful of agents erupted with laughter, and the director concluded her introduction.

"Everyone, please join me in welcoming Special Agent Joseph L. Wilson."

A round of polite applause followed, but Director Mazachek's body language told Wilson and everyone else in the room she wasn't finished speaking.

"Because Joe-L is relatively new to the bureau, I've assigned Scout Miller from my executive staff to run interference for him and make sure bureaucracy and red tape do not hinder his efforts.

"I want you to know I trust Scout to the same degree I trust Joe-L—and each of you," she said," pausing briefly to let her words sink in. "Completely."

Concluding her remarks, Mazachek turned toward the still-standing Wilson and said, "Joe-L, the floor is yours."

Though humbled by, and appreciative of, the director's display of confidence, Wilson had always considered himself something of a young Moses when it came to public speaking. He didn't relish such opportunities and, when required to speak in public, he tried to stick with a keep-it-simple approach that seemed to serve him well.

"Director Mazachek, I appreciate your confidence in me, but must emphasize that the work ahead of us goes far beyond any single agent," he began, panning the room in search of outward signs of emotion, but seeing none. "It will take all of us to figure out who and/or what is behind these deaths."

"Most of you probably know someone who died and want to find answers for those they left behind so that this kind of thing doesn't happen again. So do I."

After concluding the pep talk portion of his impromptu speech, Wilson told the assembled agents to continue analyzing the data pouring in law enforcement agencies at all levels and promised to issue marching orders by the end of the day.

Wilson closed by asking if anyone had questions. When none did, Mazachek stood, thanked Wilson, and dismissed all but two of the agents—Wilson and Miller.

As the rest of the agents filed out of The Ring, Mazachek brushed back the bangs of her bottle-blonde pageboy hairdo and turned her attention to Wilson.

"Joe-L, thanks again for coming. I hope you don't mind me throwing that curve ball at you, but I didn't want you to fret too much on your way here."

"Not a problem, ma'am. I'm always up for a challenge."

"Good. Let's go to my office and talk."

During most of the next sixty minutes, Mazachek briefed Wilson and Miller on details of the case, including several she had not shared during the meeting.

"The thing that's most puzzling about these deaths is that, apart from the quick downward spiral that follows the onset of symptoms prior to organ collapse, we're seeing few similarities between cases.

"Victim demographics run the gamut—black, white, Asian, Martian—and come from all socioeconomic backgrounds."

Opening his briefing book to a dog-eared page, Wilson shared an observation before asking a question. "I noticed the first set of toxicology reports yielded nothing worthwhile and that new reports could take up to seventy-two hours. Have we had any input from chemical and biological warfare experts about what we're dealing with?"

"Yes," Mazachek replied, "the folks at the CDC and the lab at Fort Meade have shared plenty about what's *not* involved. Unfortunately, they say we'll have to wait for higher-order tox screens to show what *is* involved."

"That being the case, I'd like to spend the next seventy-two hours putting agents in the field and speaking to people who knew the victims well," Wilson said. "I want us to focus on individuals who spent time with the victims during the days before they showed signs of being ill."

"That sounds like good old-fashioned police work to me," Mazachek replied, smiling the kind of smile she reserved for trusted friends. "I knew there must have been a good reason for bringing you here."

Giving signals the meeting was about to end, Mazachek told Miller to help Wilson draft his marching orders and then asked her lead investigator to keep her informed about any new developments, regardless of the time of day. When she picked up her phone and asked her traveling secretary to ring the attorney general, the men in the room knew it was time to depart. The meeting was over.

✝

En route to the office in which he and his new colleague expected to spend many hours together, Miller offered

Wilson a pat on the back and a question. "Did she surprise you?"

"A little bit, but I get the feeling you knew already."

"I did," Miller confirmed with a chuckle.

Wilson decided then and there he liked Miller and, more importantly, trusted him.

The duo spent much of the next hour drafting the marching orders he had promised to distribute to agents. In an electronic message sent out at 9 p.m., he instructed them to concentrate their efforts in cities with the highest death tolls and to spend their time interviewing friends and loved ones of victims and retracing the steps of those victims. It was the kind of approach that had always gotten Wilson results.

19

After thumbing through stacks of folders containing case files, Wilson removed three files he and Miller would investigate personally. The first contained details about the death of Lucille Marie Marcelli; the second about Navy Petty Officer First Class Thomas Oliver West; and the third about Pastor Ronald Edward French.

According to the case summary stapled to the outside of the Marcelli folder, the young woman's death had been the first of its kind in the New York City area. Fortunately for the FBI agents, her apartment was less than four minutes away on Flushing Avenue in Brooklyn. They would go there first.

They arrived at the entrance to the 1950s-era apartment building at 9:20 p.m., and Wilson pressed the buzzer for apartment 202. Almost a minute passed without a response, so he pressed it again.

"Who the hell is it?" came a female voice blaring through the intercom speaker in a manner reminiscent of the greeting two traveling musicians received thirty-six hours earlier.

"FBI. I need to speak with you about Lucille Marcelli."

Having not yet recovered from the trauma of losing her friend, co-worker and roommate, Rita Falcone's anxiety level spiked upon hearing an FBI agent say he wanted to talk to her. "I'll be right down," she replied nervously.

After throwing on a pair of black pajama pants and a mostly-black Nine Inch Nails sweatshirt, Falcone walked out her only door and down the hall to long stairway that ended at the entrance to the building. Already bothered by the fact that a federal agent knew where she lived, she would feel twice as bad after she opened the door and found he had a partner.

"Miss Falcone? I'm FBI Special Agent Wilson, and this is Special Agent Miller. We need to speak with you about Lucille."

"You mean, Lucy? You don't need to speak with me; you need to speak with those musicians that spent the night at our apartment that night. Lucy was fine up until they showed up."

"What do you mean when you say she was fine?" Wilson asked, careful to avoid asking questions to which she might respond with a single-word, "Yes," or "No."

"After we made it home from work that night, Lucy and I had dinner and dessert and watched TV for a couple of hours," Falcone explained in a rapid-fire burst of syllables and spit, "and then we went to bed around one. Next thing I know, these wannabe rock stars—from Mississippi or someplace like that—buzzed us from downstairs."

"How did Lucy know them?" Wilson asked.

"She answered a Craigslist ad and offered them a place to stay while they were passing through town."

"And what makes you think these musicians had something to do with Lucy's death?"

"Before they showed up, Lucy was alive. After they arrived, she was dead. Plain and simple."

"Do you have the names of the two men?"

"I do, but they're in my purse upstairs."

"Mind if we come up and take a look around while you find the names?"

"Sure, follow me," Falcone replied, motioning with her right arm while grabbing the stair rail with her left. "I warn you, though, the place is a mess."

Falcone led the men up the stairs and down the hall to her apartment where she was quick to locate her purse. After more than a minute of searching unsuccessfully for the information she wanted, she dumped the contents of her purse on her kitchen table and spotted the piece of scrap paper containing the musicians' names and phone numbers. In turn, she picked it up and handed it to Wilson who passed it along to Miller with instructions to track down the musicians.

A simple task, Miller pulled his smartphone from his coat pocket and opened a GPS locator app that had been developed especially for the FBI by sleuths at the National Security Agency. Within three minutes, he had fixes on both men; they were in close proximity to each other at an indie music bar in downtown Charlottesville, Virginia.

"Got it," Miller said, prompting Wilson to stop questioning Falcone for a moment and direct his attention toward Miller.

"Find out if one of our agents in Charlottesville can track 'em down. I'd like to hear their versions of what happened here."

"Can do, Boss."

As Miller walked away to make a phone call, Wilson turned his attention back to the apartment dweller.

"Have you cleaned the apartment since Lucy's death?" Wilson asked. Based solely on the appearance of the place, he fully expected Falcone to say she had not. And he was right.

"I washed the bed sheets and stuff, and I scrubbed the spot on the floor in the bedroom where I found her, but that's it."

"Okay, we're going to need to run lab tests on a few items. Is that okay with you?"

"Knock yourself out."

Wilson pulled a pair of latex gloves out of his coat pocket, put them on and went to work. Though the apartment had not been treated as a crime scene by the NYPD cops responding to the 911 call, the FBI agent thought a search might turn up something—perhaps many things—to aid in the investigation.

Starting in the bedroom, Wilson picked up dozens of items he thought might contain residue of the virus, bacterial agent, poison, or whatever it was that killed Lucy. Among them, a mascara brush, a cotton ball, a lottery ticket and a pair of earrings. He deposited each item into a separate plastic bag.

After placing a phone call to Charlottesville, Miller joined Wilson in scouring the apartment for clues. The list of items he bagged included a still-wrapped stick of chewing gum, an empty hair spray can, a battery-powered toothbrush and a used condom.

By 11 p.m., the men had bagged more than one hundred items in the bedroom and adjacent bathroom. From the kitchen and living room, they collected a similar assortment of items that included empty cans of beer, sofa pillows, eating utensils, unwashed dishes and a container of mystery meat that appeared to have been abandoned—perhaps years earlier—on a lower shelf near the back of the refrigerator. Whether or not any of the items would yield clues to the woman's death remained to be seen.

Satisfied they had combed the apartment thoroughly, Wilson asked a few more questions to see if Falcone's replies matched those she had given earlier that evening as well as those attributed to her by the NYPD cops one day earlier.

"How did Lucy come to know the musicians?"

"Like I said before, she answered an online ad. Their band manager needed to find the guys a cheap place to crash for one night while they were in town for a gig. That's what the guys told me anyway."

"When did they arrive, and how long were they here before Lucy fell ill?"

"I think it was about four o'clock in the morning when they got here. Of course, Lucy didn't tell me she had two complete strangers coming to spend the night, so I was kinda caught off guard when I heard someone buzzing from downstairs."

Falcone went on to explain how Lucy apologized for not telling her she was expecting guests.

"She told me she'd forgotten to let me know about the guys arriving that night. I was too tired to deal with it, so I went back to bed after she let 'em in."

"Tell us how you discovered Lucy that night."

"It wasn't night when I found her," Falcone replied, correcting the FBI agent. "It was almost nine in the morning."

"Okay," Wilson replied, noting her story was tracking well. "Tell me what happened."

"So I woke up and barely had my eyes open when I almost tripped over her." Pointing to a spot on the floor, Falcone said, "She was right there, lying in the doorway to the bedroom.

"I yelled at her for being in the way and, when she didn't move, I tried to shake her—you know, to wake her up—but she still didn't respond. That's when I turned on the bedroom light, noticed red blotches all over her body, and got really scared."

"Scared in what way?"

"I was scared she might be dead," Falcone said, her eyes beginning to tear up, "and then I remembered the musicians were still in the house and worried they might have done something to her and might want to do something to me."

"So, what did you do next?"

"I decided to risk it and screamed for them to help me. The dark-haired one came to the bedroom to see what was going on and, as soon as he saw Lucy, he shouted to his friend, the blonde, and told him to call 911. A few minutes later, the ambulance crew showed up, and they rolled Lucy out of here. I never saw her alive again."

With those words, the woman's emotions finally got the best of her; her shoulders slumped, and she began sobbing.

Wilson gave Falcone a minute to regain her composure before he continued his line of questioning. "Did Lucy have any enemies?"

"Other than the cable customers we deal with on the phone at work, probably not," she answered. "And those people never get to know our last names—security, ya know."

"Do you know if she had eaten anything odd, if she had purchased anything unusual, or if she had received any gifts during the week before her death?"

"I can't think of anything out of the ordinary. With what we make, it's not like we've ever had extra money to throw around willy-nilly at the end of the month. Plus, her birthday is—or was—still months away, and she didn't have a boyfriend or anything like that, so I don't think she would've received any gifts."

"What about family? Does she have any relatives nearby?"

"Lucy came from a family of misfits. She was the only one in her family who could keep a job, first to graduate from high school, that kinda thing."

"Do you know how we can reach any of her relatives?"

"Most of them are living on what Lucy described to me once as 'government assistance,'" she said, holding up both hands to form air quotes around her last two words. "In other words, they're locked up behind bars in correctional facilities around the country. Except for the one time I asked her about her family, I don't think she mentioned any of them ever again."

Sensing the family angle would lead nowhere, Wilson began to wrap up the visit.

"Do you have a phone number, aside from work, where we can reach you if we have more questions?"

Falcone provided her phone number and then watched as the agents began the first of several trips during which they carried bags of evidence to their car parked outside. When it appeared the agents were nearly finished, she asked two questions of her own.

"You don't think Lucy's death has anything to do with all of the dead people turning up everywhere, do you?"

"Anything's possible," Wilson replied. "That's why we're looking for answers."

"Is there anything I should know that Lucy didn't tell me? I mean, hey, am I in any kind of danger?"

Wilson looked at Miller and sensed his colleague wanted to answer the question in a rather special way.

"Ms. Falcone, I don't think you're in any more danger than anyone else in this city," Miller began. "I would, however, suggest you give your apartment a very-thorough cleaning after we leave."

"Okay, I'll do that," a puzzled Falcone replied, uncertain about what to make of the suggestion.

Of course, Miller didn't have any scientific basis for the advice he had offered; instead, he simply believed cleaner surroundings might improve her prospects.

Three hours after they had arrived at Falcone's apartment, the agents returned to the warehouse and spent another hour completing the tedious-but-necessary paperwork that would accompany the evidence bags as they were was turned over to the crime lab technicians. Showers followed, and both men were asleep on separate sofa beds inside their office by 2 a.m.

20

Three and a half hours after hitting their pillows, Wilson and Miller were awake again, focused on getting their Saturday off to a good start.

For Wilson, that meant drinking at least two cups of coffee while eating a hearty breakfast—scrambled eggs, sausage, hash browns and Greek yogurt—and taking an eighty-one-milligram aspirin. It also meant reviewing dozens of messages that had arrived during the night from agents across the country.

Miller started his day with a fifteen-minute run, followed by a regimen of pushups and yoga exercises about which his fellow agents teased him frequently. Yoga or not, Miller knew he was in better physical condition than most of the agents teasing him, and most of those agents knew the same.

After finishing their morning routines, Wilson and Miller took showers, shaved and dressed for the long day ahead. By 6:15, they were reviewing the two remaining case files Wilson had pulled from the stack the night before. By 6:30, they were en route to LaGuardia.

Thanks to Wilson's new position, he and Miller received unrestricted access to the same Gulfstream G5 that had picked Wilson up in Charlotte a day earlier. Unlike the vast majority of the bureau's fixed- and rotary-wing aircraft that had either been sold or grounded, this one remained in tip-top shape, ready to go.

Officially, FBI Director Mazachek had agreed to sacrifice her own mobility—"It's only temporary," she told members of her executive staff—so her lead investigator could be free to travel wherever the investigation took him. Unofficially, she was ecstatic about giving up the jet.

The Wilson-Miller agenda for the morning included flying to the Groton-New London Airport in Connecticut and then driving to the submarine base. There, they would meet officials from the Naval Criminal Investigations Service and try to speak with as many people as possible who had seen Petty Officer West during the last few days of his life. The bureau's resident agent in New London would be their guide.

The G5 went wheels up at 7.

After making a handful of phone calls, including one to set up an appointment with NCIS chief at the base, Wilson and Miller began perusing their email folders, hoping to find some valuable tidbits in messages received from agents across the Northeast. Most of those messages, however, turned out to be long on possibilities and short on substance.

Sadly, they also learned two agents had died during the previous week. An FBI agent in Charlottesville wasn't among them. Miller received a message from the agent in response to the request he'd made less than six hours earlier.

"Peters and Ryan appear to be clean-cut guys," the agent wrote. "They said they purchased a case of beer and a lottery ticket from a convenience store near the victim's apartment and gave it to her as a token of appreciation for letting them spend the night. They said they went to sleep soon after arriving and were awakened a few hours later by the screams of the victim's roommate. After a quick look at the victim, Ryan said he yelled for Peters to call for an ambulance, and he did."

After reading the rest of the agent's message, Miller shared it with Wilson and, together, they decided against putting the musicians on any list of suspects yet. More stones—but, in this case, not the *Rolling* kind—remained to be turned over.

Upon landing at 7:21, the men were greeted on the parking apron.

"Good morning. I'm Special Agent Carolyn Jane."

More introductions and handshakes followed before they loaded their bags into the back of a black 2012 Chevrolet Tahoe parked nearby.

"Carolyn, tell me about the NCIS guys we're gonna meet today."

"You'll be meeting Jock Martin, the NCIS special agent in charge at the submarine base in New London, and he'll likely bring a couple of guys with him. I've only worked with him on a pair of occasions, but I can't say I enjoyed either very much."

"Nutcracker? Slacker? What kind of guy is he?" Wilson asked.

"I'm told he was a Coast Guard rescue swimmer back in the day, then decided he wanted to carry a badge after someone, according to him, botched the investigation into the on-the-job death of one of his buddies. In other words, he seems to have an axe to grind."

With that, Miller took the key fob for the Tahoe from the local agent, and he and Wilson began their ten-minute drive to the base. Agent Jane, meanwhile, climbed into the only other government-owned vehicle present—another black 2012 Chevy Volt—with office manager Kaylee Hickman driving.

Arriving at the base's main entrance at 7:35, Miller showed his credentials to one of the guards who had been alerted about the pending arrival of two high-profile FBI visitors. At the same time, two other guards performed a quick walk-around inspection of the FBI vehicle. Less than thirty seconds later, Miller was waved through.

Anyone else trying to get on base that day would endure a more thorough screening that included, but wasn't limited to, the use of bomb-sniffing dogs and long poles with mirrors on the ends, used to check for explosives in hard-to-see places beneath vehicles.

While tempted to stop and investigate the area where West had crashed his SUV, Wilson's gut told him the crash was only a byproduct of the crisis and couldn't play a significant role in solving the riddle before him.

After parking in front of the NCIS office three minutes later, the FBI agents found themselves being met at the door by Martin and three of his subordinates. Quick introductions and handshakes followed, and members of the newly-formed group entered the building, made a quick left turn into a windowless, twenty-seat conference room and took seats around a long wooden table.

"What can we do for you, Agent Wilson?" Martin said, breaking the ice.

"Jock, I appreciate you going to the trouble of coming in, especially on a holiday weekend, but we're pressed for time."

Martin sensed a request was on its way, and he was right.

"I'd like to borrow one of your men—someone who knows the base well—for the next day or two," Wilson continued. "Do you have someone like that?"

"You bet!" Martin replied. "Jack Lee can help you out. He's one of my best."

At that moment, a twenty-eight-year-old, third-generation Chinese-American stepped forward from a spot in the back of the room and walked toward Wilson.

"Jack Lee, sir," the young man said, focused on making eye contact with Wilson as soon as he swiveled in his chair and stood to face him.

"Glad to meet you, Jack. Ready to go?"

"Yes, sir!"

With that, Wilson thanked Martin and his staff for their hospitality and for letting him borrow Lee. After that, the trio headed out the door.

"Wait," Martin said, half-shouting to Wilson as he was halfway out the door of the building. "You're gonna want this."

Martin caught up to Wilson and handed him an accordion-style folder featuring several compartments, each containing at least one resealable plastic evidence bag. Inside the bags were items collected from inside West's vehicle and from inside his home. After Wilson signed a form to show he had accepted custody of the evidence, Martin handed him a key to the front door of West's condo and a copy of his agency's admittedly incomplete report about the petty officer's death.

"Thanks again," Wilson told Martin before turning around and introducing Lee to Miller as the three walked toward their Tahoe.

"You drive," Wilson told Lee. "We need to go to the schoolhouse where Petty Officer West did his teaching."

"Yes, sir! We'll be there in no time."

Wilson noticed Lee's exuberance right away, but wasn't sure whether he should attribute it to youth or something else, so he didn't say anything about it. Miller, on the other hand, wasn't so hesitant.

"Jack, you seem pretty excited about getting out of the office. This isn't your first rodeo, is it?"

Caught off guard by the question from the man old enough to be his father, Lee answered carefully.

"Agent Miller, I've been an NCIS agent for six months. Before that, I spent four years as a scope dope aboard the USS Fort Fisher and then almost six years as a Navy cop. When it comes to high-profile investigations, this probably qualifies as my first."

Wilson appreciated the young man's honesty in answering Miller's question. At the same time, he wasn't bothered by the fact Martin seemed to have loaned him his least-experienced investigator.

"You're a lot like me, Jack," Wilson said, hoping to put the young man—trim and athletic at five-six and one-fifty—at ease. "I've only been with the bureau eighteen months myself."

"It sure has aged you," Miller quipped from the backseat.

"Who asked you, old man?" Wilson countered with a laugh.

"Agent Wilson, what did you do before joining the FBI?" Lee asked, breaking the silence that had momentarily filled the SUV.

"I was a sheriff's detective in Missouri, Jack."

"I see," Lee responded, trying unsuccessfully not to sound surprised.

Barely two minutes later, Miller piped up again as Lee drove through the entrance at the Naval Submarine School where prospective submariners learned survival skills.

"Senior Chief Master Diver William Cox is the officer in charge, and he's expecting us at eight o'clock at something called the Submarine Escape Trainer."

"It's right over here, sir," Lee said, pointing toward a dive tower almost six stories tall.

As Lee parked the SUV in a space marked VISITOR, Wilson and Miller saw a mountain of a man emerge from a set of double doors near the base of the tower. It was Chief Cox.

At six-six and two-sixty, Cox seemed to have muscles in places where most men didn't know they grew. And while Wilson would feel small standing next to him, Miller would find himself wondering what he would have to do to achieve similar results.

"Good morning, gentlemen, Bill Cox," the chief said before extending handshakes and completing introductions. "Follow me."

Chief Cox led the men to his twelve-by-fifteen office where nearly every square inch of available wall space was covered by framed certificates, photos, plaques and other memorabilia. Whether or not the display—referred to by military folks as an "I Love Me" wall—was intended to impress or intimidate, the visitors concluded it could do either well.

"Coffee?" Cox asked.

"No thanks, chief" Wilson replied. "We're really pressed for time today."

"Got it. How can I help?"

"We're trying to learn as much as possible about Petty Officer West and the last seventy-two hours of his life. Can you tell us about him and about what you know was going on in his life during that time period?"

"Like clockwork, he showed up by 6:30 every day, worked out for at least an hour, conducted classes all day, and went home around four o'clock. As far as I know, Wednesday and Thursday were no different."

"Did he have any enemies or anyone who might have wanted to do him harm?"

"If he did, I can't imagine who it might have been," the chief replied. "This guy was tough as nails, but as fair and as friendly as can be, always willing to go the extra mile—even for a stranger."

With tears welling up in his eyes, Chief Cox spent another five minutes sharing a laundry list of the late petty officer's career and educational achievements, special skills and other bits of information before Wilson seized back control of the conversation.

"Do you know who he hung out with and who his best friends were?"

"He and I were close, because I think he was on track to replace me here two assignments down the road, but most of his real buddies—you know, the guys around his age—were Navy divers outside the school."

"Do you know where we can find 'em, chief?"

"Over at Submarine Group 2. I'll call ahead to let them know you're on the way."

"Thanks, Chief, but I'd rather we arrive unannounced."

"Okay. Whatever you say."

The conversation ended with Wilson thanking the chief for his time and asking him to call if he came up with anything he thought might prove useful to the investigation. After departing the school, the trio drove across the base in another direction.

At SUBGRU2, the investigators found a handful of divers who seemed willing to tell all about their late friend during a one-hour session in the unit's break room. While most of what they said qualified as irrelevant, one detail caught Wilson's attention.

"Did you hear what that short, stocky guy said about West?" Wilson asked as they drove past the base's main gate en route to West's condo. "He said West wasn't a risk taker and that the only chances he took regularly involved gambling. Something about that bothers me."

Lee couldn't resist throwing his two cents into the mix.

"I don't know how it might connect to all this, but the NCIS report says there were no signs of trauma or injury on the petty officer's body except for a cut on his forehead that he apparently suffered when he hit his head on the steering wheel after his vehicle plowed into the concrete barrier."

"Interesting, Jack," Wilson replied, careful not to put out any embers of self-confidence that might be heating up in the young NCIS agent's mind. He had read the report, too, but sensed something much bigger waiting to be discovered. "Let's head to the petty officer's place and take a look around."

When they arrived at the condo a few minutes later, they found it was fairly new but sparsely decorated. Perfect for a bachelor, it had two bedrooms, one and a half baths and a small yard he didn't have to maintain. West had enjoyed that and the fact it had a park nearby where he could take his dog, Max, a three-year-old Rhodesian Ridgeback, on walks after work.

The agents put on their latex gloves again, and Lee retrieved the key to the condo's front door from one of the plastic bags inside the accordion folder.

"We've kept the place locked up tight since his body was removed," Lee told the FBI agents, "because we weren't sure what we were dealing with."

After Wilson and Miller followed him through the front door, Lee removed a handful of photos from another bag and began speaking again.

"Judging by these photos, I'd say everything appears to be the same as it was the last time we were here."

"Let me see those," Wilson said before taking possession of the photos as well as the accordion folder. "While I look through this stuff, I want you guys to take a look around this place and look for anything the NCIS agents might have missed."

The veteran that he was, Miller had already begun perusing the kitchen counters and table. Lee began his search in the bedroom that appeared to be the one used most often by West.

While his colleagues began combing the condo for more clues and evidence, Wilson sat on an armless, bar stool next to the bar-height kitchen table so he could take a look at the contents of some of the evidence bags.

Inside a bag marked "West, Thomas O. (PO1)—SUV," he found many items one might expect inside a bachelor's vehicle: an assortment of music CDs; an insulated coffee mug with a screw-in lid; a USB-tipped charger cable; and a small packet of breath strips.

Along with maintenance-related paperwork from the glove box, a dash-mounted GPS device, a pair of identical ink pens, and some loose coins from the console, nothing seemed unusual. One item, however, did raise a question in the mind of the investigator.

"Didn't we see one of these at that woman's apartment in Brooklyn?" asked Wilson, using the thumb and forefinger of his gloved left hand to hold up a coffee-stained lottery ticket.

"We did," Miller answered, his voice indicating heightened interest.

Speaking loud enough for all to hear but not expecting feedback, Wilson offered another observation after looking around the kitchen counter area where, according to the evidence tag, the lottery ticket had been found.

"This ticket is stained with coffee, but I can still make out the time stamp—July 1, 2016; 12:04 A.M."

"Evidently, yesterday wasn't his lucky day," Miller replied.

Wilson removed the remaining pieces of evidence from the folder and, with help from Miller and Lee, spread two dozen items across the kitchen table and the nearby countertop. The number of analysis-worthy items—including a toothbrush, a comb and a nose-hair trimmer—totaled seventy-eight.

Wilson knew they could submit all of the items to the FBI lab, but fought the urge to do so, hoping instead his search might produce something worthy of a "smoking gun" label. Finding nothing and realizing time was of the essence, he opted to trust his gut again and end the search.

After wrapping things up at the condo and loading their findings into the SUV, the trio headed back to the base, Lee driving again.

Because the condo was only a short drive from the base, Wilson hadn't worried about wasting time traveling from the base, to the condo, and back. To the contrary, he viewed the travel time as giving him opportunities to openly discuss matters with Miller and Lee—without worrying about being overheard by curious others.

"Next stop, the impound lot—or whatever the Navy calls the place where the petty officer's car is being kept," Wilson directed.

"Sir, his vehicle is parked inside a secure warehouse," Lee replied. "Whenever we need a safe place to leave large amounts of evidence, the logistics folks accommodate us. I have a key."

"Good, let's go see it after we grab a bite to eat."

"Does this base have anything good to eat on a holiday weekend, Lee?" asked Miller, jumping into the conversation from his passenger-side, second-row seat as he saw a dining establishment coming up on their right.

"Yes, sir. The Union Deli never closes, and it has a lot of choices—some of them healthy," Lee said, hoping his visitors would be pleased with his recommendation.

Miller said, "Lead the way. I'm starving," and Wilson didn't object. He was hungry, too.

At the deli, Wilson ordered a bacon cheeseburger sans bun; Miller an avocado salad—no dressing—with a plate of fresh fruit; and Lee his usual, a Philly cheesesteak sandwich.

Forty minutes later, Wilson and Miller knew they could trust Lee's food instincts—the Union Deli had good food.

After downing their meals and making some quick pit stops, the trio headed to a windowless warehouse where they would examine the six-year-old SUV left behind by West.

Upon arrival, Wilson and Miller got a taste of what "secure" means in the paint-anything-that-moves world of the Navy. They had to pass through two armed security checkpoints before gaining access to a poorly lit cage inside which they found the late petty officer's vehicle.

"Jack, see if you can find us some light—strong flashlights at a minimum," Wilson ordered. "We can't see squat in here."

A few minutes later, Lee returned with a pair of mobile floodlights—each the equivalent of having the sun mounted on a pole attached to a skateboard—and plugged them into wall sockets at opposite ends of the cage.

"That's more like it," said Wilson, pleased with Lee's resourcefulness.

"Boss, take a look at this," said Miller, already searching the area around the driver's seat. "Coffee stain?"

"Could be," Wilson replied after quick inspection. "What's the concern?"

"Remember the lottery ticket at the condo? It was stained with coffee."

"But his coffee cup had a lid on it," Lee interjected. "Didn't it?"

"He's right," Wilson said. "Maybe the spill is older than the ticket or the coffee that stained the ticket came from a spill in the kitchen."

"I don't get it," Lee chirped again, genuinely curious. "Why so much interest in the coffee spill?"

Miller started to let out an answer, but Wilson beat him to the punch.

"Always trust your gut, Lee. Scout's trusting his gut and, though I don't know where it might lead yet, I think he might be on to something."

Lee didn't say anything in response. Instead, he opened the vehicle's rear hatch and searched for any clues NCIS agents might have missed while the FBI agents meticulously scoured the first two rows of seating for anything unusual.

Aside from the coffee stain, the bullet holes and damage the vehicle had sustained during the crash, nothing stood out as unusual. Borrowing words his dad once used to describe an oil well that failed to produce, Wilson called the SUV a "dry hole."

"Gentlemen, I think our work here is finished," Wilson concluded. "Let's get this locked up and get out of here."

Lee located the civilian in charge of the cage, made sure things were returned to their previous state, and rushed through the checkpoints to catch up with Wilson and Miller who were walking back to their vehicle.

Ten steps behind the FBI agents as they approached the Tahoe, Lee pushed the UNLOCK button on his key fob as he narrowed the gap while trying hard not to look as if he was rushing. After climbing into the vehicle, he expected his involvement in the case would end as soon as he drove the FBI agents back to the NCIS office on base.

"Jack, I'm impressed with your work," Wilson said as Lee drove down a four-lane avenue flanked by nondescript tan buildings, "and I'm gonna ask your boss if Scout and I can borrow you a bit longer. Are you okay with that?"

"Yes, sir!" Lee replied, giddy about the opportunity. "That would be awesome!"

"Dial up your boss for me, then hand me your phone," Wilson instructed.

A short conversation followed during which Martin felt as if he had no choice but to agree to the FBI honcho's request. The conversation was so one-sided, in fact, Wilson decided he wouldn't stop to finalize the paperwork in person. Instead, he told Lee's boss to expect a phone call later that day from an FBI agent in Brooklyn who would oversee the personnel transaction.

"That was easy," Wilson said after hanging up on Martin. "Now, let's drive by your place so you can pack a few days of clothes. After that, we'll head to the airport."

"Yes, sir!"

A single man living with a fellow NCIS agent in a no-frills duplex near the base, Lee knew he could easily disappear into the world of the G-Man for as long as necessary. Best of all, he looked forward to some adventure.

Thirty-five minutes later, the trio arrived at the airport and deposited the SUV they had borrowed in a space where Special Agent Jane could easily find it. Next stop: Concord,

New Hampshire. Weather permitting, according to the pilot, they should arrive by 1:30 p.m. local time.

21

FBI Resident Agent Jim Petrie from the Portsmouth, New
Hampshire, Field Office met the G5 on the tarmac after it
touched down in Concord at 1:28 p.m. Following brief
introductions, Petrie handed Miller the key fob to a 2012
Chevrolet Suburban. In much the same fashion as his New
London colleague had, Petrie would ride back to the FBI
office in Portsmouth with his office manager, Kat Mills, in
another nondescript Chevy Volt. He would not, however, go
empty-handed.

"Jim, I need you to get these to the lab in Brooklyn
ASAP," Wilson said, pointing to the bags of evidence they
had collected in New London but had been unable to unload
on the local agent before their departure.

Petrie put the bags in the trunk and backseat of his Volt
and headed back to Portsmouth while Wilson and his
colleagues climbed into the Suburban. Their next stop: 2
Buckingham Street, the home address of Pastor Ronald E.
French.

Fortunately, the vehicle's on-board navigation system still
worked despite the fact it had been almost a year since most
government contractors, including the company providing
GPS services to the FBI, had been paid for their services.

With Miller behind the wheel, the trio arrived at their
destination at 1:45 p.m. and found nothing unusual about the
home's appearance. In fact, it seemed to mesh well with the

other three- and four-bedroom wood-frame homes in the area.

Most of the homes were at least sixty years old, and some needed painting. Most of the lawns were maintained, but not immaculate. Some of the driveways were completely paved, while others consisted of two ribbons of concrete—each about twice the width of a tire—separated by a strip of grass. And, in almost every case, one could find a driveway stretching from the street to a detached two-car garage near the back of a quarter-acre lot much deeper than it was wide. For the most part, pride of ownership seemed largely intact in the middle-class neighborhood.

Upon arrival, Miller passed up the opportunity to park along the curb in front of the two-story home, painted sky blue with white trim and located on a corner lot. Instead, he turned right at the corner a few feet beyond the house and then turned right again and parked in the home's fully paved driveway. To Miller, the side door seemed more logical as a place to knock than the Buckingham Street entrance.

The agents exited the SUV, walked toward the home's red-stained deck and, after climbing three steps, took six more steps to the side door. There, Wilson opened an aluminum screen door wide enough so he could knock on the insulated wood-and-glass door behind it.

If not for the fact they had eaten at the Navy base less than three hours earlier, the smells from early Fourth of July Weekend cookouts—steaks, pork roasts, burgers and kebabs cooking on grills—might have made it impossible for them to focus on anything but food as they waited for someone inside to answer. Fortunately, they didn't wait long. From inside the home, the agents heard the voice of a young child sound an alarm of sorts. "Mom, some men in suits are at the door!"

Seconds later, the agents saw a white-fabric curtain move to reveal half of a young boy's face behind the glass pane that filled most of the upper half of the door. Then they heard footsteps and saw a middle-aged woman's face as she peeked through the same window.

The woman turned the deadbolt lock and unlocked the doorknob before opening the door about six inches—the length of the gold-colored chain connecting the now-open door to its frame. Though Wilson couldn't believe anyone would trust one of those little chains to provide security, he said nothing.

"Can I help you?" the woman asked, striving to be polite while obviously nervous about the unexpected arrival of three strangers in suits.

"FBI," Wilson said as he held up his badge and ID. "Are you Brenda French?"

"Just a moment, please," the woman replied.

"Are you Brenda French?" Wilson repeated after the door opened all the way.

"No, I'm Lacie Hall, her sister. And who are you?"

"FBI. Is Mrs. French home?"

"Yes, but I'm afraid she's in no mood to talk. Her husband passed away yesterday, you know, and a house full of visitors just left. She needs to rest."

"Yes, ma'am. That's why we're here," Wilson continued patiently, realizing the woman was trying to protect her sister. "I understand this is a difficult time, but we came a long way and need to speak with your sister about her husband."

As Hall began to object again, the agents saw another woman appear in the doorway.

"It's alright, Lacie," said Brenda French, her voice still thick with the Southern drawl she'd grown up with in

Alabama. "These men came all that way. Come on in, please."

French led the FBI agents through a maze of rooms and hallways and, finally, through a door to the screened-in porch at the front of the house, facing Buckingham Street.

"Lacie, please keep an eye on the children for me," she asked before closing the door behind her. They didn't need to be watched, but their mother was in full-protection mode as she made the painful adjustment to life as a single parent.

"I'm sorry," she said. "I don't want the children to hear whatever it is we might need to discuss."

"I understand, Mrs. French, and we appreciate your willingness to speak with us," said Wilson who had made it clear to Miller and Lee he wanted to be the only one asking questions.

"Here, please, have a seat," the woman said, pointing for the men to sit down in matching wrought-iron chairs that surrounded a glass-topped outdoor dining table, the base of which had been made from the same materials as the chairs. "Would you like some coffee?"

"No thank you, Mrs. French."

Over the years, Wilson had interviewed hundreds of people who had seen loved ones murdered. In this case, however, questions remained about the cause of the pastor's death, so he treaded carefully.

After introducing himself and his colleagues again, he began the interview.

"Mrs. French--"

"Please, call me Brenda," she interrupted.

"Okay, Brenda. I need you to think back about the day your husband died and, in as much detail as possible, tell me what you remember about that day."

"Well, I remember waking up that morning around seven and finding Ronnie still in bed, and I thought that was strange because he never slept past six. Then I rolled over toward him and asked him something—I don't remember what—but he didn't respond," she continued, her voice trembling. "That's when I noticed he was covered in some kind of red rash. It was all over his face, his neck, his arms... so I called for an ambulance."

"Had your husband been feeling ill or acting unusual during the forty-eight hours prior to his death?"

"He had been under a lot of stress, trying to breath life into that church," she explained, pointing across the street as she spoke. "It had taken a lot more time and effort than we ever imagined it would."

"So, he was the pastor of the church right across the street?"

"Yes, the River of Life."

"Did his stress show up in any change of attitude or strange behavior?"

"I don't know if it did or not. I know he went to bed earlier than usual the night before he died, and I thought that was strange."

Wilson asked the grieving widow to recount the twenty-four hours before that night.

"Ronnie was looking forward to the Fourth of July weekend. After working Wednesday, he knew he wouldn't have to got to the office on Thursday, Friday, Saturday and Monday."

"Do you remember anything unusual happening that day?" Wilson asked, rephrasing his question.

"Not really. He always spends Friday afternoons visiting shut-ins and members of the church who were old, sick or couldn't get around very well, so he decided to go ahead and make his visits—you know, to the hospitals, nursing homes and so forth."

"Are you sure he made those visits?"

"Gosh, I have no reason to think he didn't. He left the house around one o'clock and got home a couple of hours later."

A few seconds passed and Brenda French realized she needed to ask questions of her own.

"Why do you want to know all these things? Is there something you're not telling me?"

"Mrs. French, we're investigating a large number of deaths that have occurred around the country since Friday morning, hoping to find out what might have caused them."

"Yes, I heard something about that from people who stopped by today," she replied, her voice trembling, "but we don't even own a television. Please tell me more about what's going on."

"Mrs. French, during the last couple of days, something— and we don't know what yet—has caused the deaths of at least thirty thousand people, the vast majority of whom lived in nine Northeastern states, including New Hampshire. We think your husband might have been one of them."

Upon hearing those words, Brenda French began sobbing as if her heart had been broken anew. Seconds later, she fell forward and buried her face in the flesh-and-bones pillow created by her crossed arms on the table in front of her.

Wilson knew better than to rush, so he decided to wait her out as she teetered on the brink of mental and physical collapse.

Nearly ten minutes passed before the woman began to regain at least some of her composure and Wilson felt he could ask for permission to look around the house and inside her husband's office and car.

"We're looking for anything that might help us determine exactly what it was that killed your husband," he explained.

"If you wouldn't mind, I'd like you to leave now," the woman said somewhat unexpectedly, prompting the agents to cast concerned glances toward each other. "Just pretend you're done here, and get back in your car and drive off down the street.

"I'll try to pull myself together and take the children somewhere. When you see us drive away, you can come back and look around as much as you'd like. I'll leave the side door unlocked, and my husband's keys will be on the kitchen table along with my cell number. You can call me when you're done, but I don't want the children here while you're searching the house."

"Thank you, Mrs. French," Wilson said. "It shouldn't take us more than three or four hours."

Seemingly unfazed by Wilson's time estimate, the mother of four showed the men out the Buckingham Street entrance to the house and then retreated back inside the main living area of the house to round up her children and her sister for an unplanned outing.

The investigators, meanwhile, walked across the yard and climbed back into the Suburban before driving it to a spot two blocks away and parking so they had a clear view of the family's driveway. Several minutes later, they watched as the woman and her entourage climbed into her late-model Hyundai minivan, backed out of the driveway and drove away, bound for places unknown.

As soon as the minivan was out of sight, Miller drove the Suburban back to the house and, in less than a minute, the three agents reentered the home to begin their search.

The home seemed to be kept in meticulous order—a place for everything and everything in its place. During almost thirty minutes of searching, the agents found nothing in trashcans; no papers on tabletops; and no clothes on the floor or on furniture—not even in the kids' rooms. Drawers were so neatly organized, they suspected Brenda French might suffer from OCD—Obsessive Compulsive Disorder—but they wouldn't mention it.

Relying on his gut again, Wilson told his men it was time to check out the pastor's car and office, both of which could be found across the street at River of Life Church.

Wilson picked up the set of keys Brenda French had left on the kitchen table, and the trio exited through the side door and headed toward the house of worship across the street.

After stepping off the porch and taking a few steps in the direction of the church, the men heard a voice from in front of the house next door to their right. A tiny, gray-haired wisp of a woman, whose appearance indicated she must have been in her late eighties, walked slowly across the lawn in their direction.

"Are you men from the funeral home or the insurance company?" she asked, her eyes looking down as she focused on completing each step.

"Uhh, no ma'am," Wilson replied, not in a hurry to identify himself.

"Then why are you sneaking around here on a Saturday while Mrs. French and the kids are gone?" she asked, adding, "I saw them leave, ya know."

At that point, Wilson opted to let the cat out of the bag.

"I'm FBI Special Agent Wilson," he said, flashing his credentials. "We had a friendly visit with Mrs. French, and now we're going to look around inside the church."

"Is something wrong?" she asked after finally making it to within arm's reach of Wilson and grabbing his right elbow to steady herself.

"Nothing to worry yourself over, Mrs..." Wilson replied, prompting her to share her name.

"Payne," she replied. "Lillian Payne."

"It's good of you to keep an eye out for your neighbors, Mrs. Payne," Wilson said, hoping the woman might release her grip and allow the agents to go on their way.

"So, Pastor Ronnie is dead, and FBI agents are at his house the next day?" the woman countered skeptically. "I think you're trying pull the wool over this old lady's eyes."

"No, Mrs. Payne, but we would appreciate you keeping our visit confidential. We don't want everyone in the neighborhood worrying, you know."

With that, Miller stepped forward and extended his elbow, a sign he was willing to help the elderly woman back to her porch and up its five wooden steps.

After letting out a skeptical, throat-clearing "Hmmph," Mrs. Payne accepted the towering agent's offer and began a conversation from which it would take Miller several minutes to extract himself. Meanwhile, Wilson and Lee made their way to the church across the street.

A large wooden cross, attached to the blonde-brick wall above the building's main entrance, made it easy for passersby to identify the building as a church. On Sunday mornings, however, the building's half-empty parking lot made it easy for folks to identify the church as struggling.

Wilson and Lee made it to the front entrance of the church and they found the side-by-side solid-oak doors locked. After trying several keys, Wilson found the one that worked and unlocked the door.

Once inside the church's foyer, the men followed a hallway around the side of the sanctuary opposite the parking lot. At the end of the hallway, they found the pastor's office inside a small extension of the building that appeared to be an architectural afterthought.

To reach the pastor's office, they walked through a ten-by-ten reception area and past a desk and chair—rarely used since the church's part-time secretary position fell to the budget axe after the last woman to hold that job passed away.

Compared to his orderly home, Pastor French's office looked more like a bachelor pad with stacks of papers cluttering a mahogany desk, file cabinets on the verge of bursting, and books filling most of the remaining space.

Space was at such a premium, in fact, that one almost had to turn sideways to follow the path leading from the office's door to the pastor's leather desk chair—a gift from a church member whose office furnishings store had closed a year earlier, thanks largely to the economic fallout from Black Monday.

Only two agents at a time could fit inside the office to sort through the pastor's belongings, so Wilson and Lee took on that task and began thumbing through the pages of dozens of books and looking inside drawers.

After Miller arrived, he walked out the office's private entrance at the back of his office to the spot where the pastor had parked his Japanese luxury sedan. The private entrance had made it possible for the pastor to sneak in and out on days when he simply didn't have time to be social—that is, when small crowds of church members gathered for Bible study sessions, committee meetings and other church functions.

Ready to search the vehicle, Miller pressed the UNLOCK button on the car's key fob and, instead of hearing an electronic thunk, he heard a soft electronic click—an indication the car was already unlocked. To Miller, it appeared the pastor must not have worried about crime in his neighborhood.

Within minutes of launching his search, Miller found what he would deem his first piece of low-hanging fruit—a white piece of paper crumpled on the floor mat under the front edge of the driver's seat.

Using his gloved hands to flatten out the piece of thermal paper as best he could without damaging it, he bagged it, slipped it into the left inside pocket of his suit jacket and continued searching.

Next, he dug deep into the center console Pastor French must have used as a mobile trash can, found what he was looking for, and carried it into the office where Wilson and Lee were still searching.

"Find anything interesting?" Miller asked rhetorically as he tried to keep a lid on his understated brand of excitement.

"Nothing yet," Wilson replied, suspicious of the smile forming on Miller's face. "You?"

"It just so happens I did," Miller responded with dramatic flair before offering a piece of evidence bearing the date, July 1, 2016, and the time, 1:59 p.m. "This store receipt shows someone—perhaps the pastor—purchased a thirty-two-ounce fountain drink, a large bag of salted nuts and a hundred-dollar lottery ticket at a Maple Mart in Campton, New Hampshire.

"In my other hand, I offer a lottery ticket."

"Another lottery ticket?" Wilson said. "That makes three."

Turning toward Lee, he asked, another question: "Where's Campton?"

Lee entered "Campton NH" in the search block of his phone's map app and waited. "According to the map, it's about fifty miles north of here, just off I-93."

"I wonder if he visited any hospitals or nursing homes up there," Miller chimed in, his eyebrows raised in doubt.

"Scout, call the local cops up there and ask 'em if they've had any suspicious deaths lately," Wilson ordered, sounding as if he believed he might finally have a solid lead. "If so, ask 'em how many and get details about 'em."

"Why does a church pastor buy a lottery ticket?" Lee wondered out loud. "I thought that was a sin or something."

"He was human like the rest of us," Miller answered as he pulled out his own smartphone and began looking up a phone number for the Campton PD. "He drove a ten-year-old car, worried about how in the world he was gonna send four kids to college on a pastor's salary and, oh yeah, he had to save his church from financial ruin."

"There's a story behind that ticket, and we need to find out what it is," Wilson interrupted. "It's time I call Mrs. French."

As Wilson dialed the widow's number and Miller began dialing the Campton Police, Lee packed up the bagged-and-tagged items from the office and started carrying them to the Suburban. Their all-too-brief search of the church was over.

"Mrs. French, we're done for now," Wilson said as soon as the pastor's wife answered, "but I have a couple of questions I need to ask you."

"Go ahead," she said before explaining they had gone to a local mall and her kids were with her sister at the food court.

"Did your husband have any reason to visit Campton, New Hampshire, yesterday—perhaps as part of his home and hospital visits that day?"

"I've never even heard of Campton. Why do you ask?"

"Mrs. French, we found a receipt in his car for purchases he appears to have made yesterday afternoon at a convenience store in Campton," Wilson explained after walking back into the pastor's office.

A pregnant pause followed as the pastor's widow tried to process the news, and Wilson continued.

"Mrs. French, did your husband keep a list in his office of the folks he visited each week?"

"Not in his office," she said, her voice trembling again. "It's in his phone."

"Mrs. French, I know this is confusing to hear—and it may turn out to be nothing—but I need you to help me out. Can you tell me where I can find your husband's phone?"

"I have it with me," she replied, a bit exasperated. "It's in my purse in case someone he knew tries to reach him."

"Good. Please take out his phone, look at the names on his visitation list for July 1 and let me know if there are any names you don't recognize."

Mrs. French followed his instructions and, seconds later, began sharing her findings.

"There are only five names on the list, and they all live in Concord—or very nearby," she said before begging Wilson to explain why her husband had gone to Campton.

"As soon as I find out, I'll let you know," Wilson said, hoping he would be able to make good on his promise sooner than later. Then he heard the line go dead. Brenda French had hung up on him, leaving the distinct impression he had sent the woman into panic mode, probably wondering what else her late husband might have kept from her.

Walking outside the church again, Wilson asked Miller if he'd learned anything of value from the Campton P.D.

"The police chief said ninety-six Campton-area residents, ranging in age from sixteen to seventy-nine, have died since yesterday morning," Miller replied. "Among those, five—a husband, wife and three sons—were members of the family that owned the Maple Mart."

"I think it's time to roll," Wilson said, his mind racing in an effort to process the new information. "Let's lock things up here for the time being, return the keys to the house and head out."

Wilson and Miller wrapped things up and climbed into the SUV where Lee was already waiting for them in a second-row seat.

"Have you ever been to Campton, Lee?" Miller asked, his eyebrows raised high as if expecting a negative response.

"No, sir."

"Well, you're going there now!"

22

Earlier than expected, Wilson and his colleagues departed the French home and drove down Buckingham Street for the last time at 2:45 p.m. Next stop: Campton, a town where he expected to find many clues.

"Any hunches, boss?" Miller asked as he merged into the northbound lanes of I-93, giving voice to a question Lee had wanted to ask but resisted.

"Gentlemen, we've looked at the lives of three unrelated victims in three states, and the only common denominator seems to be that each purchased, or came to possess, a scratch-off lottery ticket. Don't know about you, but I find that's a bit too coincidental."

"If I remember right, the game was set to pay one winner something like a hundred thousand dollars per month for life," Lee piped up. "They called it The National Bet, because it was happening around the same time President Rivera promised to restore everyone's retirement accounts."

"Did anyone claim the winning ticket?" Miller asked.

"I don't think so," Lee replied. "I know I didn't."

"Did you buy a ticket, Jack?" Wilson asked.

"No, sir. I don't gamble."

"Okay then, why don't you fire up your phone there and see if there's any news about a winner coming forward?"

"Yes, sir," Lee replied before launching another session of mobile surfing.

Meanwhile, Wilson tried to reach his wife at home, but she didn't answer.

It took Lee less than two minutes to find an answer to Wilson's question about the lottery.

"According to a *Boston Globe* article yesterday," he began, "the New England Lottery Council folks say no one has come forward yet, but that's not unusual with a high-stakes game like this one."

"I know you said you're not a gambling man, Jack—and I respect that—but I'll bet you lunch that the person who purchased the winning ticket doesn't claim it," Wilson said. "A family member might claim it, but not the actual purchaser."

"I'll take that bet," Lee replied, "but what makes you think you'll win."

"Gut instinct, Jack! Gut instinct!"

On their way out of Concord, Wilson asked Miller to stop at the first decent roadside food joint he spotted, noting he didn't expect there to be much in the way of choices in tiny Campton.

Overhearing the front-seat conversation, Lee again tapped what he considered the infinite knowledge of his smartphone and found what looked like a good choice two miles ahead.

"Agent Miller, there's a place called Benito's at the Lawson Road exit," Lee suggested. "It has burritos and organic smoothies."

"I'll bite," Miller replied, his sense of humor evident.

"So will I, Jack, but you'll walk home if it turns out to be a bad choice," Wilson said, a sign he'd accepted Lee as a worthwhile, albeit temporary, addition to his team.

Upon arrival at Benito's, the trio discovered the takeout-only operation, and Miller ordered a bag of eight burritos, two all-natural fruit smoothies and a cup of coffee—for

Wilson, "Black, no cream or sugar"—before parking the
SUV under a shade tree for two minutes while he distributed
the food and drinks.

"I'm saving two of these bad boys for later," Miller
advised as he distributed the first six burritos evenly among
the agents and placed the others inside a built-in cooler
between the front seats. After speaking with the Campton
police chief, he had an idea of how he might use the spare
burritos.

Five minutes later, the agents were back on the road.
During the next forty-five minutes, Wilson and Lee spent
most of their time reviewing messages while Miller drove
toward the small farming town best known for having three
covered bridges within its city limits. Arriving in town at
3:35 p.m., it didn't take long to locate the Campton Police
Department.

Located four blocks beyond the "Welcome to Campton"
sign, it occupied a small portion of a five-thousand-square-
foot single-story metal building that also housed city hall and
the local volunteer fire department/ambulance service. It
didn't need much space, since the town's police force
consisted of only one part-time officer with little experience
and even less training.

A tiny brass bell hanging inside the CPD's front door
signaled the arrival of three visitors. Hearing it, Chief Phil
Muehring rose from behind the gray metal desk he'd found
at a Navy surplus store in Concord and waddled into the
hallway outside his office to see who had entered the
building where he spent most of his waking hours despite
being a part-timer.

Upon seeing three men in suits, each looking as if he
might have traveled from Boston to see him, the chief
greeted them cautiously.

"Can I help you, gentlemen?" he asked while tucking his shirttail into the back of his pants—a challenge for a man carrying 250 pounds on a body several inches shy of six feet.

Per prior arrangement with Wilson, Miller responded first.

"Special Agent Scout Miller, FBI. We talked on the phone earlier."

"Agent Miller, I'm surprised you drove all the way up here," the chief replied, relieved to learn the men in suits had not come to question him about the string of armed robberies that had forced him to retire ten years early from his job as chief of security for an armored transport company in Boston.

"Chief, this is FBI Special Agent Joe Wilson and NCIS Special Agent Jack Lee," Miller said. "We need you to help us with a sensitive matter related to our phone conversation earlier."

"The name's Phil Muehring—sounds a lot like 'during'— and I'll help you gents with anything you need," the chief assured them, secretly hoping their needs wouldn't involve chasing armed suspects or doing anything that might test his long-lost physical abilities.

"What can you tell us about the family that owned the Maple Mart?" Wilson asked.

"Well, the Ketmerings were nice folks. They ran a real nice little business. Very friendly and conscientious, you know.

"Charles and Janet moved up here about twenty years ago from down by Manchester. Rumor has it, they sold everything they owned so they could move up here, open the Maple Mart, and start raising a family—far from the city, ya know.

"Their kids ranged in age from twenty-one to twenty-six—all boys and smart as whips. They all graduated from college early.

"The oldest just got back from teaching in China for three years, and the other two were in graduate school. Somehow, they all found time to work shifts for their parents at the Maple Mart. Good boys, they were."

"Can you tell us what happened to them?" Wilson probed.

"You'd have to ask the doctor for those de--"

"Chief, I'm not looking for specifics," Wilson said politely, cutting the chief off in mid-sentence. "Just an overview, chief. Tell us what you know."

"Well, I know Alex was the first to get sick. He worked the last shift, beginning at eight—Thursday eve, that is—and ending at one o'clock Friday morn. A few hours later, he became ill and, after things started looking real bad for him, Charles—that's his father, you know—drove him to the hospital in Concord. That must've been around 10:30 Friday morn."

The chief paused as if in thought.

"Anything else?" Wilson asked, hoping his words might jumpstart the chief's memory.

"Since Charles usually worked the first shift, five to noon, he'd asked his wife take his place before he left to the hospital with Alex," the chief recalled. "Around noon, I drove down there to grab a bite and check on things, and that's when I found the other boys, Christopher and Mikey, working behind the counter.

"They told me the hospital had called and said their dad was sick just like Alex. The boys also told me their mother wasn't feeling well and thought the whole family might have come down with food poisoning or something like that.

"I ran some errands and patrolled the area for a while after eating and, about the time I got back to my office at about three o'clock, I got a call from someone asking me why the Maple Mart was closed.

"When I drove there to check on Janet and the boys, they were all in a real bad way, so I called an ambulance, you know. We squeezed all three of 'em in and, by 5:30, they were at the hospital in Concord—the whole family in the ICU."

The chief went on to explain that Alex had been the first Campton resident to die that day and that, within twenty-four hours of the onset of their symptoms, everyone in their family had died.

"Chief, do you think we can get inside the Maple Mart and see if they have any security camera footage?" Wilson asked.

"You sure you want to go in there?" the chief asked, hoping they might reconsider. "No one's been in there since I locked it up yesterday."

"I think we'll be fine, chief," Wilson answered.

"Okay," the chief said, resigned to the fact he would probably lose an argument with the FBI agent, "but I'm not goin' in there!"

"Fair enough, chief. You let us in, and we'll do the rest."

Chief Muehring led the men to the parking lot where he and Wilson jumped into the front seat of the CPD's electric blue 2005 Chevrolet Camaro. Though the chief had played no role in the drug bust four years earlier, he had gladly accepted the keys to the car from DEA agents, courtesy of the federal asset forfeiture program. It was a giant step up from the 1999 Crown Victoria Police Interceptor it replaced.

Miller and Lee followed in the Suburban and, upon arrival at the Maple Mart, stood with Wilson as Chief Muehring held up his end of the deal—unlocking the store's side-by-side glass doors—before retreating to the relative safety of his Camaro. Wilson, Miller and Lee, meanwhile, went inside the store.

Wilson's quick scan of the building's fifteen-hundred-square-foot interior showed him that, in addition to the main entrance, it had a single emergency exit at the rear and closed-circuit video cameras mounted near the ceiling in three of the four corners of the its rectangular retail space.

After almost missing it, Wilson spied a fourth camera built into a working clock radio mounted behind the lone checkout counter and directly opposite where customers stood as they paid for their purchases. Upon close inspection, he discovered the stealth camera featured some of the latest investigation-friendly technology and seemed to have been set up properly.

"Gentlemen, we're in luck," Wilson told his colleagues. "This camera system takes digital snapshots of every customer who stands on this side of the counter. As a result, we should be able to whittle down our window of interest— let's say, from the first minute of July 1 to 6 o'clock July 2— and then take a look at the snapshots."

Thinking his youngest colleague would probably be able to get the job done more quickly than he or Miller might, Wilson turned to Lee and asked if he wanted to give it a shot.

"Yes, sir!" Lee replied.

While Wilson and Miller looked around the store, Lee found a laptop computer beneath the counter. After powering it up and being prompted to enter a password, he employed a tried-and-true technique—simply hitting the ENTER key— to get past the obstacle. Like so many others in the small town who lived without fear of crime, the Ketmerings worked without an actual password.

Lee located a STORE folder and double-clicked on a BIG BROTHER application he correctly assumed was behind the store's security system. During the next ten minutes, he figured out how to narrow the field of searchable images from tens of thousands captured during the previous thirty days to 686 snapshots taken during the forty-two-hour period in question. After saving images to a blank one-terabyte flash drive and copying them to Miller's FBI laptop, he let Wilson know they could proceed to the next step.

"Agent Wilson, we can take a look at the snapshots now. They're in chronological order, oldest to newest."

"Good work, Lee," Wilson replied before turning toward Miller. "Scout, see if you can get Barney Fife to come in here and help us out."

Miller walked out the door to find the chief using his red paisley handkerchief to spit-polish the front left quarter-panel of his vehicle. Expecting some drama, Wilson and Lee watched through floor-to-ceiling tinted glass windows at the front of the store as Miller went to work.

At first encountering a police chief adamantly opposed to going into the store, Miller became more convincing soon after he leaned into Chief Muehring's personal space, shook his head and turned around to open the passenger door of the Suburban. Wilson and Lee watched with delight as Miller resorted to using his secret weapon—the bag containing the two extra burritos from Benito's. A few seconds later, the chief walked into the store, followed closely by Miller.

"Chief, thanks for agreeing to help us out," Wilson said as he began to turn the laptop around so the chief could see the screen from where he was standing in front of the counter. "I need you to look at these photos and tell me if you recognize anyone."

"Mind if I sit down and eat while I do that?" the chief said, motioning toward a stool behind the counter currently occupied by Lee.

"No problem," Lee said before picking up the stool and moving it to the other side of the counter so all three agents could watch over Chief Muehring's shoulder as he eyeballed the images.

"Let us know each time you recognize someone," Wilson instructed, "then tell us the person's name and anything special you might know about him."

"Alright," he replied, "but this is gonna take a while."

"We'll make sure you're well compensated for your time," Wilson assured the chief.

"And the burritos?" he said, prompting Miller to remove the Mexican delicacies from the bag and, along with a napkin, set them on the counter next to the laptop.

With food in front of him and visions of extra income flashing through his mind, Chief Muehring began looking at the first image and stared at the screen for more than a minute without making another move.

"What is it, chief?" Wilson asked. "Do you know him?"

"Can't say that I do."

"So why have you stopped?"

"I don't know how to move ahead to the next photo."

Lee stretched out his arm and hit the right-arrow key on the computer's keyboard, then the left-arrow key before repeating the same steps three times. The wordless explanation seemed to clear things up for the chief, and he began moving through the images much more quickly.

"I know this one!" he explained, excited to recognize someone after striking out on the first two-dozen images he had seen. "That's Calvin Tucker, the principal at the school. What's he doing out after midnight?"

No one responded to the chief's question.

Several images passed before the chief spotted another person he could identify between bites.

"That's Mrs. Pedersen. She works at the bank. Kind of a flirt, she is."

As Chief Muehring focused on the individuals whose faces appeared largest in the snapshots, Wilson began concentrating on something else—the crowd that began to form inside the store during the last hour of the first day of July.

Immediately after the clock struck midnight, according to the time stamp on the video (i.e., "01-JULY-2016 00:00:00"), Wilson noticed the size of the crowd began to swell even more until it appeared to fill the entire frame— and, probably, the store as well. At the same time, the investigator noticed the people in line stopped allowing others to go ahead of them to finalize their purchases. Instead, they began making purchases of their own. Whatever had drawn them to the store seemed to have become available for purchase at the stroke of midnight.

"Chief, what motivated so many people to go to the Maple Mart at midnight?" Wilson asked, though he suspected he already knew the answer.

"It had to be the lottery tickets—The National Bet is what they called it. It was supposed to pay the winner a hundred grand a month for life, you know, and the tickets were only sold for one day. Yesterday."

The room went quiet for several seconds before Chief Muehring spoke up again.

"This reminds me of something I saw back when I was a kid in 1974. I remember people going crazy the first time scratcher tickets were sold in Boston. They lined up early so they'd be sure to get 'em as soon as they went on sale—at midnight!"

"That's good to know, chief," Wilson said, his suspicions already confirmed.

Chief Muehring identified two more people among those appearing in the next dozen images. Then the system seemed to have a hiccup—a noticeable pause in the slideshow when the chief hit the key to advance to another image. Lee quickly figured out that the hiccup coincided with the four-hour gap between the store's 1 a.m. closing time and its re-opening four hours later.

After a few seconds passed, the first of 484 new snapshots appeared on the screen. Captured at 5:02 a.m. July 1, it was a face Chief Muehring knew.

"John Adams! He claims he's related to the second president, but he's--" The chief stopped talking when he sensed the agents glaring at him for chit-chatting.

The chief went on to confirm the identities of about a third of the faces that followed. Regarding his failure to identify the remaining two thirds, he said many were probably travelers on I-93 who stopped for gas en route to Manchester to the south or the White Mountains National Forest to the north.

"Chief, I need you to write down the names of the folks from Campton who died during the first week of July and then put a checkmark next to the names of any who showed up in the snapshots. It's kind of a crosscheck. Got it?"

"Yes, sir," the chief replied, "but it might take a few days."

"I need it today, chief and, if it works out like I think it will, you'll get a medal for your efforts."

"A medal?"

"Something big anyway—and I'll buy you dinner tonight if that'll help you get it done today. You choose the restaurant!"

"Deal!" the chief said.

"One more thing, chief," Wilson added as he pulled a five-by-seven-inch photo of Pastor French from inside his black nylon laptop case, "I need you to let me know if you see this guy's face in any of the photos. It's very important."

"Can do, Agent Wilson," the chief said, his voice sounding as if he realized he had no choice but to cooperate fully.

"Great! We'll leave you alone, so you can get to work."

As Chief Muehring found a pen and a pad of writing paper and began the crosschecking process, Wilson asked Miller and Lee to join him a few steps away where their conversation would be less likely to distract the chief.

"Scout, I need you to do two things," Wilson said quietly. "First, prepare a BOLO message that instructs agents to be on the lookout for signs that victims had purchased these scratch-off tickets, but don't send it out until I give you the okay. I want the director to know where we're headed first.

"Second, contact the lab boys in Brooklyn and ask them if any other scratch-off tickets—beyond the ones we sent in— have been turned in for analysis. If they have, tell 'em to let us know ASAP—especially if they find anything interesting or unusual about 'em."

Stepping away, Miller decided to call the lab first, then work on the message. He knew Wilson wouldn't care about the order as long as he got both things done.

Wilson, meanwhile, gave Lee new marching orders, too.

"Jack, I want you to find someone in charge of the lottery in New Hampshire and ask how many scratch-off tickets were sold at the Maple Mart. After that, I want you to learn as much as you can about these lottery tickets. Think in terms of reverse engineering them—the paper, the ink, printing, packaging, distribution, everything—and put it into a format I can digest quickly. No need for fancy, just informative."

After looking over at Chief Muehring and seeing he was still absorbed in his work, Wilson spoke to Lee again. "I'm guessing the chief will let you use the printer at his office."

Chief Muehring had been listening while pretending to be engrossed in his work and, upon hearing Wilson's prompt, held up the key to his office in his left hand while keeping his eyes glued to the screen.

Lee took the key and turned toward the door. As he did, Miller—still on the phone with the lab boys—tossed him the key to the Suburban and, seconds later, the young NCIS agent was out the door and on his way to the police station four blocks away.

While his colleagues completed their assigned tasks, Wilson made a phone call to Mazachek's private number.

"Good afternoon, Joe-L," the director answered. "Anything yet?"

"I think we have a solid lead, ma'am. Scout and I have personally investigated three first-day deaths and found one common denominator in the lottery tickets."

"Keep talking."

"In each of the three cases—in Brooklyn, in Connecticut, and in New Hampshire—we've found hundred-dollar scratch-off lottery tickets purchased yesterday. Two were in the homes of victims. The third was in a victim's vehicle."

"Continue," the director replied, though not convinced.

"Today, we're in Campton, New Hampshire, a little town of less than four-thousand, following up on one of those deaths. Ninety-six people have died here since yesterday morning, and I'm convinced most of them who died after purchasing scratch-off lottery tickets.

"Though I don't yet know how the tickets were weaponized, I'm convinced they were. That's why I'll be sending a BOLO out about these tickets. Our people need to handle them with extreme caution."

"You never cease to amaze me, Joe-L," Mazachek replied. "Keep up the good work, and keep me informed."

"Will do, ma'am."

The director's verbal pat on the back belied what she felt inside upon hearing Wilson's report.

"If someone found a way to use lottery tickets to kill thirty thousand Americans," she wondered, "what else might they use to attack the United States?"

✝

During three and a half hours spent examining snapshots at the Maple Mart, Chief Muehring identified seventy-seven of the ninety-six recently deceased locals and confirmed Pastor French had visited the store shortly after 2 o'clock the previous afternoon.

"Why are we coming up short?" Wilson asked the chief after reviewing the numbers.

"I suspect some folks bought more than one ticket, and some may have given some tickets away as gifts. They do that, ya know."

"Bingo!" Wilson thought to himself upon hearing the police chief's answer.

"Scout, is that BOLO ready?" Wilson asked, switching gears.

"Yes, sir. It includes instructions to pay special attention to any lottery tickets purchased July 1 by any deceased person or close family member, to handle those tickets with care and to expedite delivery of any tickets found to the boys at the lab in Brooklyn."

"Good," Wilson replied. "Send it out."

Miller opened his laptop and, within seconds, had sent the agencywide BOLO message. As it began to zip through cyberspace, Lee walked into the Maple Mart and began sharing his findings about lottery ticket sales to Wilson.

"During a period of almost eleven hours, the Ketmerings sold 289 scratcher tickets at $100 each. The first ticket was sold at 12:01 a.m. Tickets continued to be sold until 12:59 a.m., and then there was a break while the store was closed from 1 to 5. Sales resumed at 5:01 a.m., and the last ticket was sold at 2:38 p.m."

"That's less than thirty minutes after Pastor French bought his ticket," Wilson said.

"And about twenty minutes before I called the ambulance," the police chief added.

"Jack, are you ready to educate me about the lottery business?" Wilson asked, his mind racing to connect details.

"Yes, sir!" Lee replied while holding up a bundle of a dozen or so pages he had printed and stapled together at the chief's office.

"Good! You can tell me what you've learned while we drive back to Concord."

"Where would you like to eat, gentlemen?" Chief Muehring interjected after sensing his FBI meal ticket was about to leave town. "There's a good place--"

Wilson cut the chief off again, this time as he began removing a twenty-dollar bill from a money clip he seemed to have produced out of thin air.

"Sorry, chief, but we're gonna have to take a rain check on dinner," he said as he handed over the twenty. "Hope this buys you a good meal. We'll be in touch!"

Though happy to receive the cash, Chief Muehring felt as if his intimate involvement in the case had come to a screeching halt. His visitors from afar were leaving his town as quickly and as unexpectedly as they had arrived. "So much for my fifteen minutes of fame."

23

"What did you find out about the lottery tickets, Jack?"
Wilson asked, wanting to learn as much as possible about the
lottery—and scratch-off tickets in particular—from Lee
while Miller drove.

"The lottery is a three-hundred-billion-dollar industry that
got its start right here in New Hampshire in 1964," Lee
began. "Because the popularity of scratch-off tickets had
fallen a lot in recent years, gaming officials across the
country got together and decided to try something new to
rekindle interest. That's The National Bet.

"They limited sales to one twenty-four-hour period to
create a sense of urgency; they used a record amount of
advertising to convince people it was, quote unquote,
patriotic to buy National Bet tickets; and they printed really
fancy tickets to make them appear to be worth a hundred
dollars. By the time the day was over, they'd set a new
record by selling more than thirty million scratch-off
tickets—so I guess it worked."

Lee paused as if needing some feedback, and he got it.

"I'm still listening," Wilson said.

"On the business side of the game, there are only a few
big players involved in running the lottery and the real
business takes place at the tens of thousands of retailers
where tickets are printed out when you pay for them.

When one looks only at scratch-off games, the lottery becomes a lot more complex.

"Keep going," Wilson said, eager to hear more.

"There are three companies under contract to print scratch-off lottery tickets for the nationwide lottery consortium that's behind The National Bet game—and, when I say 'nationwide,' I mean thirty-six states and the District of Columbia that participate. Each company is assigned a territory and is responsible for printing tickets that end up in convenience stores, gas stations and grocery stores within that territory.

"One of the companies is Monticello Printing in Columbia, South Carolina. It's responsible for printing approximately 8.6 million tickets that ended up being sold at fifty-eight thousand locations across nine states in the Northeast. For each ticket sold, Monticello earns a tiny commission—between two and three percent of the selling price—based on volume."

"What's in it for the retailers who sell the tickets?" Wilson asked.

"Not much, really. Retailers earn a small commission, from five to seven percent, on each ticket sold. Plus, they receive bonuses when they sell winning tickets and when they exceed sales goals."

Seeing Wilson lost in thought as he tried to digest details, Lee revisited the printing side of the equation.

"When I called Monticello Printing and asked the chief of printing operations if there was any way someone could tamper with the cards as they were being printed, he said there probably was. Instead of offering an explanation, he suggested I talk to the companies who supply the components that make up a ticket."

"Get to the point, Jack," Wilson said.

"He gave me the names and contacts at three different paper suppliers, two ink suppliers and one company that supplies the latex."

"Latex?" Wilson asked.

"Yes. The rubbery stuff you scratch off the front of a ticket is made of some sort of latex coating."

"What's the name of the latex company?"

"Illinois Chemical Company in Effingham, Illinois."

Wilson's mind was racing, but he said nothing.

"That's not all," Lee added. "The guy at Monticello said his company is Illinois Chemical's only customer who buys latex for scratch-off tickets."

"That will be our next stop, gentlemen!" Wilson said before picking up his phone and telling his pilot where they would be going next and to be ready to fly in thirty minutes. After that, he and Lee reviewed more incoming reports while Miller drove.

Though most of the reports came from sources in the Northeast, a few came from sources in states where death tolls were much lower.

"It doesn't shock me that a few hundred people from outside the nine-state area died," Wilson told Lee, "because a lot of people travel and some of them buy lottery tickets while away from home." A long pause followed as Wilson realized he had described himself and his colleagues remained silent.

Soon after 8:30 p.m., Wilson, Miller and Lee returned the SUV to Resident Agent Petrie along with bags of evidence collected in Concord and Campton and instructions to expedite them to the lab in Brooklyn. Soon after loading their things aboard the G5, they departed toward Effingham.

✝

Barely twenty-four hours into the investigation, Wilson took a brief power nap before waking and using the onboard phone to call Mazachek. He knew she'd want an update about his findings so far and about his plan for the next few days.

Wilson began by explaining how, based largely upon Lee's research into the lottery industry and into scratch-off tickets, all signs pointed to Effingham. "I believe someone at Illinois Chemical has the answers to our questions."

"Then what's next?" the director countered. "Do we need an executive order to halt lottery ticket sales?"

"No. The death count has stopped rising, and I don't want to tip off anyone about the connection we've made to lottery tickets."

"What do you need then, Joe-L?"

"First, I need a judge to sign off on warrants so we can raid the plant and any home, business, vehicle or storage facility remotely related to it."

"I'll get that to you before you go to sleep tonight. Anything else?"

"I'll need a mobile command post, two empty trailers and at least fifty agents in place by tomorrow afternoon so I can brief them and have 'em ready to turn this place upside down early Monday morning. And I'll need a biohazard team, a hundred masks with respirators and George Day."

Mazachek didn't raise any questions about any of Wilson's requests. "Scout knows how to make it happen. Tell him to prepare the tasking order as soon as he can, and I'll turn it around A-S-A-P."

"Will do, ma'am," Wilson said. A fraction of a second later, he heard a dial tone.

Having kept their eyes and ears tuned to their boss during the call, Miller and Lee believed instructions were coming soon—and they were right.

"Scout, you heard what I need, right?" Wilson asked.

"You bet."

"To minimize the chances of anyone knowing we're on our way, I want agents who are flying in to land in Indianapolis, Louisville or Saint Louis, secure transportation for the rest of the week and then drive to Effingham. They'll get more details within twenty-four hours."

Miller went to work, and Wilson turned toward Lee.

"Jack, I need you to find us a motel with a conference room somewhere on the outskirts of town and book enough rooms for a week. Along the way, make sure you tell every person you talk to he'll be facing serious federal charges if he breathes a word to anyone about your inquiry or about any arrangements that result from it. Understand?"

"Yes, sir."

"My goal is to brief everyone—bio guys included—by sunrise tomorrow and to have everything in place so we can be on the doorstep at Illinois Chemical by six o'clock Monday morning," Wilson concluded. "Any questions?"

"Can you estimate the number of agents to expect?" Lee asked.

"Fifty-five, but I want you to book the entire motel. That'll reduce the number of people who will see us or realize we're in town. Anything else?"

When no further questions surfaced, Miller and Lee returned to their laptops and began taking care of their assigned tasks.

Miller pecked out a seven-hundred-word tasking order not unlike the hundreds he'd prepared during previous investigations, ranging from racketeering probes and organized crime rings to white-collar crime schemes and bribery scandals. While it contained many boilerplate details, it also offered many Effingham-unique ingredients as he hoped to cover all of his bases.

Lee, meanwhile, moved to a window seat in the back of the G5's mostly-empty cabin configured to accommodate fourteen passengers. There, he looked up information about lodging facilities north of I-70 and west of I-57 in Effingham. After finding plenty of options, he used ground-level and birds-eye-view images available online to get better views of the leading contenders and narrow the field—first to four and eventually to one.

24

With Miller and Lee busy, Wilson focused his attention on reviewing reports and paid most of his attention to those that mentioned a lottery ticket being found in close proximity to a victim.

Wilson scanned hundreds of report pages for clues and began to suspect most of his agents were seeing only one kind of ticket. Then he read a report submitted by an agent at the FBI Pittsburgh Field Office.

The report offered details about a man who purchased two scratch-off tickets—the first at a Buckeye convenience store in his hometown of Hubbard, Ohio, and the second at a Kroger grocery store 7.7 miles away in Sharon, Pennsylvania.

"On the front of the ticket purchased in Ohio at 6:31 a.m. July 1," the agent wrote, "the rubbery gray material in the scratch-off panel appears to have been partially scratched. What remains of the material inside the panel appears mostly gray in color.

"On the front of the ticket purchased in Pennsylvania fifteen minutes later," he continued, "the edge of the panel— where the surface of the paper portion of the ticket became visible after being scratched—appears to be rust-colored, much different than the other ticket.

"Closed-circuit video shows subject appears healthy and normal at the time of his purchase in Sharon, Pennsylvania," the report continued. "Subject died eighteen hours later, according to the local medical examiner. Noteworthy: 8 clerks at grocery store died during the first thirty-six hours of July."

After reading that report, Wilson picked up the G5's secure satellite phone and asked the FBI operator to connect him to the FBI mobile lab in Brooklyn.

"Lab, Ronck speaking," said Donald Ronck, Ph.D., a white coat-wearing civilian in charge of the field lab's 7 p.m. to 7 a.m. shift.

"This is Special Agent Wilson. What can you tell me about the lottery tickets you've looked at so far?"

"Some of the tickets are testing positive for thallium," the sixty-one-year-old Ronck responded matter-of-factly.

"Thallium? Refresh me on this thallium stuff," Wilson replied, thinking he had heard something about it in the past but wanting to be certain he knew what he was dealing with.

"Thallium is a chemical element with symbol tee-one and atomic number eighty-one," Ronck began.

Fearful he was about to be on the receiving end of a long-winded explanation, Wilson cut him off.

"It's highly toxic, right?"

"Deadly," Ronck answered. "Thallium is the stuff that killed that Russian guy a few years back. Reports I read about that case described Yuri Sh-chekov-novich—or however you say his name—as becoming fatigued and then covered in red skin blotches before his internal organs began collapsing one by one. He lasted three days after being put on life support right away. He would've died much sooner without prompt treatment."

"How did this thallium get into the latex material on the scratch-off tickets?"

"I suspect it was mixed into it during the production phase," Ronck said. "That's how poisoning cases usually take shape."

"How much thallium would it take to kill someone?"

"Depending upon a person's weight and physical condition, it would--" Ronck began, again sounding like a professor trying to explain a precise formula, before being cut off by Wilson again.

"Ballpark!"

"Not much. Not much at all. A microscopic amount, in fact, especially when it's Thallium S-213."

"Thallium what?"

"Thallium S-213," Ronck enunciated clearly. "It's a recently-discovered radioactive isotope that's more deadly than previous versions. Breathe in the tiniest amount of vapor from this stuff, and you're dead within twenty-four hours."

"I have agents in the field handling these tickets. Two have died," Wilson explained, beginning a new line of questioning. "Why haven't more died?"

"Actually, nine agents have died. In fact, I shared those numbers with Director Mazachek a few minutes before you called." Ronck let those words settle before continuing.

"I suspect it has something to do with the fact most agents have been wearing gloves while handling the tickets; they haven't scratched the surface of the tickets while handling them; and they've put the tickets inside sealed plastic bags pretty quickly after finding them. Beyond that, I think they might have had guardian angels."

"With somewhere north of thirty million tickets sold, the number of deaths—only thirty thousand or so—seems too small, too, so why haven't more ticket buyers died?" Wilson asked.

"Agent Wilson, you may have noticed a discoloration of the latex on tickets that had the toxin mixed in with the latex. That's because the thallium starts to oxidize as soon as it comes into contact with the air.

"Because the window of exposure is extremely brief, the odds of an individual ticket buyer breathing in thallium before it oxidizes are low—extremely low in fact—but not as low as the odds of winning the lottery."

Though slightly relieved by the answer, Wilson wasn't done with Ronck.

"Where does a person obtain thallium?"

"Agent Wilson, there's only one place in the continental United States that has it, and that's the Centers for Disease Control in Atlanta."

The news didn't register as much of a shock to Wilson, because he remembered reading reports during the past two years about a half-dozen incidents involving CDC employees and the mishandling of some potentially deadly pathogens, including smallpox, anthrax, botulism bacteria, and a virulent bird flu virus. And who could forget the Ebola debacle. After receiving the news, however, he shifted gears.

"How long until I can see a report containing the information you just shared?"

"I think Mr. Drummond is planning to send it out first thing in the morning," Ronck replied, referring to the day-shift leader in charge of all lab operations.

"Does he plan to add anything to the report after he arrives in the morning or is he pretty much done with it?"

"I think he wanted to look it over one last time before forwarding it to the director."

"Then do me a favor. Send the report to me now. If you need to copy your boss on it, that's fine, but I need it now. Got that?"

Ronck wasn't certain what to make of Wilson's request, but the tone in the agent's voice convinced the thirty-five-year forensics pro he should fulfill it. Immediately.

Less than ninety seconds passed before a message arrived in Wilson's S-Drive mailbox. Not from Ronck, this one—SUBJ: SEARCH WARRANTS—came from Mazachek and contained his ticket to launch the raid.

Almost as soon as Wilson clicked the SEND button to forward the search warrant message to Miller, another message arrived. It was the lab director's report Ronck had marked it "DRAFT" at the last minute to protect his boss in case something went awry.

After giving the report a quick look, Wilson sensed his hunch about Illinois Chemical was about to pay off. At the same time, however, he knew there was plenty of work remaining to be done and decided to share another tidbit related to that work with Mazachek.

In a reply to her message, Wilson wrote: "FYI: I'm contacting the CDC director to ask him for two things. First, I'm asking him for a list of CDC employees with access to something called Thallium S-213; and, second, I'm asking him to find out if any of that product is missing. Will keep you posted."

After sending the message to Mazachek, Wilson called the CDC Command Center and was patched through to the agency director's mobile phone.

"Dr. McKinney speaking."

"Dr. McKinney, this is FBI Agent Joe Wilson. I'm heading up the investigation of the deaths in the Northeast and need your help."

"I hope you've been receiving our daily updates," McKinney replied.

"Yes, sir, I have, but I need something from you that I haven't seen in any of your updates."

"What's that, Agent Wilson?"

"I need to ask you to do something without setting off any alarm bells among your employees. Do you understand, sir?"

"I think so. Tell me what you need."

"I need you to gather some information," Wilson explained. "Normally, we'd send in a team of agents, but I don't want to tip off anyone inside your agency if, indeed, anyone is involved in some wrongdoing."

"Go on," McKinney said, wanting him to cut to the chase.

"First, I need you to put together a list of all of your employees, full- and part-time, plus contractors—anyone at CDC who has ever had access to any areas where you keep something called Thallium S-213."

"Okay."

"As you compile that list, I need you to include up-to-date contact information—mailing addresses, physical addresses, home phones, cell phones, email addresses—for each employee. Are we clear on that?"

"Yes, we're clear. Anything else?"

"I need you to find out if any Thallium S-213 is missing from your inventory."

"Do you suspect thallium from our inventory might be involved in the deaths?"

"We're investigating all possibilities, sir," Wilson said, not wanting to tip his hand too much, "and it appears your agency is the only outfit in the country that has it."

After a pause, McKinney asked if Wilson needed anything else.

"Yes, there is one more thing. I need you to have someone review your agency's phone records—bills, logs, whatever you have—to see if any calls were made to any phone numbers in the 217 area code during the past twelve months. It would help if you begin by searching records associated with individuals who've ever had access to the thallium."

"I'll see what we can find, Agent Wilson. How soon do you need it?"

"Yesterday," Wilson replied.

✝

While Wilson was on the phone, Lee continued his efforts to secure lodging in the Effingham area. Having narrowed his list of motels to three finalists, all of which seemed to offer good locations and meet his other criteria, he made phone calls to the finalist hotels.

Because it was late at night and time was of the essence, each call began with an explanation of who he was and a request to be put in immediate contact with the motel's most-senior management person (i.e., a decision-maker who could respond to his needs quickly).

Lee's first call was to a small establishment—third on his list—named after the local high school's sports teams. It took only a few moments of conversation with the motel's manager to discover he didn't have enough rooms due to a renovation project that had left him at only twenty-five percent availability. In a way, Lee was thankful he wouldn't have to explain his choice of the Flaming Hearts Inn to Wilson and Miller.

Second on his list was the Crossroads Inn, a two-story facility whose name came from Effingham's location at the intersection of I-70 and I-57. Lee learned most of the one hundred rooms were booked because of a huge influx of visitors for the community's month-long centennial celebration—which would have been held the previous year but had been postponed due to fallout from Black Monday.

None of the city fathers had thought a celebration was in order at the time.

Lee's top choice was the Premier Lodge, a budget motel also located near the junction of the interstates on the north edge of town and ten minutes from Illinois Chemical. The drawback: it was slightly farther away than the other two motels. Fortunately for Lee, the motel's proprietor, Daamodar Patel, told him he was in luck.

"A group from China canceled at the last minute and, as a result, I have sixty rooms available for at least four days," Patel explained. "That, however, is the best deal I can offer—unless you have triple A. That gets you an extra ten percent discount."

"I need the entire motel—all of your rooms—for a week," Lee insisted. "FBI Immigration Enforcement Division."

When Patel heard those words, he seemed to shift gears.

"I can make that work, and I can give you government rate. Deal?"

"Yes, Mr. Patel, but one more thing: whatever you do, you must not tell anyone about our presence in your facility. You could find yourself facing serious charges if you tell anyone—even your wife and children—about this arrangement. Do you understand?"

"Most definitely," Patel replied, his voice crackling with anxiety. "I will tell no one. You have my word."With that, Lee thanked the man and told him his first guests would arrive in less than three hours and the remainder would trickle in during the day Monday. Patel assured him he would begin to relocate all guests scheduled to stay beyond that night.

†

After reviewing the lab report, Wilson tried to reach Lori again. When she didn't answer her cell phone this time, he began to fear the worst.

25

Upon landing in Effingham at 11:15 p.m., Wilson, Miller and Lee were greeted by FBI Special Agent Gerald Scott. Almost immediately, the local agent's mode of transportation caught Wilson's eye.

"Looks like our luck ran out," he said, loud enough for all to hear as Scott emerged from the driver's seat of another black Chevy Volt. "What happened to our Suburban? Our Tahoe?"

"We haven't had any of those in ages," said Scott, fresh off a ninety-minute drive from the FBI Chicago Field Office in Fairview Heights, Illinois.

After quick introductions, Wilson surprised everyone— including the plane's crew—by telling them he had another trip to make and hoped to return within a few hours.

Fortunately, both the pilot and his co-pilot got plenty of time to rest during the day, so fatigue wasn't a problem when Wilson introduced his change of plan and told them to get the plane refueled and ready for an immediate flight.

As Miller, Lee and Scott slept in adjacent rooms at the Premier Lodge, Wilson's flight—which seemed to take forever—arrived in Charlotte at 1:33 a.m., and he told the crew to sit tight and wait for further instructions.

After running into and through the general aviation building at the airport, Wilson hailed a cab to whisk him toward his home in the suburbs. En route, he made two phone calls to his wife. Both went unanswered. He feared the worst.

As the cab came to a stop in his driveway, Wilson tossed a twenty-dollar bill into the front seat, dashed toward the garage door and entered the security code. Ducking beneath the door as it opened, he ran inside, turned on the light in the kitchen and began looking for Lori.

Within seconds, he found her lifeless body—bluish-white skin, cold to the touch and covered with a red rash—stretched out on the living room sofa. Clutched in her left hand, he found the letter he'd written and mailed to her less than forty-eight hours earlier. On the coffee table in front of her, he found a shiny nickel and The National Bet lottery ticket he'd left inside the cookie jar, most of its latex panel scratched off.

As the gravity of the situation developed fully before his eyes, Wilson began sobbing uncontrollably, blaming himself for buying the ticket and, more importantly for not finding a way to warn her after he began suspecting lottery tickets had been weaponized.

More than twenty minutes passed before he regained enough composure to dial 911.

"Sir, what's your emergency?" the dispatcher asked.

"This is FBI Special Agent Joe Wilson. I need you to send a patrol officer, a HAZMAT team and the coroner to my house right away."

"Sir, please describe the nature of your emergency," the dispatcher pressed.

"Have the shift commander call me ASAP," Wilson said. "I'd rather describe it to him."

He gave the dispatcher his street address and cell phone number before ending the call. Less than a minute later, his phone rang.

"Agent Wilson," he answered.

"Major Frank Williams, Charlotte P-D. I understand there's some kind of situation at your place."

"Yes we do, and I need you to help me keep a lid on this."

Immediately, the shift commander suspected he might be dealing with a case of domestic abuse involving a fellow law enforcement officer asking for special treatment. It wouldn't be the first time he'd seen someone with a badge crack under the pressure of his work.

"Why don't you tell me what's going on first, Agent Wilson?"

"Major, I'm the FBI point man on the investigation of the deaths up in the Northeast," Wilson explained while struggling to maintain his composure, "and I came home tonight and found my wife dead in our living room.

"It appears she's a victim of whatever's been killing people up there, and I don't want any of your men to suffer the same fate."

Wilson went on to describe how he'd found his wife in their living room and, without giving too many specifics, how the circumstances mirrored those of cases he'd investigated during the previous two days. After the shift commander began to show signs he understood the special nature of the situation and no longer suspected foul play, Wilson continued.

"I need you to make sure your first responders speak with me as soon as they arrive and before they enter my home," Wilson explained. "Is that clear?"

"Yes, sir, Agent Wilson," the major answered.

Minutes later, Wilson identified himself to the two police officers first to arrive. In turn, they told him they had received a call from their supervisor and understood the delicate nature of the situation.

"Make sure anyone who goes inside this home wears a full-protective suit with gloves and a mask with a respirator," Wilson said, repeating what he hoped their supervisor had already told them, "and tell everyone to keep their time inside to a bare minimum."

"Yes, sir," the patrol officers replied in unison.

"And anyone who speaks to the news media about this situation *will* face federal obstruction of justice charges. Do you understand?!"

Nervously, the two officers assured Wilson they did. Having seen enough national news coverage of the mysterious deaths in the Northeast, they weren't about to do anything stupid. And when the hazardous materials crew arrived, the officers shared the FBI agent's instructions to the letter.

Though willing to comply with Wilson's instructions, the first responders soon found themselves bothered by one thing they witnessed during this late-night call: Wilson wasn't taking any precautions or following any of his own instructions.

Still, no one challenged the FBI agent; instead, they simply kept their distance, hoping to finish the job at hand and to live to see another day.

✝

A few minutes after 4 a.m. July 3, 2016, technicians placed Lori's body inside a black plastic bag and zipped it up before removing it from the home and transporting it to the coroner's office. Though an autopsy would be conducted later that day, Wilson didn't plan to ask the coroner for his cause-of-death determination. He knew already what had killed his wife.

Two hours later, Wilson shared the news with Mazachek before making a request.

"Madame Director, I need to withdraw from the task force."

"I understand, Joe-L, and I'm so sorry about Lori. Take some time, and let's talk again in a couple of days. Okay?"

Wilson didn't respond, and Mazachek spoke to him one more time.

"Take care of yourself, Joe-L. Do what you need to do, and I'll talk to you again in a couple of days."

After ending the call, Mazachek made another.

"Scout, I need you to be prepared to put the raid on hold for twenty-four hours and let the G5 pilot know he needs to sit tight for a couple of days. Joe-L's wife died, and I want to give him some time and see if he comes back."

"What happened to her?" Miller asked, shocked at the news that interrupted his morning review of message traffic.

"He bought her a lottery ticket for their anniversary and, sometime after he left Charlotte, she died after scratching it."

"Do you really think he'll be any good to anyone after only a few days?"

"I don't know, Scout, but I want to give him every possible chance to bounce back. Meanwhile, I want you to use this time to make sure all of your agents in Effingham are ready to conduct this raid. It looks like it might become your game to manage."

26

Normally, Miller would have dispatched a small team of agents to conduct surveillance of a facility like Illinois Chemical for at least twenty-four hours before launching a raid. Now, because the plant would be closed on Independence Day, he realized he would have to accept more risk than usual by going without the surveillance and relying on non-FBI sources for help instead.

After hanging up with Mazachek, Miller called Effingham County Sheriff Doug Johnson's cell phone.

"Sheriff Johnson?" Miller asked when he heard someone had accepted the call but not said anything.

"Yes," the forty-two year old replied without a hint of politeness. "How'd you get my number?"

"This is FBI Special Agent Scout Miller," he said, ignoring the sleepy sheriff's question. "Sorry to bother you so early, but I need your help."

"You're right, it is awfully early Agent --"

"Miller. Scout Miller."

"Well, it's awfully early and a holiday weekend to boot," the sheriff continued. "I hope this is damn important."

"Actually, it is," Miller replied, pausing a moment to let his words sink in, "but it's not the kind of thing I can discuss over the phone."

"Are you serious?" the sheriff asked.

"Yes, and I need you to stop by Room 112 at the Premier Lodge at 7 a.m. so I can fill you in on the details."

Sensing something exciting about Miller's invitation amidst the backdrop of the mass murder deaths that were all over the news, the sheriff agreed and said he would hurry out.

"And, sheriff, there's one other thing," Miller continued. "I need you to do me a favor and contact the police chief and the fire chief and let them know I need to see them, too. Can you do that for me?"

Without hesitation, the sheriff said he could. In fact, he was so eager to make the calls—and to find out the rest of the story—that he'd gotten dressed and was ready to walk out the door by the time he'd hung up the phone.

Thirty minutes later, one knock yielded three men outside Miller's motel room door.

"Gentlemen, come in and have a seat," Miller told them.

Introductions followed, and Police Chief J.O. Plosky, Fire Chief Willie Gamble and Sheriff Johnson took seats around a small table as Miller began to provide a quick overview of the situation.

"What I'm about to tell you doesn't go public. Understand?" Miller began, continuing only after seeing three heads nod in agreement.

"FBI agents will be arriving in Effingham during the next twenty-four hours. Once they're in place, we'll be conducting a no-knock raid at Illinois Chemical. Along the way, I'm gonna need your help."

"What's this all about, meth or something?" Sheriff Johnson asked, figuring his was a safe guess.

"No," Miller responded, "something much bigger."

Hearing that, the three locals leaned forward, eager to hear more.

"We believe there's a connection between someone at the plant—possibly more than one someone—and the deaths back East that have been in the news so much. Now, I need your help as we plan this raid."

"Anything you need," the police chief said, followed by affirmative nods from the fire chief and the sheriff. Secretly, all three relished the thought of being involved in such a high-profile investigation.

"First of all, I need to know contact information for the company that handles the alarm system at Illinois Chemical. Anyone?"

"There isn't one," Sheriff Johnson replied. "The place is open twenty-four-seven, so they don't need an alarm system."

"The sheriff's mistaken," the police chief interjected, eager to correct his colleague. "My neighbor works there, and he told me the plant closes three times each year— Christmas, Easter, and the Fourth of July."

"Okay, gentlemen, thanks," Miller continued. "How about incident reports? Have any of you had to send units to the plant recently—let's say, during the past five years?"

"I can check, but I don't recall any incidents out there," Chief Plosky said.

"Me neither," the sheriff added, "but I'll check."

"Great," Miller said before making contact with the two law enforcement officers in the room. "Now, I need you to search your databases to see if anyone you've dealt with— let's say, during the past five years—listed Illinois Chemical as his place of employment."

"I can have Wanda go through the records, but it might take a while," Sheriff Johnson explained. "Our computer system crashed a while back, and we haven't been able to replace it since our federal grant dollars dried up. That means Wanda has to go through the files by hand."

"I can check, too," Chief Plosky said, "but can't guarantee I'll find anything."

"I don't need guarantees, gentlemen, just effort," Miller explained, "even if it means calling people in to work on a holiday weekend."

"Fair enough," the police chief replied as the others nodded.

"Another thing," Miller continued, "Early Tuesday morning, I'll need you to help us block traffic at the end of the entrance road leading from the highway service road to the plant."

"We can do that for ya," Sheriff Johnson offered before pointing out that the plant, because of its location a stone's throw beyond the city limits of Effingham, was within his department's jurisdiction and not that of Chief Plosky. "How long do you think you'll need us?"

"Plan for a week, but don't worry about the cost. We'll cover your regular and overtime for as many men as you can provide."

"Sounds fair," a relieved sheriff replied as Miller turned his focus toward the fire chief.

"Chief Gamble, I need your help in obtaining a floor plan of the plant. Am I right to believe you guys keep one on file?"

"You bet. With all of the chemicals out there, we're required to know our way around and to know what's stored in their tanks and such."

"Great! I'd appreciate you getting me copies of the plant's floor plans ASAP," Miller said, "and, if you have any other useful information about the building, I'd like that, too."

Standing up and hoping to give the impression he wasn't interested in further discussion, Miller asked if anyone had any questions. Hearing none, he shook three hands and gave out three business cards while emphasizing the confidential nature of the work ahead and ushering two of the three to the door.

"Chief Plosky, can you hang around a minute?"

"You bet," he replied, pleased the FBI agent had singled him out for a one-on-one consultation.

After the other two local officials departed, Miller began following up on something he'd heard a few minutes earlier.

"Chief, you said your neighbor works at the plant. What's his name?"

"John Komorowski."

"And does he work days or nights?"

"He works days. Has for years."

"Can you take me to meet Mr. Komo--"

"Komorowski. He's Polish like me," the chief said before answering the question with a question. "Why on earth do you want to meet him?"

"I need help from someone who knows the place inside and out," Miller said, realizing he needed someone with firsthand knowledge of the early-morning operations at the plant and hoping Komorowski might be his man.

"Let me call him and see if he's awake," Chief Plosky said as he took out his phone and began looking for his neighbor's number in his contacts list.

"If you don't mind, chief, I'd rather we just show up. You drive?"

"Sure."

Ten minutes later, Miller and the police chief were knocking on the front door of the Komorowski residence. A few seconds passed before they heard footsteps approaching from inside the three-bedroom Tudor home. Then the door opened.

"What in tarnation is goin' on here, J.O?" Komorowski asked as he opened the door, appearing as if he'd crawled out of bed seconds earlier. "Don't ya know it's a holiday?!"

"Hold your horses, Ski. I'm here on business."

"What kind of business?" the man barked, prompting Miller to step forward and speak.

"Special Agent Miller, FBI. I need to talk with you about something very important, Mr. Komorowski."

Sixty-four years old and a widower only a few months from retirement, Komorowski felt his arthritic knees begin to wobble and didn't hear a thing Miller said after uttering the three-letter acronym of his employer.

"Do I need a lawyer?" Komorowski whispered after turning his eyes toward his neighbor.

"No, Ski," Chief Plosky replied.

"Okay then, come on in," the still-nervous Komorowski said before leading the visitors to his kitchen where they sat down around a small table, the knotty pine surface of which needed a thorough cleaning.

"Ski, Agent Miller needs to ask you some questions about the plant's--"

"I don't have any plants!" Komorowski interrupted, his eyes big as saucers. "Not even for medicinal purposes!"

"Calm down, Ski. He wants to ask you questions about the plant where you work, that's all."

Though slightly amused at how Komorowski's hearing loss briefly derailed their conversation, Miller remained straight-faced as he tried to get the near-retiree back on track.

"Mr. Komorowski, I need you to answer a few questions about what goes on during a typical day at the plant. It's a matter of the highest national security."

"National security? Really?"

"That's right," Miller explained, careful not to mention the word, raid. "I need you to tell me what my agents might expect to see when they arrive at Illinois Chemical tomorrow morning. Let's start with the employees first. When will the first workers arrive?"

"Well, if you're talkin' about the day-shift folks, they won't be there," Komorowski explained. "Neither will the mid-shifts. But the graveyards will get there around 10:45 that night."

"So only the graveyard shift workers go to work on the Fourth of July?"

"Eleven to seven. That's how our contract worked out this time around."

"Okay, let's look at Tuesday," Miller continued, shifting gears after confirming that the plant would be closed until the final hour of the day Monday. "Assuming everyone shows up for the graveyard shift Monday night and the day shift Tuesday morning, how many employees will be at the plant at shift change Tuesday morning?"

"About forty-four, I'm guessing. Eighteen on each shift, and eight or nine front-office types during the day."

"What about deliveries? Expecting any tomorrow?"

"We accept small deliveries every day. I couldn't tell ya exactly how many might come during the day shift, but the big deliveries—two tanker trucks full of chemicals—show up like clockwork every Tuesday evening."

"Okay, so tell me about the midday shift and when those people come in."

"Not much goes on between three in the afternoon and eleven at night. After the economy tanked two years ago, most of the 'middies'—that's what we called them—got cut, and all we do anymore during those hours is receive shipments that can't be accepted at some other time during the day."

"Who accepts those shipments?"

"Dan, Gary and Burt take turns doing that," Komorowski said before explaining that the names he mentioned belonged to the plant manager and his two shift managers.

"That's good to know, Mr. Komorowski," Miller continued. "Now, let me ask you about the folks you work with. Any troublemakers?"

"Besides me, you mean?" Komorowski chuckled, having grown comfortable with the FBI agent who didn't appear the least bit interested in laughing. "Not that I can think of. That random drug testing seems to keep most of the bad apples away."

The conversation continued for a few more minutes with Miller asking Komorowski about security cameras and guards at the plant. As the conversation came to an end, Miller gave the man a stern warning.

"Mr. Komorowski, I appreciate your help today, but must make it crystal clear that you can't speak with anyone about our conversation today. If I find out you have, you will find yourself facing charges of interfering with a federal criminal investigation, and that could bring you stiff fines and jail time. Do you understand?"

"Yes, sir," Komorowski replied, now wishing he'd never agreed to help.

"One slip of the tongue," he thought to himself, "and my retirement money might end up in the hands of a lawyer."

†

By the time Miller and the police chief left Komorowski's home en route to the motel, neither had any reason to believe the man would say a word about their conversation.

"I think you might have made him soil his pants, Agent Miller," the police chief chuckled. "I've never seen him turn so many shades of pale."

Mostly ignoring the chief's comment, Miller asked the chief to tell his sheriff and fire department colleagues the raid would be delayed a day.

"That'll give 'em more time to search their records," Miller added. "And be sure to remind them to keep quiet. Got that?"

"Yes, sir," Chief Plosky replied, sensing the FBI agent was dead serious about the matter.

27

Unable to sleep and still struggling to comprehend his loss at 10 o'clock Sunday morning, Wilson thumbed his way through old photo albums for a while before entering the walk-in closet of the master bedroom and spending most of thirty minutes touching and smelling Lori's clothes. And crying. He couldn't believe she was gone. And he couldn't believe he had lost yet another loved one to a senseless crime.

After enduring a handful of condolence visits from friends, colleagues and neighbors, Wilson mustered the mental energy to call one of the local funeral homes and make arrangements to have his soulmate's body cremated. The phone call turned into a long conversation during which a funeral counselor helped him draft an obituary.

Despite falling far short of conveying the right words to describe the love of his life, the obit was finished and would appear on the funeral home's website within twenty-four hours. It would also grace the pages of the *Charlotte Observer* and the *Arrington American* and probably remain in obituary archives at each newspaper forever, sharing these words:

> *Lori Ann (White) Wilson died at her Charlotte, North Carolina, home July 2, 2016.*

Lori was born in Clovis, New Mexico, August 1, 1978, and moved with her family to Arrington, Missouri, in 1981.

After graduating from Arrington High School in 1996, she earned a Bachelor of Science degree in elementary education at Lindenwood University in Saint Charles, Missouri, in 2000.

Lori enjoyed serving her community as an elementary school librarian in Arrington, Missouri, for more than a decade. She was devoted to her students and shared her love of reading with them. She also served one term on the local school board before she and her husband relocated to Charlotte, North Carolina, in January 2015.

Lori is survived by her husband of 16 years, Joseph L. Wilson, of the home.

No memorial service is planned. In lieu of flowers, the family asks that contributions be made to your local school library.

A funeral service didn't make much sense to Wilson, so he opted against holding one. After all, neither he nor Lori had siblings, both had lost their parents years earlier, and neither had any living relatives with whom they'd maintained contact over the years. On top of that, only a handful of others—mostly neighbors and FBI Charlotte staffers they barely knew—were likely to attend.

After the phone call with the funeral home counselor, Wilson tried to take his mind off his loss. Nothing on television offered anything remotely capable of distracting him, so he turned it off and walked into the kitchen to see what other mail, if any, had arrived during his most-recent absence. He found something that would change everything.

On top of the small rolltop desk that served as the household business center, Lori had placed two wicker baskets to hold their mail—one for incoming, the other for outgoing. In the incoming basket, Wilson found the usual assortment of bills and junk mail. In the other, however, he spotted a single pink envelope, the odd-sized kind his wife always used when she wrote to him while he was away.

Stamped and addressed to him at the Quantico address at which she knew he could receive mail while working on the task force, the envelope contained the last letter Lori ever wrote—one her husband would cherish.

Wilson sat down at the kitchen table, used a nearby letter opener to tear open the envelope at one end and carefully removed a one-page handwritten letter from inside.

Smelling Lori's perfume and seeing the outline of her lips in red lipstick at the top of the otherwise-blank pink stationery, he almost lost control before reading the words she'd written in perfect, flowing cursive:

Dear Joe-L, Thank you so much for the ring and for our first 17 years together. As I write this letter, I want you to know I haven't checked to see if the lottery ticket you sent me is a winner. Why? Because I already feel like I won the biggest and best prize any woman could ever win... YOU!!! I am so proud of you for being selected for such an important job. (I always knew you were the best cop around!), and I hope you can come home soon. If not, please know that, no matter where you are, I'm yours forever! Love always, Lori.

To Joe-L, it seemed as if his wife had written the letter with full knowledge of how it would be received. She had given him permission from the grave to go back to work and put all of his energy into solving one of the greatest crimes—or acts of terror—ever. Still troubled by the fact that no one had ever been arrested for the murder of his parents, he made a silent vow to find the person—or persons—responsible for killing his wife.

Putting the letter back inside the envelope and into his coat pocket, Joe-L took a deep breath before picking up his phone and dialing a familiar number.

"Joe-L," Mazachek answered. "How are you doing?"

"I'm ready to go back to work," he replied, shocking the FBI director with the news."

"Are you sure, Joe-L? It's so soon."

"One hundred percent. Lori wrote a letter to me before she died. Probably before she even knew she was going to die," Wilson paused. "Long story short, she always wanted me to do my job, so I'm going to get back out there and do it. For her."

"I wish I had gotten to know her, Joe-L," Mazachek said, struggling to keep from displaying any outward emotion. "She must have been very special."

"She was," he replied, fighting back tears and not wanting to dwell on the subject that made his heart ache. "Let me clean up, and I'll be in Effingham as soon as possible."

†

After arranging to have a neighbor boy check his mail and take care of his yard, Wilson took a cab back to the airport and boarded the G5 again at noon. He had, after all, instructed the crew to sit tight—and they did. Two hours and a short nap later, the G5 touched down in Effingham. Miller, Lee and Scott met Wilson as he stepped off the plane.

"Welcome back, boss," Miller said, making a point not to sound cheerful while thoroughly surprised to see Wilson return to the field so soon. "So sorry about Lori."

His emotions still raw, Wilson nodded slightly as if to say "thank you" and then changed the subject.

"Refresh me, you are?" Wilson asked, unable to recall the name of the Chicago-based agent standing next to Miller.

"Special Agent Gerald Scott. From Chicago."

"Thanks for being here," Wilson replied as he and the other agents climbed into the car. "Scout, how do things look for tomorrow? Everyone here?"

"The last few agents should arrive by six tonight and be ready to go by sunrise," Miller replied, "but the raid will have to wait until Tuesday if we want to have most of the employees there when we do it."

"What's the problem?" Wilson asked.

"Fourth of July, boss. The plant is closed all day until the graveyard shift workers arrive before eleven o'clock Monday night."

"Okay. Give me a few minutes to get my things put away, then stop by my room," Wilson said as they came to within sight of the Premier Lodge. "Before we meet, let everyone know I want them to meet us in the conference center at eight for a pre-brief."

"Can do, boss!" Miller replied.

While walking toward his first-floor room, Wilson took a quick look around and concluded that Lee had done a good job in selecting the motel. Across the street from a Walmart Super Center on a dead-end road not far from the bustling interstate, it provided agents a mostly-out-of-the-way location that would allow them to operate without tipping their hand to any Illinois Chemical Company employees who might not appreciate their presence in town.

After Lee gave him a keycard for his room, Wilson realized he'd eaten little since his first brief visit to Effingham and asked Lee to help remedy the situation.

"Jack, I need you to find me some good take-out," he said.

"Already done, boss. It should be arriving at your room any minute."

"Thanks, Jack."

Five minutes later, Lee's prediction proved accurate.

Wilson heard a knock at his door and soon found himself face to face with a pimple-faced, sixteen-year-old delivery boy. In the boy's left hand was a paper sack. The words printed on the outside indicated it was full of Chinese food from the Hu-Nan Deli.

"Nine-seventeen," the delivery boy said, wide-eyed at the site of a sharp-dressed man wearing a Bianchi Model X-16B Agent X-Harness and holsters cradling two Glock 23C pistols, one on each side of his chest. "Are you a cop?"

"Kind of, but don't tell anyone I'm here," Wilson said in an unmistakably-firm tone followed closely by a wink of his left eye. "Do you understand?"

"Yes, sir," the boy said as he reached out and took a ten and a five—plus a "keep the change"—from Wilson.

"Don't worry, boss," Lee said as he walked over from his room next door and saw the blank look on Wilson's face. "This is healthy food—no MSGs, no trans fats, no gluten--"

"Does it have any flavor?" Wilson interrupted.

"We had some two hours ago, and it was excellent."

"Who knew one could find good Chinese food in Southern Illinois on the Fourth of July," said Wilson before motioning for Lee to follow him into his room.

Miller and Scott arrived a few minutes later and, between bites of free-range chicken and quinoa, Wilson began talking shop with them.

"Gentlemen, I talked to one of the lab guys and had him send me a copy of their draft report about any lottery tickets found on or near victims' bodies. It shows a lot of tickets tested positive for a radioactive isotope called Thallium S-213."

"Whoa!" said Scott, the only agent in the room who had not heard the details of Wilson's airborne phone conversation with Ronck. "Is that stuff deadly?"

Silently answering Scott's question, three sets of eyes looked back at him in disbelief and prompted him to realize the foolishness of his question. "Of course. My bad."

Deciding against saying anything out loud about Scott's miscue, Wilson offered more details.

"Our guy at the lab said he suspects the thallium, in the form of a very fine powder, was added during the production process used to make the latex that people scratch off the panels of lottery tickets.

"The latex is gray when it's applied to the surface of the already-printed ticket, then it gets painted over with a thin layer of ink to match the design scheme of the ticket. On The National Bet tickets, the stuff was covered with the colors of ink found on the newest hundred-dollar bill—mostly green, purple and orange.

"In all three cases we investigated personally, we found lottery tickets among the victims' belongings, and each ticket had what appeared to be rust along the edges of the scratch-off panels. And that makes sense, according to the boys at the lab, because the thallium that got mixed in with the latex is a ferrous-thallium compound that starts to oxidize as soon as it comes into contact with air."

Wilson paused to let the information sink in. "Your heads spinning yet?"

"How does the thallium get into its victims?" asked Lee.

"Apparently, the scratching process causes the thallium to separate from the latex," Wilson explained. "When it separates, the thallium breaks into microscopic particles, some of which become airborne. Inhale enough of those particles—and the lab folks say it doesn't take much—and you begin to suffer the consequences soon after."

"Did the lab guy say anything about agents getting sick after handling the tickets?" Lee asked, despite being comfortable knowing he had not handled any tickets not already sealed in plastic bags.

"He said that as long as you eat healthy—you know, Hu-Nan Deli three times a day—you should be fine," Wilson answered, causing his fellow agents to erupt in nervous laughter. He didn't mention anything about the agents across the country who had died during the investigation. Didn't figure it would help.

"Seriously, I think we avoided trouble by wearing gloves, by not scratching any tickets, and by quickly bagging the ones we found," he said before taking another bite of his dinner.

At that point, Miller decided his boss could use an update about some of Lee's findings.

"Boss, Jack found some information about possible suspects during the flight here."

Hearing Miller's teaser, Wilson turned toward Lee and raised his eyebrows as a silent prompt.

"I searched the archives of the Effingham newspaper for the phrase, King Chemical, and the words, employee or work," Lee began. "It turned up two persons of interest."

Wilson nodded slowly as if to say, "Keep talking."

"Gary Kastens is a Gold Star father whose only son was killed in combat in Africa," Lee explained before noting that the local newspaper had published a couple of stories about it back in April 2014. "It was a pretty big deal here."

"We're fighting in Africa now?"

"Yes sir, we are."

"What makes you think this dad might be involved?"

"A couple of things he told a reporter in Effingham caught my attention. Nothing screamed out loud or anything, but I think he might be worth a look.

"Here, take a look," Lee said as he handed a printout of the newspaper article to Wilson who quickly seemed to become transfixed by what he was reading under the headline, ***Father of Fallen Hero Vows to Keep Promise***:

A blue sedan with government plates.

It was the last thing Gary Kastens expected to see April 7 as he mowed the lawn in front of his rural Effingham home. Occupants of the vehicle came bearing bad news: his only child, Air Force Master Sgt. Joshua L. "Josh" Kastens, 30, had been killed in combat somewhere in Africa less than 24 hours earlier. It was the kind of news no father ever wants to hear. News no father ever forgets.

A 2002 graduate of Effingham High School, Sergeant Kastens was only weeks from marking the 12th anniversary of his enlistment.

After serving only two years as a life-support specialist assigned to an air rescue squadron, he applied for and was accepted into the grueling training program known as "Superman School." After almost 500 days of training that included survival school, parachute training, medical training and more, he reached his goal of becoming a pararescueman (a.k.a., "PJ") and was assigned to the 31st Rescue Squadron at Kadena Air Base on the island of Okinawa, Japan.

A longtime Effingham resident and employee at Illinois Chemical Company, Gary Kastens said his son discovered his calling in life early and died doing what he had always wanted to do.

"Josh saw a movie, Blackhawk Down, in which bodies of American Soldiers were shown being dragged through the streets of Somalia in 1993," Kastens explained, "and he asked me why no one tried to save them. Not long after that, he told me he would be joining the Air Force after high school.

"He saw something in the teamwork and camaraderie of the military and, at the same time, saw his job in the Air Force as an opportunity to save lives."

Sergeant Kastens died, according to an Air Force news release, after sustaining multiple gunshot wounds during a mission to rescue the pilot of a single-engine F-16 fighter jet that went down in an undisclosed location in Africa during a routine combat air patrol mission.

Though Air Force officials would not identify the pilot or those believed responsible for the death of Kastens' son, they did confirm that an American F-16 had crashed in Somalia—but only after authenticated photos of the plane's wreckage appeared in several African newspapers within 24 hours of the crash.

Military experts in Washington piled on to the news, saying they believed members of the al-Shabaab terror group were responsible for Sergeant Kastens becoming the first reported Air Force combat death tied to American military involvement in Africa. Gary Kastens, meanwhile, had more pressing matters with which to deal.

Gary Kastens would work to keep memories of his son alive and to fulfill a promise he had made to Josh via letters exchanged while the airman was serving his country in places such as Iraq, Afghanistan and Africa.

"Josh told me to remember the promise I made to him in a letter last summer," the father recalled. "He asked me if, in the event he didn't return from this deployment, I

*would do everything in my power to prevent the United
States from settling for defeat against Islamic extremists.
Of course, I told him I would, never thinking I would ever
have to fulfill that promise."*

*Gary Kastens acknowledged the fact that fulfilling the
promise appears to be a tall order for one man, especially
in a small town like Effingham. Asked how he planned to
fulfill the promise, he couldn't offer specifics.*

*"I'm going to do everything within my power to fulfill
that promise," the elder Kastens said. "I know one man
like me, working alone, cannot singlehandedly overcome
the type of evil we've seen from the Islamic terrorists in
Afghanistan and Iraq and now Africa. If others join me in
this cause and let the president and members of Congress
know how important this effort is, then I believe I will
succeed—we will succeed—in keeping the promise I made
to my son."*

Editor's Note: *It is the policy of the* Effingham Courier
*staff to respect the privacy of family members who've
suffered the loss of a loved one by not interfering in their
lives during the period immediately following their loss of
a loved one. If, however, we are contacted by a family
member interested in speaking with a reporter about his
or her loved one, we will, on a case-by-case basis,
consider assigning a reporter to the story.*

"That's quite a story," Wilson said, all the while realizing
the emotions flowing from the father were not much
different than the fresh ones he carried in his mind about the
death of his wife. He fully understood the desire of a father
to bring justice to those who kill good people. People like
Josh and Lori.

Wilson was pleased with Lee's raw analysis of Kastens,
but still had more questions before he could determine who

might be the mastermind behind the deaths. "Okay, who else?"

"There's a Filipino kid by the name of Yusaf Abdul Sharif," Lee explained. "According to a brief in the student newspaper at Benson Wood College, he started out working as a night janitor at Illinois Chemical Company in May 2014 and landed an engineer apprenticeship with the company a few days after Christmas.

"Basically, the company pays for his graduate studies, and he promises to work for the company part time while in school and for six years after he completes his master's degree."

"Aside from the Muslim angle, what makes you think this Sharif fellow is worth questioning?" Wilson asked.

"When I searched the newspaper's online archives for more about him, I learned he majored in chemical engineering and, barely one month before the end of his senior year, converted to Islam *and* joined the Muslim Students League."

"Interesting," Wilson replied. "Is there more?"

"When I ran a few searches about the MSL chapter on campus, I found one of its leaders is a guy from the island of Mindanao in the Philippines, a real hotbed for radical Islam. He goes by the name, 'Manny,' but his official Muslim name is Mohamed Abu Nadal.

"Being from Mindanao, it's very possible he's affiliated with the Moro Liberation Front, an extremely dangerous Islamic militant group that ranks one notch below Abu Sayyaf in the hierarchy of terror groups operating in that country."

"Isn't that spat over now?" Wilson asked, recalling that the Filipino government had signed a peace accord of some kind with the Muslim extremists in their country's southern region two years earlier.

"The peace agreement didn't last long," Lee replied.

A pause followed before Wilson spoke again.

"You might be on to something, Lee. Anyone else?"

"Sir, there might be one more," Lee said, prompting Wilson to tilt his head back and raise his eyebrows before saying, "Okay, talk."

"In the newspaper article about Illinois Chemical awarding the apprenticeship to Sharif, the Filipino kid was quoted as saying he was thankful that the managers at the company had recognized his potential. In addition to Kastens, he mentioned Dan Christie and Burt Abramov as the other two managers.

"I couldn't find much of anything about Dan Christie, except that he's the plant manager and is a longtime member of the local Rotary Club."

"Okay, then what did you find out about the other guy, Abramov?" Wilson asked.

"Well, I couldn't find any other mentions of Abramov in connection with Illinois Chemical, but I kept digging and found an entry in the Legal Briefs section of the December 6, 2013, edition of the local newspaper. It shows Burtran F. Abramov and Ruth M. Abramov had their divorce finalized four days earlier."

"A lot of guys get divorced," Wilson countered, playing Devil's Advocate.

"Understood, but I ran a search for the origin of the last name, Abramov, and one result pointed me to Chechnya," Lee continued. "Ever heard of that place?"

"Good work, Lee," Wilson said. He'd definitely heard about the Islamic republic that had long been a thorn in the side of Russian President Vladimir Putin and his predecessors.

The foursome spent most of the next three hours reviewing and tweaking the plan for the raid. After that, Wilson told them to get some rest. Everyone in the room could tell, however, that he was mainly speaking to himself.

At two minutes before 8 p.m., a rested Wilson arrived at the motel's conference center in time to begin a one-hour briefing during which he shared details of their plan, including the special attention they would pay to the three Illinois Chemical employees Lee had pegged as persons of interest. The session ended with Wilson telling his fifty-four agents to be ready to do the same thing the next morning at eight. And they were.

✝

The Monday morning briefing took place as scheduled and lasted two hours. Wilson gave his agents copies of the one-page outline for how they would execute the raid and told them to become intimately familiar with it.

Wilson ended the meeting by instructing his agents to keep poring over leads and reading messages while also taking time to get plenty of rest before the raid.

28

Almost ninety-six hours had passed since the first mysterious death had been reported, and life was about to get more serious in Effingham—but not before breakfast.

Wilson drank coffee and reviewed messages while Miller jogged around the perimeter of the motel property and did some yoga stretches. Lee, meanwhile, worked out in his room, knocking out a fifteen-minute P-90X cardio routine— the kind he thought *might* kill Miller and *would* kill Wilson. Other agents completed their morning routines as well.

On orders from Wilson, Lee made sure the buffet line in the motel's lobby/dining area included eggs, bacon, sausage, fresh fruit and energy bars—as well as plenty of coffee. It would, Wilson said, "power them through" the long, grueling day that followed.

After breakfast, agents finished preparations for the raid, making sure their equipment, including heavy (i.e., bullet-proof vests, sidearms, etc.) and not-so-heavy gear (i.e., digital cameras, evidence bags, latex gloves and face masks with respirators), was ready to go.

Though Wilson knew the masks would frighten some employees, including the vast majority whom he suspected were unaware of any criminal activity that might have taken place—or was still taking place—at the plant, he decided such a precaution was necessary. Except for him.

Per the plan, Wilson arrived at the facility alone, behind the wheel of Special Agent Scott's Volt. After passing through the unmanned front gate at 5:58 a.m., he parked in a space near the front entrance and waited two full minutes before getting out of the car and walking into the building, a nylon briefcase in his left hand.

"Can I help you?" came a question from an unseen male whose voice carried into the hallway from an office adjacent the entrance.

"Yes, I'd like to speak with the manager," Wilson said as he walked toward the voice.

"I'm the night-shift manager, Burt Abramov," the voice repeated seconds before appearing in the doorway, dressed in a heavily starched long-sleeved dress shirt, crisply ironed khaki slacks, and black leather shoes bearing a mirror-like shine. "How can I help you?"

"I'm FBI Special Agent Wilson," the investigator said as he flashed his ID. "Can we talk in your office?"

"Sure, we can talk," came the reply as Abramov turned to led the unexpected visitor back to his office, all the while trying to figure out exactly what it was that had brought an FBI agent to Illinois Chemical.

Though Wilson recognized Abramov's name as one Lee had dug up, he said nothing while following him into the office from which one had a clear view of the plant's main floor and most of its production employees.

"How can I help you?" Abramov asked as he motioned for Wilson to take a seat.

"Mr. Abramov, I have a search warrant signed by a federal judge that affords the FBI broad powers of investigation per provisions of the Patriot Act of 2001," Wilson said while remaining on his feet and pulling a thick and official-looking envelope from his briefcase, now resting on the edge of Abramov's desk. "In less than an hour, a team of FBI agents will arrive to search your facility and conduct interviews. I'm going to need your complete cooperation."

"What's the prob--" Abramov started to ask before Wilson cut him off.

"Before they arrive, Mr. Abramov, I'm going to need you to help me ensure everyone remains safe and calm while we're here. Understood?"

"Sure," Abramov replied, not wanting to upset the man whose sidearms he had spotted under his coat as he reached into his briefcase. "Anything you need."

"First, I need to know where the master controls for the security camera system are located," Wilson said.

"It's right here," Abramov answered before picking up what could have been mistaken for a television remote control from on top of the desk in front of him and turning on a large, flat-screen monitor mounted on the wall to his left. "We hardly ever pay attention to the cameras unless we have someone from headquarters paying us a visit."

"Does anyone else in the building have access to these feeds?" Wilson asked as Abramov surfed through a variety of closed-circuit video feeds before pushing a button that resulted in four separate feeds appearing on the screen, each occupying a quarter of the sixty-inch-diameter viewing surface.

"No."

One feed appeared to come from a camera mounted above the front doors through which he'd entered the building, and two others appeared to be located along the building's exterior and showed views of two nearly identical shipping and receiving docks. Wilson wasn't sure about the location of the remaining feed that seemed to be coming from a camera inside the building.

"Where is this camera located?"

"That's in accounting, to keep track of the accounting people who manage company money."

"And this is the only place where the feed can be viewed?"

"Yes, sir."

"Mr. Abramov, I'm going to need your help with several important matters very quickly," Wilson continued. "First, I need to know the exact number of employees who reported for work today and if all of them here."

"Counting me, we have eighteen on the premises."

"Are you absolutely certain about that number?"

"Of course. We run a lean operation, and I always know when someone is missing."

"And is anyone missing today?" Wilson asked, wanting to ensure no misunderstandings arose.

"No. Everyone's here."

"How many employees are there on the day shift?"

"Including the plant manager and the office staff, twenty-seven."

"What if I asked you to shut down your plant today. Tell me if it's safe to do and explain what's involved."

"Shutting it down isn't dangerous, and it won't take much in terms of action, but it will take time."

"How long?"

"About thirty minutes."

"How many people need to be involved?"

"I can do it by myself, but I'm not authorized. Unless it's an emergency, only the plant manager can do that—he'll be here in twenty minutes or so—and only after he receives approval from headquarters. In Chicago."

"Don't worry about getting approval," Wilson said, waving the search warrant envelope. "I already have that."

"As soon as your plant manager arrives, I'll explain to both of you what has to happen today," Wilson said, making a mental note—the clock on the wall showed ten minutes had passed since he entered the building—before removing an iPad from his briefcase. "Until then, I need you to take a look at something for me."

Wilson handed his iPad to Abramov and asked him to look at a diagram of the plant's layout and tell him if it appeared to be accurate.

"Yes, it appears to be correct," Abramov said after looking over the diagram for about a minute. "The fire department inspectors visit the plant quarterly because of all the chemicals we have, so they tend to stay on top of things."

As Abramov finished speaking, something in the feed from the top-left monitor caught Wilson's attention. It was a car pulling into a parking space next to Wilson's car outside the front entrance.

"Who's that?"

"That's Mr. Christie, the plant manager. He's early."

"Early is good," Wilson thought to himself before speaking to Abramov again. "Let's meet him as he comes in the door."

Wilson followed Abramov into the hallway and to the foyer where they met Christie as he entered the building.

"Boss, we have a visitor," Abramov said as Christie came through the door.

Before Christie could respond, Wilson spoke.

"Mr. Christie, I'm FBI Special Agent Wilson, and I have a search warrant signed by a federal judge. In less than an hour, FBI agents will begin searching your facility and interviewing your employees. Under the provisions of the Patriot Act, my men and I will operate with broad powers of investigation. Do you understand what I've said so far?"

"Yes, sir," a shocked Christie said, fearful the tightness in his chest might be the first sign of the heart attack his wife had been warning him about for years.

"As I've already told Mr. Abramov, I'm going to need to have you do several things for me before my agents arrive," Wilson continued. "First, I need you to instruct all of your graveyard-shift employees to report to the break room for a mandatory meeting that begins in five minutes. Can you do that via intercom or the PA system?"

"Yes, sir, but what is this all about?" Christie asked, still in a state of shock.

"In due time, Mr. Christie. Right now, I need your full cooperation. Understand?"

Christie nodded, and the three men returned to the office where Abramov and Wilson had already spoken briefly.

"Excuse me a second," Wilson said as he removed a satellite phone from the holster on his left hip, sent a quick text message, and returned the phone to its holster. "Okay, Mr. Christie, I need you to make your announcement without giving any indication as to the purpose of the meeting. Got it?"

Christie didn't reply, opting instead to let his actions speak.

"Good morning, everyone. Please listen up," Christie began, speaking over the plant's intercom system. "I need everyone to gather in the break room for a mandatory meeting in five minutes. Again, stop what you're doing and head toward the break room immediately. The meeting begins in five minutes. Please do not be late. Thank you."

On the production floor, several employees grumbled upon hearing the announcement and immediately tried to call their spouses, parents or second-job bosses—to let them know they might be late. Much to their dismay, their calls did not go through, because the text message Wilson had sent moments earlier contained instructions for Miller to remotely activate a cell phone-jamming device in the backseat of the Chevy Volt parked outside the plant's front entrance.

Tensions were high as employees began to gather in the break room. Several even considered voicing their concerns in the direction of Christie and Abramov as they stood in the front of the room. They abandoned those thoughts, however, upon noticing Wilson's dark suit-and-tie presence as he stood next to their managers. Thinking he might be from headquarters, they decided it would be wise learn more before they said anything that might get them in trouble.

Though some arrived as many as two minutes late, all of the graveyard-shift workers made it to the break room by 6:20, and none had been chewed out for their tardiness. Had any of them known Wilson was responsible for both the meeting and the fact that their mobile phones had stopped working, they might have behaved differently.

Wilson whispered in Christie's ear before pulling out the only phone in the building that still worked and sending another message to Miller—one he would share with members of the task force: *"Go!"* After returning his phone to its holster a second time, he instructed Christie and Abramov to say nothing until he did.

Graveyard employees watched nervously as Wilson walked across the room in front of them until he was standing next to the exterior wall. There, he pulled on a nylon cord and closed the blinds over four windows, preventing anyone from seeing much of what would soon transpire in the parking lot outside.

Seconds after Wilson had returned to a spot in the front of the room, the people in the room heard the sound of a single vehicle as it pulled into a parking spot outside. Through cracks in the blinds, some were able to see Gary Kastens had arrived early to begin his job as day-shift manager.

Entering the building curious about who might own the Chevy Volt parked outside, Kastens followed the sounds of voices to the break room.

"Take a seat, please," Wilson told Kastens firmly while making direct eye contact with the man as he stuck his head through the door of the break room.

"What's going on?" Kastens replied.

"Please take a seat, sir," Wilson answered while maintaining his serious, all-business approach. "You'll learn soon enough."

After spotting his management colleagues in the front of the room, Kastens located some space near the back. There, he would show a bit of defiance by leaning against a wall instead of sitting in a chair as instructed. Only after Wilson told him one more time to find a seat did he do so.

Soon after Kastens sat down, the air filled with the sounds of more than a dozen large SUVs arriving in the parking lot.

After parking their vehicles in what seemed like a carefully choreographed effort, a dozen agents dressed in full protective gear—including masks with respirators—entered the building and made their way to the break room. There, they used their appearance and their weapons to send clear messages: no one would leave the room without the FBI's express permission. Without Wilson's permission.

Ten more heavily-armed agents took up positions around the outside of the building; two three-agent teams manned the loading dock doors on the west side of the building; and six additional agents kept watch over the main entrance from inside the double-glass doors.

Sixteen more agents, easy to spot in their dark blue FBI windbreakers with maize-colored agency acronyms screen-printed on their left chests and across their backs for all to see, entered the building next. Aside from latex gloves, most wore no protective gear.

Dispersed among Illinois Chemical's eight administrative offices, the last group of agents began turning on computers and using proven techniques, including software "backdoors," to gain access to password-protected files and fly past firewalls inside the company's network.

Rather than follow traditional FBI protocol that called for loading hundreds—maybe thousands—of boxes with files and other possible evidence and carrying the boxes out of the building so they could be searched and held as evidence, Wilson had instructed his agents to focus first on downloading as many files as possible to portable hard drives. He believed such an approach would allow examination of documents to take place much more rapidly than manual eyeballing would.

Last to enter the building were Miller, Lee and Scott. Like Wilson, they had opted against wearing masks or protective gear other than latex gloves. They had, after all, managed to remain alive this long.

"Ladies and gentlemen, please be patient as we wait for day-shift employees to arrive," Christie said after Wilson whispered the instructions in his ear. Both men sensed the employees were growing increasingly nervous about their situation, not knowing why they were being held in a room while surrounded by gun-toting FBI agents.

Fifty minutes passed before the plant manager confirmed for Wilson that all of his employees had arrived for work and were inside the break room.

In the wake of Black Monday-driven downsizing, none had dared call in sick. Today, however, many wished they had, especially after seeing so many dark-colored SUVs in the parking lot. Instead, they packed themselves into the break room where some sat on the floor due to a shortage of chairs.

Wilson didn't care that the room was designed for only thirty-five people at a time, according to the "Maximum Occupancy" sign hanging on the wall above the sink. He had "bigger fish to fry" and, amidst a sea of nervous faces— including the one belonging to John Komorowski—he began speaking.

"Ladies and gentlemen, I'm FBI Special Agent Wilson," he began. "I have a search warrant signed by a federal judge that authorizes me and my colleagues to search this building and detain anyone while we conduct this search."

He didn't mention the word "indefinite" as he thought it might upset someone. But he believed he had wide discretion.

"I want you to know each of my agents is equipped with audio and video recording devices to record today's activities. In addition, I want you to know we'll provide you with an opportunity to speak to an agent if you have special needs—things like a medical condition or medication you must take.

"At this time, however, I need each of you to do something important, so please pay attention. If anyone has in their possession any type of weapon, carried legally or not, please raise your hand."

When two men and one woman raised their hands, Wilson wasn't surprised. A record number of Illinois residents had signed up for concealed carry permits and taken the required training classes as soon as it had become possible to do so in

January 2014, thus opening the floodgates for pro-Second Amendment citizens in the final state to legalize such permits.

"Okay," he continued, eyeing the three who had raised their hands, "please keep both hands visible at all times and walk out into the hallway. The men at the tables in the hallways will take custody of your weapons until such time as we can return them to you."

Wilson paused for a moment while the trio of gun owners walked into the hallway where agents relieved them of their firearms, asked them for their names and contact information, and allowed them to return to the break room.

"Next, I need everyone to slowly, very slowly, remove from your pockets, handbags or backpacks any mobile phones, tablets, laptop computers or other electronic devices you might have in your possession. In just a moment, beginning with those of you in the front and working our way toward the back, I'll ask you to turn in your electronic devices in the same manner as the folks with the firearms did. Again, we'll move from front to back, table by table, and so forth.

"Please know your property will be returned to you as soon as soon as possible. Whatever you do, please do not hand a device to anyone who is not an FBI agent."

After instructing his agents to begin the collection process and leaving it up to them to ensure it was completed without incident, Wilson motioned for Christie and Abramov to follow him into the hallway.

Upon seeing his management colleagues walking out of the room, Kastens stood and intended to join them when an FBI agent standing by the door stopped him in his tracks.

"Sir, please sit down, now!" the agent barked.

"I'm the day-shift manager, Gary Kastens, and I think I should be going with those men," he countered while pointing toward Christie and Abramov.

Hearing the commotion behind him and recognizing the man's name from Lee's research, Wilson turned and nodded to the agent at the door—his signal to let Kastens join his group.

"Follow me, gentlemen," Wilson said before leading the three men into the office where he'd met Abramov more than an hour earlier.

"Mr. Abramov, you told me earlier that the plant could be shut down without a problem, right?" Wilson asked.

"Yes, sir."

"Okay then, I need you to shut it down."

After shrugging his shoulders, Christie nodded to Abramov, giving his subordinate permission to follow Wilson's order. At the same time, the plant manager realized he might be in for the longest day of his life.

"You know this will cost us tens of thousands of dollars, don't you?" Christie asked, knowing he could now tell his boss in Chicago he'd tried but failed in his effort to stop the FBI from shutting down the plant.

"Not my problem," Wilson replied.

With that, Abramov logged on to his company's intranet and began a shutdown sequence that involved responding to a series of on-screen prompts, each of which was the equivalent of asking, "Are you sure you want to do that?" In response to each question, Abramov moved his cursor to the YES icon and hit ENTER on his computer's keyboard. After twenty-five minutes, he assured Wilson the job was complete and Illinois Chemical was shut down.

"Alright, gentlemen," Wilson said, "you can return to the break room and have a seat."

As the three men walked down the hallway toward the break room, they slowed their pace while passing the front doors and seeing more FBI vehicles arrive to join the sixteen already there.

Had they been allowed to loiter, they would have seen two unmarked big rigs—each towing fifty-three-foot trailers—arrive and back into positions so that the rear end of each trailer was less than twenty feet from the building's main entrance.

They also would have seen the arrival of an FBI Mobile Command Post, a modified Winnebago motor home on which no expense had been spared when it was obtained by the bureau during the fat-budget days before Black Monday.

Parked parallel to the building and sixty-five feet away, it stood perpendicular to the two tractor-trailers. Together, the building, command post and two trailers formed a loose box within which much work would be accomplished.

†

Wilson, Miller, Lee and Scott returned to the break room after being notified that agents there had completed the process of collecting electronic devices from plant employees.

"Ladies and gentlemen, please raise your right hand if you hear your name called," Wilson said before reading off a list of fifteen names, last names first. Among them, he interspersed the names of three in whom he had more than a passing interest: Kastens, Gary; Abramov, Burtran; and Sharif, Yusaf.

Upon hearing their names called, the employees felt their hearts begin to race and began raising their right hands.

Among Wilson's three prime suspects, Kastens was the first of the three to have his name called and his hand went up. It was followed soon after by Sharif (a.k.a., Rosy), and the last name called was Abramov.

"Those of you with your hands raised, please stand up and follow me," Wilson said before walking out into the hallway and turning his focus back toward those inside the room to ensure they were complying.

Once they made it into the hallway, the employees were divided into three groups of five persons each and escorted to separate holding areas throughout the plant. By design, each group included only one of the three prime suspects.

Wilson waited several minutes for the groups to reach their designated holding areas before pulling out his sat phone again and sending the first of three new text messages to the agents in charge of the special groups. Then, one at a time and at least ten minutes apart, he told his agents to escort Kastens, Rosy and Abramov to separate offices along the single long hallway in the plant's administration area.

His goal was to make the employees in each group believe the three men had been selected at random. Most importantly, he wanted to ensure none of the three realized he'd been singled out.

The remaining Illinois Chemical employees in each of the three special groups were held for almost an hour before being allowed to return to the break room one at a time, fifteen minutes apart and with instructions against speaking to anyone.

By noon, all of the non-management employees in the break room were told that, in order to leave, they would have to sign individual nondisclosure forms. Appearing very official and featuring the FBI logo top and center, each form contained several paragraphs of strongly worded legalese via which potential violators of the terms and conditions outlined on the form were warned they would face the most severe penalties allowed by law.

Wilson delivered the same message in a serious, but less-threatening manner.

"Ladies and gentlemen, I appreciate the patience and understanding you've shown me and my agents today. At the same time, I must warn you that you are not to discuss anything about what has gone on here today until or unless you're informed otherwise by a representative of the FBI. Not with any of your coworkers, friends, neighbors or family members. Anyone who violates this gag order *will* face federal criminal charges.

"As a means of demonstrating your understanding of what I just explained to you, each of you will need to sign and date a nondisclosure form before you leave this room," he continued. "After you sign your form, my agents will return your phones and/or firearms to you and you'll be free to leave. My only request is that you leave as soon as you sign the form and do so in a safe and orderly fashion. At some point along the way, I expect you'll understand and appreciate our efforts here today. Thank you."

With those words, Wilson left the break room and walked outside the building to call his boss.

"Shoot," Mazachek ordered, not wanting to waste a second on formalities after accepting Wilson's call.

"We've found three possible suspects, and all are Illinois Chemical employees," he began. "One's a Gold Star dad who lost his only son in combat two years ago. The others are transplants—one from the Philippines and the other from Chechnya."

"Anything solid on these guys yet?" Mazachek replied.

"Not yet," Wilson answered, "but I'm optimistic."

"Keep me posted, Joe-L," the director said, hanging up before Wilson could say more.

29

In television crime shows and action movies, criminal investigators always seemed to mention three words—means, motive and opportunity—as keys to solving crimes. Wilson, however, had found the words of criminals—whether spoken, written on paper or transmitted electronically—usually did them in as often as anything else.

Accompanied by Miller and Lee, Wilson exited the break room and walked to a small office near the end of the long hallway. Upon entering, he found most of the contents of the room had been removed, per his instructions, leaving only a small lamp table, two chairs and a video camera on a tripod to record the conversation about to take place. Seated in one of those chairs, Kastens looked up at Wilson as he entered the room.

"Please, keep your seat," Wilson said as he sat in the chair across from Kastens, who'd shown no indication he was about to stand up. "Sorry this is taking so long, but I need to ask you a few questions."

"I'll help any way I can."

Wilson liked the man's apparent willingness to cooperate, but he wasn't quick to jump to any conclusions. After all, he'd seen murderers and other violent criminals act in similar ways.

The session began with Wilson informing Kastens of his Miranda rights (i.e., to remain silent, to have an attorney present, etc.) and, in return, Kastens telling him he had nothing to hide. To Wilson, the man sounded as if he was being honest and sincere, and Wilson took that as a good sign. But not proof.

"Mr. Kastens, I understand you suffered a tremendous loss a couple of years ago," Wilson said. "Do you blame anyone in particular for the loss of your son?"

"What do you mean?" he replied, caught off guard a bit by the directness of the question. "He was killed in combat! In Africa! Of course, I do!"

"Mr. Kastens, I'm deeply sorry for your loss, but I'm looking for someone who might have an axe to grind, and you fit the bill."

"Does this have anything to do with the letters I sent to Washington?" Kastens asked as he began to feel his face heat up while imagining one of Senator Slott's staffers turning his name over to the FBI as someone who was threatening them. "Or is it because I've attended a few Tea Party gatherings?"

"Why don't you start by telling me exactly what took place between you and your elected officials," Wilson said, ignoring Kastens' questions.

"I made a promise to my son, Josh," Kastens told Wilson as Miller and Lee took notes a few feet away. "In the event he didn't return, I promised I would do everything in my power to keep the American people from settling for defeat in our war against radical Muslims wherever they were— especially in the United States.

"Ever since he was killed, I've been trying to fulfill that promise," he continued. "First, I wrote letters to Washington and tried to convince my elected officials not to withdraw our troops prematurely. When they replied with form letters, I became angry.

"During several phone calls and a trip to Washington, I got angry, but I never threatened anyone, and I didn't do anything worthy of an FBI investigation."

Wilson wasn't eager to pursue the Tea Party angle Kastens thought might have gotten him in trouble. As a detective at the sheriff's office years earlier, he had received great assistance from Tea Partiers and didn't hold anything against them to this day. Likewise, he shared Kastens' disdain for most politicians. So he changed directions.

"How long have you worked at Illinois Chemical, Mr. Kastens?"

"About thirty years."

"And you're a manager?"

"Yes. Day shift."

"And you've done that for how long?"

"Except for the seven months or so right after my son was killed, I've been day-shift manager for about twenty years."

"What did you do during those seven months?"

"Dan decided to move me to the graveyard shift for a while, thinking it would be less stressful for me as I was trying to deal with Josh's death."

"Did it help?" Wilson asked.

"I suppose," Kastens replied, opting against explaining how nothing really helps a man get over the death of his only child. Having lost his parents to violent crime, Wilson believed he understood what the man was saying and what he wasn't.

"Have you ever been involved in or associated with anything illegal going on at Illinois Chemical, Mr. Kastens?" Wilson asked, shifting the discussion dramatically.

"No, sir. Why?"

"Have you ever added anything toxic or poisonous to any Illinois Chemical product?" Wilson asked, ignoring Kastens' question.

"Absolutely not!" Kastens said, sounding as if he was insulted by the question.

"Okay, Mr. Kastens, I don't have any reason to believe you're lying, but I need you to do one more thing for me—take a polygraph exam. Will you do that for me?"

"You can test me all you want."

"Great," Wilson said as he stood up from his chair. "Before I go, there's one last thing I need to tell you: you must not speak about these matters with anyone—not your coworkers, not your friends, and not your family—about our conversation in this room today. If I find out you have, you could face charges of interfering with a federal criminal investigation and go to prison. Do you understand?"

"Yes, sir," Kastens said, a bit stunned by such a warning.

"Good. Until it's time for the test, you can sit tight and let one of the guys outside the door know if you need anything."

With that, Wilson and Lee left the room, followed by Miller after he had collected the video camera.

"Make a note," Wilson told Miller. "If we decide to search Kastens' place, we'll need to look for any letters he wrote to his elected officials and anything he received in return. Now, I'm gonna talk to the Filipino kid."

Miller dutifully entered the note on his iPad screen.

"So that's how it's done?" Lee whispered as the trio walked.

"Every interview is different, Jack," Wilson replied. "Let's go do another."

The agents' next stop was a cleaned-out corner office across the hallway and two doors down. There, they walked past another pair of FBI agents keeping an eye on the twenty-five year old they knew as Sharif as he sat nervously.

Miller and Lee, never introduced, entered the room first. Finding an identical set up, Miller powered up the video camera, hit RECORD and stood against the wall next to Lee and behind the chair Wilson would soon be using. Seconds later, Wilson entered the room and sat down directly across from his interviewee, again separated only by a small lamp table.

"Good morning, Mr. Sharif," Wilson began, noticing the young man's hands and knees were shaking, his eyes the size of saucers. "I need to ask you a few questions."

"Sure, but what is this about?"

"Do you mind if I call you by your first name—Yusaf, right?" Wilson asked, dodging the young man's question.

"Sure, you can call me Yusaf, but everyone here calls me Rosy."

"Rosy? Where did that name come from?"

"My last name, before I converted to Islam, was del Rosario."

Sensing the fledgling Muslim who allowed coworkers to call him by his old nickname might hold some regrets about his conversion to Islam, Wilson decided to exploit that possibility by addressing him as Rosy at every opportunity.

"Before I continue, Rosy, I want you to know you have the right to remain silent and that anything you say can be held against you in a court of law," Wilson explained. "Likewise, you have the right to an attorney and, if you can't afford one, one will be appointed for you. Do you understand your rights, Rosy?"

"Yes, sir, but I don't understand," he answered, his voice trailing off.

"Rosy, tell me about your involvement with the Muslim Students League."

"I joined right after I converted to Islam and right before I began working here," he answered, wondering how the FBI agent knew he'd joined MSL.

"You told me what your last name used to be. What was your full name before you converted to Islam?"

"Michael. Michael Archangel del Rosario."

"What is your father's full name?"

"Juan Hector del Rosario."

"And what does he do for a living?"

"He runs a printing business. Metro Printing. In Manila."

"Okay, Rosy, new subject. Are you familiar with the Moro Liberation Front and Abu Sayyaf?"

Caught off guard by the question, Rosy's mind began to race as he struggled to decide how to answer the question, and then he blurted out his answer. "Every Filipino has heard of those groups!"

"Are you familiar with Mohamed Abu Nadal?"

"You mean Manny? Yeah. He introduced me to Islam."

"Did you know Manny is a member of the Moro Liberation Front?" Wilson asked, fishing to see if a link could be made.

"No," he answered, now regretting ever leaving the faith of his father and wondering what else Manny might not have told him. "Manny mentioned the group to me many times, but he never said he was a member!"

Seeing Rosy's eyes well up with tears as if he was about to break down, Wilson switched directions again. "What is your job at Illinois Chemical?"

"I am an apprentice engineer."

"Tell me about that job."

"The company is paying for my graduate education. In exchange, I work for the company part-time until I finish my master's degree and then for six years after that."

"A master's degree in what?"

"Chemical engineering."

"Tell me about your duties, your work as an apprentice," Wilson continued, sensing he might be on a worthwhile trail.

"I shadow different employees at the plant," Rosy said, appearing to calm down a bit as he realized the FBI agent wasn't going to beat him or inflict any other form of violence on him. "Every six months, I work with a different manager. Right now, I'm working with the night-shift manager, Mr. Abramov."

"Do you like your job, Rosy?"

"Oh, yes! Very much."

"Have you ever been accused of, or convicted of, breaking any laws, Rosy?"

"No, sir," the young man said eagerly. "Never!"

"Have you ever been involved in or associated with anything illegal or know about anything illegal going on at Illinois Chemical?"

"No, sir."

"Have you ever added anything toxic or poisonous to any Illinois Chemical product?"

"No, way!"

"Okay, Rosy, I don't have any reason to believe you're not telling me the truth, but I'd like to ask you to do one more thing—take a polygraph exam. Can you do that for me?"

"I guess so," Rosy replied, fearful of being perceived as uncooperative if he refused and wishing his father was nearby to offer advice.

"Good. We'll take that test in a little while. First, I need you to understand that you're not to speak with anyone about our conversation today. If I find out you have, you'll face federal charges of interfering with a criminal investigation and you'll probably go to prison. That means you can't talk to Manny or anyone else about it. Not at work. Not at school. Not anywhere. Understand?"

"Yes, sir," Rosy said, now more frightened than ever.

Wilson and Lee left the room, followed soon after by Miller now toting two video cameras.

"He said he didn't know Manny was affiliated with the Moro Liberation Front," Wilson said as the three agents walked down the hallway toward a third office.

"Do you believe him?" Lee asked.

"Hard to say, Jack, but my gut tells me this kid is lonely and far from home and may have fallen in with the wrong crowd."

"Should we search his place now?" Miller asked.

"Let's wait until after we speak with Burt Abramov—and after you speak with Rosy's father," Wilson answered.

Taking that as a signal he should contact Juan Hector del Rosario, Miller headed to the command post.

†

Wilson still didn't believe he'd found the person or persons responsible for tampering with the latex after two cursory interviews, so he moved on to the third interview, counting on his patience to be the trusted ally it had always been.

Walking down the hall again, Wilson and Lee found two FBI agents standing watch outside another interview room set up identical to the first two. After Lee entered the room and hit RECORD on the video camera, Wilson followed him in.

"Good morning, Mr. Abramov," Wilson said, intentionally making eye contact while ignoring Lee's presence in the room and opting to stand instead of sit as he had during the first two interviews. He didn't know why he had opted to stand, but it seemed like the right approach at the time.

"Good morning, sir," Abramov replied, standing briefly in a show of respect. "How can I help you today?"

"Mr. Abramov," Wilson began, again without introducing his colleague.

"Please, call me Burt," Abramov interrupted, his words showing no hint of either his native Chechen language or the Russian in which he was also fluent.

Wilson acknowledged Abramov, offered him a Miranda warning and asked him if he understood his rights.

"Sure, no problem," he replied. "How can I help you?"

Ignoring Abramov's question, Wilson began asking his own questions. "How long have you worked at Illinois Chemical?"

"Almost nineteen years."

"And your job right now is what?"

"I'm the manager of the overnight shift," he explained, having never liked using "graveyard" to describe anything related to his job. "Eleven at night to seven in the morning, Tuesday through Saturday."

"How long have you held that position?"

"About ten years."

"And before that?"

"I started here as a custodian in 1997 and worked my way into management."

"I'm sure you prefer the daytime shift, right?"

"Oh, yes! I worked the day shift for almost eight months last year and hope to return to it again one day."

Abramov didn't mention the fact the current day-shift manager would likely have to be fired, retire or die for him to assume that position on a permanent basis.

"Because it gives you more time to spend with your five children, right?" Wilson continued.

"Yes," Abramov answered as hesitance turned into anger. "How did you know I have five children?!"

"That's not important right now, Burt."

"How did you know I have five children?!" Abramov asked, showing signs Wilson had struck a nerve with the personal nature of his inquiry. "And why do you want to know so much about them?!"

"No particular reason, Burt. I just want to know you better."

"What is this questioning about, Agent Wilson?"

"We believe someone at this plant might be involved in a plot to commit mass murder," he answered matter-of-factly. "Know anyone like that, Burt?"

"Oh, my God!" he replied, appearing to show more interest than anger. "I bet this has to do with that fifty-million-dollar reward the attorney general announced on television! Am I right?"

"Is there anything you want to tell me, Burt?" Wilson asked, sensing his interview subject might know more than he was letting on.

"To get the reward, you mean?" Abramov replied. "No. I mean, I don't think I know anything. That would seem impossible, right?"

"What would seem impossible?"

"That I might know anything about terrorism in tiny little Effingham?"

"Who said anything about terrorism, Burt?" Wilson asked sharply.

"You did," Abramov replied. "You said mass murder, right?"

"I used that phrase," Wilson replied, hoping Abramov might elaborate on his previous statement.

"To me, they're the same thing, and that kind of thing doesn't happen around here, does it?"

Wilson ignored Abramov and decided to change direction.

"What made you leave Chechnya, Burt?"

Though the question surprised Abramov, he seemed to answer it in stride.

"Things were becoming dangerous there, especially where I lived in Grozny, and I didn't want to die," he said, conveniently failing to mention other circumstances that had played a role in his abrupt decision to leave the war-torn region the day after Christmas 1991, only weeks before the breakup of the Soviet Union of which Chechnya was a reluctant member.

"Do you have any Chechen friends in this country?"

"Of course," he replied. "Many people from Chechnya fled to the United States just like I did."

"Have you communicated with any of them recently?"

"Not that I recall," he answered, adopting the vague style of response made popular in recent decades by members of the American political class while testifying under oath.

Wilson shifted gears again, this time getting personal.

"Burt, I understand you went through a pretty tough divorce a while back, and you even had the police come out to your house a couple of months ago to break up an argument you were having with your wife," Wilson began. "How are you holding up these days?"

"First my children, now my wife," Abramov replied with an unmistakable hint of hostility. "Who told you about my divorce? That has nothing to do with my work here, and it certainly has nothing to do with terrorism or mass murder."

Wilson couldn't believe Abramov had used the "T" word again. Using one of his favorite interrogation tricks, he decided to throw Abramov a curve.

"Burt, have you ever heard of Kevin Bacon and six degrees of separation?"

"I don't eat bacon, Agent Wilson," Abramov answered, "but I know you must use a higher temperature than six degrees to cook it."

The unconventional tactic worked. Abramov seemed to become more perturbed—some might say angrier—with each passing minute, and Wilson kept pushing.

"Have you ever had a restraining order issued against you, Burt?"

"Absolutely not! Why?"

"Have you ever been accused of, or convicted of, a crime, Burt?"

"In Chechnya, yes. Everyone was a suspect, according to the corrupt government there."

"What about in the United States?"

"Of course, not," he answered, unable to hide sweat stains that had appeared under the arms of his long-sleeved dress shirt.

Hearing Abramov's response, Wilson began pacing back and forth across the room. Four steps in each direction. Never taking his eyes off Abramov. On his final pass, he saw Abramov turn his head away, prompting the investigator to stop walking, slap both hands down on the table and regain the man's attention.

"Burt, have you ever been involved or associated with anything illegal going on at Illinois Chemical?"

"I don't think so," he replied, the tone of his voice rising as he spoke.

"Have you ever added anything toxic or poisonous to any Illinois Chemical product?"

"That's ridiculous! Of course, not!"

Wilson paused for a second before adopting a softer tone.

"Burt, I don't have any reason not to believe you, but I need to be certain you're telling me the truth. Would you be willing to take a polygraph?"

"Sure, I'll do that!" Abramov said. And why not! He was familiar with myriad countermeasures one could use, such as putting a tack in one's shoe during an exam or tightening one's buttocks muscles, to throw off the findings of a polygraph exam. Years earlier, he had ordered a book and DVD series about polygraph countermeasures produced by a polygraph examiner in Oklahoma City. Of course, he didn't see any need to mention that—or a handful of other things he knew—to Wilson.

"Alright then," Wilson told Abramov, "wait right here."

After opening the office door, the FBI agent whispered to his colleagues outside the door to keep a close eye on Abramov while then he walked down the hall and out the front doors of the building. Lee, meanwhile, collected the video camera and caught up to Wilson as he was about to enter the mobile command post.

30

After locating Rosy's personnel file and learning he had listed his father as his primary emergency contact, Miller stepped into one of the command post's three soundproof micro-offices, each of which was barely large enough for two people standing shoulder to shoulder, and closed its sliding glass door.

Displaying no concern about the fourteen-hour time difference between Effingham and Manila, Miller dialed the father's number and, moments later, heard the phone at the del Rosario residence begin to ring.

"Hello?" a tired male voice answered in English while noticing the clock radio on his nightstand showed 9:32 p.m.

"Is this Juan Hector del Rosario?" Miller asked.

"Yes, who's calling?"

"This is Special Agent Miller," he began, not letting the Filipino know that technicians inside the command post were recording the call. "I'm with the FBI, the Federal Bureau of Investigation, in the United States, and I need to speak with you about your son, Yusaf."

"You must have the wrong number," the Filipino replied. "I don't have a son by that name."

"Excuse me," Miller regrouped, "but do you have a son by the name of Michael Archangel del Rosario?"

"Yes, why?"

"Mr. del Rosario, we suspect your son might be involved in criminal activity," Miller explained before pausing to give the father a moment to absorb the gut-wrenching news.

"This can't be! Michael would never hurt a soul. You must have him confused with this other person."

"That's possible, sir, but..."

"What is it you think he's done?" the father interrupted, hoping and praying it was something minor, though he feared it might have something to do with news reports that had been broadcast worldwide about the huge death toll in the United States.

Rather than respond to the question, Miller changed the subject.

"Mr. del Rosario, did you know your son recently converted to Islam?"

"No," came the shocked father's answer, followed by four softly spoken words: "I don't believe you."

"Mr. del Rosario, your son converted to Islam more than two years ago. Have you spoken with him recently?"

A long pause followed, and Miller could tell the man at the other end of the line was struggling to maintain his composure.

"No," the distraught father replied. "The last time I spoke to him was two years ago. I told him we couldn't afford for him to come home until after he finished his graduate studies."

"Was he upset over that?" Miller asked.

"Yes, he was upset, but I told him his education was more important than spending Christmas with his family—and I have five other children to support and a business to run."

"And you haven't spoken with him in two years?"

"I've written letters and sent him email messages."

"Has he replied or communicated with you in any way?"

"No."

"Mr. del Rosario, has your son ever been in trouble with the police?"

"Never! He has a big heart, my Rosy. Always makes me proud. You must have the wrong boy!"

"Sir, it might turn out that he isn't involved, so…"

Sensing Miller was about to end the call, the father interrupted him by asking for his phone number and email address and then pleading with the agent to keep him updated.

"Sir, please promise me you'll let me know if anything happens to my son. You will, right?"

"Mr. del Rosario, I'll try to keep you posted, but feel free to contact me anytime."

After ending the call, Miller exited the micro-office, walked outside the command post and found Wilson in conversation with other agents near the front entrance to the plant.

"Boss, I spoke with the kid's father," Miller began, "and I'm leaning against him being any kind of psycho killer."

"Tell me more," Wilson replied.

"Rosy didn't even have the guts to tell his father he had converted to Islam and changed his name," Miller said, "and he hasn't communicated with his family since his conversion."

"Any idea why he converted?"

"His father wouldn't pay for him to come home for Christmas a couple of years ago," Miller explained, "and this was his way of getting back at his father."

Thinking it might be time to search Rosy's apartment, Miller asked Wilson if he was ready to "release the hounds."

"Almost," Wilson replied, recognizing Miller's reference to members of his team who, by this time, were chomping at the bit to begin searching the homes of the three prime suspects. "I want to keep everyone here until we finish up the polygraph exams."

31

"Mr. Kastens, would you come with me, please," Lee said after leaning his head into the room where the Gold Star father had been sitting for well over an hour.

Without speaking, Kastens stood and began following Lee into the hallway and to another office.

"We need you to take that polygraph test Agent Wilson mentioned earlier," Lee explained. "It shouldn't take too long."

Acknowledging Lee with a slight groan, Kastens remained silent as he followed the NCIS agent down the hallway to another office.

Many questions filled Kastens' mind as they walked, and one, in particular, floated to the top: "Should I submit myself to the polygraph?" Before he could answer that question to his own satisfaction, he found himself alone inside the exam room, standing a few steps in front of a man he'd never seen before.

George Day had conducted hundreds of polygraph exams during more than twenty-five years in uniform. Typically, he would set up a video camera on a tripod and plug it into a nearby power outlet so that he could record his examinee's every move and evaluate his own work. This day would be no different.

"Have a seat right there, Mr. Kastens," Day began, pointing to an ordinary, armless chair on the other side of the desk that separated the two men. "May I call you Gary?"

"That's fine with me."

"Before we begin the exam or get into any of the technical details, I'm going to check your ID to make sure you are who you say you are. After that, I'll explain what's going to happen during the exam and have you sign a release form—that kind of stuff. Anytime you need to take a break to use the restroom or get a drink of water, just let me know."

Kastens confirmed he was listening with a slight nod of his head.

Day continued by asking Kastens for some form of identification and received the man's Illinois driver's license in return. After taking a look at it, he moved on.

"Now, I need to ask you a few questions about your medical history and any treatments you've had or medications you take that might affect the outcome of your exam. After that, I'll tell you a few things about the polygraph so you have a general understanding of how it works. Then we're going to discuss why you're here, and you'll have a chance to explain anything you might know about any efforts to tamper with products produced at Illinois Chemical.

"After you've had your say, I'll put together a series of yes-or-no questions that will allow you to confirm the things you shared with me. After I load the questions into my computer, I'll read each of them to you so that you won't be surprised when I ask you to answer them during the polygraph exam. Are we good so far?"

Kastens nodded again.

"After we finish reviewing the questions, I'll hook you up to the polygraph and give you a chance to answer the questions—several times each if necessary—until I have enough data upon which to make a solid decision.

"Among the sensors I'll attach to your body, you might find the blood pressure cuff a bit uncomfortable. It'll be inflated for about five minutes at a time and might make your arm fall asleep, but it won't be painful. Any questions so far?"

"No."

"I understand you're nervous, but that's not unexpected, and your nervousness won't change the outcome of the exam," Day continued before explaining details about the release forms Kastens would have to sign and telling him about how the polygraph works. For Kastens, the session reminded him of a junior high school biology class.

"During the polygraph exam, I'll pay particular attention to how your Sympathetic Nervous System responds, because it's the system over which you don't have much control."

Kastens sat motionless, listening to Day ramble for a bit until finally getting to the heart of the matter.

"When people lie on polygraph exams, they do so for one reason and for one reason only: they broke the law, made a mistake or basically did something wrong, and they know they'll be punished if they get caught. Hoping to avoid the consequences of their actions, they lie. Unfortunately for those who lie during a polygraph exam, they can't hide their SNS responses, and they get caught. Questions?"

Kastens shook his head, and Day moved on.

"Gary, I understand you've worked at Illinois Chemical for quite some time. Is that correct?"

"Yes, almost 30 years."

"And you're a shift manager in charge of things like manufacturing products, right?"

"Yes. Day shift."

"And Illinois Chemical makes a number of specialty products, mostly for the printing industry. Is that right?"

"Yes."

"We believe someone at Illinois Chemical tampered with the formula used to make one of those products. Have you ever done something like that?"

"No," Kastens replied calmly.

"Do you know if any of your fellow employees have done that or talked about doing that?"

"No, I don't, but I only manage the day-shift employees."

"Are you telling me you think someone on one of the other shifts might have tampered with a formula?"

"I'm not saying that at all. I'm saying I have no way of knowing what happens during shifts when I'm not working."

"Have you ever done anything during *your* shift that your employer would frown upon or that would get you in trouble?"

"I probably have, but nothing close to criminal. Nothing serious."

Sensing Kastens might be on the verge of making some kind of admission, Day asked, "Can you give me an example?"

"Sure. A couple of times, I was late submitting EPA forms about how we disposed of some outdated chemicals, so I changed the dates on a couple of forms."

Day accepted the answer and continued.

"Now, I'm gonna cover the questions I'll ask you during the test."

Kastens listened but said nothing as Day went through the short list of questions, not expecting any answers.

"The first question is have you ever been involved, in any way, in adding any toxic or poisonous substance to an Illinois Chemical product? And the second question is have you ever altered any Illinois Chemical product so that it became toxic or poisonous?

"That's it, Gary," Day said. "Would you please move over to the exam chair?"

Without saying a word, Kastens stood, walked a few feet across the floor and sat down in a padded, black leather chair with a stainless-steel frame. According to Day, someone had designed it especially for conducting polygraph exams.

In addition to unseen activity sensors built into the seat, the adjustable arms and the black rubber floor pad upon which Kastens couldn't help but place his feet while seated, a number of visible sensors—rubber tubes around his chest and abdomen, a cuff around his left bicep, and wires connected to the fingers of his right hand—would record his breathing, blood pressure and galvanic skin response, respectively.

As Day returned to his seat, he made sure his computer was ready before offering Kastens a final set of instructions.

"You'll need to remain perfectly still in order for the test to be accurate, and you'll need to keep your head still and your eyes focused on the wall in front of you. Understand?"

"Yes."

Before asking the first question, Day also reminded Kastens he would need to respond to each question with a "yes" or a "no" and that there would be pauses between questions.

The polygraph test began, and Day asked each of the questions, in order, four times before being satisfied that he didn't need to ask the questions again. After a few minutes spent examining the results, referred to by polygraphists as charts, Day ended the session.

"That's all for now, Gary," he said before standing, walking around his desk to disconnect Kastens from the blood-pressure cuff and remove the other visible sensors. "Agent Lee is outside and can take you back to your waiting room."

Kastens was relieved to have the test behind him, but nervous Day had not told him whether or not he passed it.

After sending Kastens back to his waiting room, Day called Wilson, who was working inside the command post.

"D.I.," Day said, the acronym for Deception Indicated.

"Are you sure?" Wilson countered.

"That's what the charts tell me."

Per Day's instructions, Lee returned Kastens to his waiting room and waited another fifteen minutes before he retrieved Rosy and escorted him to the polygraph exam room.

When Rosy walked into the room, Day followed the same pre- and post-test steps with the very-nervous young man as he had with Kastens. It was, however, what happened during the exam that left the examiner befuddled.

He had never seen a person perspire as much as Rosy had. Likewise, he had rarely seen a person fidget and squirm and look at the video camera so often. As a result, Day had to review the ground rules more than once and ended up running through the set of test questions six times before concluding he had done as much as possible to ensure accurate results.

Asked if he'd ever been involved, in any way, in adding any toxic or poisonous substance to an Illinois Chemical product, Rosy answered, "No." And when asked if he'd ever added anything to any Illinois Chemical product so that it became toxic or poisonous, he gave the same response.

After reviewing Rosy's charts, Day reached one less-than-helpful conclusion—inconclusive—and shared it with Wilson after sending the Filipino back to his waiting room.

"I'd like to say I could rule him out, but I can't. He was all over the place."

"Okay," Wilson replied. "Let's give Abramov a shot."

✝

"Good afternoon, Mr. Abramov," Day said as his third examinee entered the office fifteen minutes later. "May I call you Burt?"

"Sure. No problem."

Unlike the previous examinees who could best be described as nervous and extremely nervous, respectively, Abramov gave the impression of a man who couldn't have been more relaxed and more confident, seemingly unfazed by the fact his every sound and movement was being recorded and scrutinized.

Day made his offers about water and restroom breaks and verified Abramov's ID in much the same manner as he had twice before, then asked his examinee if he was familiar with the polygraph.

"Certainly, I've heard of the polygraph."

"Have you ever taken a polygraph exam?"

"No, but I have been subjected to many different types of interrogation?"

"Really," Day said before going silent and waiting for Abramov to fill the dead air.

"It was many years ago—before the collapse of the Soviet Union and before I came to America," Abramov said, causing Day to pay close attention.

"Why were you interrogated?"

"Because I liked to hang around with a group of men the communist leaders had declared subversives, you know. In America, you would call such people Tea Partiers, I think."

As he had during his interview with Wilson, Abramov opted against telling Day the whole truth—including the fact he was familiar with several different types of interrogation and had, in fact, witnessed many interrogations during a previous chapter of his life.

Day finished jotting down Abramov's comments and went to work, conducting Abramov's polygraph exam in much the same way he had the two earlier ones—sandwiching it between pre-test and post-test phases. After more than an hour, the exam ended, Lee escorted Abramov to his waiting room, and Day called Wilson.

"Agent Wilson, I've conducted hundreds of poly exams, but I've never had someone beat the machine the way this guy did."

"Explain."

"He said he's never taken a polygraph exam, but I don't believe him. He was too calm and casual, and he passed with ease."

"What do you suggest we do then?"

"I think it's time to try CVSA," Day said.

"I agree."

32

Though investigators at nearly two thousand local and state law enforcement agencies across the country had stopped using the polygraph and made the Computer Voice Stress Analyzer their credibility assessment technology of choice, only a few federal investigators were familiar with CVSA. Wilson was one of them, and Day knew it.

It was after the two met at a CVSA examiners conference two years earlier that Day learned Wilson had become the first law enforcement officer in the Missouri certified to conduct both CVSA and polygraph exams while serving as a sheriff's deputy/detective. Unbeknownst to Day, Wilson had learned something about him during the same event.

A rumor had circulated at the conference about Day being the retired Army Green Beret whose exploits with CVSA had been highlighted in a then-new nonfiction book, *The Clapper Memo*. Not surprisingly, Day had refused to confirm or deny the rumor. As a result, most conference attendees concluded it must be true.

Now, with Day cornered in Effingham, Wilson decided he would try to confirm whether the rumor about him was true.

On a web site run by former and/or retired Special Forces operators, Wilson found a year-old discussion thread about *The Clapper Memo*. It centered on a portion of the book in which the author shared details from his extensive interview with a retired Army Green Beret, whose name could not be revealed for security reasons, about his successful employment of CVSA in combat zones.

According to one thread contributor, the author reported the Green Beret had served in the U.S. Army Special Forces in several distant lands, including Iraq and Kuwait, and had conducted more than five hundred CVSA exams on enemy combatants, suspected terrorists, third-country nationals, and other individuals suspected of being hostile toward Westerners.

According to the same thread contributor, the author reported the Green Beret had credited CVSA with helping him and his brothers-in-arms prevent planned enemy attacks, break up theft and contraband rings, and save American lives. In addition, the author had quoted the Green Beret as saying his success with CVSA began in 2004 and continued for five years—even after top DoD officials had issued no fewer than three memos containing instructions for all DoD personnel to use only the polygraph and after CVSA had proven more effective and reliable.

When one thread participant asked why the Green Beret had kept using CVSA and, in effect, disobeyed orders, another person responded with an answer that appeared to have been based upon something in the book: "He and his boots-on-the-ground commanders knew the Pentagon directives were based on flawed academic studies conducted by pinheads who couldn't produce the one element required to produce accurate CVSA exam results: jeopardy. And we all know saving lives is more important than following orders from f---ing bureaucrats thousands of miles from the front lines of war."

While none of the quiet professionals participating in the thread had mentioned Day by name, the author of the jeopardy comment did refer to the Green Beret in question by the screen name, Knight73. And that tidbit had caught Wilson's eye, because it matched the first portion of a personal email address Wilson had seen spelled out on Day's notepad during the conference.

No doubt about it, Wilson believed Day was *that* Green Beret!

†

It was only after post-Black Monday anger swelled to never-before-seen levels that Americans outside of law enforcement, military and intelligence circles began showing more than a passing interest in any proven alternatives to the polygraph.

Much of their interest arose following national news reports about the alleged involvement of several high-ranking officials at the Departments of Justice and Defense in a massive bribery and corruption scandal. While those early reports emphasized the fact that all of the officials alleged to be involved in the scandal had passed polygraph exams, later reports revealed indisputable paper trail and video evidence—most of which had been collected by freelance investigative reporters and wannabe journalists.

While a few brave souls in Congress highlighted the above-described news reports in long-winded speeches on the House floor, one took things a step further. U.S. Representative Mario Diaz-Balart had one of his staffers contact the author of *The Clapper Memo* and ask for help in arranging to have the Green Beret who had been interviewed for the book (Day) to speak about CVSA during a late-October meeting of the House Appropriations Committee on which the Florida representative served.

When the Green Beret spoke, his words landed mostly on deaf ears, but they did not go completely unnoticed.

FBI Director Mazachek paid attention that day. Though unfamiliar with CVSA before the hearing, she came to believe there had to be something legitimate about the technology if a retired Green Beret was willing to stick his neck out so far in front of members of Congress.

Within thirteen days of Day's testimony, Mazachek had located him, flown him to the capitol and convinced him to join the bureau and help her procure CVSA technology and training for the FBI. It would be one of many "cultural" changes she put into motion after taking the helm.

Both Wilson and Day knew their use of CVSA in such a high-profile case could signal the beginning of the end for the polygraph, but that wasn't their primary objective. Instead, they simply wanted to get to the truth about who and/or what had killed so many Americans. If CVSA could help them reach their goal, then so be it.

33

"Mr. Kastens, I need you to come with me, please," Wilson said after opening the door to the room where the Gold Star dad had been sitting for well over an hour.

"Where are we going?" Kastens said before standing and following Wilson into the hallway.

"It's time for you to take another exam. It shouldn't take long, and it's completely painless."

Though he remained silent as he followed Wilson down the hallway, Kastens had many thoughts run through his mind as he anticipated taking the test Day had felt the need to describe as "completely painless."

Moments later, they reached their destination.

"Right in here," Wilson said before motioning for Kastens to enter the office where Day was waiting, this time seated behind a nondescript wooden desk.

As Kastens entered the room, he expected Wilson to follow him. Instead, Wilson closed the door behind him and remained in the hallway, leaving him alone with Day and the unblinking eye of the video camera as it sat atop a tripod, looking over the examiner's left shoulder toward him.

"Take a seat," Day instructed, prompting Kastens to step toward the empty chair across the desk from the examiner and being to sit down.

"Gary, do me a favor before you sit down," Day said without standing or reaching his hand out to shake. "Move that chair so it's directly opposite mine."

Kastens complied.

"That's good," Day said, prompting Kastens to sit. "Again, my name is George Day, and I'll be conducting your truth-verification exam today."

"I thought we were done with tests?" Kastens remarked, somewhat snarkily.

"We're simply covering all our bases, Gary," Day replied. "Again, I have water out on the table for you in case you get thirsty. My only request is that you don't drink it during the actual exam. Deal?"

"Sure."

"If you need to use the restroom anytime during this process, just let me know."

Though uncertain about what was about to take place, Kastens believed firmly that the truth would win out, so he didn't object or decide to "lawyer up."

"Before we begin, I need to take care of a little red tape that's required for this test," Day continued. "I need to see your ID again, and then I need you to sign this release."

Kastens showed Day his driver's license as he had earlier in the day, and Day transferred the pertinent details to a form before handing it back to Kastens. In turn, Kastens signed his name on a line next to a red X Day had scribbled near the bottom of the form.

"Can you refresh me as to why you're here today, Gary?"

At first astonished by the question, Kastens realized it was part of the drill and decided to play along.

"Agent Wilson thinks someone tampered with something we make here, and you're trying to figure out if I had anything to do with it. Whatever 'it' is."

"That's right," Day continued. "Now, let me tell you about what we'll be doing today. Did you notice I called what we're doing today a truth-verification exam rather than a lie detector test?"

Kastens nodded.

"That's because I personally feel like you've come in here to tell me the truth, and I like to give everyone the benefit of the doubt," Day continued. "I want to give you the benefit of the doubt. Instead of a polygraph machine, which some people erroneously refer to as a lie detector, I'll be using a different tool; basically, it's a laptop computer that's equipped with a proprietary software program that follows our conversation and can tell me whether or not a person is being deceptive as he answers my questions."

Day didn't go deeper into explaining how CVSA works by measuring frequency changes in the human voice shown to be indicative of stress. Instead, he stuck to the basics.

"Unlike the polygraph, this technology isn't susceptible to countermeasures," Day explained, "and, best of all, it's painless. So if you stick to the truth, everybody wins. Ready?"

"The truth shall set you free," Kastens replied, remembering the words he had heard so many decades earlier as a young boy attending Vacation Bible School at a local church.

"Now, we all make mistakes once in a while," Day explained. "We tell little white lies, make errors in judgment, act out of character, you know, once in a while. Right?"

"I suppose we do."

"The key to your success with this exam is for you to be honest and upfront with me at every step of the way, because a lot of important folks—judges, attorneys, prosecutors and so forth—will be seeing the results."

"The truth shall set you free," Kastens repeated, this time with a thicker dose of sarcasm in his voice. "I get it."

"Good. So, if you are, or were, involved in adding any toxic or poisonous substance to any Illinois Chemical product, it's important for you to be upfront with me about it."

Kastens said nothing.

"You might have noticed over the years that big Hollywood stars, pro athletes, CEOs and politicians admit their mistakes all the time and receive forgiveness, so it's important for you to be upfront about everything if you are, or were, involved in some kind of illegal or criminal activity."

"I understand."

"Before I joined the bureau, I had opportunities to use CVSA technology to conduct exams on a lot of interesting people, including members of the Taliban and al-Qaeda. The one thing each of them now shares in common is that they all ended up telling me the truth."

Though nervous and insulted about being lumped in with Islamic terrorists, Kastens said nothing.

"Again, if you are, or were, involved in adding any toxic or poisonous substance to any Illinois Chemical product, it's important for you to be upfront with me about it. You'll do that, right?"

"Yes," Kastens answered.

"It's certainly going to look better for you if you do," Day said before pausing to stare at his computer screen for a few seconds before continuing.

"Alright. You know, sometimes I find people who would rather skip answering a bunch of questions and just tell me the truth," Day continued. "So, if I ask if you've ever altered any Illinois Chemical product so that it became toxic or poisonous, how would you answer that question?"

"I would say I have not."

"As I mentioned earlier, stuff does happen and people make mistakes, errors in judgment and so on. We all do. I want you to know, however, that when we finish with this exam, I'm going to know whether or not you've been honest with me."

"I understand," Kastens said, though he had not been asked to respond.

"So, if I ask you if you've ever altered any Illinois Chemical product so that it became toxic or poisonous, how will you answer?"

"I'll say no, of course!" Kastens replied while growing more irritated with each passing moment.

"As part of the exam, I'm also going to ask you some easy, yes-or-no questions both of us already know the answers to. Just for practice, you can go ahead and answer them now," Day said. "Are you in the state of Illinois?"

"Yes."

"Are you sitting down?"

"Yes."

"Are the lights on inside this room?"

"Yes."

"Is today Tuesday?"

"Yes."

"And is your name Gary Kastens?"

"Yes."

"Great," Day said. "Are we doing okay, now?"

"I'm okay."

"There will also be some questions such as, 'What color is that wall?' Go ahead and answer."

"Beige."

"During the exam this morning, I'm going to ask you if the color of that wall is beige, and I want you to answer with a lie," Day explained. "Another question I'll ask is if you've ever driven faster than the posted speed limit. We all have, right?"

Kastens offered a less-than-enthusiastic nod of agreement.

"When I ask you today if you've ever driven a car faster than the posted speed limit, I want you to think back to a time when you were going ten to twenty miles per hour above the posted speed limit and then spotted a police cruiser waiting to catch you on the side of the road. Understand?"

"Yes, I think so."

"Okay, please know I won't ask any trick questions. No tricks."

With that, Day picked up the business end of a clip-on microphone that was connected at the opposite end of a six-foot cable to his laptop computer.

"Gary, clip this onto the front of your shirt there, please."

As soon as Kastens had done it, Day asked him to move it up another couple of inches, and they continued to the next step.

"I just want to make sure everything is working properly so that, if you're being truthful with me, you'll pass the test," Day said, "because I want you to pass and, as long as you're completely truthful, you have nothing to worry about."

Day went through the handful of questions again and received the appropriate answers before informing Kastens that everything was working fine.

"Any questions before we start?"

"No."

"One last thing: remind me of the two questions I asked you to lie about."

"The color of the wall and the speed-limit question."

"Okay, great! Let's begin. Is your name Gary Kastens?"

"Yes."

"Is the color of the wall beige?"

"No."

"Is today Tuesday?"

"Yes."

"Have you ever been involved, in any way, in adding any toxic or poisonous substance to an Illinois Chemical product?"

"No."

"Are the lights on in this room?"

"Yes."

"Have you ever altered a Illinois Chemical product so that it became toxic or poisonous?"

"No."

"Are you sitting down?"

"Yes."

"Have you ever driven faster than the posted speed limit?"

"No."

"Are you in the state of Illinois?"

"Yes."

"Alright, that marks the end of the first half of the test. Now, I'm going to ask you the same questions again. Over the years, we've found that stress will increase in a person who is being dishonest and decrease in a person who is being honest. Before we start again, please remind me of the two questions I asked you to lie about?"

"The wall color and driving over the speed limit."

"Perfect. Let's begin."

Day went on to ask the same questions in the same order and received the same answers.

"We're done, Gary. Now, you can return to the office you came from."

Day led Kastens to the door, and Lee escorted him back to the spartan office where he had already spent so much time by himself that morning. Then Wilson walked in to chat with Day.

"How'd he do?" Wilson asked Day, who was busy returning the "hot seat" to the spot where it had been before Kastens had arrived.

"He seemed a little perturbed at being put through the process, but he didn't lie," Day said. "Flying colors, I'd say."

Wilson hoped Day was right.

34

Having spent much of the day trying to calm his nerves, Rosy became increasingly nervous as he heard footsteps approach from down the hall and stop outside the door seconds before it opened.

"Rosy, we're ready for your next exam," said Wilson after he took one step into the room and looked at its occupant. "Follow me, please."

"But I already took an exam," Rosy objected softly, a bit of confusion in his voice.

"This is a different type of exam," Wilson explained without adding details. Rosy stood and followed the FBI agent, hoping the test—whatever it was—would help him clear his name.

The duo reached the office, and Wilson left Rosy with Day, who was waiting behind the desk, prepared to administer his second CVSA exam of the day.

"Good afternoon, Rosy."

As he had with Kastens, Day invited Rosy to sit down and, moments later, asked him to move his chair over so that it was directly opposite his. Again, Rosy complied.

"Again, my name is George Day," he explained without standing up or extending a hand to shake. The introduction was followed by a brief note about restroom breaks and the same explanation by Day about how water was available but not to be enjoyed during the exam.

"Before we start, I need to do some paperwork again," Day continued. "Do you have your ID again, Rosy?"

Without speaking, he handed Day his student ID card. A nervous glance at the video camera followed.

"Refresh me. Why no driver's license?" Day asked.

"I don't drive."

"Right." Day glanced at the card, pretending he'd forgotten that fact since giving Rosy the polygraph exam earlier in the day. "Now, if you can just sign this waiver, we can get started."

Without reading the form, Rosy signed it and handed it back to Day, prompting the examiner to ask his first question.

"Rosy, can you tell me why you're here today?"

"I don't really know," he replied before glancing at the camera and back again.

"Didn't Agent Wilson tell you something about the reason why he and his men are here today?"

"Oh, yes. It has something to do with questions about tampering with formulas or committing any crimes while working here."

"That's right, so let me tell you what we'll be doing in just a minute."

As he had with Kastens, Day explained the differences between the CVSA exam he would administer to Rosy soon and the polygraph exam the young man had taken earlier in the day before launching a short discussion of human foibles.

"Have you ever made a mistake, told a lie or acted out of character, Rosy?"

"Of course. Everyone has."

"That's right. We all make mistakes. And if you've made any of these mistakes, the most important thing you can do is be completely honest and upfront with me about them during this exam, right?"

"I don't know what mistakes you think I've made, but I will answer all of your questions truthfully."

"Good, because the results of this exam are going to be seen by a lot of people, including FBI investigators like Agent Wilson, federal prosecutors, judges, attorneys and so forth. So, if you are, or have been, involved in any kind of illegal or criminal activity, it's important for you to be upfront with me about it, right?"

"Yes, sir."

As he had with Kastens, Day encouraged Rosy to follow the lead of so many famous people who, after confessing to doing wrong, were forgiven. After that, he again recalled his CVSA experiences around the world with high-profile Muslims who ended up telling him the truth. The stories, in turn, produced feelings in Rosy nearly identical to those Kastens had felt. In short, he felt as if Day believed he was some kind of terrorist.

After pausing to let those feelings circulate in Rosy's mind, Day continued the pre-exam conversation and received all of the right answers, all of which were accompanied by voice, body language and emotional indicators appropriate to the subject matter.

Next, Day offered an explanation of how the yes-or-no questioning would work and included specifics about how the young man would be asked to lie in response to two questions. Though he did not mention it to Rosy, one of those questions turned out to be different than one he asked Kastens. Because Rosy had told Day he did not drive, the examiner decided he couldn't ask about driving over the speed limit and, instead, asked the question, "Am I wearing a watch?"

During the first run through the questions, Rosy answered affirmatively to those about his name, about the door being closed, about the lights being on in the room and about whether he was sitting down. In addition, he gave negative responses to questions about the color of the walls and about whether Day was wearing a watch—despite the fact Day's watch was clearly visible on his wrist.

Most importantly, Rosy denied any involvement in and/or knowledge of efforts to tamper with products made at Illinois Chemical.

Day stood up, walked around his desk and removed the microphone clipped to Rosy's shirt before opening the door and speaking to his examinee.

"Thank you, Rosy. Agent Wilson will discuss the results with you when he's ready."

Soon after Lee began escorting the young man back to his waiting room, Wilson walked into the office and asked Day a question as he repositioned the interviewee's chair for the second time. "Well?"

"He appeared nervous," Day replied, "but his charts are totally clean, and he's not being deceptive."

"Thanks, George." With only one prime suspect remaining, Wilson knew he was either on the right track or far from it.

Now leaning back into the doorway of Day's temporary office, Wilson told the CVSA examiner to take a break while he checked his messages and made a phone call. "I'll have Jack bring Mr. Abramov down in thirty minutes."

35

While his fellow agents had been busy with the first two CVSA exams, Miller had kept himself busy inside the command post, checking message traffic for leads from agents around the country. One message from an unexpected sender caught his attention:

Agent Wilson: I had my executive officer do some digging, and he found one of my lab employees, ALI IBRAGIM, made 14 calls during the past year to two phone numbers in the 217 area code. Nine of the calls were made during the month of June, and five of those were made to a single number at Illinois Chemical in Effingham, IL. I've attached the phone data as PDF #1. I've attached more information about Mr. Ibragim as PDF #2. Also, it appears one-dozen vials (about 85 grams each) of the material we talked about is missing from the CDC inventory. It was listed on one report as having been incinerated, but other documents that are part of the paper trail don't show evidence it had. Please let me know if you need anything else. Hope it helps. Let me know if you need anything else.—Dennis McKinney, M.D., M.P.H., and Ph.D

Quickly realizing the importance of the message from the CDC director, Miller returned to the Illinois Chemical building in search of Christie. He found the plant manager in the break room where, after cooling his heels for more than an hour, he was more than willing to help Miller if, that is, it meant he'd be able to get up and walk around. Contrary to what his sizable girth might lead one to believe, Christie had long ago embraced the management-by-walking-around approach to leadership. Sitting around an office was not his "cup of tea."

The two men walked to Christie's office, and Miller closed the door behind them.

"I need help understanding your phone system," Miller said. "I know of nine phone calls made from an out-of-state phone number to the main number at Illinois Chemical. Do you have a way of finding out where the calls coming into the building were routed?"

"I'm not sure I can without looking at the phone bill for June," Christie replied, "and we don't get that until next month. Even then, I won't be able to tell you who was actually speaking on the phone; I'll just know which phone was used."

Expecting that might be the case, Miller asked Christie for his phone service provider's name in case it became necessary to subpoena the phone records sooner. Christie gave him the information without delay, and Miller escorted the man back to the break room.

Information in hand, Miller returned to the command post to find Wilson and Lee inside. Both had taken up positions inside separate micro-offices, but only Wilson had closed his sliding glass door.

"Jack, we have work to do," Miller said before describing the content of the message received from Dr. McKinney. "We need to compare five non-Illinois Chemical phone numbers dialed by Ali Ibragim in Atlanta to the contact information we have for Illinois Chemical employees."

"Who is Ali in Atlanta?" Lee asked.

Miller showed him the message from Dr. McKinney.

"Doesn't the FBI have a way of running the numbers to find out who owns the phone numbers and stuff like that?" Lee asked after reading the message.

"Yes, and I've already sent a request to Quantico," Miller replied, "and while we wait for them to run the numbers, we're gonna check 'em out and see if we get the same results."

Miller divided the dozen or so pages of contact information into two equal stacks and, along with instructions to begin comparing them to area code 217 phone numbers written down on his note pad, handed one stack to Lee. After several minutes of looking, neither had found any matches.

"Because that didn't yield any fruit, it's time to play a little cat-and-mouse game," Miller said before reaching into a nearby cabinet door and removing something small and black from a small plastic container. Lee figured out what it was when he saw the words, THROWAWAY PHONES, written with a black marker on faded-yellow masking tape.

"We use these when we don't want the people we're calling to realize who's calling them," Miller explained. "If someone answers, we try to develop a rapport with them and keep them talking long enough to trace the call. Then we pay 'em a visit."

Lee followed Miller into the micro-office where he had been working moments earlier and watched as the veteran agent nodded to a nearby call-trace technician before closing the door and dialing the first of five numbers on his list. After four rings, Miller pushed the SPEAKER button on the phone up so his colleague could listen along with him to the recorded voice of a female: "You've reached Express Parcels. Please hold for the next available agent."

Miller ended the call without waiting for an agent. Instead, he wrote a short note on the screen of his iPad: *Express Shipping. Used to ship TS-213?*

Next, he tapped on the door, nodded to the technician and followed the same steps with the second number, but reached a different kind of recording: "The number you dialed is no longer in service. If you think you've reached this number in error, please try again." Miller did try again and got the same result.

After dialing the third number, Miller heard the phone ring three times before a woman answered. "Hello."

"Yes, ma'am. I'm trying to reach Mrs. Higgins. Do I have the right number?" Miller asked.

"Mrs. Wiggins? I don't know a Mrs. Wiggins," the woman said, giving Miller the distinct impression she was old and hard of hearing.

"I'm looking for Mrs. Wiggins. She lives on Pine Street."

"I don't know Mrs. Higgins, but what does that have to do with my feet?"

Miller ended the call politely, telling the woman he must have dialed the wrong number. Then it hit him.

The number he had dialed was, save one digit, identical to the number he still needed to check. Quickly, he dialed the fourth phone number and heard someone answer on the third ring.

"This is Manny," said the voice on the other end of the line.

Though drowned out by loud music in the background, the voice sounded to Miller as if it belonged to a young man.

"Hello, my name is Omar," Miller replied. "I'm transferring down from Chicago and hope you might help me."

"How did you get my number, Omar?"

"I was walking around the campus this morning and asked a young guy who looked kind of like me if he knew anyone in the Muslim Students League," Miller explained, weaving a tale as he went along. "The guy—I don't remember his name—gave me your number."

"Cool," Manny replied, no longer concerned about the validity of the caller's identity. "Are you a Muslim, Omar?"

"Of course, I am. Salam," Miller said, recalling one of a handful of Arabic phrases—an informal greeting—he'd learned over the years.

"May peace, mercy and blessings of Allah be upon you," Manny replied.

"And upon you," said Miller.

"How soon do you plan to transfer, Omar?"

"I just enrolled and will begin classes next month."

"Okay, hey, I'm tied up this afternoon, but I'd like to meet you tonight if you'll be around."

"Sure. When and where?"

"Let me call you back in a few minutes," Manny said, ending the call before "Omar" could get out another word.

†

"While we wait for him to call, let's see if we can connect this number with a first and last name," Miller told Lee.

"I think I can do better than that," Lee replied. "Remember the information I found online about the Muslim Students League chapter at the college?"

"I'm listening," Miller answered.

"One of the guys in charge was Mohamed Abu Nadal, right? And when I was in the room during the interview of Rosy, Agent Wilson mentioned the guy's name and Rosy said Mohamed Abu Nadal goes by the nickname, Manny."

"You're probably right, Jack, but we have to be absolutely sure it's the same guy," Miller cautioned while curious to see what tricks his young counterpart might play.

"Okay, hold on," Lee said.

Rather than use any proven FBI protocol or technique for locating a person by a phone number, Lee pulled up a popular online search engine on his smartphone, entered the phone number into the search block and waited for results. Within seconds, dozens of results described as "relevant" appeared on his screen. Several appeared to be promising, because they showed the phone number as being connected to the website of the MSL chapter at Benson Wood. After checking three of the top results, however, Lee was confident enough to share his findings with Miller.

"I found him! Mohamed Abu Nadal is the MSL point of contact at the college, and this phone number appears next to his name."

"Good work," Miller replied, impressed with how fast Lee found the information. "Any physical address for the guy?"

"Nothing comes up right away, but I bet Rosy can tell us where to find him."

"Right," Miller said. "Let's go talk to him."

The duo made their way back to the office where Rosy was waiting anxiously for something—anything—to help relieve his stress.

"Rosy," Miller said upon entering the room, "I'm Agent Miller, and I need to ask you a question."

"Okay," the young man replied, his nervousness on display after the two men who'd been present during his polygraph exam reappeared.

"Where does Manny live?" Miller asked.

"You mean Mohamed Abu Nadal, right?"

"Yes."

"He lives in the same building where I live. Same apartment—702 East Broadway Street, Apartment 2-B."

After Miller confirmed the address to ensure it matched the contact information the company had for Rosy, he and Lee left the room. Before sharing the news with Wilson, the veteran agent decided one more call was in order.

With Lee by his side, Miller returned to the command post to dial the fifth non-Illinois Chemical phone number. Like the others, it belonged to someone in area code 217 who had received calls from the CDC employee during the previous month.

Once inside and behind a closed micro-office door with Lee, Miller nodded to the call-trace tech, dialed the number, and listened to it ring.

"Agent Miller, look!" he said seconds later as he pointed toward a phone on a shelf just outside the micro-office door.

Among the nearly three-dozen phones collected from Illinois Chemical employees and run through airport-style security screening (i.e., x-rays and swabbing for explosives and chemical residues) before being transported to the command post for temporary safekeeping, one phone had lit up—a sign it was receiving a call.

"I think we have a live one," Miller said, "but let's make sure."

He ended the call and hit the REDIAL button on his phone. Seconds later, the same phone on the shelf lit up again, indicating it was receiving a call.

"Bingo!" Lee said.

After ending the call, Miller exited the micro-office and picked up the suspect phone—a ten-year-old Motorola flip phone—and began reading from the tag that had been placed on it hours earlier. "It was turned in by Abramov, Burtran F."

Armed with the new information, Miller took two steps and tapped on the glass of the other micro-office where Wilson was hard at work.

"Good news, I hope?" Wilson said after sliding open the door to his micro-office.

"News? Yes. Good news? Probably," Miller replied. "We tracked down the names of two individuals; both are tied to personal phone numbers in the 217 area code, and both received phone calls from the same CDC employee in Atlanta. One of the men works here, while the other is a student at the local university."

"What's the name of the employee?"

"Burtran F. Abramov."

"And the student?"

"Mohamed Abu Nadal. His friends call him Manny."

"Good work, gentlemen," Wilson said, his mind trying to connect dots as he exited the command post. "How did you track that down?"

"Among the thousands of messages you've received today, one came from Dr. McKinney at the CDC," Miller explained as he opened the message from McKinney and displayed it on his iPad before handing the device to Wilson. "He included phone numbers made by a lab employee at CDC to this area code. We double-checked the numbers and expect 'em to be confirmed by the folks at Quantico soon."

Wilson read and processed the information for a full two minutes before saying another word.

"It appears our Dr. McKinney deserves every letter after his name," Wilson said, referencing the three scholarly acronyms that appeared after the CDC director's last name in his email signature block. "Let me know what else you turn up."

With that, Wilson closed his micro-office door and made another call to his boss at FBI Headquarters.

"Anything yet?" Mazachek asked her lead investigator.

"The first two CVSA exams showed no deception, but I expect the third might."

"Why?"

"Because I just learned from Dr. McKinney at CDC that one of his people—a lab worker with access to the thallium—made more than a dozen phone calls to numbers in the Effingham area code during the past year."

"Who did he call?"

"Nine of fourteen calls to the 217 area code were placed during the month of June. Out of those, five were made to someone at Illinois Chemical. The other four were made to others in the area code, and that's where things get interesting."

"Keep going."

"So far, we've been able to determine one call was made to suspect number three, Burt Abramov, another was made to a friend of suspect number two, and a third was made to a shipping company in Effingham."

"So what's your next step, Joe-L?"

"First, I'll share this information with George Day and see if it changes the way he wants to approach the CVSA exam on Abramov."

"Need anything else from my end?"

"No ma'am. We're good for now."

"Okay, Joe-L. Keep me posted."

Though Wilson got out a "thank you," he wasn't sure his boss heard it before she ended the call.

As he exited the micro-office, Wilson asked Miller and Lee to join him as he walked back to the office where Day was waiting to conduct his third CVSA exam of the day.

36

"Change of plans, George. It seems we've learned more about Mr. Abramov," Wilson said as he entered the CVSA exam room.

"I'm all ears," Day replied.

"He received a call from the man we think supplied the thallium that was mixed into the batch of latex at Illinois Chemical. We also learned Manny, the college buddy Rosy mentioned as playing a big role in his conversion to Islam, received a call from the same man."

"So, rather than ask Abramov if he's ever been involved in shady dealings at Illinois Chemical, do you want me to focus on the phone calls?" Day asked.

"I want to know what you think, George. If you think it might scare him into lawyering up, let's stick with the original set of questions."

Leaning forward in his chair, Day surprised Wilson with his reply.

"I recommend we stick with the originals and, after I finish the first CVSA exam, we can ask him about the phone calls. If we think it's necessary after that, we can conduct another exam. If you're on the right track, I think he'll be more afraid of answering questions that link him directly to the supplier."

"Alright, George, I'll take your advice. Let me know as soon as you're done with him," Wilson said.

Wilson and Miller returned to the command post while Lee retrieved Abramov from his waiting room and turned him over to Day.

"Good afternoon, Burt," Day said from behind his desk as Abramov entered the office.

As he had during each of the previous two CVSA exams, Day remained seated and did not reach his hand out to shake. In addition, he asked Abramov to move his chair slightly as he was about to sit down.

"That's fine," Day said. "Again, my name is George Day and I'll be conducting your exam today. I've set out a bottle of water for you in case you get thirsty, but ask that you don't drink from it during the exam. Okay?"

"Sure. No problem," Abramov replied, noticing the red light on the video camera as it recorded everything.

"If you need to use the restroom anytime during the exam, just let me know."

As Abramov nodded his understanding, Day sensed his examinee was feeling a bit less confident than he had during the polygraph exam earlier in the day.

"Before we begin, Burt, I need to take care of a formality again. Can I see your driver's license, please?"

Abramov reached into the front left pocket of his slacks and removed it from his tri-fold leather wallet before handing it to Day who, in turn, transferred pertinent details from it to the form.

"Okay, now I need you to sign the form," Day said, using his right index finger to point to a line next to a red X he'd scribbled on the paper. "It says you agree to tell the truth under penalty of law."

"I need a pen," Abramov said, prompting Day to hand his pen to the man who then signed the form without reading it.

"Tell me why you're here, Burt."

"For the same reason you made me take a polygraph test. You're investigating a mass-murder scheme or something like that."

"Yes, we are conducting an investigation," Day continued. "Now, let me give you an idea of what we'll be doing here this afternoon."

"Okay."

"You may have noticed earlier that I described what we're going to do today as a truth-verification exam rather than a polygraph exam."

"Yes, I noticed that."

Day talked about how he liked to give people the benefit of the doubt before describing the basic differences between the polygraph and CVSA.

As Abramov continued to listen, he began to realize he was about to face something much different than the polygraph machine with which he was so familiar.

"I'm using CVSA, because it's more accurate and more reliable than the polygraph, and it's not susceptible to any countermeasures like the polygraph is," Day explained. "I can assure you, however, that it's completely painless and, if you stick to the truth, we all win. You agree?"

"Sure, no problem," Abramov said as beads of sweat formed on his brow.

"I've learned over the years that everyone is human, and we all make mistakes, Burt. We tell little white lies, we make judgment errors, and we do things we usually don't do. Once in a while, right?"

Abramov nodded slowly.

"For you to be successful during this exam, I need you to be honest as you answer each question," Day continued, "because a lot of people—at the FBI, in the court system and all over the place—will see the results of this exam."

"Like I said before, no problem," said Abramov, his anxiety increasing by the minute.

"So, if you know anything that might help Agent Wilson and his men with their investigation, it's important for you to be upfront with me about it. Okay?"

Abramov nodded again.

"Hollywood celebrities, professional athletes, CEOs and politicians admit their mistakes all the time and are forgiven by the public, so it's important for you to be open and honest with me today, especially if you know something that would be of value to Agent Wilson."

"I understand. When will the test begin?"

Day continued as if he'd not heard Abramov verbalize his impatience.

"Before I joined the FBI, I conducted CVSA exams on a lot of interesting and unusual people, Burt, including members of the Taliban and al-Qaeda and detainees at Guantanamo Bay. I even had the chance to interview some of Saddam Hussein's friends—Remember the 'Deck of Cards' in Iraq? Thanks to CVSA, every one of them ended up telling me the truth."

Abramov said nothing as myriad thoughts raced through his mind, especially after Day had the nerve to lump him in with Islamic jihadists and a dead Iraqi dictator.

"Again, if you know something, just tell me," Day continued. "It's very important for you to be honest and upfront with me. You'll do that, right?"

"Yes."

"Everything will turn out much better for you as long as you cooperate."

As he had during the previous exams, Day stared at his computer screen every so often to allow his message to soak in.

"Sometimes, Burt, I find people would rather skip having to answer a laundry list of questions and just tell me the truth. So, if I ask you if you've ever been involved, in any way, in adding a toxic or poisonous substance to any product made at Illinois Chemical, how will you answer that question?"

"I will tell you I didn't do that!" Abramov replied with a recognizable air of contempt.

"As I mentioned earlier, stuff happens. People sometimes make mistakes. At the end of this exam, you need to know that I *will* know whether or not you've been honest with me."

"I un-der-stand," Abramov said, exaggerating each syllable.

"What if I ask you if you've ever altered an Illinois Chemical product so that it became toxic or poisonous?"

"I will say I didn't do that!"

Day walked Abramov through the list of nine yes-or-no questions, including the two critical ones, three times—once for practice and twice for real—and heard the same responses during each round.

"That's it, Burt. Agent Wilson and I will discuss the results with you shortly. Meanwhile, you can step outside."

Struggling to appear relaxed, Abramov waited in the hallway and watched as Wilson arrived and entered the room, carrying only his iPad.

"Well?" Wilson asked.

"As far as tampering with the latex is concerned, I'm afraid he's not our man," Day explained. "He's just like the others."

"We must be missing something. Did you ever run into any cases like this while you were using CVSA in the Sandbox, Mr. Knight73?"

"Yes, I did," Day replied. "And, by the way, you're quite the detective, Agent Wilson." Day was impressed Wilson had connected the dots and figured out his online identity. He had never knowingly shared it with anyone.

Wilson looked at Day with an inquisitive expression on his face and said, "Can you tell me about any of those cases?"

"Sure," Day began. "I had a guy in Iraq who was the driver for an Iraqi Special Forces colonel, and I suspected he was working as an informant for forces loyal to Saddam Hussein and his crew.

"When I asked the guy if he'd relayed any information about a pending attack to an enemy contact, he said he had not even after we'd caught him red-handed with a phone that he wasn't supposed to have. It was only after we subjected ninety six people—including the colonel, his sergeant major and his driver—to CVSA exams that we were able to blame the colonel for letting the enemy know we were coming."

"What about our three prime suspects? Do any of them— or someone close to them—have a reason to lash out?" Wilson asked Day after hearing his war story.

"Kastens strikes me as too much of a loner," said Lee, answering the question aimed at Day and continuing after no one stopped him, "and I could see one of Rosy's new Muslim friends as a possible suspect, but my gut tells me it's probably someone close to Burt Abramov."

"Go on," Wilson replied, impressed with Lee's thought process as well as his willingness to speak his mind.

"Abramov seems to be a bit of a hothead," Lee continued, "and someone who knows him well might try to capitalize on that for personal gain. For what exactly, I don't know."

"George, any thoughts?"

"The most-obvious possibility, if we follow Jack's train of thought, is Burt's ex-wife," Day said, "but I'm a little fuzzy when it comes to her having the means, motive and opportunity to pull it off."

✝

As more minutes passed, Abramov found himself growing increasingly uncomfortable about what might happen during his next interaction with the FBI. Then the door opened, and Lee asked him to return to his seat inside the room as Wilson and Day eyeballed him.

Looking away from the agents, Abramov turned his attention to the red light on the video camera and took a deep breath as he sat in the same chair he'd used during his CVSA exam.

"We need to talk, Burt," Wilson said.

"Sure. I'd like to get this whole mess cleared up."

"Okay, Burt, I'm going to proceed from this point forward on the premise you've been telling me the truth. Deal?"

"But I have been telling you the truth!"

Ignoring Abramov's brief statement, Wilson began pursuing a new theory.

"Burt, is there anyone in your life who would like to do you harm?"

"Besides my wife? I don't think so."

"Tell me about your wife, Burt."

"She's what people in my homeland call a 'gham-sag'—a witch-human," Abramov began, "able to depart from her body and haunt others, including me."

Ignoring the paranormal tilt of the man's statement, Wilson pressed for more details. "Why would your wife want to do you harm, Burt?"

"Because I made her leave Chechnya with me," he replied while looking down at the reflection of his face in his well-polished shoes. "She's held it against me ever since."

"Why didn't she just leave you and go back?"

"That's not the way we do things as Muslims. I wouldn't allow it, and her family couldn't have taken her back."

"So why did you go through with the divorce?"

"Because I had no say in the matter, and she knew that. In fact, I think she began planning for it the day we set foot in this country."

"Why didn't you have a say, Burt?"

"Three years ago, she told me she wanted a divorce and, soon after that, I found out she had taken almost all of the money out of our savings to pay for her divorce lawyer—a very expensive divorce lawyer whose commercials are on television all the time! When I realized I couldn't afford to fight Ruth and her lawyer, I signed the papers."

"What kind of ruling did the judge make?"

"She got half of everything I owned, plus half of everything I make each month," Abramov said before pausing as if still in shock. "Since the divorce and Black Monday, I've become a slave—to Ruth *and* to Uncle Sam!"

"Who got the children?"

"We both did. Six months after the divorce was finalized, we went to Family Court, and Judge Cotton granted us five-two-five custody. That's when Ruth became very angry."

"Five-two-five. That's pretty much equal custody, right?"

"Yes. Judge Cotton named me the Monday-and-Tuesday-nights parent and Ruth is the Wednesday-and-Thursday-nights parent. I get the kids every other weekend."

"You said something earlier, Burt. Tell me what makes you think Ruth had been planning the divorce for a long time."

"Because she's considered me a coward ever since we left Chechnya, and she's told me a million times she doesn't want her children raised by a coward."

"How do you know she took the money out of your savings?"

"Because she was the only person who could have done it," he explained, growing more animated and incensed with each reference to her that came out of his mouth. "Only she and I had access to the account information."

Pacing back and forth now, Wilson paused briefly before asking his next question. "What makes Ruth tick, Burt?"

"Living here so long, Ruth has become completely Westernized, even having a Facebook account and a Twitter—whatever that is," he said, not familiar with the social networking tool known as Twitter which allows people to share their snippets of their lives in 140-character messages known as tweets. "She's more interested in watching television than she is in attending to the needs of the household."

"Does she have any friends in town or people she socializes with in person?"

"Of course, she does! Have you seen her, Agent Wilson? She uses her beauty to open many doors."

"Before the divorce, did she ever tell you about her day when you got home from work?"

"No. Never."

"Okay, Burt, we're done for now," Wilson said. "Jack, take him back to his waiting room."

37

After waiting a few moments for Abramov to be out of earshot, Wilson turned toward Miller and Day. "Gentlemen, I think it's time we release the rest of the employees and--"

Wilson stopped in mid-sentence when he heard a phone ring and saw Miller give the universal sign to be quiet—his index finger raised to his lips—and then made sure the door to the room was shut before removing the throwaway phone from his coat pocket and answering the call on the third ring.

"Omar," Miller told the caller, making no effort to disguise his voice. *After all, what does a Muslim sound like?*

"Salam," said the caller.

"May peace, mercy and blessings of Allah be upon you," Miller replied.

"And upon you," Manny countered.

"Can you meet me at 8:30 in the prayer room at the Student Union?"

"I can, but how will I recognize you?"

"I'll be wearing a red barong," the caller replied, giving no thought to the possibility Omar might not know that a barong was an embroidered shirt traditionally worn by Filipino men.

"Okay, I'll see you there," Miller said before hanging up abruptly.

"Was that who I think it was?" Wilson asked.

"If you're thinking it was Mohamed Abu Nadal—Manny for short—the answer is yes, and he wants to meet me in the student union prayer room at eight."

"I think it would be wise to intercept him before he enters the student union," said Day, the only man in the room who had experience living and working in a predominantly Muslim environment. "No matter what, we need to keep him out of the prayer room."

"Before we head over there, we need to talk to someone familiar with the landscape," Wilson said.

Everyone in the room knew who that someone was, and Wilson led the way as they walked down the hallway to the room where Rosy was killing time. Lee joined them en route.

"Rosy, we need your help," Wilson said as he entered the room to find the Filipino sleeping on the carpeted floor.

"What's wrong?" he replied, wiping his eyes.

"How many entrances are there to the Student Union at the college?"

"Three, I think."

"Which one would you use if you were coming from your apartment?"

"The one closest to the gym. On Benson Wood Avenue. Why?"

Wilson and his colleagues walked out and returned to the CVSA exam room without answering Rosy's question.

"Jack, I need you to become a Muslim college student," Wilson said, turning to face the NCIS agent.

"You want me to meet Manny at the Student Union?"

"Yes, you're the only one of us who's young enough to pull it off, but you can't go dressed like that."

"Let's lose the jacket and tie," Miller added.

"And move the gun," said Day, thinking the holstered SIG Sauer P229 semi-automatic pistol might cause Manny to think Lee wasn't a college student. "Take off the holster and stick the Sig in the small of your back, under your shirt."

"Anything else, gentlemen?" Lee asked sarcastically.

"That's it, Jack," Wilson replied, "and all you have to do is meet with him outside the entrance and confirm it's him. When you each out to shake his hand, we'll take that as our signal to join the party. Got it?"

"Yes, sir," Lee replied, excited about taking on the first undercover assignment of his young career.

Realizing he had only fifty-five minutes until the meeting was set to take place at the college almost five miles away, Wilson decided to stick with simple.

First, he called Chief Plosky and scheduled the use of an interrogation room at police headquarters.

Next, he and Miller dropped Lee off three blocks from the student union on the west side of the performing arts hall. Afterward, Miller parked their SUV in a lot next to the school's five-thousand-seat basketball arena. From there, Miller had an unobstructed view of the student union entrance located directly across Benson Wood Avenue and about one hundred feet away. Wilson, meanwhile, exited the vehicle, walked across the street and found a table inside the student union coffee shop.

With a fresh cup of coffee in one hand and a discarded copy of the *Wall Street Journal* in front of him, he looked the part of a well-dressed professor—suit, tie and all. More importantly, his East-facing seat looking out the shop's large tinted window offered a clear view of the building's entrance as well as the sidewalk path via which he expected Manny to arrive—if, that is, he came from his apartment eight blocks away.

Doing his best to look like a visitor unfamiliar with the campus, Lee strolled along the sidewalk of Benson Wood

Avenue, stopping a few times to take in the scenery and taking as much time as he could en route to the building's entrance.

Arriving with more than twenty minutes to spare, Lee pulled a free copy of the final spring issue of the student newspaper from a bin and positioned himself beyond the radius of the infrared sensor above the entrance's automatic sliding glass doors. Then, with the day's last rays of sunshine serving as his reading light, he pretended to be digesting the latest happenings on campus.

As Lee finished turning the next-to-last page of the eight-page tabloid, he heard the sound of automatic sliding doors opening and a voice calling his fictitious name.

"Omar?"

Lee turned to find himself face to face with Manny, a twenty-something Filipino with dark brown eyes and shoulder-length black hair atop a body weighing close to two hundred pounds.

"Boss, someone just came out of the student union," said Miller, his voice breaking the silence inside Wilson's earpiece.

"I'm heading out."

"They shook hands," Miller said as he began to climb out of the SUV, "and it looks like Manny's wanting Jack to follow him inside, but Jack's stalling."

Wilson arrived while the doors were still open, and Miller showed up moments later.

"Mr. Romanillos?" Wilson asked.

"Who wants to know?" Manny said, turning to see a well-dressed man with a serious look on his face staring him down.

"Special Agent Wilson, FBI. We need to talk."

"What's going on, Omar?" Manny asked as he turned his head toward the man he'd been led to believe was a fellow Muslim.

Lee identified himself as an NCIS agent and flashed his credentials before seeking confirmation of the Filipino's identity. "You are Mohamed Abu Nadal, formerly Manuel Romanillos or Manny, correct?"

"Yes, sir."

A look of fear appeared on Manny's face as he found himself surrounded by three men carrying badges and, more than likely, handguns.

"Mr. Nadal, you have the right to remain silent," Wilson said as Miller began patting him down in a search for weapons. "Anything you say can and will be used against you in a court of law. You have the right to an attorney and, if you can't afford one, one will be appointed for you. Do you understand these rights as I've explained them?"

"Yes, but what did I do?" Manny asked, his body trembling.

"He's clean," Miller said.

"Mr. Nadal, we need to talk," Wilson said as he gripped the Filipino's left bicep—Miller had the other—and motioned for him to walk toward the SUV across the street, "but not here."

"I haven't done anything wrong," Manny pleaded. "I have a student visa that's good for another year!"

Wilson, Miller and Lee remained silent until all had climbed into the SUV—Lee behind the wheel, Wilson in the front passenger seat and an imposing Miller sitting next to Manny in side-by-side second row seats.

"Mr. Nadal, we're going to go someplace where we can talk in private, so you can hold your questions for a few minutes," Wilson advised.

Ten minutes and five miles later, the SUV arrived at the downtown headquarters of the Effingham Police Department where he pulled into a parking spot marked "VISITOR" behind the single-story brick-and-mortar building.

Miller retrieved his recording equipment from the back of the SUV while Wilson and Lee escorted Manny through a rear entrance, down a hallway and into an interrogation room.

"Have a seat, Mr. Nadal," Wilson said before stepping out into the hallway to confirm EPD was recording video and audio inside the room. He returned to the room and began the interview as soon as Miller had let him know the FBI video camera was up and running as well.

"I'm FBI Special Agent Wilson, and I'm about to conduct an interview today with Mohamed Abu Nadal—formerly Manuel 'Manny' Romanillos—inside the Effingham Police Department headquarters in Effingham, Illinois. It is now 2045 Central on July 5, 2016. Mr. Nadal, I've already read you your rights, and you said you understood those rights, correct?"

"Yes," Manny replied nervously.

"What can you tell me about your relationship with an Ali Ibragim of Atlanta, Georgia?" Wilson began.

It took Manny a moment before he could think of anyone he knew by that name. "I believe he's on the national board of directors of the Muslim Students League, but I don't remember exactly what he does. As vice president of outreach for MSL at the Wood, I receive mail from the national headquarters all the time—and sometimes they call me!"

"Do you remember what you talked about with Mr. Ibragim the night of June 13, 2016?"

Again, Manny thought for a few seconds before an answer came to him. "He was helping me complete a grant application I wanted to submit to the U.S. Department of Education on behalf of the local chapter. Back then, no one knew the new president would shut down the Department of Education like he did."

"Is that the only time you spoke with him?"

"No. I talked with him a long time ago—maybe a year and a half ago—about how to organize an interfaith workshop on campus, but he didn't help much."

"New subject," Wilson continued. "Do you know anyone who works at Illinois Chemical Company?"

"Yes, sir. My friend Rosy works there."

"Is he the only person you know there?"

"I think so."

"Tell me about your affiliation with the Moro Liberation Front?"

"I'm not!"

"I'm not what?"

"I'm not affiliated with MLF!"

"What about Abu Sayyaf? Are you a member of that group?"

"No! I've told a few people I am, but I was lying!"

Wilson grilled Manny for almost thirty minutes before concluding the young Filipino's communications with Ibragim seemed coincidental at best. Then he changed direction.

"Mr. Nadal, do you know Burt Abramov?"

"I think he's one of Rosy's bosses, but Rosy doesn't like him."

"Have you ever spoken with Mr. Abramov?"

"No, sir."

"Mr. Nadal, we're done for now, and I'm going to have a police officer take you back to your apartment." Wilson said. "Before I do, however, I need you to understand one very important thing."

"Sure! Anything!"

"You can't speak to anyone about this conversation of ours today. If I find out you've discussed this with friends, family members, classmates or anyone, you'll find yourself facing serious federal criminal charges. Prison time. Understand?"

Manny told the FBI agent he understood and wouldn't breathe a word to anyone. And they believed him.

38

After arranging for Manny to be returned to his apartment and put under round-the-clock surveillance, Wilson called Day and asked him to put Christie on the phone.

"Can you tell me if Burt Abramov ever has the opportunity to spend time alone at the plant?" Wilson asked.

"Sure, he does."

"When was the last time he did that?"

"According to the schedule, the last time he came in was the night of June 17, to accept tanker truck deliveries. Two trucks."

"How long do you maintain video footage captured by your surveillance cameras?"

"Those cameras? We keep the footage on twenty-four-hour digital spools, so to speak, then it's automatically downloaded to a DVR and kept for another twenty-four. After that, it's erased automatically unless we override the presets for some reason. As far as I know, we've never done that."

"You said, 'those cameras,' as if you have others. Do you?"

"Yes, we have one more, but I'm the only person at the plant who knows about it."

"Why didn't you tell me about it earlier?"

"You didn't ask."

"Where is it?"

"It's mounted inside a light fixture in the ceiling of the clean room," Christie said before explaining that the risk managers at the company's headquarters had ordered the installation of the tiny surveillance camera in an effort to reduce the company's potential exposure to product-liability lawsuits.

"It records everything inside the clean room after a person goes inside, and the video is then stored—forever, I think—in the company's password-protected cloud storage system. The only people with access are the folks at headquarters and me."

"Can we look to see if that camera recorded any footage on the evening of June 17?" Wilson asked.

"You bet. When do you want to see it?"

"Pass the phone back to Agent Day."

Wilson instructed Day to take Christie back to his office, allow him to access the cloud storage and queue up the video. "We'll be there as soon as we can."

Ten minutes later, Wilson, Miller, Lee and Day watched with anticipation as a frozen, time-stamped surveillance camera image appeared on the flat-screen monitor on the office wall.

"Before I show you this video, I want you to know Burt was the only person at the plant at the time it was shot, according to records kept by the RFID badge system," Christie explained. "He entered the building at 2033, almost thirty minutes before the first truck was set to arrive, but he would not have had any reason to visit the clean room."

Seconds after he pressed the PLAY button on the remote control, Christie nearly fell out of his chair.

"Son of a bitch, he used it!" Christie said as watched the video—an overhead view of someone inside the clean room. "He used The Sucker!"

"The Sucker" was the informal name workers had given the hands-free device used to insert chemicals into the mixing vat.

Christie rewound the tape and began offering a sort of play-by-play commentary about what the men in the room were watching.

"After he placed some kind of container—it looks like a quart-sized plastic bottle—into the receiving chamber of The Sucker, the sensor detected the container, calculated its exact dimensions and initiated the wrap."

Pausing the tape, Christie explained that the wrap process involves robotic grips adjusting to the precise size and shape of the container so that a hole can be punched in it before high-pressure suction removed its contents and, within seconds, transferred them to the mixing vat.

"Is it unusual for small quantities of stuff like that to be added to the mix from the clean room?" Wilson asked.

"Not at all. The mixing process sometimes involves adding several chemicals, some of which come in quantities too small to include in a large automated process. What's unusual about this, however, is that he added something after the batch had already been mixed by the day shift and was in the process of curing. In other words, it didn't need anything added to it."

"Can you tell me what was in the vat that night?" Wilson asked.

"That one? Just latex."

"And what is that latex used for?"

"It's the kind they use on scratch-off lottery tickets."

"Can you tell me the exact date on which the batch in that vat was shipped and the name of the company it went to?"

"Each batch takes about thirty-six hours to cure after the stabilizer agent is added," Christie explained as he scanned a log sheet on his computer screen and clicked a button to make his desktop appear on the flat-screen monitor. "We call it the stir and cure."

"The date!" Wilson interrupted. "When was it shipped?"

"The truck carrying this batch arrived at Monticello Printing on Wednesday, June 22."

Wilson thanked Christie for the eye-opening information before giving his key agents a fresh set of instructions as they walked back toward the building's entrance.

"Lee, make sure we don't leave without copies of that video," Wilson ordered.

"Scout, tell Gary and Rosy they're free to leave, and remind them not to talk to anyone about the case. After that, give me a ring as soon as you have the video ready to record another chat with Burt.

"George, we need to go to the command post and talk."

†

"If this video is as clear as it appears to be, I can't help but conclude the CVSA results were off," Wilson said, speaking to Day inside a micro-office inside the command post. "Am I missing something?"

"I know it looks bad, and I can't explain it," Day replied, "but I read the charts from the exam, and they showed clearly that Burt wasn't being deceptive."

"Let's keep this between us for now, because I don't want to submarine the CVSA based on one exam result," Wilson said, "but I hope Burt can explain away what we saw on the video."

Wilson received his call from Miller and returned with Day to the room where Abramov was twiddling his thumbs.

"Burt, you lied to me!" Wilson shouted as he entered the room. "You told me you didn't add anything toxic to the products you make here, and I have video that shows me you did!"

"You're out of your mind," Abramov shouted back after quickly standing to his feet.

"Sit down and shut up, Burt!" Wilson countered just as loudly, prompting Abramov to sit down slowly and cross his arms while feeling as if his heart might beat out of his chest at any moment.

"Burt, I have video evidence showing you inside the plant on the night of June 17," Wilson offered, "*and* I have proof you've been in contact with Ali Ibragim, your Chechen friend in Atlanta."

"Yes, I was here on the seventeenth, but I don't have a Chechen friend in Atlanta!"

Wilson ignored Abramov's denials and kept pressing.

"Burt, the video shows you in the process of using The Sucker to put something into vat number twelve, a vat used only for latex, at 8:33 p.m. on June 17. Was it thallium, Burt?"

"Thallium? I don't know what you're talking about! I think you're making things up!"

"Burt, I think you want the day-shift manager position so badly you're willing to do whatever it takes to get it! In fact, I think you were willing to go so far as to frame Gary Kastens as a mass murderer. Am I right, Burt?"

Abramov couldn't believe what was happening and blurted out the only thing he could think of. "Then show me the video and prove you're not making this up!"

The next few seconds seemed to last a lifetime as he waited for Wilson to respond.

"Okay, Burt, I'll show you the video," Wilson said, trusting his gut and realizing the entire investigation could hinge on the content of the video. "Come with me."

Because his people had not yet placed the digital version of the video in a format Wilson could access, the entire group of FBI agents escorted Abramov back to Christie's office and had the plant manager play the video again.

†

As Wilson and his men escorted Abramov back to Christie's office, the sound of another ringing phone filled the hallway. It was Miller's smartphone, not the throwaway.

"Agent Miller, Chief Plosky here," the called said. "I'm at the scene of a homicide and have something you might wanna take a look at."

"What's that, chief?" Miller replied, a bit skeptical.

"One of my men found an Illinois Chemical ID badge at the crime scene, and I thought --"

"Who's the victim?" Miller interrupted.

"It's a Family Court judge. Richard Cotton is his name."

Miller got the street address of the judge's home and told the chief he'd be there soon.

Sensing the need to hear details about Miller's call, Wilson had Lee take Abramov into Christie's office while he and Miller remained in the hallway.

"Boss, the local police chief is at the scene of a homicide," Miller said as soon as he was alone with Wilson. "The victim is a local judge."

"What kind of judge?"

"Family Court."

"Anything else?"

"They found an Illinois Chemical employee ID at the crime scene."

Upon hearing that news, Wilson stuck his head inside the office where Lee was babysitting Abramov.

330

"Jack, keep an eye on him until we get back," Wilson said. And, with that, he and Miller left. Abramov would have to wait a little while longer before he could watch the video.

After a few minutes on the road, Wilson and Miller arrived at the judge's home, a four-bedroom ranch on a tree-lined, one-acre lot surrounded by yellow crime scene tape and police cars.

"Chief, tell me what you know," Wilson said as he met the police chief at the front door.

"We received a call from the folks at the county courthouse, asking us to check on the welfare of Judge Cotton, because he didn't show up for court today. I sent one of my men by his place and, when he got here, he saw the judge's car in the driveway and several lights on inside the house. After no one answered the door, my officer tried calling the judge's home and cell numbers, but got no answer, so he called me. Based on the judge's track record, I told my officer I'd have him check again near the end of the workday. When no one answered the second time, I told my officer to break in."

"And that's when he found the judge's body?"

"Yes, sir, around 5 o'clock," the chief said before pointing to several evidence bags spread out on a table for Wilson and Miller to inspect. "So far, we've found three things within a few feet of the body: a .38 Special, an ID badge and a scratch-off lottery ticket that hasn't been scratched yet."

"Why didn't you call us earlier?" Wilson asked, noting it was almost 10 p.m.

"This looked like a local crime to us until we found the ID badge," the police chief replied.

As if operating on the same wavelength, the FBI agents showed no visible reaction after seeing Burt Abramov's name and photo on the ID badge. Instead, Wilson asked the police chief another question after noticing the judge's body had already been removed from the scene.

"Did the judge's body appear to be covered in a rash or look strange in any way?"

"No, sir," but he had a hole in his head big enough to drive a truck through. Looks like a suicide."

"Any idea how long the judge was dead before his body was found?"

"The medical examiner said he thought it had probably been a day or two. Three tops."

Changing directions again, Wilson asked Miller if he had a copy of the news article Lee had found about the Abramov divorce. Without saying a word, Miller pulled out his iPad and executed a swipe and several keystrokes before handing the device, complete with the legal brief on its screen, to Wilson.

"Judge Cotton handled the divorce," Wilson said. "If the CVSA was right, then we might owe Ruth Abramov a visit."

Wilson shifted gears again. "Chief, what can you tell me about Judge Cotton?"

"He was forty-five and still single," the chief said. "A lot of people thought he was gay, but I know for a fact that's not entirely true. My men have caught him in compromising positions several times—sometimes playin' for the other team if you know what I mean, and sometimes with women."

"How did he manage to remain on the bench with all that baggage?"

"In Illinois, there's a group of lawyers at the state level who get to decide whether or not other lawyers keep practicing law—or, in the case of judges, stay on the bench—after being caught doing illegal or unethical things."

"Exactly what kind of trouble had he gotten himself into?"

"Drugs, prostitution, campaign violations, you name it. Rumor has it he used up all the favors his friends on the state review board could offer, and he was gonna lose his judgeship if he screwed up again."

"That certainly changes the complexion of this investigation," Wilson said. "Chief, I need to speak with your men."

After a quick introduction by Chief Plosky, Wilson began.

"Folks, we need your help finding any photos or other evidence that might link Judge Cotton with Burt Abramov and his ex-wife, Ruth Abramov," he said. "We have photos of both of them, so come and take a look and then let me know if you find anything."

Thanks to Lee, Wilson and Miller were able to show photos from Ruth Abramov's Facebook page that showed she was still stunning at forty-four and looking like a woman half her age. To show the officers what Burt looked like, they held up the ID badge found at the scene.

"Sir, I think I might have what you're looking for," said a forty-something detective sergeant who appeared to have been in charge of the crime scene before his boss and the feds arrived. "Judge Cotton's smartphone has a lot of photos in it."

The detective showed Wilson how to access the folder where the photos were stored on the phone and then pointed out the judge in one photo before handing the phone to Wilson.

While perusing dozens of photos showing Judge Cotton in a variety of compromising positions with both men and women, it didn't take long for Wilson to spot one that would link the judge to an Abramov. Then, abruptly, he said, "I think it's time to go, gentlemen," and they started to walk out the door.

"Before you go, sir, I think you might want to look at this," said another officer before handing Wilson a plain white envelope bearing no stamp and no address for either a sender or a recipient. Inside was a single sheet of Illinois Chemical letterhead upon which someone had printed out a note:

Judge Cotton,

The actions you took against me in the Family Court are inexcusable. Not only did you take it upon yourself to humiliate me and portray me as a monster not worthy of involvement in more than half of my children's lives, but you also dishonored me in my role as husband, father, and leader of my family.

The steps I plan to take to get back my honor will make me look very bad in the eyes of most Americans, but I don't care. Those people who fail to see the need for my actions mean nothing to me. Honor means everything to me!

Please know your actions will not stand and that you AND the system that allows you to serve as a judge will be made to pay a heavy price. Prepare to answer for your actions! Prepare to meet your infidel god!

At the end of the missive was a signature in black ink: *Burtran F. Abramov.*

After reading the letter, Wilson changed his mind from thinking it was time to speak with Ruth Abramov to thinking he'd better speak with Burt again. Not only did he want to ask Burt about the letter to Judge Cotton, but he also wanted to ask him more questions about his ex-wife.

"Chief, let me know as soon as the ME finishes his report on the judge's death, will ya?" said Wilson, sounding more like he was asking a favor than making a demand.

"You bet, Agent Wilson!"

39

"Follow my lead, gentlemen," Wilson told Miller and Day as they walked through the front doors at Illinois Chemical and down the hall toward Christie's office. Once there, they found Abramov, still under the watchful eye of Lee, staring at the ceiling while Christie thumbed through a trade magazine.

"Is the video ready?" Wilson asked, giving his colleagues an indication of the subject matter he wanted to tackle first.

"Yes, sir," Lee replied.

"Not yet, Dan!" Wilson said after seeing Christie reach for the remote control he'd use to start the video.

"Burt, before we watch the video, I want you to tell us more about your wife, your divorce, and your relationship with Judge Cotton," Wilson explained, realizing and accepting the risks involved in holding this conversation in a room where it wasn't being recorded.

"Why are you so interested in my family and my personal affairs? And why do you care about the judge?

"I have more than thirty thousand reasons to care, Burt," Wilson said, referring to the latest figure he'd received about the number of deaths he believed were linked to latex. "One of them has to do with the judge being found dead."

Though Wilson noticed the blood seem to drain from Burt's face after hearing the news, he continued to press the man for answers. "Tell me about your ex-wife, Burt."

"Like I told you, we were married in Chechnya and came here soon after. I was 27, and she was 19. She's hated me ever since I made her leave our homeland. And, frankly, I'm surprised she hasn't tried to kill me yet."

"Okay, play the video," Wilson told Christie.

No one had to tell Abramov to pay attention to the video and Wilson's color commentary that began a few seconds after Christie pressed PLAY on the remote.

"Burt, that's you adding thallium to the batch of latex, isn't it?"

"Only if I'm missing a finger on my right hand and wearing filthy tennis shoes," he replied, holding up both hands and wiggling all ten fingers for added visual impact.

Wilson was shocked. He had not noticed the index finger missing from the right hand of the person inside the clean room or anything about the person's shoes.

"Dan, can you excuse us, please," Wilson said, prompting Christie to leave the room, accompanied by Lee.

"You owe me an apology, don't you?" Abramov said.

"Not so fast, Burt. Someone used your employee badge to get inside the building that night," Wilson explained.

"And you think I gave it to someone?" Abramov replied.

"I want to know who you allowed to use your badge," Wilson pressed.

"I came here around eight-thirty that night and accepted delivery of the first truckload at nine o'clock and the second at nine-thirty. After that, I went home for a quick shower before returning for the start of my shift."

"I want to believe you, Burt," Wilson said, not sharing the fact that he now believed the CVSA exam had been accurate, "but I'm having trouble with a few items we found at Judge Cotton's house. Perhaps you can help me out."

Rather than hold up the employee ID badge found at the judge's home, Wilson held the letter, protected inside a clear plastic evidence bag, two feet in front of Abramov's eyes.

"Don't touch it, Burt, but look at it and tell me if that's your signature," Wilson said.

"No, it's not mine."

"Then who forged it?"

"Ruth did. She learned a long time ago how to forge my signature."

"And that's how she lifted money from your bank account, I suppose?" Wilson asked.

"Exactly," Abramov replied. "She never could write English words in cursive as well as I could, but she was good enough to fool the bank."

There was a pregnant pause in the conversation as Wilson gathered his thoughts.

"And that's why she typed this letter on the computer," Abramov added, hoping to bring an end to the silence in the room.

"I see," Wilson replied.

"Would you like to know something else, Agent Wilson?"

"Try me," Wilson replied, unprepared for what Abramov was about to share.

"When I was going through the divorce proceedings, I paid close attention to this judge who would decide the fate of my family. If you go back and take a close look at his body, I think you'll see something I noticed during our custody trial."

"Let me guess," Wilson said with a heavy sigh. "He's missing a finger."

"You're a quick study, Agent Wilson," Abramov said with a chortle. "My lawyer told me the judge lost it thirty years ago while playing with fireworks."

40

After concluding that Burt Abramov appeared to be innocent, Wilson made an executive decision—"Gentlemen, it's time to visit Ruth Abramov"—that set into motion a flurry of activity.

Miller handpicked two dozen agents who would soon be dispatched to search the home, and Day packed up his laptop and video gear, anticipating Wilson might want to subject the disgruntled Chechen woman to a CVSA exam. Not sure what to do, Lee opted to stay close to Wilson and be ready to assist.

Thirty minutes later, one Chevy Volt and six black SUVs came to a stop within two blocks of Ruth Abramov's home and Miller used his favorite throwaway phone to punch in the phone number to a nearby home and waited for an answer.

"Hello, this is Ruth," came a woman's voice.

Hearing an answer, Miller said, "Sorry, wrong number," and hung up. Less than thirty seconds later, the FBI agents arrived at their destination, confident Ruth Abramov was inside.

Alerting everyone inside the home he had a search warrant, Wilson shouted "FBI!" and banged loudly on the front door. Seconds later, the door opened and the lead investigator had his first up-close look at Ruth Abramov. He had to admit she was beautiful in a creepy murder suspect sort of way.

"Ruth Abramov, you're under arrest. First-degree murder. Thirty-one-thousand counts, possibly more," Wilson said as he grabbed the woman by the left arm and turned her around before placing her in handcuffs and advising her of her rights.

"I wondered how long it would take until you showed up here," the woman said, surprising Wilson with words that sounded like a confession as she sat on her living room sofa.

"You were pretty sloppy, Mrs. Abramov," Wilson replied. "It seems like you wanted to get caught."

"Think whatever you want, but you don't have proof I've done anything!"

"We'll see," Wilson countered, keenly aware he had not told her the purpose of their visit and that everything she said had been captured on video by Lee and Day. "Scout, I want at least three agents keeping an eye on her at all times."

During the search of her home, agents not only found the computer Ruth Abramov had used to draft the threatening letter to Judge Cotton, but they found a blue ink pen they believed was the one she had used to sign it.

In addition, they found evidence of a month-old email conversation Ruth Abramov had with a female friend from Chechnya living in New York City. As soon as he read it, Wilson called The Ring and had an FBI agent there visit the woman and ask her about that email conversation.

Less than an hour later, the agent reported to Wilson that the Chechen friend confirmed Ruth Abramov purchased a $150 money order in early June and mailed it to her along with instructions for her to use the money to purchase a National Bet scratch-off ticket on July 1, mail it to Richard

Cotton—Ruth Abramov had described him as a "friend"—
and keep the change for her troubles.

While that information wasn't enough to tie Ruth
Abramov to the mass murder scheme, it was a good place to
start.

While the search of the home turned up little else of
value, the state medical examiner's findings about the
judge's death pointed to Ruth Abramov's guilt.

The trajectory of the bullet as it entered the judge's skull
convinced the ME the gun was fired by someone shorter than
the victim. Someone about five-seven. Ruth Abramov's
height.

In addition, the ME cited the lack of gunpowder residue
on the judge's hands as making it highly unlikely he had
killed himself.

It was another observation by the ME, however, that
carried the most weight and quickly convinced the ME to
rule the death a homicide.

"A left-handed judge who was missing the index finger of
his right hand would not, in my opinion, use his right hand to
shoot himself in the right temple."

Two more findings helped paint Ruth Abramov as a
guilty party: her fingerprints were found on several items at
the murder scene, including the judge's .38 Special; and an
analysis of her handwriting matched exactly with the forged
signature of her husband that appeared on the letter to the
judge.

✝

At 12:54 a.m. July 6, 2016, Wilson began a heart-to-heart
conversation with Ruth Abramov.

"Mrs. Abramov, the way things look, you can either
confess that you killed Judge Cotton and that you somehow
managed to kill thirty-one thousand other Americans or you

can fight the charges in court," Wilson explained. "Fight it, and I guarantee you will face the death penalty when you're found guilty—and you will be found guilty. Confess, and you might live to a ripe old age without fear of being put to death by lethal injection."

†

To say Ruth Abramov confessed was an understatement. By 2 a.m. July 6, 2016, she had done so much more after being told she might live to an old age behind bars without fear of lethal injection *if* she cooperated.

First, she implicated Ibragim as the CDC employee who supplied the Thallium S-213, telling Wilson her childhood friend from Grozny "would do anything for me."

Next, she admitted to blackmailing Judge Cotton and threatening to expose his continued involvement in drugs and prostitution if he didn't agree to use one of her ex-husband's old RFID badges—Burt Abramov thought he'd lost it—to get into the plant and follow her instructions for adding the toxin to the batch of latex.

Finally, she told Wilson she had learned how to use The Sucker by observing carefully as her husband showed their young children what he did for a living during one of the family's occasional trips to the Illinois Chemical plant.

†

"Give me some good news, Joe-L," Mazachek said after seeing Wilson's now-familiar number on her mobile phone's screen.

"None of our prime suspects were involved, Madame Director," Wilson told his boss. "Instead, Burt Abramov's ex-wife, Ruth, was behind the whole thing."

"What on earth was her motive, Joe-L?"

"She tried to frame her husband, because she considers him a coward for the way they left Chechnya twenty-five years ago, and she's been wanting to get back at him ever since."

"Is there something wrong with Effingham?"

"It's not Grozny, I guess."

"I'm sure we'll find out more as this plays out, but I'm ecstatic that you caught her," Mazachek said.

"I hope the Attorney General will be agreeable to offering Ruth Abramov thirty-one thousand life sentences, instead of the death penalty, in exchange for the information she gave, because I kind of told her he might."

"I think he will, Joe-L, and I can't begin to tell you how thankful and impressed I am for your efforts on this case."

"It was a team effort, and I'm glad you let me be part of it."

"Joe-L, I know it's probably not your cup of tea, but you're about to become a national hero."

There was silence at the other end of the line after she said those words, and the FBI director's star agent wasn't sure how to respond. The next day would be anything but silent.

41

Never before had Effingham residents seen so many news reporters and satellite trucks converge on their small community. But July 6, 2016, wasn't a typical Wednesday in Southern Illinois.

Promptly at 9 a.m., Attorney General Daniels stepped up to the cluster of windscreen-covered microphones attached to a portable podium in the parking lot outside Illinois Chemical Company. Behind him, FBI trailers served as a backdrop while also obscuring anyone's view of the facility's entrance.

"Good morning. I'm joined by Homeland Security Secretary Argus McQueen, United States Attorney for Southern Illinois Frank Williams and, from the FBI, Director Pamela Mazachek and Special Agent Joseph L. Wilson.

"On behalf of everyone here with me, I want to begin as I did four days ago by expressing heartfelt condolences to those Americans impacted by the events of the past week. It's been a difficult week for all.

"Four days ago, my colleagues and I told you we had launched an investigation into the deaths of several thousand Americans that began July 1.

"We told you most of the deaths had occurred in nine Northeast states—Connecticut, Delaware, Maryland, Massachusetts, New Jersey, New York, Pennsylvania, Rhode Island and the District of Columbia.

"We told you we did not know exactly what had caused the deaths and that we would work nonstop, along with local, state and federal agency officials in several states, to find answers.

"Today, I'm pleased to inform you that we have important news to share. For that news, I'll turn the podium over to FBI Director Mazachek."

"Thank you, Mr. Attorney General. Before I continue, I want to express my agency's deepest appreciation for the cooperation we've received from individuals at all levels at Illinois Chemical Company, at the Centers for Disease Control in Atlanta, from law enforcement agencies across the country, and from local officials, including the Effingham County Sheriff's Department and the City of Effingham Police and Fire Departments."

Mazachek paused for a moment to look out over the crowd of faces and lenses staring at her, waiting for her to share what they suspected would be news of monumental importance.

"During a news conference in Washington four days ago, I shared three items worth reviewing now.

"First, I said we believed the immediate crisis was over, because the rate at which deaths were being reported had declined significantly. That turned out to be accurate.

"Second, I said we did not believe the unusually high number of deaths during the first thirty-six hours of the month were natural or accidental in nature. That turned out to be accurate as well.

"Finally, I told you I had assigned every available FBI agent to this case. Today, I want to share as many details as I can about the results of their hard work during the past week.

"A nationwide investigation effort led by FBI Special Agent Joseph L. Wilson," Mazachek said, motioning toward

Wilson who was standing to her left seemingly emotionless, "led us to the Illinois Chemical Company production facility behind me.

"Early yesterday morning, a team of more than fifty FBI agents from across the country raided this facility in search of evidence that might be connected to the deaths of more than thirty-one thousand people during the past week. Under the incredible leadership of Special Agent Wilson, that raid yielded much fruit.

"Late last night, Special Agent Wilson informed me that members of his task force had arrested two individuals whose actions are suspected to have resulted in the deaths of at least thirty-one thousand, two hundred individuals in fourteen states during the first three days of this month.

"We believe these individuals conspired as many as twelve months ago to devise a plan that would involve tampering with the chemical formula used to produce a type of latex that is later applied to the surface of scratch-off lottery tickets during the printing process."

Gasps arose from among the crowd of reporters and bloggers, some of whom were tweeting live from the news conference.

"We believe these two individuals began executing the final steps of their plan during the last two weeks of June.

"We believe these two individuals knew the tainted latex material printed on the surface of the lottery tickets could, after being scratched off, become airborne for a short time.

"And, finally, we believe these two individuals knew that anyone who inhaled the tiny airborne particles of the tainted latex would die."

Sensing members of the news media were growing impatient for her to utter the names and pertinent details of the individuals who had been arrested, the FBI director didn't keep them waiting long.

"The first individual arrested Tuesday evening was Ruth Madina Abramov, a forty-four-year-old female resident of Effingham, Illinois.

"The second individual arrested was Ali G. Ibragim, a fifty-one-year-old male resident of Decatur, Georgia, who is employed at the Centers for Disease Control in Atlanta.

"Please be advised we believe these individuals committed these heinous acts while acting on their own and *not* as agents of any terrorist group, foreign nation or other enemy of the United States. As always, I advise you to remember that the defendants are presumed innocent until proven guilty."

With that, Mazachek ceded the podium to Attorney General Daniels.

"Because of the nature and scope of the allegations, I will be working closely with U.S. Attorney Frank Williams and his counterparts in fourteen states to prosecute this case to the fullest extent of the law. I trust you will understand that, in order to preserve our case for trial, we might not be able to answer all of your questions in as much detail as you might like at this point as this case moves forward. Questions?"

Dozens of hands went up, and even more questions followed.

Anticipating such a cacophonous reaction, the AG seized the opportunity as one during which he could offer an answer to a question he had hoped to hear though he wasn't even sure it had been asked.

"Yes, I'm asking lottery officials nationwide to discontinue their sales of scratch-off lottery tickets until we complete a more-detailed investigation into security factors involved in their production."

Satisfied he had won the first volley, Daniels surveyed the crowd before pointing to a young female reporter in the center of the pack and offering her the opportunity to ask the first genuine question of the day.

"J.C. Champlin, Effingham Courier," she began. "Can you tell us where the two individuals are being held and tell us more about them?"

"Regarding your first point," Daniels began, "I will not divulge the location or locations where these individuals are being held due to security concerns. Regarding your second point, I can tell you both of the accused are legal permanent residents of the United States who immigrated to this country from Chechnya during the early 1990s."

A barrage of mostly-predictable questions followed.

"Are they Muslims?" one reporter shouted.

"Do you suspect they represent a terror sleeper cell?" shouted another.

"Can you describe for us how they tampered with the latex formula?" shouted a third.

And there were more questions—so many, in fact, that the news conference continued for more than forty-five minutes.

Not surprisingly, most of the answers to the questions left members of the Fourth Estate wanting after it became apparent that the people on the receiving end of the questions were less concerned about headlines than they were about finishing the case well. For them, that meant putting Ruth Abramov and her co-conspirator behind bars. For a long time. Or worse.

"Some things never change," Wilson thought to himself after he managed, with Mazachek's permission, to extricate himself from the Q-and-A session and duck into the command post a few yards behind epicenter of the news conference.

†

While it may have appeared to the American public that the FBI's job was done, Wilson knew plenty of work remained to be done on the case. On the plus side, however, his boss had told him he could continue to use her G5—a nice perk for a guy who expected to do a lot of traveling between Atlanta, Charlotte, Effingham and D.C.

Along with Miller and a smaller core of FBI agents— Lee's NCIS boss recalled him to New London, saying he could no longer get by without his young agent—Wilson continued working on the investigation for nine months as the prosecution built its cases against Ruth Abramov and Ibragim.

While one set of arguments would seek the death penalty for a decidedly uncooperative Ibragim, a completely different case would be made regarding the prosecution of Abramov. She had, after all, fingered the trusted government employee who had supplied the Thallium S-213 used in her deadly plot.

42

Though almost a year had passed since the news conference marking the beginning of the end of his investigation, Wilson expected his involvement in the case might continue for several more years. In fact, he expected to be called upon to testify during court proceedings at some point in the not-too-distant future. Until that day came, he vowed to enjoy the present, being treated as a most-honored guest at the White House.

After learning several days earlier that he would soon be receiving the Presidential Medal of Freedom from President Rivera, Wilson had called the White House and asked the president's chief of staff to let the president know that each of his three close colleagues deserved to receive the same medal—the highest honor a civilian in the United States can receive. The president agreed.

During a nationally televised Rose Garden ceremony July 4, 2017, President Rivera noted the heroic actions of Miller, Day and Lee before presenting them with their medals. Taking Mazachek's advice, he reserved his highest praise for Wilson.

"Despite his own personal hardship that came one year and one day ago when he lost his dear wife Lori, FBI Special Agent Joseph L. Wilson made it his mission to find those responsible for his wife's death. In so doing, he also found those believed responsible for my dear Juanita's death and for the deaths of more than thirty-one thousand other Americans, each of whom was loved by someone.

"For his boundless courage, tenacity and wisdom in the face of adversity, I present this award to FBI Special Agent Joseph L. Wilson with the heartfelt thanks of the American people."

Soon after the president placed the medal around Wilson's neck, Wilson thanked the president, the FBI director and his fellow agents and his wife for making the award possible.

Due to the presence of hundreds of politicians and other top-tier dignitaries, Wilson endured dozens of interviews, grip-and-grin photo opportunities and endless handshakes during the four hours that followed the ceremony. When the smiles began to wear off, he saw Mazachek approaching him.

"I think it would make sense to move you up here, Joe-L," Mazachek said. "We're gonna need you in court, you know."

"I suspected that," he replied while observing his colleagues savoring the rare and unusual spotlight, "but I'll need to go back to Charlotte and take care of a few things first."

One thing he needed to do was pick up his wife's ashes and dispose of them somewhere. He didn't where exactly, but one year was long enough for them to be sitting on a shelf at the funeral home.

And then there was another thing.

"I'd like to bring somebody on board with the bureau," he told Mazachek, nodding toward Lee who was busy posing for a photo with President Rivera.

"Is he as good as you, Joe-L?"

"Probably better. He just doesn't realize it yet."

"Okay. I'll make him an offer he can't refuse."

Wilson watched from a distance as Mazachek ambled over to Lee and engaged him in conversation. After only a few moments, a look of shock appeared on the young man's face. Then came a smile. It was obvious to Wilson that his accidental understudy had accepted the offer.

"What are you so happy about, Jack?" said Wilson after closing the room-sized gap between them.

"The FBI director asked me to join the bureau! Can you believe it?"

"Yes, I can, Jack. You deserve it. Congratulations!"

Before saying another word, Wilson noticed Lee breaking eye contact with him and coming to attention of sorts. Wilson knew someone prominent was approaching from behind. Then he felt a tap on his right shoulder.

"Agent Wilson, I wanted to thank you again for all you and your team did this past year," said President Rivera. "Is there anything else I can do to assist you as we wrap up this nightmare?"

"Thank you, Mr. President," Wilson replied before pausing a moment. "There is one thing."

After outlining his request, Wilson heard the president say, "I'll make it happen."

✝

An unusual sound for a Friday morning, the noise coming from outside his office window caused Campton Police Chief Phil Muehring some concern. The chief looked out his window and saw a large tractor-trailer rig had parked along the curb. Though he didn't know the driver or what he might be hauling, the chief was certain about one thing: that driver wasn't going to park his rig in the no-parking zone outside his office if he had anything to say about it. And, as chief of police, he knew he did.

Chief Muehring saw someone walking from the cab toward the back of the trailer and decided to meet him before he could unload whatever it was he was hauling.

"Whaddya think you're doing here, buddy," the chief said. "This is a no-parking zone."

"Are you Chief Phil E. Muehring?" the driver asked.

"Yes, and who are you?"

"Stand by, please." Not answering the chief's question, the driver punched a speed-dial number on his smart phone.

Chief Muehring was, to say the least, as perplexed by the unusual situation as he was curious.

"Yes, sir, I'll hand him the phone," the driver told someone before turning back to the chief. "Chief Muehring, someone would like to speak with you. Please hold the phone in front of you like this and look at the screen as you talk."

Chief Muehring watched as a video image appeared on the phone's screen, and he couldn't believe his eyes.

"Good morning, Chief Muehring," said President Rivera. "How are things in Campton today?"

"Uhh, fine, Mr. President," the chief replied nervously, realizing it was too late to comb his hair or to otherwise try to improve his appearance. "This is quite a surprise, sir."

"I understand chief, but I'm told this nation owes you a debt of gratitude for the way you assisted the FBI last year about this time," the president explained. "Chief, would you mind asking Jeff to raise the door on the back of his trailer, please."

Realizing the president knew the name of the truck driver was Jeff, the police chief said, "Certainly, Mr. President," and forwarded his request.

A moment later, Jeff released the latch at the bottom of the trailer's rear door and allowed it to slide up and out of the way.

The police chief could hardly believe his eyes as he was nearly blinded by the glare of the sun shining off the grill of a sparkling new Cadillac Escalade. Black with CAMPTON POLICE in gold and white lettering, the SUV was decked out with the latest in crime-fighting technology, most of which the chief would never need or use.

"It's yours, chief," the president said, "on behalf of a grateful nation and a generous donor. I hope you make good use of it."

"Thank you, Mister President," the chief said as a range of emotions swirled through his mind. "I'm sure we can."

At Wilson's request, President Rivera did not mention the FBI agent as having anything to do with the award. Wilson thought the police chief would appreciate it more that way.

✝

In a private ceremony one week later, President Rivera presented Burt Abramov with a five-million-dollar check, his reward for helping the FBI solve the case. Though far short of the fifty-million-dollar reward announced by the government, the Chechen immigrant was pleased to receive it. After all, it was more than enough to replace what his gham-sag had stolen, and it would allow him to spend more time with his children while happy *and* Ruthless.

Author's Note

On the copyright page, I noted this book is a work of fiction. Aside from a few things, such as the erroneous figures used to represent the number of scratch-off tickets sold, most of the details of this story are real. Chief among them is the Computer Voice Stress Analyzer, or CVSA, which received a great deal of attention in my second nonfiction book, *The Clapper Memo*.

If you find yourself intrigued by the manner in which fictitious FBI agents used CVSA to help solve the latest crime of the century on the pages of *The National Bet*, order a copy of *The Clapper Memo*. It contains real-world examples of how law enforcement, military and intelligence professionals have used the technology.

About the Author

A native of Enid, Oklahoma, Bob McCarty graduated without honors in May 1984 after earning a Bachelor of Science degree in journalism from Oklahoma State University. During the next twenty-plus years, he served stints as an Air Force public affairs officer, a political campaign manager, a sales consultant and a corporate public relations professional before turning to writing full time in 2006.

Bob's first nonfiction book, *Three Days In August: A U.S. Army Special Forces Soldier's Fight For Military Justice* (October 2011), chronicles the life and wrongful conviction of Green Beret Sergeant First Class Kelly A. Stewart.

Bob's second nonfiction book, *The Clapper Memo* (May 2013), reveals what he uncovered during an exhaustive four-year investigation into the federal government's love affair with the polygraph and the turf war that has raged silently for more than four decades between polygraph loyalists and all challengers to the century-old technology.

Bob is married and the father of three sons, one of whom is married and living abroad, and two cats. He makes his home near Saint Louis.

Acknowledgements

Thanks to everyone online and offline for your encouragement as this book advanced from the stage of being a twinkle in my mind's eye to a lost file and back again.

Special thanks go to my wife and sons for continuing to put up with this writing obsession of mine. In addition, I owe a debt of gratitude to the following individuals who offered to serve as second sets of eyes as I approached the end of this project: Carrie Fatigante, Mike Marshall, Jane McKinney and Kathleen Logan Smith. Your efforts are much appreciated!

Finally, I offer thanks to a man whose words were cited by David Warsh in his *Boston Globe* article, "A rising gorge (March 4, 1997)":

"No politician, however troubled by the lottery's harmful effects, would dare raise taxes or cut spending sufficiently to offset the revenues a lottery brings in. With state hooked on the money, they have no choice but to continue to bombard their citizens, especially the more vulnerable ones, with a message at odds with the ethic of work, sacrifice, and moral responsibility that sustains democratic life." – Professor Michael Sandel, Harvard University

Connect

Stay up to date with news and info about Bob McCarty by visiting BobMcCarty.com and connecting with Bob through Facebook, Twitter and other social media.

After reading *The National Bet*, please post a review of the book online and send us photos of yourself holding your copy of *The National Bet* so we can share them with the world via social media. Email your photos and anything else you would like to share to:

BobMcCartyWrites (at) gmail (dot) com

Thanks in advance!!!